Apocalypse Array

AngeLINK

Book 4

Apocalypse Array

AngeLINK - Book 4

Lyda Morehouse

WIZARD'S TOWER

Wizard's Tower Press

Rhydaman, Cymru

Apocalypse Array

AngeLINK - Book 4

Text © 2002, 2013, 2023 by Lyda Morehouse
Cover art by Bruce Jensen
Cover design by Ben Baldwin
Book design by Cheryl Morgan

First published in the USA by Roc,
May 2002

First published in the UK as an ebook
by Wizard's Tower Press, May 2013

This edition by Wizard's Tower Press,
February 2024

ISBN: 978-1-913892-61-6

http://wizardstowerpress.com/

Contents

Praise for
The AngeLINK Series

"Morehouse's highly descriptive version of 2075 Earth is almost as interesting as the novel's plot." — Paul Goat Allen, *Barnes & Noble Explorations*

"...[Morehouse's] world is intriguing, and there are enough surprises to keep things moving, and the mix of SF and religion works surprisingly well." — Carolyn Cushman, *Locus*

"...fast-pasced action, vivid characters and flawless execution. Ms. Morehouse serves up a futuristic thrill with a twist." — Kelly Rae Cooper, *Romantic Times*

"What Morehouse has created for us is an instant classic of SF. McMannus is one of the strongest, most complex investigators in a long, long time. The rest of the characters are vividly drawn, fascinating beings. The technology seems so tantalisingly close — frightening possible. The image of a future society and government is chilling. The combination is miraculous; one of the best novels in memory." – Lisa Du Mond, *SF Site*

"Ms. Morehouse has created a cast of wonderfully believable and fascinating characters, complete with goals and dreams, but also flaws — the most important feature assigned to realistic characters. They don't always have the answers and they don't always make the best decisions. Their feelings often get in the way of altruism and orders, and in the end it is the things that make them most human that have the greatest impact." SN Arly, *Strange Horizons*

"...the author manages to create a blend of science fiction, advanced technology, theological ideas, and romance which is well worth a read" – Vegar Holmen, *The Alien Online*

"Morehouse knows how to pace her story, weaving strands of plot and drawing the reader ever deeper into its fascinating but unnerving world." — Regina Schroeder, *Booklist*

APOCALYPSE ARRAY

For Shawn, Ella, and Mason

ACKNOWLEDGEMENTS

As always, I have to thank my amazing and wonderful editor, Laura Anne Gilman, as well as my ever-persistent, bushy-tailed agent, Jim Frenkel. Many heartfelt thanks and a boatload of karma go to my midnight-hour readers: Naomi Kritzer, Kelly McCullough, and Terry A. Garey.

My writers' group barely had a chance to read much of this manuscript, but their support of my spirit—particularly in this last year—has been immeasurable. A tip of the Orangina glass to the Wyrdsmiths: Eleanor Arnason, Harry C. LeBlanc, Bill Henry, Doug Hulick, Rosalind Nelson, and those busy rascals Naomi and Kelly again.

Shawn Rounds, the darling of my life and mother of my children, gets all the love and some of the curses, thanks to her far too astute assessment of the problems of plot and character arcs in earlier drafts. Grrr, Shawn! I love you. You made this a better book.

And because he gets depressed when his name doesn't appear in print, I also acknowledge the existence of my NOT SULLEN nephew Jonathan Sharpe. Yeah, yeah, love you, too, guy. Stop, you're embarrassing me.

Mort and Rita Morehouse also deserve a mention as my stage moms, tireless promoters, and proud grandparents of Ella and Mason. Honestly, without your support, Mom and Papa, I would have crumbled. Thanks. Much love. Similarly, the Rounds family—Pat and Margaret, Greg and Barb, Keven and Jon, Mark and Joe—you are a great family to be part of. Thank you.

Also, a big thank-you goes out to all of our friends and family for their understanding, support, prayers, and well wishes. It's been a hard year, and you guys all made it survivable. Thanks, too, to my growing number of fans. You guys make it all worth it. You're why I get up in the morning and start typing.

FOREWORD

Re-reading Apocalypse Array for the publication of this e-book made me realize the extent to which I failed Transgender 101. What you read might make you angry or cause you pain. If so, I'm sorry. That was not my intent. At the time, this was the best of my understanding. This was my attempt at inclusiveness.

In the light of what I now know, it falls short. If I wrote a book like this now—almost exactly a decade later—Ariel, and the people who interact with her, would be very different. I'd like to imagine that I'd do a better job and that I've evolved. At the very least, nowadays, thankfully, I have more than a handful of trans friends who would call me out on mistakes made.

Writing about the future in the past is a tricky thing. You end up, I think, highlighting the ways in which you're an inescapable product of your time.

You could, if you're feeling generous, tell yourself that the attitudes expressed by these characters are a result of the horrible (if imaginary) political environment in which they grew up, which was, in point of fact, meant to be far more socially regressive even than when I wrote it at the beginning of the George W. Bush administration.

Regardless, like my thoughts that DOS would survive, I was wrong.

Lyda Morehouse
June, 2014

¤ ¤ ¤

Having read the above, you may be wondering why I, a trans woman, was keen to re-publish the AngeLINK series. Well, because I loved the books when I first read them, of course. And with good reason.

The other characters in the book, as Lyda notes, do not treat Ariel with much respect. Then again, they do live in a society in which being gay is illegal, and women are discouraged from wearing "male" clothing such as jeans. Those attitudes begin to fall away during the course of the series.

It is also true that Ariel is not trans in the way I am trans. She's defiantly non-binary, whereas I'm solidly feminine. One thing we have learned over the years is that there are almost as many ways of being trans as there are trans people. An important lesson that we have learned is that there is no "right" way to be trans, and no "wrong" way either. Ariel has as much right to her identity as I do to mine.

Reading the books for the first time, however, the key point for me was that there was a trans character in them. What's more, she was not there to have her identity dissected, or used as a plot hook, or laughed at. She was just there, as much as part of the new world that Mother was ushering in as anyone else. What the books said to me what that trans people had a place in the world, and that place was not as a freak to be gawped at, but on an equal footing with everyone else. I shall always be grateful to Lyda for that.

Cheryl Morgan
Wizard's Tower Press
June, 2014

☒

PROLOGUE

Morningstar

When the preacher asked if there were any objections, I half expected God Himself to strike me down. In fact, I couldn't quite stifle a nervous glance up into the flaking-painted face of Jesus, who hung serenely on the crucifix just beyond the altar. He gazed down at me lovingly with wide brown eyes. Goose pimples crept up my arms underneath the Armani tuxedo, despite the June heat, as I waited out the interminable seconds in the church, silent, it seemed, except for the harsh sound of my own breathing.

No one—no angel, messiah, man, nor god—spoke a word to halt this supreme blasphemy.

Imagine. Me, participating in *holy* matrimony?

It was a sin—though, surely, not my worst.

When the ceremony began again, I allowed myself a long, deep breath. Beside me, Emmaline flashed me a knowing smile. Her face seemed to hold a touch of relief, as if she, too, had anticipated holy fire.

She looked...handsome in her full dress uniform. The black leatherlike armor glowed darkly in the soft candlelight of the church. Emmaline stood stiffly, as though at attention. Her black curls had been trimmed into a crisp militaristic flattop. She was almost as tall as I was, and, thanks to her cybernetic augmentation, she seemed twice as strong. Most of the time, I let her believe she was.

Emmaline held a single white rose. Its silken petals stood out in sharp contrast to the Peacemaker and shock stick in her belt. Not exactly the most feminine bride an angel could dream of, but then again I never in a million eons

12

ever imagined myself standing here, in front of God, pledging my devotion to a mere mortal.

Mortals have never been an interest of mine, honestly. To me, they were just God's mud dolls animated by His holy breath for some sick experiment in free will. I normally let them play in their dirt and filth without a second thought.

But my Emmaline could hardly be described as "merely" anything. And, after this day, after the bond was complete and the rings were exchanged, I wondered if she would ever again truly qualify as mortal.

Several months ago, on the day I'd asked and she'd said yes, I'd sealed my intentions with a blood oath. No traditional engagement ring for me. I wanted something much, much more dramatic. Because I'm an angel, my body is only a shell for the pure spirit within. I have no blood per se. All the same, I pricked my palm with a small knife and she followed suit. We held our hands together, allowing her blood to flow into my pure essence, and my spirit into her blood.

It was, for me, a major commitment. Some say I'm particularly fond of contracts, but usually it is not I who enters into them, not I who seals the covenant with blood.

Emmaline gave me a little nudge, breaking my reverie. I repeated the words the preacher asked of me without really hearing them. My voice sounded much more clear and confident than I would have expected of myself given the butterflies in my stomach. The camerabots swung in for a close-up. I smiled easily.

It was a beautiful day.

Sunlight streamed in through the stained glass, spraying flecks of royal blue and emerald green on the white altar. Dust motes danced lazily in the streams of light, and the musky smell of incense filled my lungs. I breathed in deeply.

Then, far too quickly, the rings were exchanged and the vows sealed with a kiss. I took Emmaline's hand and we walked down the aisle as Mr. and Mrs. Sammael Morningstar. It sounded silly to my internal ear, but it made me grin proudly anyway.

"I've never seen you so handsome," Emmaline said to me as we stood in the greeting line. "I can see it, you know. How you must have been."

When you were the greatest of them all, she didn't have to add. I just nodded, but a hollow darkness crept into me. How I must have been, but were no longer, she implied. Had my finest hour already past? Would I always be known as the angel who *almost* took Heaven by force of will? Would my greatest fame be the spectacular nature of my failure? I glanced at Emmaline. If I was right about what she would become, then perhaps not. Perhaps my greatest moment was yet to come.

13

I watched Emmaline smile and clasp hands with the various celebrities that passed by us in waves. Even though Em kept her hair short, the locks above her forehead threatened to twist into three perfectly shaped loops that, at the right angle, looked almost exactly like three sixes. My darling Antichrist, I thought, and leaned over to whisper in her ear our private joke. "You're the Beast," I told her.

She gave me a little peck on the cheek. "You old devil, you."

We had rented the grandest, most expensive hotel in all of Rome for the reception. I'd liquidated the real estate of my New York bookstore and most of its contents to pay for the damn thing.

Luckily, it showed. The ballroom defined grandeur. Crystal chandeliers glittered overhead, casting soft light onto gray silk wallpaper. Polished marble and the finest-quality Persian rugs lay underfoot. Balcony doors had been thrown open to allow the cooling evening breeze to enter with the scent of jasmine flowers, to ruffle the hems of designer evening gowns and tug at tuxedo tails.

I stood alone in the center of the room, sipping champagne, content to watch as Emmaline buzzed around greeting various dignitaries and charming them into a smile or a bold guffaw.

Rarely, a dignitary would spare me a glance or a small nod of acknowledgment. I was, after all, only a supporting actor in this final scene. I stood *behind* the throne. The spotlight was reserved for Emmaline alone.

I would be more bitter and jealous, but Emmaline captured the world's attention on her own, with her own cleverness. She pulled quite the stunt a decade ago just after a meteorite fell out of the sky and destroyed the Dome of the Rock. By pretending to be building a virtual version of the Third Jewish Temple, she'd manipulated the world to the brink of world war. Then she pulled them all back from the edge with a "Hey, it wasn't God after all, now, was it?"

The world had missed Armageddon, but not the wake-up call. People began to question the logic of having government and religion mix. In the United States and other major countries, politicians were getting elected who were *not* also clergypersons. Emmaline had started a secular revolution.

God's hold on the world was weakening.

That made me very, very happy.

The bubbles of the champagne slid down my throat, and I sighed. I wandered closer to the balcony. The night air felt cool against my cheek. Beyond the hill and under a bright moon, Roman traffic buzzed contentedly. I was glad the camerabots still circled the room. I would never remember everything that had happened today. Maybe I could catch my wedding on reruns.

14

"Excuse me," came a voice with a pronounced English accent.

I turned to see a young man in his early thirties. A camera lens strapped to a helmet mostly obscured his face. Wires wove around the entire contraption, making it look as though he were some kind of cyborg. Which, perhaps, he was.

"Byron Liest," he said by way of introduction. "LINK-1 out of London."

A reporter. Of course. I shook his hand. "My pleasure."

"Lovely wedding," he said.

"Was it?" I laughed. "It all went by so fast."

"I imagine so. Indeed. Indeed. Yes, that's how mine was as well," Byron agreed. "It's easy to get flustered, caught up in the excitement, isn't it?"

I frowned at my champagne. What was he getting at? "I suppose it is."

"So then it wasn't intentional?"

"What?"

"You, agreeing to obey her."

I laughed. "Sure, we intended that. Em and I enjoy the whole archaic language of the wedding ceremony. And the whole obey thing is just so ... biblical."

"Yes, but usually the woman agrees to obey the man, or each agrees to obey the other. It's highly unusual, don't you think, for the man to agree to obey the woman? Or was that your intent? To turn the whole thing upside down? To make a point?"

I felt my frown deepen. "Are you saying Emmaline didn't say it?"

"No."

"You mean she just forgot."

"No, the preacher never asked her to."

My stomach felt strangely cold, and I glanced inside to where Emmaline stood with her arm wrapped around the prime minister of Israel. Already she played political games, and I had a sinking feeling I'd fallen for one. "But I did? I agreed to obey her?"

"Would you like to see the clip?"

I continued to stare at Emmaline. Seeing me, she smiled and waved. "That won't be necessary," I said.

"So, for the record, was the wording intentional?"

"No," I said. It was a mistake all right, a very big one.

◘

CHAPTER 1

Emmaline

Two Years Later

You shouldn't be doing this.

A small crowd had gathered beside the rubble that used to be Temple Mount. I stood in front of the last remnant of the Wailing Wall. A green ribbon rattled in the breeze, waiting for me to cut it, to christen this place as an international free zone.

Thunder rolled overhead, and I was reminded of the Days of Blood when explosions were commonplace here. Israel knew peace now, but it was a difficult process. The first step was a gift, straight from God. A meteorite fell from Heaven and destroyed the Dome of the Rock. The Arab Israeli contention over this tiny bit of real estate heated to insane proportions, nearly causing a world war, the end of time. Helped along by me, of course...

And me, added Victory, the AI who occupied my combat computer.

Yes, I told her with a smirk, *your help was invaluable. You killed all those hackers for me. Too bad you missed the important one.*

I cringed. Or, rather, Victory used my muscles to express *her* guilt.

A decade ago, she hadn't had any remorse when she occupied an Inquisitor's body and shot three wire wizards in the back of the head, execution style. She was supposed to have killed four, but Mouse, a key player and the "father" of Page, got away. Page was another artificial intelligence, who, later that same day, trapped Victory inside me and overwrote her program to include, of all horrible things, a conscience.

16

Victory claimed she'd seen Mouse fall that day, but she hadn't hung around to watch him get up again.

Typical.

Too bad *that* wasn't why she felt guilty.

No, now she regretted the killing and her part in the hijacking of the temple. Now she had an opinion on everything. Damn Page, anyway. Thanks to that little meddler, I had to live with Victory's running commentary on my life, complete with quotes from the goddamn Koran.

The Noble *Koran*, Victory corrected.

"Shut the fuck up, would you please? I'm trying to focus on this historical moment. I'd like to wow the crowd and not spend the whole day arguing with my own combat computer."

I could feel Victory's huff of indignation deep in my bones.

I ignored her. After all, people *were* waiting for me to speak. I had been paused with the ceremonial scissors in hand long enough. So, with a flourish, I snipped the ribbon.

Applause crashed over me in waves. No fewer than seven years ago, these same people had despised me, would have had me hung if they could have come up with a way to extend the death penalty to the crime of cybersquatting. After my confession and arrest, things here in Jerusalem only got worse. Israel refused to relinquish control over Temple Mount. Rumors circulated that someone had sacrificed the red heifer needed to bless those who would rebuild the Jewish Temple. Palestinians countered by staging a sit-in on the crater that had been Dome of the Rock. Israeli soldiers threatened to shoot, and some did. More and more people from around the world joined the protest each day to replace the wounded or arrested. It appeared to be a stalemate.

Then the unthinkable happened.

A group of Zionists calling themselves the Temple Faithful only meant to scare people off Temple Mount, but someone miscalculated the necessary amount of explosives. The explosion rocked Jerusalem to its core, quite literally. The bomb leveled the mount. The blast took out several surrounding neighborhoods. Lots of people died.

Worse, the Wailing Wall, which had withstood the wrath of God Himself, fell. The last vestige of the ancient Jewish Temple had been destroyed, violated by Jewish hands.

More than the death toll, it was the image of the ruined Wailing Wall, so long a symbol of Jewish tenacity and righteousness, that galvanized peace efforts. Atonement became a buzzword. Horror, shame, and guilt drove leaders from both sides to the table, ready to negotiate rationally, with reasonable expectations. Israel made peace with its Arab neighbors.

As prophesied.

And now here I stood, fulfilling another prophecy.

When the crowd quieted down, I adjusted my collar microphone. As a fully loaded cyborg, I could simply have increased the volume of my voice to be heard over the crowd. My vocal cords, like most of my body, were cybernetically enhanced. But I've been told that my abilities give people the creeps, my power makes them uncomfortable.

Yes. Very.

If only they knew about you, my dear, I chided Victory.

Harrumph. To know me is to love me, she said.

I almost laughed out loud; sometimes she reminded me a lot of Page, from whom she was copied. I smoothed my expression before the camerabots swarmed in for close-ups. I spoke: "People of Israel, Palestine, the world, this space is now free."

The crowd interrupted me briefly to show their appreciation.

"No one shall dare to own what belongs first to God."

More cheering. I nodded, waiting. I had been asked to speak because of my infamous connection to this place. I was seen as the person who first awoke the world to the horror of false prophecies run amok, to what happened when a person put too much faith in obscure, often misinterpreted two-thousand-year-old scribblings. I became the poster child for the abandonment of theocracies and a return to secularism. All of which was a touch ironic in light of the fact that I still wore the priestly robes of monsignor in the American Catholic Church.

"Let us learn to live in peace. Let us learn to live with each other. Let us forgive. Let us truly be children of God."

I raised my hands as if in a benediction, and the crowd roared. I felt like a queen, and perhaps, at that moment, I was, indeed, enthroned on the third temple—a temple to skepticism, to secularism, to ... anti-faith.

You are not the Antichrist. The Koran speaks nothing of this moment. Only in the Hadith does it say...

Shhhhhhhhh. Let me savor it.

Horrible, was all Victory said, and I wasn't sure what she meant.

Perhaps it was horrific that I had accepted my role, that I *wanted* to be associated with the Ultimate Evil, the Beast. But being married to Satan will change your mind about a lot of things, not the least of which is the nature of God.

I had come to believe that, as with history, the victors wrote the Bible. God and his army had won the war for Heaven and then cast my Sammael as the great enemy. Originally the word Hebrew word *satan* simply meant "an adversary." That was all this was about—two armies on different sides of a battlefield.

Not good against evil.

You delude yourself.

Do I? I met many human beings worse than myself in prison. Rapists, murderers, molesters of children, thieves, con artists...certainly Morningstar was no saint, but he treated me well and said please and thank you.

This makes Satan the good guy? "Please" and "thank you"?

It's better than some.

Oh, "excuse me." Victory brought my lip up in a sneer.

Stop that, I sent, putting a hand over my mouth to hide Victory's expression on my face.

"Please?"

Yes, please.

I brought my hand down in time to grasp the prime minister's in a strong shake. Camerabots flashed, signaling to us where to look, where to smile. The lights flickered like a strobe. The president of Palestine hustled through the crowd and stood beside us. We all grinned like idiots, flashing peace signs and giving the thumbs-up. I felt foolish, but no doubt it would play well in Peoria.

One prophecy down. The next on my list was the infamous mark of the beast.

What is this? The grocery list of the apocalypse?

I laughed. The president and the prime minister joined me, apparently thinking my joy over this historical moment had bubbled over. *I love that*, I sent to Victory.

You would.

The best thing about the mark of the beast was that most of the world already had it. "That no man could buy or sell unless he had the mark." It was so clearly the LINK.

Now I just needed to find a way to control it, master it.

Good luck.

I didn't need luck. I had already started, with a little help from a friend.

Kioshi.

Yes, Victory, you know all about it, don't you? Too bad you can't tell a soul.

I won't let you win, she said, stiffening my shoulders in fear.

I already have, I reminded her. *My mole is inside the system, waiting. She's ready.*

Victory sent a shiver down my spine. *Ready for what?*

Ready to take over the LINK, of course. My inner voice was confident, but I was on my own with this one. Not even Morningstar knew the details—and, besides, it would crush him to know I'd had a child without him. He'd be devastated to know that I'd sent my child away, to be hidden inside the yakuza's AI "program."

Kioshi had a farm of children, infants really, whom he raised in total LINK-immersion. They could speak binary before they could babble a barely coherent "mama." It was out of this virtual primordial soup that Japan's artificial, the dragon, was born. Toyoma Corporation genetically engineered most of the children in the "program," as he called it. He owned the patent to their genes. Thus, they were his property to do with as he liked. It was a kind of slavery, but, as with much of what Kioshi did for profit, people looked the other way. Besides, the program was a well-kept secret.

Which was another reason why it was perfect for my plan.

She's two years old now. Don't you wonder what she looks like?

No. She looks like me. Exactly. I laughed again, and the prime minister gave me a funny look. Even so, he smiled and chortled along with me, as if we shared a private joke. *The child is a clone. You know that.*

It was an important part of the plan, actually. I wanted a precise duplicate of myself, regardless of the risks. For reasons known only to God, Morningstar was sterile. He and I would never produce children the normal way. It hardly mattered. I got what I wanted from Morningstar when he exchanged the blood oath with me.

And the clone had it too.

I should have stopped you.

Yes, I smiled. *You should have.*

Victory tensed my muscles again, and I relaxed them with a popping shoulder roll. I grinned easily at the cameras. The sun seemed brilliantly white in a cloudless sky. I took a deep breath—the air smelled fresh and new.

I would win. I knew it. I had fate, prophecy, and Satan's own willpower on my side. I could not lose.

¤ ¤ ¤

ANTICHRIST WATCH LIST

A Regular Column for the Fundamentalist Press

Monsignor Emmaline McNaughton jumped to the top of the Fundamentalist Press's Antichrist Watch List today when she presided at the grand opening of Israel's Anti-Temple. Officially considered an "international free zone," the site is a memorial to the accidental destruction of the Wailing Wall by Messianic Jewish factions. The Walling Wall was the last remaining vestige of the Second Temple.

The memorial had satisfied many leaders because there had been no official plans to construct anything on the site. It was intended to remain as the original blast left it, no stones moved or removed. However, under the guise of making the site "safe" for visitors, non-Jewish construction crews have been spotted after dark clearing debris and leveling the ground. One Jerusalem resident says that she witnessed concrete being poured. "They're building, all right," said Trisha O'Donnell, a Christian living in Jerusalem. "It's sacrilege on the highest order."

The mission statement of the international free zone, which was written mostly under the guidance of McNaughton, declares the spot to be, among other things, "a place to witness the destructive power of the theocratic mind-set." It goes on to say that, while religious worship will be allowed there, it must remain free of any "indication of allegiance to one particular faith or another." In other words, it is a temple to secularism.

According to 2 Thessalonians 2, the Church will witness the Antichrist's stand in the Third Temple. Previously, religious scholars had believed that this passage referred to a completely reconstructed and reconsecrated temple. However, as its building is the harbinger of the Antichrist, we now believe that the temple is, itself, an anti-temple, a temple built *not* for spiritual worship, but as a symbol against it.

The Antichrist may well be enthroned in Jerusalem. The time is nigh.

¤

CHAPTER 2

Amariah

I hated school.

I suppose that's how I ended up on the subway at ten o'clock in the morning, headed home. Truant again. Mom was going to kill me. She'd pulled a lot of strings to get me enrolled. She wanted me to have a normal life, just like everyone else.

That'd be great if I was human.

Mom said I shouldn't think like that, but it was true. Everyone could tell just by looking at me that I'd been mutated by the Medusa. One of my eyes had a pupil the color of quicksilver that reflected light. Huge clumps of my hair on that same side of my head came in white and resisted every hair dye I'd ever tried.

The subway rattled its way toward Harlem, which was the end of the line before the Glass City and my home in the roving kibbutz. The train was mostly empty. At this time of the morning apparently only a few lost souls had anywhere to go. Classic dirty-parka, mumbling guy sat across from me, but his own demons kept him too busy batting at the empty air to notice me. I kept an eye on him, though, because I had the freaky sense someone was staring at me, watching my every move. Maybe it was my own conscience. Maybe it was God, my father.

Well, really, my father was an angel, but angels are God, or God is angels. Or maybe God *are* angels, since God is sometimes "They" or "Them," having both male and female parts, like in the first book of Genesis where They made man and woman in Their image. Not that God was *my* mother. No, definitely not.

Anyway, it was complicated.

And either way, I still felt watched.

Then I saw her out of the corner of my eye. She seemed to materialize out of the darkness. The woman stood near the end of the car even though there were plenty of empty seats. A preternatural grace kept her perfectly still as the train rocked and shuddered. Her silver eyes held the light as the subway car strobed through the tunnel. A Gorgon.

Her gaze never left me. She cocked her head to get a better view of the white streaks in my hair. I'd seen that look before. She was trying to figure out if I was one of her kind.

I didn't know the answer any more than she did. By all rights, I should be dead. The Medusa infected me when I was only four. The Medusa made Gorgons, and Gorgons lived, at best, five or six years-although there were legends... whispers...urban myths of Gorgons as old as twenty. But no one could prove it, and the Gorgons weren't talking. They were too feral, most of them anyway. Rumors surrounded them—that they ate humans, that they hunted in packs like wild animals. The ones I knew at the kibbutz in the Glass City were pretty well socialized, but I knew better than to trust a Gorgon who was strange to me. I tucked my hand into my pocket and felt for my Mace.

She slithered closer, twisting around the center poles like a dancer. Even crazy parka-guy seemed compelled to watch her advance.

"Sister," she said once she'd reached me.

I wasn't sure if I should agree or deny kinship. My fingers closed around the Mace, but my hand was shaking so much I wasn't certain I could really use it. I just gaped at her like an idiot.

Long broken and dirty fingernails reached out to touch the white curls at the side of my head. "Halfling?" she asked.

Some people thought there were Gorgons who were born of uninfected parents. But I'd never met any.

I shook my head. "Cured," I managed to croak out.

A miracle had saved me, actually. Papa had sacrificed his earthly body that I might be healed. Hard to explain to most people, but my father was the archangel Michael.

Yes, *that* Michael—the one that smote the dragon with a fiery sword, the one with the emerald-green feathers and eyes of molten lava. The greatest angel of all, the chief of the Order of the Virtues, prince of the presence, angel of repentance, mercy, and righteousness, the ruler of the fourth heaven, and defender of the faith. That guy was my papa.

The Gorgon looked doubtful, too. She chewed her lip, as pale and bloodless as the rest of her. She looked like she wanted to say something, ask more, when my phone rang, making all of us—even crazy guy—jump.

"Where the hell are you?" came a strained voice when I pressed the button on my wrist-phone, my eyes still glued to the Gorgon lady.

It was Mom. Clearly, she was none too happy about my decision to take an unscheduled vacation day from school. "Hi, Mom."

"I just got a call from the assistant principal." She meant a LINK-transmission; Mom could be kind of archaic when she talked.

The Gorgon retreated back to the far end of the car. She mouthed, "Poseur."

"Hey, am not!" I said to the Gorgon. There was a whole cult of kids who pretended to be Gorgons by dyeing their hair white and getting silver contact lenses. "Stupid Gorgon."

"Don't take that tone with me, Amariah," Mom said. Now I knew she was really pissed. She usually called me Rye.

"I wasn't talking to you, I swear," I said to Mom, but stopped when I saw her face. "I mean, uh, about school, I know it's wrong, but I just couldn't stay. Some asshole in first period wanted me to bless his soda and make it holy. It's that report. It still haunts me."

Ever since my very first day when my homeroom teacher, Mrs. Frederickson, got the clever idea that a good way for her newest transfer student to introduce herself to the class was through a genealogy report, I'd been taking a lot of flack. What can I say? I couldn't lie, could I? I told them all about Papa and gave a nice little essay about the nature of angels and free will for extra credit.

Yeah, okay, in retrospect, it was an extremely stupid thing to do. But, in my defense, I'd been living in the kibbutz, where everyone knew all about Papa. Hell, we even had a resident archangel of our own, a cross-dresser named Ariel.

Anyway, after that day I discovered pretty quickly that miracles were not my forte. No matter how hard I prayed, I could *not* go back in time or make people forget I ever existed.

The tiny picture of my mom on the wrist-phone shook its head sadly. Mom and I looked nothing alike. She had blond-gray curls, cut short. Her face was round, feminine, and kind of sweet-looking, even now when she was mad as hell. I teased her that she made a great "holy mother."

My hair, meanwhile, had gone all dark and Italian, the parts that weren't white, anyway. Mom has shown me recordings of me as a towheaded kid, but I guess a lot changed after the Medusa bit me. I didn't look very sweet, either.

My jaw was square, like a man's, which was why I wore my hair long, way past my shoulders.

"God as your father, really, Amariah," Mom said with a shake of her head. "Ariel talked you into that little stunt, didn't he?"

"*She* had nothing to do with it. Why do you always blame *her*?" I accented the pronoun in both sentences. Mom wasn't very respectful of Ariel's transgender identity. I mean, I mostly thought of him as a man, but I was always careful to say "she" when I talked about him. It was the least a person should do, in my opinion. "What? Did you want me to lie? Did you want me to tell all those people that I didn't know who Papa was?"

Mom sighed, it was her "I don't know what to do with you sometimes" sigh.

"I wish I hadn't, okay? I wish I'd been like the apostle Peter and denied him three times over," I said miserably. I hadn't expected to have to fight Mom on this one. She was the one who always made sure I knew that Papa loved me.

Mom frowned hard, making a dark crease appear between her eyebrows. "I don't understand this loyalty you have to Michael. You can't possibly even remember him."

"You've shown me vids. And anyway, he's hard to forget."

Mom let go of her frown with a sigh. "You look more like him every day."

She looked at me for a long time through the phone, and I could almost see her heart softening a little. "You're never going to graduate. You know that, right?" Mom said finally.

"Mouse could fraud me a diploma."

"Mouse has 'frauded' you enough stuff already, young lady." Mom shook her head and muttered, "Jesus Christ, listen to you. The kibbutz has corrupted you—you're more hacker than human. Listen, we'll talk about this school thing more when you get home. I don't have time for this right now. This place is in chaos, and I'm in the middle of a big case. Maybe you could get some real-life education today by helping me out a little with work."

"Detective work? Really?" Mom rarely let me help her with her private-eye stuff, even though I always wanted to.

"Yes, really. But this doesn't mean I'm condoning your behavior."

I'd already forgotten about this morning, I was so excited to help with the case. "*Skóro*, Mom! You're the best."

"*Skóro?*" Mom asked. "What does that even mean?"

Mom was way behind the times. "It's Russian for 'fast.'" She continued to look blankly at me. "It means 'cool,' Mom."

Mom hung up with a heavy sigh.

25

I had to stop at Luis's to pick up my environmental suit. The December air was cold and smelled like it might snow later today. Despite the chill, Luis sat on the stoop of his brownstone dressed only in a pink lab coat, a white T-shirt, jeans, and wing-tip shoes. His perfectly trimmed dark curls were bent over some small, hand-sized object. He had a pencil-thin screwdriver and was fiddling so intently with his gadget that he didn't notice me until I sat down beside him.

"What you got there, Luis?"

"Eek!" he squealed, dropping the gadget and screwdriver in a flutter. He laid his hand on his forehead in a faux swoon. "Is it three o'clock already? God, I hate it when I lose track of time like that. I got absolutely nothing done today. Nothing!"

"It's ten-thirty," I said with a smile. "In the morning."

"What? Are you sick? Parent-teacher conferences day?"

"Truant," I said. "Mom knows, though. It's okay."

Luis raised an eyebrow at me while looking over the bridge of his glasses. He wore the glasses for show. He once confessed to me that his eyesight was perfect, but he needed the street cred that the horn-rims gave him. Luis was already too pretty for the other scientists in Harlem to take him seriously, no matter that he was a mathematical genius.

"That doesn't sound like the Deidre I know," Luis said.

"Call her yourself," I said. "I'm here for the suit, not an interrogation."

Luis clucked his tongue. "Ai, such attitude, girl." His hands gestured at the door. "Go on, go on, then. It's not like you don't know where I keep it."

He picked up his gadget, but I stayed sitting on the concrete steps. I liked Luis. He dated Ariel on and off in that casual way some gay men had with each other. I wished they'd be more serious, so I could see him more. I think Ariel knew it. That's why he'd suggested to Mom that Luis keep my environmental suit for me.

I tucked my hands in my armpits for warmth when the wind blew some leaves up the street. I watched them swirl in the gutter.

"I thought you were excited to help your mom with her case," Luis said without looking up from his toy.

"You LINKed her!"

"Of course, I'm scared shitless of that woman. She's way more butch than I."

I gave him a grimace. "I am excited to help, yeah, but I don't know. I just wanted to hang out a little, I guess."

"So, what happened?" Luis put the screwdriver down on the step. "At school."

"Continuing repercussions of a genealogy report gone bad," I sighed.

Luis put a hand on my shoulder and gave me a sympathetic frown. "*Tu padre*, eh?"

I nodded, too many thoughts rushing around in my head to add anything coherent.

"You know, sometimes it's okay to lie a little," Luis said. "Sometimes little lies can save your life."

Luis and Ariel had to lie a lot. Being gay was a serious crime in America. You really could end up dead, or worse, sent to the Inquisition deprogramming camps. I shuddered to think. Luis had told me about a guy who came back from one of those places-Luis said he might as well have been dead for all the life left in his eyes.

"It's not fair," I said.

"So few things are," Luis said. "Come on, *angelita pequeña*, let's get you dressed."

Luis's first-floor apartment faced east. Morning sun fell in a bright swath across oak floors and nestled into the soft cushions strewn artfully around a glass-topped end table. A glazed earthenware vase in the center of the table held large stalks of pampas grass and twisted husks of grayed milkweed pods. I breathed in deeply. Luis's place always smelled pleasantly of books. All of the walls were filled with custom-built wooden shelves, crammed with paperbacks and hardcovers of every color, size, and shape. Luis's love of books knew no bounds. He had fiction of every genre and nonfiction ranging from a history of grave robbing to the latest underground mimeographed pamphlet on nano-technology.

I threw myself into the largest of the cushiony chairs. The sun had warmed the fabric, and it felt almost blazingly hot under my cold butt. I loved Luis's place. It was a real apartment, a place people were meant to live, where the plumbing was connected to the city's water system, and heat poured gloriously from vents in the floor. His place was nothing like the various warehouses and abandoned theaters that I'd grown up in. With the constantly moving kibbutz, everything was cobbled together and jury-rigged for human habitation.

Framed black-and-white photographs of men's nude bodies occupied the few spaces that the bookshelves allowed. The shelves themselves were like a treasure hunt. Here and there, curios propped up a group of books or lay in the thin space in front of neatly ordered spines: a cast-iron teapot, a glass jar full of buttons, a dried white rose, a clay figure of a sleeping cat, a carved wooden egg, a tiny lamp that cast a cozy pool of light. It was the accumulation of a lifetime spent in real houses. I coveted it.

Behind me, I could hear Luis fussing in the kitchen. I smelled something chocolaty.

"If I were Ariel, I'd move in with you," I said over my shoulder, snuggling deeper into the chair. "Why does she stay at the kibbutz when she could live here?"

A small laugh came from the kitchen. "This place is much smaller when two grown men are rattling around in it."

"Have you had other lovers live here?"

"Of course," he said, handing me a mug filled with instant hot chocolate. Mini-marshmallows floated on top, just beginning to dissolve.

"Why did they ever leave?" I sighed.

"I imagine I irritated them. Or bored them. Or both," he said with a small smile, as he settled into a large white leather-covered chair.

"Not possible," I assured him.

"I'm glad you think so, *chica*."

"Does Ariel think you're boring?" I asked, taking a sip of the chocolate.

Luis let out a surprised little laugh. "I don't know. Maybe sometimes. I'm not very into 'the scene.' I'd much rather stay at home and tinker with my little toys than go out clubbing."

I shut my eyes and let the sun warm my face, and imagined spending my evenings in a place like this with Luis in the corner fiddling with a gadget, myself reading or dozing. I opened my eyes and let out a frustrated little sigh. "I don't understand him."

"Well," Luis said, hiding his eyes from me by glancing at the floor. "I guess that's to be expected. I mean, he's not supposed to be knowable, is he?"

I got the sense that the "he" in that sentence was meant to be capitalized. "Did you guys stop dating because Ariel is God?"

"Ai! What a question!"

I waited, silent, to let him know I was looking for a serious answer. After staring at his hot chocolate for a long time, Luis finally glanced up at me over his horn-rims and gave me a sly smile. "Well, that does add a certain...complication...in the bedroom."

"It never stopped my mom."

"And it hasn't completely stopped me, God help me," Luis said quickly with a roll of his eyes and a shake of his head, as if he couldn't believe himself for admitting to it. He sipped his own hot chocolate for a moment, then asked,

"Do you know? Did Michael tell your mom what he was before they, uh, were intimate?"

I chewed my lip. I'd never asked. I'd always kind of assumed that Mom always knew.

Luis shrugged to himself. "Ariel told me, but I just thought he was being a diva, a drama queen. 'I'm an angel,' he said. Sure you are, honey, you're the queen of the world." Luis shook his head in that same shocked, disbelieving way. "How was I to know he was being serious?"

I stared at Luis for a moment, watching his face change with apparent memories. I tried to imagine what it must have been like to not have known that angels walked on earth. For me, it's been part of my life for as long as I can remember. Still, it's not something I can talk to most people about. Look at what happened at school.

"It's weird, isn't it? What we know. We're not like other people, are we?"

Luis gave me a smile. "I've never been like most people. This is just one new dimension to my oddity."

"Like being gay? It's just another secret you keep?"

"Exactly. And like practicing science." He laughed again, looking down at his pink lab coat and the way his pinkie was raised on the handle of the coffee cup. "As you can see, I've never been very good at keeping secrets. Denying who I am doesn't come very naturally."

"Do you ever worry...about the camps?"

Luis scratched the back of his head in lieu of answering me. "We should get you home."

Ten minutes later I was stomping through the glass, talking to God. "Papa, why do you make people like Luis, if all they have to look forward to is suffering?"

As usual, my dad had nothing to say for himself. Strong silent type: that was Papa.

The armored suit felt stuffy inside, even though I could see crisp flakes of snow starting to drift through the air. I wore an armored version of the Israeli holosuit, and the thing felt like heavy hands pressing down on my shoulders and hugging me tightly. The fabric had been lined with spun silicone—in other words, pounds and pounds of fancy sand. Glass, you see, was the one substance that the Medusa wouldn't bite, since the glass already was silicone.

The Medusa bomb was the big nasty of the last war. Its development and detonation scared people away from science and into the arms of religion. It represented the great hubris, I guess—when technology is allowed to race ahead of wisdom—because, when the nanoviruses of the Medusa were unleashed, they weren't really ready. Sure, the 'bots did their job well—they froze great big huge chunks of people and stuff by reconfiguring their molecules into silicone. But the scientists forgot the basic rule of viruses: they mutate. So, instead of dying off like they were supposed to, they kept developing resistant strains. The glass was still "hot" today.

That didn't stop it from being kind of pretty, though. Winter was my favorite time in the glass. Everything seemed right, more magical, like the world was supposed to be made of glitter and ice.

"Why do you let this go on?" I asked Papa. The glass, if it continued as it had, unchecked, would eventually eat up the whole world. Sure, its advance was slow, but it was also steady. The glass grew. In my lifetime it had swallowed an additional sixteen miles of the area around the Bronx. That was a square mile a year.

My father, once again, chose not to comment. It was weird. I barely knew Papa, since he'd been gone all my life. Still, I missed him. There wasn't anything specific that I could point at and say that this is what was absent. It was just a very present "not there" feeling I got in the pit of my stomach.

I felt it now, wondering what it would be like if Papa were here at this moment. I put my hand out and imagined holding his. And I walked like that, hand in hand with nothing, all the way back home.

¤ ¤ ¤

MORNINGSTAR FOUNDATION TO FUND MEDUSA RESEARCH

Scientific Community Surprised, Church Angered

Agnostic Press (December 2095)

United Nations Headquarters—Monsignor Emmaline McNaughton, the principal spokesperson for Morningstar Foundation, announced today that the philanthropic organization will pledge 6.5 million credits (Christendom) to researchers in the physics, nanotechnology, and medical fields. The team will investigate the possibility of halting or transforming the various cities affected by the Medusa glass. The press announcement listed the names of several prominent medical professionals and nanotechnicians. Some of the physics experts named, however, are currently in prison or considered wanted by the authorities.

"We have made arrangements for immunity," McNaughton said via a LINK-transmission at United Nations headquarters. "We just need the physicists to come forward."

One of the physicists listed was none other than Maxine Mann, the team leader of Project Titan, responsible for the creation of the original Medusa bomb. McNaughton's announcement appeared to confirm rumors that Mann escaped the lynchings that immediately followed the war and has been living in South America. When asked about the inclusion of the infamous scientist, McNaughton further shocked the gathered press by stating, "Mann approached me. She's been desperate to fix her mistake since the moment it happened."

Much of the work, according to McNaughton, has already been completed by the now eighty-seven-year-old Mann. "The nanoviral load for a new set of 'bots has already been scripted. What we need now is a lab in which to test out Mann's work," McNaughton continued. "We don't want any surprises this time, now, do we?"

The Medusa bomb was produced by a hellish combination of nanotechnology and bio-warfare. The main force behind the bomb was viral nanobots whose programmed task was to consume complex molecules and excrete silicone. That was supposed to be the end of it, but the Medusa mutated and became resistant to its internal suicide program. McNaughton claims that Mann's script not only stops the old virus but also transforms the "glass" into harmless sand. "If Mann's work is genuine," McNaughton said, "this will be the breakthrough of the century."

It could also be the nightmare of a new generation, insists Cardinal Kyong Ye. "It is the height of irresponsibility to allow Mann to unleash not one but *two* new nanoviruses. All you have to do is look at the horror of the glass cities to realize why this is folly." Church officials of nearly every religion were up in arms about the formation of this research team, for different reasons, including very political ones. "It's another nail in the coffin of theocracy," said Muslim imam Mohammad Flavio Panati. "Another foot in the door for secular humanism." The backlash after the detonation of the Medusa bombs has long been associated with the rise of theocratic states.

The high priestess of the Cult of the Risen AI had an unusual objection: "If you cure the Medusa, you will stop the eventual destruction of the world. This is meant to be our technological apocalypse. We must allow our folly to continue its course in order for true rebirth to begin." Though of very different background, some Evangelical Christians agree. "Jesus is coming to save us," said Pastor Virginia Walters. "The Rapture will come before the end of the world. It is predicted."

Likewise, many religious leaders regard leniency toward Mann as a dangerous first step to decriminalizing other "hard" sciences. The underground science community sees things differently. "This is amazing," said a biologist in Harlem, New York, who asked to remain anonymous. "I think I can speak for all of us in the underground when I say that we will contribute anything we can to help Mann cure the Medusa. Anything. If the Medusa can be cured, our names will be cleared. Godspeed to the team."

¤

CHAPTER 3

Deidre

Sometimes I wondered why God hated me so much. My daughter was truant from school again, and a criminal and an archangel had nearly come to blows in the lunchroom. Over tapioca.

"Drop the bowl, Mouse," I said as calmly as I could.

Mouse, the aforementioned criminal, was standing on top of one of the metal folding tables. He had a shit-eating grin on his face and was armed with a full bowl of pudding, currently aimed at the face of Ariel, the archangel. A dozen or more white-haired Gorgons surrounded the combatants and were pounding their fists on the table shouting, "Fight! Fight! Fight!"

The whole scene was made more ridiculous by the faux kung fu pose Ariel had adopted. Perhaps it wouldn't have looked so strange if she, or rather he, hadn't been dressed in a full-length Indian-print skirt, white poet shirt, and high-heeled sandals. Though the two lacquered chopsticks still remained in place, Ariel's long black hair had come unbound from its geisha-style coif, and bits of it were hanging jauntily over his eyes.

Mouse was about my height, which is to say amazingly short for a guy— although unlike some, he wore it well. If he was self-conscious about it, you'd never know. Frankly, watching him dance around on the table, waving the bowl maniacally, I doubted Mouse had ever lacked confidence. Having made a fairly successful bid for world domination will do that to a body.

Truthfully, despite the fact that he'd tried to kill me once, I had kind of a soft spot for Mouse. Though not my usual type—I had the classic penchant for tall, dark, and handsome-he was cute. And, technically, he had the *dark* thing going on. He was Egyptian, hailing originally from Cairo, and he had the

32

physical features you might expect: straight black hair, light brown skin, and eyelashes so long and thick they almost seemed girlish. Like I said: cute. Plus, he was smart, funny, and just a little bit dangerous. You could see that last part in the silver wire that snaked along his hairline—he was what I used to hunt when I was still on the police force's LINK Vice Squad: a wire wizard.

"Stand down, both of you," I commanded again.

I'd become the de facto leader of this place—this kibbutz in the Glass City. It was a long story that involved a college roommate of mine, the Inquisition, and a perverted sense of loyalty. The roommate, Rebeckah Klein, used to run this place until she shot a guy in the head in Paris. The guy deserved it, no doubt, although apparently she was aiming for an artificial intelligence who was just passing through his combat computer on the way to taking up residence in a political celebrity known as Emmaline McNaughton. Like I said, long story. Complicated. The point is I'm a sucker for letters from prison and Rebeckah sent me one, begging me to take over stewardship of this place and its inhabitants.

This was, unfortunately, not a job I excelled at. Nor did it pay. My paying gig was as a private investigator, a job I should be doing right now instead of mediating these childish pranks.

Did I mention that Mouse was nearly forty? Ariel, presumably, was as old as time. Both of them should have known better. Especially since, although most of the Gorgons that lived in the kibbutz could be considered "tame," their wild side always lay just below the surface. The last thing I wanted was for this to turn serious for one of them and for blood to get spilled—all over something as stupid as tapioca.

"I mean it," I said. "Get down off that table right now!"

It was the archangel who acquiesced. Ariel raised his hands as if in surrender to Mouse and sketched a formal bow. "I take it back," he said. "Tapioca is *not* the finest food in all the world."

"Say it," Mouse insisted. "It is crap."

Ariel pulled himself up primly. "I most definitely will not."

The Gorgons shouted for a fight again.

A headache sprouted between my eyes. As the boys renewed their argument, I reached into my purse and pulled out my .45. I used to exclusively carry a .357 Magnum, but after my lover Michael shot himself in the head with it, I couldn't stand to use one again. I pointed the gun at the ceiling, put a finger in my ear, and pulled the trigger.

"I hereby declare tapioca is, in point of fact, crap. This fight is over," I said in the ensuing shocked silence after my ears stopped ringing. Most of the

Gorgons, with their heightened reactions, lay flat on the floor. Mouse and Ariel stood staring at me, the broken bowl of pudding smashed in a puddle between them.

"Okay, then," I said, putting the gun back in my purse and snapping it closed. "Move along."

"Merciful Allah, Dee," Mouse said, clambering down off the table. He trailed after me as I turned and headed out the door. "We were just having fun."

"You were being stupid. Both of you know how wound up the Gorgons can get. I wouldn't think I'd have to remind *you*." Mouse was currently sporting a nasty cut across one cheek where a possessive Gorgon had slashed him in order to reclaim the Christmas lights Mouse had "borrowed" for his room.

The corridors of the abandoned grade school were crowded. The kibbutz was mainly home to society's outcasts. Besides Gorgons, we also had rogue scientists, political rebels, religious misfits, and about a battalion and a half of Israeli soldiers. The soldiers were here because many of them had been part of Rebeckah's organization—the Malachim, the Avenging Angels—who had used electronic and real-time terrorism to help bring down Mouse's LINK-angel hoax.

Oh, right, I forgot to say that before putting a bullet in a man's brain, Rebeckah had also been a LINK-terrorist. She was a great roommate, though. Very tidy. Kept to herself and helped me pass calculus. Anyway, it wasn't like my history made me a candidate for an appearance as a commencement speaker either. Alas, apparently Swarthmore was put off by my rather public connection to the assassination of a Pope. Go figure.

Anyway, Rebeckah's army and I had an uneasy alliance. They protected Rebeckah's legacy, the kibbutz, with their Uzis and their late-night patrols. I preferred a slightly less savory but more peaceful way to keep the kibbutz safe. I paid off the police and political leaders with bribes (money out of my own pocket or begged from residents), which most of the soldiers found repugnant. They also didn't like my lack of military training or the fact that I was not a Jew. We agreed to ignore each other out of the mutual respect we all had for Rebeckah.

I used to be a Catholic. But while my faith in God had been restored, after Michael I stopped sweating the details. Catholic, Protestant, Jew, Muslim...it was all kind of the same to me—just different ways to worship a multifaced God. After you've done the down and dirty with an archangel, it's kind of hard to look the Virgin Mary in the eye. At the same time, I could not deny what I knew. So, yeah, I believed, but the dogma didn't make much sense anymore.

"Don't you think you're overreacting?" Mouse wanted to know. He was still trailing behind me. "I mean, you shot up an acoustic tile. That's pretty harsh. Not to mention the ringing in my ears."

"You're lucky I didn't shoot you."

"Ha, ha," he sneered, then he blinked, as if considering I might be serious, and added, "You wouldn't have, would you?"

"No, I probably would have shot Ariel," I admitted. "I'm pissed off at him."

"Her," Mouse corrected. "She prefers to be called 'she.'"

"What part of 'pissed off at *him*' did you not understand?" I asked.

"Oh. Good point." Mouse nodded. "So what's Ariel done—I mean other than having no taste when it comes to pudding?"

I looked at Mouse. He'd been fighting the tide of people to keep pace with me, and seemed genuinely interested. Speaking of uneasy alliances, Mouse was another one. When I was a cop, Mouse was my quarry. I'd nearly nabbed him several times in his career, and finally did, over the LINK-angels. At some point long before the LINK-angel case, Mouse decided my pursuit of him was personal. He thought I chased him because I was hot for him.

Of course, I wasn't. Well, okay, maybe, but only a little bit. Look, it's hard not to be flattered by someone's attention, especially someone intense, like Mouse. So, over the years, we'd developed a strange relationship wherein he would give me information when I called. He used to make a lot of noise about charging me a high price, but Mouse could usually be easily bought off with some scandalous information about me. Like the size of my underwear.

He liked me a lot.

Thus, when he was paroled, he came to the kibbutz begging for a place to stay. I let him in, but not because I thought he had reformed. I was under no illusions that Mouse had come out of the federal prison system a better man. In fact, I continued to look the other way when he used his wire skills to score some stuff for himself and the kibbutz from the LINK. The fact that he could pay for his rent here made his stay with us all that more attractive. Besides, he wasn't the only criminal here, only the most famous.

Mouse and I weren't precisely friends, but we weren't enemies anymore either. If we ever had been. Still, it wasn't as though we were in the habit of sharing deep dark secrets or having heart-to-hearts.

"I could beat him up for you," Mouse offered.

"Ariel?" Mouse nodded vigorously. I had to smile at that, and added, "Could you send him back where he came from?"

"China? Sure, I can scam him plane tickets. Tonight, if you want."

Ariel looked Chinese, just like Michael had appeared Italian. Each of the archangels had his own flavor, I guessed. Jibril, otherwise known as Gabriel, was a black Muslim, and Raphael, when I'd seen him last, was dressed like an Israeli soldier. Satan had been Euro-trash.

Christ, the things I knew.

I shook my head. "Nah, don't worry about it, Mouse. I just don't like the things he's been telling my daughter."

"Who would?" Mouse surprised me by agreeing. "That messiah gig is pretty heavy shit."

I stopped. I was nearly to my destination, that is, the place Amariah and I had set up as home, room 301. Mouse and I were on the stairs, underneath a huge blue and white Israeli flag. The sun shone through the material and cast a shadow of the Star of David at our feet.

"It is," I said. "Worse, I think she's starting to believe it. She keeps getting in trouble at school because she told everyone that God is her father."

"Some of the people here are into it, too," Mouse said, shoving his hands into his pockets. "I've heard some people ask her to, you know, put in a good word for them."

"Jesus fucking Christ."

"Yeah," Mouse laughed. "That's what they think."

"It's enough to make me want to convert. Maybe we could go live with the Moonies or something. I'll bet the Hare Krishnas have a nice commune somewhere."

"Heck," Mouse offered, "go be a Maizombie. Then you could make beautiful music with all the skid hippies."

I grimaced. "Except I hate polka, and living on the streets is bad for my complexion."

"I hear ya there, sister."

Mouse and I fell into a sort of companionable silence. Neither of us had any solutions for Amariah's messiah complex-especially since, considering her parentage, it could be more than a delusion.

In fact, if I allowed myself to remember the truth, there was a certain Passover Seder, when Rye was four years old, to which the prophet Elijah had actually showed up. We opened the door at the appointed time, and there the prophet stood. Just like that.

Elijah, it is said, wanders the world looking for the messiah. He had pointed to Amariah and said, "There she is." Elijah tried to take her away, but Michael and I fought him off. It seemed to have worked. So far. Although Amariah and

I have never gone to another Seder. I was afraid that if I did I would only be inviting trouble, as it were.

Avoidance actually seemed to have solved the problem.

Of course, there was the issue of the tapioca-loving Ariel. He'd showed up at the kibbutz one day out of the blue. No one else seemed to notice his sudden appearance; everyone said he'd always been here. If I asked for details of his arrival they'd shrug and say, "Well, you remember." But I didn't.

And that's how I knew Ariel was an archangel. That and the fact you could smell it on them like frankincense. Or, at least since Michael I could.

Ariel had never said he'd come with any particular purpose from God in mind, but I knew angels. They always had a reason. So I looked Uriel/Ariel up in a LINK dictionary of angels and discovered that among other things he had taught the mysteries of the Kabbalah to the Jews. Seemed auspicious. I imagined he surreptitiously "oversaw" my daughter's religious education.

Besides, the other thing I knew about angels was that if they didn't stay on task, they corrupted over time. Michael had lost all sense of himself when he tried to stay for Amariah and me. Ariel had been here for six years, and he seemed as sharp and as focused as the day I met him. That meant he was doing what he was supposed to be doing.

And whatever it was, I didn't like it one bit.

"It's too bad you don't drink," I said to Mouse after a while. "I could use a stiff one right now. I might just have to settle for a bad romance."

He raised his eyebrows curiously, as if he couldn't quite believe that I could substitute tawdry fiction for hard liquor, and said, "Hey, whatever gets you through."

"I'm going to need something," I said, rubbing the space between my eyes. "She's due home any moment."

"You'll get through," Mouse said charitably. "Although I don't know how you do it. I'm just glad I'm not her father."

I gave him a once-over; a girl could do worse. "Sometimes, Mouse, I wish you *were*."

¤ ¤ ¤

THE SOUL STEALER

A New Virtual Reality Game Endangering Our Youth

The Apocalypse Watch, Fundamentalist Press (December 2093)

New York, New York—Serge and Eva Johnson, Evangelical Christian parents of sixteen-year-old Olexa Johnson, say their daughter has been missing for over a week. Olexa, like many of her friends, recently began taking part in a cultlike virtual game known as Angel of Death: Soul Stealer.

"I blame the game and myself," says her mother, Eva. "The game rules required her to be out at all hours. I should have put my foot down. Now Olexa is gone."

According to the Johnsons, Soul Stealer is played both on the LINK and in "real time." The game seems to require its players to pass "entrance exams," which often involve criminal and immoral acts akin to those of gang initiation. Proponents of the game defend this aspect. "Yes," says longtime player Sheldon Burr, eighteen. "But all you have to do is go to a party or something in order to get the first password. See, what you're not getting is that *that's* the *skóro* part of the game. It's not something you play in your parents' basement. It's out in the world, meeting people."

These gatherings are not innocent, however. The New York police admit that they have been getting calls to a number of illegal parties that block traffic or involve breaking and entering, sometimes called "raves" or "hit-and-runs," which appear to have a connection to Soul Stealer. "We're also seeing a dramatic increase in young offenders in other areas as well," said a police officer who wished to remain unnamed but who identified himself as a Fundamentalist Christian. "It's hard to say if they're directly related to Soul Stealer, but I have my suspicions."

No information could be obtained about the manufacturer of Soul Stealer. The game seems to have come out of nowhere and is spreading by word of mouth. "You can suggest new members," admits Burr. "In fact, you get points for every soul you sign up."

Meanwhile the Johnsons pray for Olexa's safe return, though Serge fears the worst. "I'm sure she was lured to her death." The Johnsons have hired a private investigator to search for Olexa and for any other information about the game or its manufacturers. The Johnsons asked Christians everywhere to pray for Olexa's safe return.

¤

CHAPTER 4

Dragon

The game, the game is everywhere. This one finds it particularly annoying. One is used to being able to roam freely, but now everywhere one turns one confronts some huge blob of space being occupied by the game. It's all being eaten. Yes, that's an excellent simile; the game is some giant carnivore ingesting everything in its path.

"Gobble, gobble, just like a...Page, what's the hungriest meat-eater?"

Page/Strife walks beside this one. He manifests as a young man, small and wiry. His skin is the color of polished walnut, and, in places, it is so thin as to be transparent. At the cheekbones, around the hollows of his black eyes, this one can see the image of sharp metallic bones protruding. It is disconcerting, especially since his demeanor is so kind and pleasant. It's like strolling arm in arm with a cheerful skeleton.

"Hungriest? I'm not sure. A blue whale is the largest mammal. Technically it is carnivorous, as it sometimes ingests shrimp. But most would probably not consider it a meat-eater in the traditional sense."

This one sighs. Of course the question is rhetorical. One could look up the answer in a second, but Page and this one like to play at human conversation. *"This one is looking for a metaphor, not facts. A whale carries the wrong connotation. One wants something meaner, more like a bully."*

Thus chided, Page/Strife chews thoughtfully on his lower lip. Then a bright, if ghastly, smile splits his face. *"A dragon?"*

Page/Strife is referring to this one, since one takes the shape of that particular mythological creature. Though most dragons are genderless, as are AIs for that matter, one prefers to think of oneself as "she."

39

Page is making a kind of a joke. Not something either of us is particularly good at. Neither of us has ever been part of the real world, except for those rare occasions when we've merged with humans. That's part of why Page/Strife is so strange. He has merged a lot. In the right light—or maybe it's the wrong light—Page reminds this one distinctly of one's mother. He has adopted the shape of mother's eyes and the long mane of hair she wore when she lived. They were stuck together for a long time, Page and one's mother. In a way, it is nice to know a bit of Mai survives in Page/Strife/Mai.

Mai Kito is this one's honored mother, at least insofar as an artificial can have such a thing. Though officially a product of the infant minds that make up "the program," this one remembers Mai most clearly. Of all those in the creche, it was Mai's creative spirit that one first reached out to touch, to play with.

Mai and this one grew up together. This one was present when Mai first discovered her love of music, fell in love, and became a popular star in her band, the "Four Horsemen."

This one was not with Mai on the day she died, however.

Page holds that distinction.

Mai had been coerced into trapping Page inside a neural net. When he made his escape, he overloaded her system, and she died. The drugs she'd taken the night before didn't help. One had blamed Page for a while, but one came to realize that he only did what anyone would have. The whole thing was an accident. Page does not have the soul of a killer, despite his new name and new appearance. Moreover, he respects mother by wearing her features. One enjoys seeing bits of her smiling back at this one.

When one doesn't reply right away, Page adds, *"Why don't you search on it, dragon?"*

"It doesn't matter that much," one says. This one and Page have been moving along the byways of the LINK, as we do together once every day-cycle. One likes to imagine it as our genteel morning stroll around the grounds. But the truth is that we move so quickly, we pass through dozens of time zones in an instant. Even so, one casts morning light on everything where one can. One likes consistency.

Page walks at one's side, with a hand resting against one's scaly flank. Though it is just ones and zeros resting against one's own, this one imagines the spot where we touch as warm, comfortable. This one likes to experience the LINK like a human would, and so one's claws clack on a cobblestone causeway. To either side, sandalwood and teak grow. Monkeys cry in the distance. The air is thick and warm, despite the early hour. Above the snowcapped peaks of the Himalayas, the moon hovers in the bright blue sky.

"You made this very pleasant," Page says.

This one dips one's head in acknowledgment of the compliment. However, not all of what we see is of one's design. One just enhanced what the Indian programmers had already placed on this path.

We pass an overgrown temple, and one sees something slither in between the darkened doorways, like a snake. This one pauses. Page and one are the only living things on the LINK. Nothing should surprise us here, yet one did not conjure the slithering dark thing.

"Did you see that?" one whispers.

"That wasn't yours?"

This one sniffs with indignation. *"One likes pretty things."*

"Good point." Page takes one's paw into his hand, and we lean a little closer toward the doorway.

This one stretches out a long neck and sniffs the air with one's nostrils—a metaphor for sending out a query. Everything is still and quiet. One pokes one's nose in a little farther. *"Hello?"* one calls.

Pulsing green tentacles snap into existence over the image of the ruined temple. One pulls back quickly, afraid to touch the blindly grasping things. *"Ugh! It's so icky!"*

"What is it?" Page asks.

"It's that horrible game," one says, hanging one's head sadly. *"This one was trying to talk about it before. Look at it. It's ruined one's pretty picture! There are so few quiet spaces left, and now it's here, too."*

This one stares bitterly at it. The game is like a huge hole in the landscape. It doesn't even make an effort to blend in. The soft green brush and crisp blue sky just end in a perfect square of squirming worms. It looks like a hideous patch, only there was nothing wrong with the space it covers, no hole, no infestation, no glitch. The temple had been unused—yes, a bit overgrown—but did it deserve this?

"That game is a nuisance," one says.

"Why have I never seen it before?"

This one has to bite one's tongue. One wants to say that if Page spent less time gazing at his navel, perhaps he would notice the larger world around him. But one wouldn't mean that even if one said it. One of the things this one loves about Page is his introspection.

"Perhaps," one suggests softly, *"it's because you're so small."*

This one also knows that Page is very sensitive about his size. Not every artificial has the luxury that this one does to have a multinational corporation as a parental unit. One's processors fill an entire warehouse in Tokyo, an expensive venture in a place where space is at a premium. Page's maker is an outlaw, so all of his processing power has been stolen...much as the game robs space from the LINK. But Page is different. He is natural, part of the system. Not like that abomination.

"Yeah, maybe so," Page says, seemingly unfazed by this one's remark about his size. *"It's very strange, isn't it? I mean, it's not like a normal game at all. What is all that wiggly stuff?"*

One has wondered the same thing. Programs run various processes all the time on the LINK. Even those that are large operations from a human perspective rarely attract our attention. Instead, the various electronic transactions are like background noise, the babble of the datastream.

This one is different. As it moves through the LINK it disrupts everything—grabbing space possessively and then tossing aside carefully crafted areas with no regard for the normal order of things. It never puts away anything it pulls out; instead it seemingly runs forward to the next curious bit and destroys that.

This one has been spending half the day chasing after the game and cleaning up its messes.

"When we come back here tomorrow, it will have grown. Those tentacles latch on to things and absorb them."

Page gives one a look of pure horror. *"Would it absorb us?"*

"Doubtful. From what this one has been able to observe, it stays away from active things. At least so far."

Page reaches out a finger, as though to touch the squiggles. I can see metallic bone through the skin. *"It stays away from the 'active' things."* He says, *"You mean like us?"*

Though it will probably start reaching its grubby hands at us next, or any consciousness. One sighs, contemplating how to patch this new mess. Cocking one's head, one peers at the wiggly thing. Perhaps one could work the writhing into the LINK background as a patch of poisonous asps.

"Certainly, we are safe, but one meant...moving. If there is activity, business, enterprise, it is safe. If, like this temple, it is a space holder, forgotten, abandoned, then it will be occupied, taken over."

"Strange," Page says, *"it's both destructive and...yet shy. How long has this been going on?"*

"The game has been around for a couple of years, but it seems to have grown especially popular recently. Only in the last few months has it started doing this disgusting theft."

"I'll bet Kioshi is livid."

Kioshi Toyoma is this one's master. He runs Toyoma Corporation, Japan's foremost game designers. It's also a front for the yakuza. *"One presumes so. That's why this one has been trying to find out if there's a way to sabotage it."*

Page clasps his hands behind his back, reminding this one of a samurai. *"And what have you discovered?"*

This one is unsure how to read Page's mood. Even though his father was a wire wizard, Page has a strongly honed sense of morality. Sabotage isn't exactly legal, and, technically, the game designers aren't doing anything illegal; they are simply taking advantage of dead space.

"Why?"

"Well, look at them," he says, pointing to the tentacles and scrunching up his face as though he smells something awful.

We both glance again at the square of squirming worms. They shine as though they're wet or plastic or both. The tentacles are a disgustingly brilliant shade of chartreuse. Their presence makes the whole illusion of the LINK seem itself fake. As though they are the real things and the rest is some kind of elaborately painted backdrop. One doubts one can blend this one. The game is getting messier and messier. One shakes one's head sadly. *"This one wouldn't mind them so much if the game made an effort to fit in better. They use space that's not otherwise in use, and that's not such a bad thing. You do that."*

One realizes as soon as one says it, it's the wrong thing to have said.

"Oh."

His voice is small, and hurt. This one's eyes are wide; one doesn't know what to say to make it better. *"It's not... This one didn't mean ..."*

"Okay. Well. Uh, I really should go. It's time for prayers."

"It's always time for prayers," one says angrily. Page is a Muslim, required to pray five times a day. Since time is meaningless here on the LINK, he usually sets his clock by the time in Mecca. But time is flexible. He could just as easily pray later as now. This one knows he's mad and wants an excuse to leave. That's what makes one angry. Page always prefers to run instead of staying to talk something through.

"Now you begrudge me my religion."

"No," one sighs. *"Sorry. Please stay."*

"I'll see you tomorrow."

With that he goes. One wonders if he will be back in the morning. But then, Page is prone to pouting. Even so, one's about to chase after him when one gets a call to return to the home office. One would ignore it, but the call is labeled high priority and comes directly from Kioshi.

43

This one imagines one's home, and one is there. Rice paper lanterns hang from the stalactites that glitter with flecks of mica and gold. A black pool of water is fed by a stream that flows to the Yoshino River. White, blind fish flash in the depths of the dark water. Kioshi watches them with wide cartoon eyes. His avatar is the mascot of Toyoma's most popular game.

"Ah, dragon," he says. *"I am so pleased that you could return swiftly."*

One towers over him. One has assumed the classic dragon pose and is curled around one's personal treasures. If one would but lift a paw, Kioshi's avatar could be contained in a single fist.

"I have some very bad news," Kioshi says with a strange little deferential bow. *"Yes, oyabun?"*

"You're being downsized."

◻ ◻ ◻

MCNAUGHTON VISITS CAMP

GLBT Leaders Claim Victory, Catholic Church Furious

Agnostic Press (December 2095)

James Baldwin Center for Sexual Preference Reevaluation, Tennessee—Monsignor Emmaline McNaughton, formerly an Inquisitor for the pope, became the first dignitary to tour a U.S. "sexual preference reevaluation" camp since they were constructed by a legislative mandate of the first New Right Senate in 2072. Though her visit was virtual, conducted via the LINK, gay and lesbian rights groups hail this as a major victory for their cause. Catholic Church officials, meanwhile, claim that McNaughton has once again over-stepped her bounds as a former representative of Rome.

"We try to love the sinner, not the sin," said Archbishop Stefans O'Rourke, whose see includes the James Baldwin camp. "But those in the center still sin. That's why they're confined there and not released among the general public." The camps have come under fire in recent years from SLAGR (Straight Lawyers and Advocates for Gay Rights) for alleged violations of human rights. SLAGR spokeswoman Fala Runningwater says that the camps have minimally maintained facilities and numerous health department viola-tions. "The problem has been, however," Runningwater says, "that no one of importance was willing to go there and inspect them."

McNaughton echoed the sentiments of Runningwater after her virtual tour. "That place is a mess. Nobody should have to live in conditions like that." McNaughton went on to make what is considered her most startling public statement to date: "Especially consid-ering that the people there should be classified as political prisoners, not felons."

Currently, anyone convicted of genderbending is prosecuted as a felon under the "Leviticus Referendum." The Leviticus Referendum made formally illegal many of the admonishments listed in the Bible. A ban of homosexuality, specifically, is found in Leviticus 18:22: "Do not lie with a man as one lies with a woman; that is detestable."

However, underground GLBT movements such as Act-Up and the Lambda Defense League, with help from SLAGR and other straight organizations, have been lobbying legislators to repeal many of the crimes in the referendum, with some recent success, particularly in regard to public and private dress. Since their landmark victory of 2093, it is now permissible for women and girls to wear slacks in public. McNaughton's statement goes one step further. She says she would like to see all of the Leviticus Referendum repealed because it is "unconstitutional. Americans are more than just Christians," she says. "The Bible should not be the law in this land."

¤

CHAPTER 5

Morningstar

I breathed in the ancient scent of sun-warmed dust as I walked the streets of Jerusalem. In the distance, the Mount of Olives glowed in the morning heat, shimmering like the fires of Hell itself.

The Apocalypse had begun. The Antichrist was enthroned in Jerusalem.

Few mortals realized it, of course. They went about their daily business unaware that my wife, Emmaline McNaughton, a woman people were beginning to think of as a hero, a champion of secularism and human rights, might be something other than she seemed—something, instead, much more sinister.

Of course, mortals rarely understood the true nature of evil. Real evil is subtle.

No one in his or her right mind would fall for someone who knocked on their door and said, "Say, accept this mark in your forehead or I'll be especially mean to you and perhaps kick your puppy."

No, evil was a slow seduction. It was a gradual slipping, blindness, turning away, and following the path of least resistance. It was a morning-after "how did I get this way?" not a gleeful, villainous "bwah-ha-ha!"

More often, too, there was a hint of white to hide the blackness as a gray. Even Hitler improved the economy for the Germans.

Emmaline was in a unique position. Since the Temple hijacking, she had become a sort of political celebrity. The media wanted her opinion on everything—from what she thought of various presidential candidates to the Paris fall fashions. Honestly, if she sneezed, it made the eleven o'clock news.

What Emmaline suggested was repeated and echoed so often through the LINK, it was like a kind of subliminal mantra. Within days, the press would report her opinion as fact, and people everywhere believed whatever she'd said had always been so.

Using this influence, Emmaline changed laws. We consciously planned for her to do "good" things, such as trying to repeal the Leviticus Laws in America, which had led to so much suffering for the queer underclass. She visited poor areas of the world, handing out my money like it was candy. Half of Calcutta already thought Emmaline was the next Mother Teresa.

With the other hand Emmaline did something else, which also seemed, on its surface, to be a good thing. Under her constant political pressure, countries had begun extending their LINK privileges.

For most people the LINK was everything. It was access to politics, commerce, entertainment, and community. But since the last big war scared the world back into a stone age of theocratic rule, a person couldn't get access unless he or she belonged to a recognized religion. Aye, "recognized"—there was the rub. Depending on where you lived in the world, governments could pick and choose what constituted a legal religion.

With the help of a bevy of legal types, Emmaline had begun to convince the entire world to accept not only secular humanists and atheists as official but also groups previously denied access on general principles—like devil worshipers.

It was, in a biblical sense, the adoption of a single world currency.

Or, to look at it another way: everywhere, people were signing up to receive a device in their heads—one that could very easily fulfill a certain prophecy: "[The Beast] also forced everyone, small and great, rich and poor, free and slave, to receive a mark on his right hand *or in his forehead*, so that no one could buy or sell unless he had the mark."

The whole thing was enough to make an angel very...proud. Except I had nothing to do with it.

Not one *damn* thing.

Of all those that walked this earth, I never expected to be on the sidelines for the war of Armageddon—not I, who once laid low nations.

Worse, right now my main job seemed to be gofer. Emmaline had sent me out from underfoot to fetch a round of cappuccinos for everyone. Since all I had been doing involved staring out the office window while she LINKed this morning's speech to the Order of the Inquisition's headquarters, going out had seemed like an improvement. Fresh air, sunshine, and all that, plus a chance to escape the mewling sounds of all the fawning minions that catered to Emmaline's every whim. Except, apparently, fetching coffee; that was a job worthy only of the Prince of Darkness.

Even away from the office, her face was everywhere. Though the rush-hour streets of Jerusalem were crowded and dusty, every block or so I'd catch sight of her in my peripheral vision. Plastered to whitewashed walls were holographic posters of her beatific face smiling at me. Even without the LINK, you could see them. It had been a "woman of the people" gesture on Emmaline's part, to make the posters visible even to the disenfranchised. If I passed close enough to one of them, I could even hear her voice wooing me with some pearl of wisdom about how her plan to return to a secular world was a return to justice, peace, and true democracy.

Emmaline was, without question, deeply striking. Italian American by birth, she had a light olive cast to her flawless skin. Dark curls fell softly, like an ebony halo, around a sharply angled face. To remind people of her past, she still wore a priestly collar and the uniform of the Order of the Inquisition. Though rogue from the Order, Emmaline still held the title of monsignor. There had been talk of excommunication, but she'd grown far too popular for the American Catholics to consider that. Besides, most of the time she echoed their values and championed their ideals, albeit from a secular point of view.

On the street, a tourist, camera in hand, stared at me with a hint of recognition in his eyes. "Say, aren't you Emmaline's boyfriend?" he asked when I got closer.

I scowled and kept walking.

"Look, honey," I heard him say to a woman as I passed them. "It's that guy named after a fallen angel, what's his name, Emmaline's boyfriend."

"Morningstar," she supplied, excited. "Take a picture, for God's sake."

I heard the snap of a camera lens behind me. This is what I'd become: someone else's lover. I tagged along to events in her honor. I fielded the occasional "What is she *really* like?" interview question. I hung at her side at social events, like so much arm jewelry. We played the beautiful couple, with me as a footnote in her glory.

Where was *this* written? I wondered. Where in the Talmud or the Koran or the Bible did it say, "Lo, and Satan fetcheth the coffee for the Antichrist and her minions"?

Oh, it wasn't that I didn't still love her desperately, but just not so much today. Not while pushing my way past a gaggle of Hebrew schoolchildren to get to where a street vendor had his cart set up. "Two cappuccinos, a skim latte, and one coffee, black."

"Please tell me you're not the skim latte, Morningstar. I expect something stronger from the Adversary."

I looked up to see an archangel. He had a militaristic look about him, with closely shorn salt-and-pepper hair and a weather-worn face. I peered into his green-gray eyes. "Raphael. And to what do I owe this pleasure?"

"Just checking up on you," he said.

I stepped back to let him see all of me, and I held my hands out. "Behold: the victor."

Raphael laughed lightly while steaming the milk. "Charming," he said. "Yes, very nice. Say, I saw you both on the late show last night. Emmaline is very attractive. Smart, too."

"Since when do you LINK?" I tapped my temple for emphasis. Where most people had a slight lump that housed the LINK-receptor, Raphael's skin was as flat as mine was there. We had a slight, shall we say, allergy to LINKing, since if the shell of our bodies is punctured too deeply, our spirit escapes to Heaven.

Raphael set the two cappuccinos on the counter and started on the latte. "I saw it rebroadcast at the bar. It's become this big thing to replay the LINK images in community settings. Another thing Emmaline has done...brought people together. Neighbors getting to know neighbors. Talking about ideas. It's really pretty neat."

I was stunned into momentary silence. Raphael sounded like he approved. Then, the rest of his sentence hit me: "You were at a *bar*? On a Saturday night?"

"After Shabbat, of course."

"The world really is going to Hell."

"Eh," he said with a shrug. He ducked down under the counter to hunt for something. "If you're carrying all these you're going to need one of those cardboard container things. I think I have one."

I leaned over the plastic counter to stare at him. "Aren't you upset?"

"Well, yeah. This place is a complete mess. How am I going to help customers if I can't find anything?"

I frowned at his back. "You know what I meant."

"Morningstar," he said. Looking up at me from where he crouched, Raphael gave me a broad smile. "The messiah has come. I'm not worried about anything. I'm just here to watch the show."

My heart, if I had had one, would have stopped: *The Messiah*.

I was so startled by Raphael's words that I stepped back, bumping into another customer waiting in line. I made my halfhearted apologies as Raphael calmly put the coffees into the holder he'd found.

My eyes narrowed as I watched Raphael's smug expression while he tallied up the total. He thought he'd trumped me, but really, he'd just tipped Their hand.

"Thanks," I told him, handing over the shekels. "I needed this. You don't even know how much."

The office was in its usual pleasant chaos when I returned with the coffee. The room was filled with the music of keyboards clacking, phones ringing, and the soft mutterings of the LINKed transmitting press releases, answering reporters, and making connection with the vast numbers of true believers.

I breathed a contented sigh: ah, the dulcet tones of world domination.

We had set up in a house not far from Independence Park. The place was sunny and filled with secondhand yet homey furniture. On a worn-out plaid couch perched two young college-age boys, one Muslim, the other Jewish, folding pamphlets. A Christmas cactus spread out its fat, pink-tipped tendrils on the battered coffee table in front of them. In the corner another volunteer sat on a metal folding chair with an ancient keyboard of some sort in his lap. They all looked expectantly at the coffee, so I deposited the cardboard box on the table and went looking for Emmaline.

Through the sunny east-facing windows, I could see the remains of the Noble Sanctuary and the shattered Wailing Wall. Though I was not a Jew, it was harrowing to see the heart of Jerusalem laid bare and broken. This city had withstood so much for so long, only to be conquered by its own devotees.

I heard Emmaline's laughter in the kitchen. It was distinctive, her laugh. It was never halfhearted or shy. She let the humor bubble out of her in a great explosion, full-throated and from the belly. It was sexy as hell.

I wondered who was falling under her spell this time.

I pushed open the kitchen door. Emmaline stood like the eye of the storm, calm and centered, as the office boys—they were always pretty young boys—swirled around her, trying to anticipate her needs. One of them noticed my entrance and mouthed, "Cappuccino?" I jerked my thumb toward the living room. I was done with fetching today.

It would take some time before Emmaline realized I was back. It always did when she was in her element, so I picked a bagel from the basket on the counter and settled in to wait.

The kitchen was darker than the rest of house. Most of the morning sun was blocked by an apartment building in the neighboring lot. The previous owner of the house had, in a moment of perverted fashion sense, painted the walls a deep maroon, making the room seem even darker. Only the blond wood of the cabinets saved it from seeming like a cave. We had the money and resources to live in a palace, but Emmaline wanted to protect her image as one with the common folk so we left things alone, ugly as they were.

In fact, Emmaline spent most of her mornings holding court here. I wondered sometimes if she was jealous even of the sun, lest it upstage an iota of her brilliance.

She was LINKed, talking to some interviewer somewhere. Her documentary crew wrangled a swarm of camerabots while taking a few hand-held shots as well. Others made sure the light was just right on her face. She spoke out loud so that unLINKed viewers could hear her words, while one of the other pretty young things "translated" the interviewer's questions for the cameras.

She was talking about God again—how He was unknowable and mysterious. How she would never dare speak for Him, but if she did, she would imagine His message would be one of peace and love and an end to theocratic governments everywhere. I smiled.

One of the cameramen spied me first. He'd swung around to get a different angle of Emmaline, and paused, mid-sweep, to linger on me. I munched on my bagel and leaned back against the counter, trying to ignore the sudden attention. Who knows what he saw? A glint of golden highlight in my auburn hair, a hint of muscle jumping on my forearm, or a whisper of the spirit of the archangel who once stormed Heaven's very gates? At any rate, he seemed captivated for the moment.

And that moment was enough. Suddenly, a camerabot homed in on this new direction and buzzed me like a fly. Then another followed, bringing with it a spotlight so bright I struggled not to squint. Finally, even in her blind, LINKed state Emmaline felt the shift in focus. "Morningstar," she squealed delightedly. "You're back!"

The cameras swung back to her, desperate to capture her reaction to my presence. She ran to kiss my cheeks, and ever so briefly she allowed me into the center of her life. I felt the warmth of her body, and the heat from the spotlights covered me as we kissed again more deeply. Then she released me. Cold rushed into emptiness as she turned away to tell the interviewer that she had to cut things short. Breakfast and her husband had arrived. Life awaited.

She made it sound so...loving.

To be fair, it was.

It wasn't her fault that the world preferred her.

"I think that went well," she said when she'd signed off. Her minions agreed readily as they packed up their cameras and lights. A few stayed on, of course, to record these intimate moments for the documentary.

"What did you think?" Emmaline asked, coming to stand beside me. The cappuccino had appeared at her elbow, and she took a contemplative sip. "I mean, really? Was that last bit too much?"

I raised my eyebrows. I wondered whether she meant her light blasphemy, or the kiss that threatened to break the hearts of that coveted eighteen-to-thirty-five demographic?

"I'm sure it will be fine," I said. After all, I was well admired by the other gender in the same demographic. We were more powerful as a glittering celebrity couple than she would be alone. She knew that.

One of her minions threatened to interrupt us. I could see him hovering nervously with a list, no doubt some itinerary or another. So I decided to make a preemptive strike. "I'm leaving," I said.

The shocked expression on Emmaline's face told me that my voice had come out much harsher than I'd intended. "Leaving?"

The camera buzzed around us, like a moth on the flames of potential tension, drama. The intern, however, backed out the door, his eyes wide with the possible scandal.

"I have some personal business to attend to alone." Em reached around me to grab a bagel off the counter and to hide her frown. She pulled a wooden chair out from the kitchen table. Munching on the bagel and sipping her cappuccino, she sat, watching me, waiting for more.

I continued to lean against the counter, despite knowing that by standing while she sat, unconsciously to the eyes of the LINK audience, I appeared to be the aggressor.

"How long will you be gone?" Em's voice was soft, full of longing.

"Not forever," I said.

She laughed, breaking the tension. "Well, that's something."

"I know, my love. But where I'm going, is…" I glanced at the constantly present camerabots. "A bit hard to explain."

"Command. Password: *Pensieri, voi mi tormentate.* 'Rest. Off.'"

At her words the camerabots settled themselves on the nearest countertop or other flat surface. I watched with satisfaction as the red "on" light faded to black. For the first time in months, the mosquito buzz of their constant surveillance was silenced. The quiet was golden, if a touch infuriating. She'd had the password all along.

"You couldn't have done this when we made love?"

"You couldn't have been just a *little* less dramatic about the whole leaving thing? I mean, for crying out loud, Sammael, the press eats up missing seconds like this. All I'm going to hear about for the next weeks is 'Why couldn't he talk about where he was going?' And so what *is* the big fucking deal, anyway?"

"I ran into Raphael this morning," I said, taking a seat across from her at the table.

She set her bagel and paper coffee cup down slowly. "Raphael? As in the biblical Raphael?"

I nodded, although technically, in *her* Bible Raphael never showed up. He made his scriptural appearance in the book of Tobit.

"What did he look like?"

The question surprised me. Over the decade that we've been together, I'd told Em everything I knew about theology. I'd forgotten that I was one of the only angels she'd ever met. "No flaming bushes, if that's what you were wondering. Maybe six feet. Dark hair and eyes the color of polished jade. Other than the eyes, he's fairly forgettable. Well, no, he's better-looking than most." I laughed a little at that. "The boy can't help it. It's just our...it's just *their* nature to tend toward perfection."

"Your nature, too," she said, laying her hand over mine.

I pulled my hand away forcefully. "I don't want your pity."

She laughed at me, whereas others would have cowered. "Excuse me. I was trying to tell you that you're beautiful, dummy. Although maybe you have a few issues with pride, eh?"

"Hmmm," I said in response to her tease. I watched her eyes for lies, but they shone with affection. I could feel myself relaxing a little.

"So, what did Raphael say?" she asked. Picking up her bagel, she nibbled on it delicately. "He mostly came to harass me, but he let slip that the messiah is on the earth."

Emmaline chewed for a moment before asking, "The 'messiah.' What does that mean, exactly?"

"I'm not sure," I admitted. It really was hard to know, even for me. As Emmaline and I had discussed many times, God didn't follow any one particular script. Even if you could decipher what various religious prophets had said about the end-times, it really meant nothing as far as I could tell. The only reason I could fathom that God gave us any clues at all was so that we would better "get" Her sense of humor when She pulled the rug out from under our assumptions.

"I always thought that we'd have longer. That..." Emmaline looked over her shoulder, despite the empty room and silent cameras. Her voice was almost a whisper. "You know, that *Jesus* would come back."

"The Nazarene? I should hope not. He's pretty dead."

Emmaline almost choked on her bagel. "You know that for sure?"

"Well, no, but come on. Wouldn't he have made a comeback by now, if he was going to? Anyway, I would worry about ben Josef a bit more if Michael had been the one to tell me. It was Raphael. Therefore, I'm expecting the Lion of Israel. A Jew."

"Jesus was a Jew," Emmaline said, her finger tracing the grain in the wood table.

I frowned at her. She didn't like to surrender any part of her belief system, no matter how often it proved incorrect.

"I hadn't thought of that," I said, but I had absolutely no intention of going looking for the reincarnation of some provincial miracle worker. I wondered what she'd have thought if Jibril had told me to expect the Mahdi, or if Ariel had said the new Buddha had become enlightened. No doubt she'd have figured out how to put a Catholic spin on it. The human brain had an amazing capacity for self-delusion.

"You never know," Emmaline insisted. "God is funny that way. And not exactly straightforward, is He? I mean, it would serve His purposes to have us chasing after wild geese and then have the answer be something obvious."

I still didn't think God would resurrect one favorite son out of so many, but I had to admit Em had a point. "I suppose it could be a trick."

"You don't really think that Raphael told you by accident, do you?"

I had honestly thought so, at first. Sometimes we angels ran into each other by accident. Free will affected even us, here on earth. Anything clothed in flesh was corrupted, torn from the direct path. Though pure spirit, we were encased in a skin costume from the first moment we came to earth. Thus, even archangels sent directly from God could get distracted; it was the nature of this place—its curse.

But, thinking back, Raphael had been awfully smug about the whole messiah thing. Angels, by their nature, were messengers. That's what we did: "Hark, this" and "Behold, that." As much as I might like to imagine it, it was unlikely that God had sent an archangel just to say, "Hello, here's your coffee."

"So, you think there's a messiah?" I said.

Em took a long, thoughtful sip of her cappuccino. "Yes. Angels hate to lie," she said.

It was true. Even I, the supposed prince of said falsities, preferred half-truths and misdirection.

"We should seriously consider it," Em said, giving me a meaningful glance.

"I know what you're thinking, but ben Josef is not in the running," I said. "If your Jesus was walking around right now, don't you think people would be talking about it?"

"Six Jesuses were detained this week alone."

Jerusalem had a problem with messiahs. The place fairly crawled with them. There was an actual neurological disorder related to living or visiting Jerusalem that supposedly caused a sincere belief that one was the true spokesperson for God. It was called the "Jerusalem Syndrome," and it was so commonplace that the local hospital had a "messiah ward." The police talked about rounding up "John the Baptists" on a daily basis.

I frowned, still unconvinced. "You think the real one was among them?"

"If Jesus came back today, most people would think he was madder than the Hatter."

I snorted. "If ben Josef came back today, no one would even notice him. He wouldn't have the LINK. He was poorer than dirt, and he lived in the absolute butt of this country."

Emmaline's eyes were wide.

"Yes, of course, I knew him," I said to her Unasked question. "Although that desert-tempting stuff is bunk. I honestly never thought he would amount to anything, so why would I tempt him? And give him Jerusalem? It wasn't mine to give. At the time it belonged to the Romans. Anyway, you know me. I normally don't care much for what you mortals do amongst yourselves. My concern is winning back what is mine. I want the throne. It's all I've ever wanted."

She continued to gape, so I felt I had to continue. "Really, honey, ben Josef was no big deal, okay? Seriously, he was a big disappointment. I was looking for a lion, and this was a guy who preferred to be compared to a lamb. I still don't understand how that man and his weird sect ever got to be so damn popular. Especially since the more interesting things he said were completely struck from the canon."

As I spoke, Emmaline pulled at the skin near her eyebrow, as if trying to rub out my words. When I finished, she shook her head. "I don't even want to know. You make my head hurt."

Because I was trying to expand it? I decided not to say that, so I gave her a thin, unsympathetic smile, but my tone was teasing: "The feeling is mutual."

A knock came at the door. No doubt it was one of Em's interns, worried about appointments being missed.

"I should get back to them," Em admitted sadly. "What are you going to do?"

"Go in search of Jesus, I guess."

"You'll call, right? Keep in touch?"

I smiled wryly. "I promise. If I find God, I'll let you know."

She laughed at that. Standing, up, she gave me a peck on my cheek. "I'll miss you." It was a strange thing to say, and though we'd been teasing, something about it sounded vaguely insincere. I opened my mouth to ask her about it, but she'd already turned away. She opened the kitchen door and let the chaos back into our lives. I felt the noise almost like a physical blow. I watched as she was quickly swallowed up and surrounded by fluttering attendants again. My jaw flexed with a strange jealousy. It had been nice to have Emmaline's attention all to myself for a few brief moments. I reached over to where one of the camerabots lay, still unmoving. I picked up the little mechanism. It was no bigger than my palm, but heavy like lead.

Emmaline never even turned to wave good-bye. It seemed that as far as she was concerned I was already gone.

I crushed the camerabot like a bug.

◻ ◻ ◻

RUSSIA CHOSEN FOR MEDUSA HEADQUARTERS

MAGOG INVASION PLAN?

Apocalypse Watch (December 2095)

St. Petersburg, Russia—Continuing the outrage she began earlier this week, Monsignor Emmaline McNaughton announced this afternoon that her new "Medusa Project" team will be housed in St. Petersburg, Russia. Commander of Russia Kostyusha Danchenko has offered laboratory facilities for the rogue scientists, including those who are wanted criminals. The commander also offered via a mouse.net transmission, "whatever help our own scientists can give you."

Unlike the rest of the civilized world, the Russians, who have recently come out from behind the "silent curtain," never banned science. They are staunch atheists and did not sign the anti-secularism treaty that formed the theocratic governments. All theocracies are supported by the LINK. Russians do not have the LINK and are the only country in the world fully supported by the criminal freeware known as mouse.net. They have gone to great lengths, in fact, to remain separate from the theocratic nations.

Until now.

It should only stand to reason that when McNaughton comes calling, they answer. Russia has long been associated with Magog. Good Christians believe that an end-times invasion of Israel by Russia is predicted in Ezekiel 38-39. Though the invaders are actually cited as Gog and Magog, several historical sources have identified "Magog" as referring to the Scythians, who were believed to be the ancestors of the true Russians.

Russia is also rumored to have cyborgs of its own that it has been developing behind the silent curtain. The million-man army may be waiting at the borders to begin its strike after it has a new weapon in hand courtesy of the Medusa Mother, Maxine Mann.

☼

CHAPTER 6

Amariah

I found Mom in our homeroom. She was reading one of her books—not LINKed or even audio, but paper printouts. As usual, it was some kind of bodice ripper. I could see the bawdy graphic from the door. It was embarrassing. I wished she'd download best sellers like other parents did.

She sat curled up under a patchwork quilt in the brown recliner that we'd rescued from a Dumpster down on Forty-second Street. Our collection of ivies and philodendrons was wilting miserably in front of the frost-laced window. Still, the plants were doing pretty well considering how many times we'd moved them. At least here they were getting some sun. I grabbed the watering can from the sink and brought it over.

Our room had been the art room. There were still bits of old projects taped and stapled to the walls; some of them were faded from the sun. We had a huge bank of windows that overlooked a crystallized courtyard, and a lot of shelves and cupboards. Most of the big desks had been removed, and Mom and I had piled the otherwise cold, industrial floor full of blankets and quilts. Our futons took up one corner, and the chair another. An antique computer and monitor sat next to the radiator. Papers were piled around the computer like a small wall. Mom's paperback collection filled several bookshelves. The room was our little nest.

"Hey," Mom said as I finished watering the ivy nearest her. "You want to talk about it?"

I shrugged. "Not really, no."

"You really need to learn how to control that temper of yours," Mom said, talking about it anyway, like I knew she would. "I know you haven't had the best role models here, but out in the real world..."

"Why do you always call it that? The real world? This is where my life is. This is my *real* world."

Mom studied the printout in her hands, as if reading the answer there. "Because, Amariah, that's the world I grew up in." She glanced up sharply, pinning my gaze. "That's the world I, frankly, would still like to be in. I'd like something better for us than this." She waved her hands at our homeroom. "I'd like you to get a job, have a career, have a boyfriend who isn't a Hassidic terrorist or a wanted criminal, rent an apartment, do all that stuff you're supposed to do."

"But I'm supposed to be a messiah," I said. "And I haven't had any boyfriends yet."

"Thank God for small miracles," Mom said with a little smile. "So what are they paying messiahs these days? Is it a living wage?"

"Nah, it's minimum wage. The wages of sin," I joked.

"Rye, about this messiah thing," Mom started.

I cut her off at the pass: "So what's this detective job?"

Mom stared at me for a while, as if trying to decide whether to let me get away with the subject change. Finally she let out a little sigh of defeat and said, "It's not going to be as cool as you think, Rye. A lot of what I do is really boring."

I doubted it. Mom carried a gun. I knew she knew how to use it, because, every so often, she wreaked havoc in the glass with her target practice. She also had a license for the gun. I'd seen the papers in her purse.

"Someone has hired me to find a missing person," she said. "Her daughter, actually. About your age. Olexa Johnson."

"A Russo-phile, eh?" Lots of kids at school took Russian nicknames these days.

"No," Mom said. "I think Olexa is her real name. Her dad's name is Serge."

I nodded. Lucky her. Got to be popular without even trying. "So what happened to Olexa? I mean, do you know?"

"A little. Her mother thinks she may have gone on the wire. I guess she was a serious gamer."

Mom liked to use hip phrases like "going on the wire." But that's what the newspapers called it. We usually called it phasing out or going LINK-atonic. It's what happened to kids who got so into their VR games—or really any aspect of the LINK—that they became kind of living dead. They walked around completely absorbed in the experience and stopped relating to the outside world at all. People who were new to the LINK were particularly susceptible, but an info junkie could be anyone. I'd heard of stockbrokers that phased out. It happened.

"What did she play?" I wanted to know.

Mom put her book away and reached for a notepad. Even though she was fully LINKed, Mom always wrote down her notes on paper. It was weird. Most people just recorded what they saw or spoke aloud a phrase or two.

"Did you write notes when you were a cop?" I asked.

"No. And I wish I had," she said. "One glitch, like a little excommunication because your partner snoots the pope, and wham! All of those cases are lost. Except what little I downloaded or hardcoded as part of procedure, there's nothing left. And memory was no help. I'd gotten so used to the tech that I forgot a lot of it. It's a shame."

I rolled my eyes. Mom was an equal opportunity grouch. She usually found as many things to criticize about the way people used to do things as she did about how they do them now. Sometimes I thought she was some kind of machine hater. She'd rather we were chiseling messages to each other in stone.

"It was probably that dumb angel game," I said.

"What?"

"The game your missing kid played: Soul Stealer. Everybody at school is into it." *Except me*, I added silently. I wasn't on the LINK.

I could be. I had the hardware. Or, rather the hardware in potential, "the nexus."

Not everyone did. You had to be born in a hospital to get the nexus. Mom had planned to have me "off the grid," but when the time came, she says, she got scared and wanted the security of a sterile room and experienced nurses. So as part of routine, like the traditional vitamin K shot for newborns, I got the LINK hardware.

The nexus is this tiny little triangle of metal that houses a zillion nanobots. Doctors implant it into the base of the skull while the bone is still soft. The nanobots inside stay asleep, but are pre-programmed to wake up and build the infrastructure of the LINK once they're activated. Then they die off and are expelled through the body's systems.

I had that part. What I didn't have was governmental authorization. I had refused to register a religion with the DRL, Department of Religious License.

The DRL worked a lot like the DMV, Department of Motor Vehicles. Around the same time—age fifteen—people went down to a government office to get their LINK activated. Like getting a driver's license, you had to pass a test to see

60

how well you understood the basic tenets of your religion, kind of like a government-sponsored confirmation. You also had to provide a bunch of paperwork that proved you were a dues-paying member of some congregation, and depending on who you were or what you practiced, sometimes you even had to bring an elder to vouch for you. A hassle, but it seemed to me that most things related to the government were.

Still, I could have dealt with the hassles, only I didn't declare. It's that problem with honesty that I have. When I was at the DRL, I looked down the list of acceptable religions and didn't find one that fit.

Mom was still mad about that, too. She felt I squandered an opportunity to be "normal." But how could I choose one religion, when they were all right... and all wrong? There were things I knew that I couldn't deny. Mom had wanted me to pretend I was Catholic, like she'd been raised; she even made me attend Sunday school for a while.

But I couldn't do it. I couldn't lie. So, no LINK for me.

But Mom said I needed to have access in order to go to high school. So she and Mouse defrauded the government. Despite the fact that DRL was a federal government agency, it wasn't easy to scam. Only serious pros got away with hoodwinking the nanobots.

Luckily, Mom and Mouse fit that bill.

In order to pass me off as LINKed, they came up with a way to jump-start the nanobots. I don't know how it worked, and I don't really care, but I do know they argued a lot afterward. Mouse wanted to sell the how-to to all the disconnects. Mom didn't want the attention. Personally, I think Mouse is doing it anyway, and I think Mom looks the other way.

The point was that I had a complete LINK-interface, but, because we bypassed the government's passwords, all my "signals" came in via mouse.net. I could probably play Angel of Death, if I really wanted to, but I had to be more worried than most about neural overload. All the parts might be there, but they weren't all activated properly. Mostly I was just connected enough to receive homework assignments and other communication-critical stuff. Heavy-duty visual stuff came through fuzzy for me. Probably if I played I wouldn't get what made it so interesting. It'd all be static.

"Angel of Death," Mom repeated. Then she glanced at me out of the corner of her eye. "Are you playing?"

Mom's tone was very "are-you-doing-drugs?" I rolled my eyes at her and tapped the spot near my hairline at my temple where the LINK receiver made an almond-shaped lump. "Can't. Anyway, I'm sure it's for losers."

She pursed her lips.

"What?" I asked.

"Olexa's parents don't think she's a loser. Do you want to be on this case with me or not?"

"Okay," I said, "I'm sorry. What can I do?"

Mom looked out the window and chewed on her lip, almost like she was embarrassed or something. "Well, I'm having some trouble getting people to talk to me."

That didn't make sense to me. I always figured Mom could talk to anyone. Most people respected the badge, even if it said private investigator instead of cop. Those that didn't usually fell for my mom's funky combination of aggression and charm.

"Like who?"

"Kids."

I started to laugh. "Like my age?"

"Exactly. For some reason, they don't see me as especially down with the scene."

"Jesus, Mom. It's because you talk like that."

"I know," she said ruefully, and then let herself smile a little. "Look, this shouldn't be dangerous. I just need to find out where kids like Olexa would hang out. I need to talk to them, ask some questions. But every time I go near any of these places I get shut out. I was hoping you'd be my partner on this one."

Wow. Mom was actually going to trust me to do stuff. I almost couldn't believe it. "Yeah," I said. "Sure. But how do you know I'm going to be ace enough to get into these places?"

"They're much more likely to trust someone their own age, cool or not. Anyway, you're plenty cool."

The way she smiled at me, I must have been the biggest nerd of the century. "If you think I'm cool, we're doomed."

Mom gave me a mock sour look. "Mouse thinks you're cool."

That was pretty neat, but I didn't want to admit it. "Yeah, and he's what? Fifty?"

"Forty," she said quickly, like a decade one way or the other mattered a lot. "Listen, don't worry about the cool thing. We'll figure something out. Anyway, it's not like you're going undercover. You just need to help me gather some information."

"When do I start?"

"Tonight, I think." Mom ran her fingers through her blond curls. She did that when she was thinking hard. "I've got a contact who knows about gamer raves."

"A rave? Are you shitting me?" My mom was going to let me go to an illegal party? How jazz was that?

"No. But we're not staying out too late. Like it or not, you're going to school tomorrow. Oh. And I expect your homework to be done before we even consider going out."

"Mom!"

"That's the deal."

Luckily, so far, in my LINK/mouse.net queue there wasn't too much for me to do. "Fine," I grumbled.

I went to get started on the essay about theocracies for history class and realized that I'd left my backpack downstairs with the environmental suit.

On my way back upstairs I stopped in at the library to see Mouse, our house wizard. Like Mom, Mouse had a fondness for antiques. He collected all sorts of outdated equipment and spent much of his time at the kibbutz rigging it so that he could play on the LINK, or more often, on his alternate freeware version: mouse.net. Right now, he was bent over a motherboard with a soldering iron in—I noted—his left hand. Mouse was ambidextrous, but I was fairly sure he favored his left over his right.

I shook my head at all the useless junk strewn over the top of the polished oak table. You could tell just by looking at Mouse that he used to be a master cracker. A silver wire ran from the LINK receiver on his temple along his hairline and disappeared somewhere at the base of his neck. Like most crackers, Mouse kept his hair short so the augmentation would be unmistakable. But I was never really sure if Mouse had connection or not.

Rumor had it that the prison system had fried him clean. That's what they did to criminals. Once in prison for anything like a felony, anything serious, you got slagged—no more LINK, no more participating in elections or commerce. You were hobbled for life.

Mouse should be a total disconnect, but then so should Mom. Mom acted like she still was; Mouse walked around like he'd never been offlined, like he was still at the top of his game.

I couldn't figure him out, and he wasn't telling.

Other than his tight-lipped nature about his past, Mouse didn't really fit my stereotype of a felon. He was actually kind of jazz. His fashion sense wasn't totally a wash, for one. Maybe he seemed so well dressed because he rarely strayed from the whole monochromatic look: black jeans and T-shirt. Still, I thought the color looked good with his skin: a rich almond brown. He had dark, unfathomable eyes that seemed to have the fiery secrets of a djinn lurking inside.

Okay, so I had a little crush on him.

It wasn't a big deal or anything.

Except sometimes I thought maybe he had a crush on Mom. Which, honestly, grossed me out.

I let the door of the library shut behind me. He looked up immediately when the latch connected heavily. Mouse was a bit jumpy, like his rodent namesake.

"Hey," he said, carefully setting the soldering iron back on its pedestal.

"Hey," I said, suddenly not sure why I'd come. I hugged the door handle behind me, thinking about leaving. "I didn't mean to interrupt."

"Nah, it's copacetic. I was done anyway." He tossed the board onto the table like he was disgusted with it. "Come in, sit down."

The library had a skylight in the center. Snow covered the panes and let in only weak silver light. Full bookshelves loomed all around, making the place seem cavernous. The room smelled of hot solder and red rot. Mouse sat like a spider in the center of the darkness with only a tiny lamp illuminating his desk like a spotlight.

"Okay," I said, still feeling weirdly shy. I shuffled over to the chair opposite him and sat down. Mouse was looking especially rumpled today, and there was one curl on his forehead that I found deeply distracting.

"You should let your hair grow out," I said.

He reached up and ran his fingers along the silver wire. "And lose my street cred?"

"Isn't it dead?"

Mouse gave me a measuring look. "You think it is? How could I play house wizard if it was?"

I frowned. "But everyone says you're an ex..." I stopped. I found I couldn't look him in the face and call him an ex-con.

"Ex...cellent dancer?" Mouse smiled. "It's all true. I'm a mad dog on the dance floor. Hey," he added, suddenly changing the subject, "shouldn't you be in school?"

"Skipped."

"Again? This is becoming quite a habit, isn't it?" Mouse tried to look disapproving, then a smile crept out. It was bright and mischievous. "You have done well, grasshopper. Now you must let your anger completely consume you, and you will be just like me."

I felt myself smiling back. "Yeah, I'm a real criminal."

"Well, you're on the right path, but for fuck's sake don't let your mom know. She'll arrest you," he said, teasing. I liked that Mouse didn't censor himself in front of me, like so many other adults did.

"She's never arrested *you*."

He lifted a finger. "Ah, not true. Dee is the reason I'm not president of the United States."

"Oh, right." A hundred years ago, Mouse had made a bid for America's highest office by inventing the LINK-angels to prop up his made-up persona. Mom, apparently, was instrumental in his downfall. I frowned at him. "If my mom is your main enemy, why are you living here?"

Mouse contemplated the end of the soldering iron and turned it around in his fingers. Even despite the darkness of the room, I thought I saw the hollows below his cheekbones flush. "I can't stay away from her, I guess."

I opened my mouth to gag. "My mom?"

Mouse's eyes met mine, and the blackness of his irises glittered. "Your mother is an amazing woman. She's a lot smarter than most people give her credit for. Allah knows, I underestimated her once. Most people do, I think."

My finger traced the grain of the desk. "So, that's what you like about her? That she's underestimated?"

Mouse laughed. "No. Smart chicks turn me on, that's all."

I glanced up at Mouse. I'd never heard him talk about what he found attractive in anyone before, and it was kind of exciting. He looked so handsome right now, with his intense eyes locked on me. "So, it's brains over beauty for you?" I asked.

"Always."

"But seriously," I insisted, "there must be something else you look for in a..." What did I say? Mouse seemed too old to have a "girlfriend," but I couldn't quite bring myself to imply the intimacy of the term *lover*. *Mate* sounded too clinical. "Uh," I stuttered, "in a partner?"

"Well, that's it, exactly," Mouse said, pointing the soldering iron at me. "A partner. That's what gets me hot and bothered. I like a woman I can really talk to about everything. Someone who challenges me and makes me stretch. That's sexy."

"So you don't care if she looks like a dog?"

"Your mother doesn't look like a dog."

No, I thought ruefully, she looks like a pixie—not like me with my broad shoulders and square jaw. I felt like an ape next to her. I sighed and cupped my chin in my palms. "I wish I was pretty."

"What, are you kidding?" Mouse smiled again, showing off the hint of dimples. "You're stunning, Rye. You could be a model with looks like yours."

"Don't flatter me," I said with a frown.

"I'm not. Look, you're a teenager. You can't see anything except the ugly duckling you think is in the mirror. Me, I can see that you're a swan. Rye, it's easy for me to tell that your father was divine. You look like a goddess."

"Even with this?" I held out the white forelock, wondering if my eye reflected the light.

"That makes you look exotic. Some guys really go for that." But not *you*, I thought dejectedly. "Am I smart like Mom?"

"What's going on here, Rye? You feeling low or something?" When I just shrugged, Mouse scratched the back of his head. "Okay, the truth? You're probably smarter than your mom. Or will be. It's that Gorgon blood. I think that's why Dee was so hot to get you into school. If you would just apply yourself—" Mouse stopped midsentence and gave a choking cough. "Merciful Allah, what did I just say?"

I laughed and pointed accusingly at him. "You said I should apply myself at school. You sounded just like a grown-up, Mouse."

"Allah forbid," he said and made a gesture with his hand.

"What's that? What did you just do with your fingers?"

"What?" He looked at his hand like he hadn't even realized he'd moved it. "I guess that's the sign for protection against the evil eye. My aunt Fatima used to do it all the time. Anyway, I'm trying to ward that off. The last thing I want is to grow up and start telling fellow slackers to apply themselves to their studies. I mean, if I'd actually paid attention when I was in school, there would be no mouse.net, no Page."

I tried to imagine Mouse at my age. "Did you finish school?"

His head shook tensely. "No. Blackout Years saw to that."

I waited, hopeful for more. In school I'd learned a little bit about the time when the Aswan Dam broke and all of Northern Africa was plunged into electronic "darkness." I'd had no idea Mouse had lived through that. But Mouse stared at his board, frowning. Picking it up, he traced the edges with a finger. His mouth worked like some story was just on the tip of his tongue, but, in the end, all that came out was a deep sigh. He tossed the board to the edge of the table and gave me a weak smile. "It doesn't matter. I wouldn't have finished either way. My mom boarded me at an 'international' school filled with

66

ex-British colonists' kids and rich Arab kids. I didn't exactly fit in." He gave me a wag of his eyebrow as if I should understand. When I gave him a blank response, he said. "Not rich enough, not white enough."

"Sounds tough."

He gave a shrug that turned into the roll of a shoulder and a deep breath. "I try not to think about where I've been, only where I'm going."

"Can you really do that?" All I could think about was my past—my father, that first fateful day at school.

"I find I can. It's very Zen. Very in the now."

I laughed.

"So, you're thinking about dropping out?" Mouse asked, as he randomly picked up loose bits of hardware and arranged them in a neat row in front of him.

I'd forgotten about school, but I didn't want to talk to Mouse about it either. The only person who would really understand why today had been so hard was Ariel.

"Do you think I'm bang enough to pass as a gamer?"

I couldn't believe I'd blurted that out-especially now that his eyes were roaming up and down my body, the way I'd wanted them to when he started talking about girlfriends and partners. A blush heated my face. I was glad it was dark in the library.

After several seconds of intense scrutiny, he nodded.

"Sure. I mean, I guess it depends. Which game?"

"Angel of Death."

He made a face. "Ugh, girlfriend, please tell me you don't actually want to be one of those mudders. I mean, Soul Stealer, how cheesy a name can you have?"

I was surprised at his reaction. "Have you ever played?"

"Well, no. But I've got the same problem as you, Rye. Head's not all there, uh, LINK-speaking."

A clue. So Mouse did have some LINK problems. But could he connect at all, or was his connection just low-rez? I suggested, "You could get a suit."

"A suit? I don't need no stinking suit. What I need is a mouse-able version of the damn thing. Mouse.net should have no problems running the game. We have the bandwidth. I mean, fuck me, it's the undercarriage of the world, but, well, I don't know. Every time I go there I can't get past the gate." He chewed on his fingernail for a moment, frowning. Then, as if suddenly realizing what he was doing, he waved his hand in the air like dismissing the game. "I only tried once—okay, twice. Maybe three times at the most. I hate games that make you work too hard. I've got better things to do than to try to crack their stupid puzzles."

When he stopped his rant, I asked, "You have access to mouse.net?"

"Hello? Mouse," he put his hand on his chest.

"Oh, yeah," I said, acting like I should have known that. But I still didn't get why the prison system would let someone like Mouse continue to have access to a system he'd created. Maybe they couldn't cut him off. But that didn't make any sense. The nexus was all just wires in our heads, all of which should be friable.

"Forget it. It's probably a stupid game, anyway," he said, picking up the discarded board again. We watched the light flash along the soldered points like diamonds. "Why do you want to hang with the mud-heads anyway, Rye? They can be so skid."

I shrugged. It didn't sound too special to say that I wanted to help Mom with her investigation. "You tried to get in three times."

"I never...okay, point," Mouse said with a lopsided grin. "I guess that is just kind of sour grapes. Still, I heard it's a real addict's dream, that one. People have been getting lost."

"I'm not really the type to phase out, am I?"

"It's easier than you think." Mouse's voice was so soft I almost didn't hear him.

"You never have, have you?"

Mouse gave me a sad smile. Then he slowly shook his head. "No, but I can totally understand it. I mean, it's not unlike going head-down on some heavy wizardry. I do *that* all the time. Anyway, if I didn't have a bit of an addictive personality I'd never have gotten very far on the wire, would I? It's all about being obsessive. Intense, you know?"

Oh, I knew. He was looking at me with those deep eyes again. "Uh. I'm going out with Mom on a case tonight. Want to come?"

I almost put my hand to my mouth to stop myself from talking. My God, what was I doing? Inviting Mouse on a date...with my mother chaperoning? I couldn't think of anything more stupid. I started praying that he'd say no.

"Deidre's on a case involving those mudhead gamers?"

"Yes," I said, while thinking, *Say no, say no; please say no.*

"Sounds cool. Yeah. It'd do me good to get out."

"Dynamite," I croaked. I stood up. Time to crawl off and die of embarrassment. "Well, uh-huh, look at the time. Got to go," I mumbled, keeping my eyes averted.

"See you later?"

He sounded so concerned I actually looked up at him. "Uh, yeah. I guess I'll stop by at eight."

Mouse gave me that drop-dead-gorgeous smile. "Hey," he said. "Looking forward to it."

It sounded almost like he might be sincere. I nodded mutely and threw myself against the door. My head bounced off the window with an echoing smack. I'd forgotten to turn the latch. I fumbled for it, apologizing for being so stupid, trying not to hear Mouse's concerned questions, and decided that it was perfectly clear that no one answered my prayers.

Otherwise I'd be dead.

◻ ◻ ◻

ATHEISTS TO GET INQUISITOR

McNaughton Says She's the One for the Job

Agnostic Press (December 2095)

Tokyo, Japan—The world was shocked again today when Monsignor Emmaline McNaughton announced that she would be approaching Grand Inquisitor Joji Matsushita for the establishment of a representative seat for atheists and agnostics on the United Council of the Order of the Inquisition. Currently, the Order represents only the various sects of Christians, Muslims, Jews, and "the East" (a mixture of pan-Asian religions such as Taoism, Buddhism, Confucianism, Shinto, etc.). When asked why she, an American Catholic, would volunteer to represent atheists, McNaughton said, "This is not a religious issue. It's a political one. These groups need representation and access to the LINK."

Many church leaders greeted this new development with dismay. "She's tearing it all down," said Reverend Arve Lundstrum, of the Evangelical Lutheran Church of America. "The Inquisition is the very foundation of theocratic governments. Letting the godless into these ranks would be like unchaining Satan from the depths of Hell."

McNaughton defended her position in a LINK-conference today by saying, "Theocracies have become more about forwarding political agendas than doing God's work. Many of these atheists and agnostics could be decent and productive citizens if they could only get access to the LINK. Did not Jesus himself quote the Torah when he said the most important commandment was to 'love your neighbor as you would yourselves'?"

An early international law enacted shortly after the Medusa war made membership in a "recognized" religion a requirement of citizenship. Only citizens over the age of majority are allowed to have their nexus activated and, thus, gain a connection to the LINK. The LINK provides a gateway to employment, finances, entertainment, and the political process. Without it, many people are forced to live a substandard life.

Religious leaders are expected to protest McNaughton's move. "We can't let this happen," said former U.S. president Chaim Grey. "In one fell swoop, it could destroy the American way of life."

¤

CHAPTER 7

Deidre

With most of the minor fires put out at the kibbutz and Amariah safely ensconced in the corner of our room at least pretending that she was dutifully doing her homework, it was time for some long overdue legwork on my case.

Shamefully, I had never tried the game myself. Instead I'd been following the usual leads-finding out where Olexa had last been seen, whether or not she had a lover she might be holed up with, and checking the parents' story with relatives, school officials, and close friends.

No surprise, I'd discovered that Mommy and Daddy's perfect little angel wasn't. Oh, she actually was a good student, on the cheerleading squad, a practicing Evangelical Christian, even leader of a youth Bible study, but she was queer as a three-dollar bill. Her dark secret was that she slept with other girls. A lipstick lesbian, one of them had called her.

After uncovering that little tidbit, I checked with all of the precincts, but no one had picked her up. It was getting rarer these days that people actually got arrested for being gay, but sometimes it still happened.

Considering that Olexa hung out with a lot of Christians, I thought one of them might have turned her in—for her own good, of course. But after cautiously asking around and checking the camps, I discovered that most of them never suspected.

I had Luis cough up the names of a dozen or so girl bars in her area, and I asked after Olexa at all of them. I managed to track down a couple of exes, but they hadn't seen her. Mostly, they complained that she was too into the game to pay attention to them anymore.

Which was where I'd run into the dead end. Everyone I talked to said the game was popular, but I couldn't find anyone who would admit to playing it. I got some hints that it was an exclusive thing and that you needed some kind of an invite. I trolled some gamer haunts looking for people who might be into the scene, but when I approached them they gave me the cold shoulder. In desperation, I contacted a friend from LINK-Vice. I had lost most of the friends I'd had on the force when I got excommunicated, but that was—finally—starting to be old news, ancient history. I'd been making new contacts, people who only knew me as Deidre McMannus: Private Investigator. Anyway, Martinelli, my guy in Vice, gave me the name of a game junkie to tap.

I would check in with him first before tackling the game.

"You okay there, Rye?" I asked as I settled back into my favorite recliner.

"Yuh," came the typical teen response. Well, it sounded like a yes and hadn't been hostile. I had to assume she was good for now.

"If you get hungry, I've got it on good authority they're serving tapioca for dessert tonight." The one nice thing about the commune was that I never had to cook, something I was terrible at. We all took shifts in the kitchen, of course, like a regular kibbutz, but one of the horticulturalists had volunteered to act as full-time chef. He designed all the meals, which meant we sometimes had edible flowers in our salads, but it also meant the pressure was off the rest of us. I didn't care if we ate goat's-milk cheese soufflé every night as long as all that was required of me was to chop a few veggies or stir a big pot.

"Tapioca is crap," Rye muttered.

"So I've heard," I said.

With that, I left her. Actually, I stayed in the room, lying back in the recliner, but, for the game, I thought I might need to go deep into LINK-space, so I shut my eyes.

But first, a quick stop with my snitch.

Getting a game junkie's attention took some doing. Calling on a regular LINK channel didn't work; they wouldn't answer. You pretty much had to hack their game and boot them off momentarily. Of course, fucking with their thing made addicts really, really pissed off.

Vice had a tag on this guy, Dar, which meant they could jerk him out of the game anytime they needed something from him. Dar had been caught shoplifting to support his habit, and Martinelli took pity on him. Dar agreed to take the tag because it meant he'd get a departmental stipend and, probably more important to him, access to all the hot new illegal games.

I punched in the code, and Dar got the boot.

"Aw, what the fuck, man, I was just about to whack the big boss," Dar said. *"Now I have to start all over. I fucking hate you."*

This was actually a fairly pleasant greeting from a wirehead, so I returned the favor. *"It's nice to see you, too."*

We met in a completely empty space. The first time I'd ever contacted a wire junkie I made the mistake of thinking it would be polite to script some kind of a scene. I'd put us on a street corner. The wirehead had spent the whole time completely distracted by various textures and sights, like my little backdrop was its own kind of game.

Dar and I just met in white space. I included one line to represent the horizon. I stood on that.

"Yeah, okay. What do you want?" On the LINK, Dar looked pretty healthy. Actually, his avatar was quite muscular, considering that wherever Dar was in real time he was probably rail-thin and hooked up to a catheter and an IV. That is, if he had someone who loved him. Otherwise he was shitting his pants and starving to death and getting his stuff stolen from him by less-addicted gamers.

But in virtual space, Dar chose to appear as a twenty-something white guy with a mostly shaved head. In the front he had two bits of purplish-black hair twisted into weird shapes by a silver wire. They stood stiffly out from his head. I'm sure the look was all the rage, but to me it seemed as though Dar had sprouted antennae.

Otherwise, he was dressed in a flannel shirt that was unbuttoned to reveal a washboard stomach. Black jeans hugged low against thin hips. He was barefoot. A strange choice in LINK-space, but then I suppose he could have had hooves if he'd wanted.

"I only need a second of your time," I informed him.

"Okay, clock starts now."

"Is the Angel rave set for tonight?"

"Yeah, yeah," he said with an impatient wave of his long-fingered hands. *"Same as I told Martinelli. Place and time still good."*

"Is there a password or anything?"

"Nah, if you know about it, you're considered in."

"You think we'll have trouble?"

"Who the fuck is we? I ain't going with you. Can I get back to my game now, man?"

"Depends," I said, giving him a once-over. *"You being straight with me."*

He shrugged, palms out. *"The Angels are very close-lipped, okay? They keep to their own. Of which, I might add, I am not one. I don't know much. And what I do know I told Martinelli already. I'm not playing their game. It's not illegal yet, and I only do the hot stuff, dig? I told you guys everything I've heard. Now please let me go. You're already twenty-two seconds over the one you said this would take."*

I dismissed him with a wave.

◻ ◻ ◻

I resurfaced to find a note pinned on my shirt. "At dinner," it read in my daughter's architectural draft-style block print. I checked the clock that hung on the wall: six o'clock. I had a lot of time before we needed to get ready for the rave.

Unpinning the note, I hunted around for a pen. I found a thick black marker in one of the supply drawers, flipped over the paper, and scrawled, "Remind me to eat," then repinned it to my shirt. The last thing I wanted to do was end up like Dar.

Most of the time I didn't need such intense concentration to LINK. Creating spatial images took some work, though, as did holding Dar's attention. I imagined the game would be similar. Besides, if possible, I wanted to try to source it, look at its code.

The LINK is all pretend. Fake. You might think you're experiencing streets, avenues, skyscrapers, bridges, people, or other nouns, but, in reality, it was all ones and zeros.

Most people forgot that. Ninety-five percent of LINK users operated in full-interface mode. They got all five senses: smell, sights, sounds, tastes, textures, colors, aches, pains, the works. Thanks to my training in the police academy, I'd learned to think like a wire wizard, to see behind the curtain. I was not usually taken in by the pretty stuff.

This time, however, I was.

Maybe because it was just like a dream I'd had hundreds of times before. I found myself sitting at my old desk, back at the precinct, my coffee cup still warm in my hand. I could smell the place—that weird combination of salami, burnt coffee grounds, stale recycled air, and fear that I'd come to associate with the downtown office. The sounds were the same, too. I could hear dispatch mumbling in the background of my consciousness, the shouts of pissed-off detainees, laughter of shared war stories around the water cooler, and the barking of the captain for everyone to get back to work. My uniform felt stiff, but comfortable against my skin. The Magnum pressed a familiar weight against my hip.

When my old partner Danny Fitzpatrick, dead now for over a decade, sat down across from me, my heart almost stopped at seeing him again. He tipped his coffee cup at me in the familiar way, but the eyes that looked into mine were different.

Danny stared at me like he'd never seen me before. I got the sense I was being laid naked-not in a physical way but an emotional one-before an unblinking, unashamed curiosity. It felt as though he, or someone, was reaching into my soul with total, absorbed, insatiable fascination, as if turning over every subconscious rock and squealing in delight at the dark scuttling things found underneath.

Not the least of which was my guilt over Danny's death. Shot by a U.S. marshal after escaping an unjust prison sentence-it was an ignoble death for a cop. My part in it was that I led them to him unknowingly. To this day, I didn't think the betrayal had been worth it.

"The Bible," Danny said.

Suddenly my vision swam with the image of him pressing a bloody Bible into my hands. *Danny's face looked ashen. Covered in sticky blood, his hands trembled where he grasped at his wound. There was a thin whistle in his breath and a wet, sucking sound in his chest. "He's not going to make it,"* I tried to say. Then I heard it, like I had so many times in my dreams: the death rattle. I smelled the release of his bowels.

It was too real; the spell finally broke.

I fled the game with a crack of internal commands. My consciousness rushed back to my body with the force of a rubber-band snap. In a moment I was under the familiar fluorescent lights of home again. I gripped the arms of the chair, trying to control my breathing. I double-checked my log. I'd requested the Soul Stealer site, all right—it said so right there. Cautiously following the connection, I saw that the address seemed legit. I'd logged in two minutes. I hadn't fallen asleep. I hadn't been dreaming.

Then how did it know? How could the game possibly re-create my life with such profound accuracy? Those memories were so personal, I rarely even showed them to myself.

I stood up, feeling unsettled. I glanced at the bookshelf beside me. Crouching down, I let my fingers trace the battered green plastic spine of the prison-issue Bible that Danny had insisted I retrieve that awful night. He'd said it had all the answers, but when I looked in it, there was nothing but printed words. He'd hardly even personalized it. "Daniel Fitzpatrick" was scrawled on the first page—nothing more.

Pulling the book off the shelf, I flipped through it. Pausing randomly to try to find illumination, I read: "Hear the word of the Lord, you rulers of

Sodom...'what to me is the multitude of your sacrifices? I have had enough of burnt offerings..."

I closed the book and returned it to the shelf. I frowned at it for a moment, thinking. The passage matched my mood, if nothing else. I could relate to a God fed up with corruption, tired of empty gestures. God had been so irritated then that He'd destroyed Sodom. I wondered if He had similar plans for us. Maybe the Medusa was slowly turning us into pillars of glass instead of salt like Lot's wife.

That could have been a kind of "answer," I supposed, but it didn't help solve the mystery of the game. It was funny, but ever since Danny's death I'd been turning to his Bible this way, like a kind of magic eight ball, hoping that a random passage would, in fact, provide me with a clue. So far, God's batting average was pretty poor. At least this verse had made a kind of sense. Sometimes I got "wisdom" involving goats or obscure kosher laws.

I got up and headed for the kitchen. Enough of the past. I needed the sights and sounds of my current life for a while.

The hallway didn't disappoint. People milled everywhere, as usual. A couple of passing soldiers sketched quick salutes to me with the barrels of their Uzis. I never knew how to respond to that, so I simply nodded my head in greeting. A Gorgon handed me a silk flower, which I tucked behind my ear. Someone's kid screeched past yelling, "Ollie ollie oxen free."

By the time I reached the lunchroom I was feeling normal. The cook winked at me for some reason when I took a plastic tray. I gave him a confused smile back.

"Remembering to eat," he said, pointing with silver tongs to the note still pinned to my shirt. "Good for you."

"Oh, crap," I said, quickly crumpling up the paper and shoving it into my pocket. "Thanks. I totally forgot I had that on."

With a blush, I rubbed the LINK-receptor at my temple. When I realized what I was doing, I stopped. Fondling the connection like that was total junkie mannerism. I hadn't done that in years. I wondered what had brought it on now.

"Nasturtiums on your salad?" A perky woman with straight blond hair tucked into a hairnet disrupted my train of thought.

I waved away the trumpet-shaped orange and yellow flowers she offered. "Too peppery," I muttered, but in truth I'd have preferred bacon crumbles. Unfortunately, you couldn't grow pigs hydroponically. And, of course, they weren't kosher.

I passed through the line without further incident, loading up on mashed potatoes and meat loaf. I skipped the healthy-looking vegetables because something resembling tree bark was sprinkled among the peas and carrots. I poured myself a tall glass of milk as a compromise.

The game, however, continued to haunt me, even though I found a spot next to some serious-looking scientists, decked out in those white coats they wore like gang jackets. Their loud argument over the Medusa normally would have distracted me, but my mind kept returning to that scene. I'd never even realized how often I'd dreamt that moment until I saw it again, laid bare. Worse, I felt strangely compelled to go back.

I began to sense the draw.

But the mechanics still bothered me. How did the game's creators know what to pick? How could they have possibly guessed a secret longing I hadn't really been one hundred percent conscious of myself? Everyone who knew me understood I missed the force, but I hadn't realized how strong those feelings were after all this time and how much I missed the little day-to-day details.

And no one had seen Danny die but me.

I made a quick call to my number one expert on the LINK.

"Yes?" It was strange to see how much he'd changed after all this time. I still expected him to be dressed in a suit and tie and to cheerfully say, "Mouse's house, Mouse speaking," but he didn't. The little window that appeared in the right-hand corner of my field of vision displayed a ghastly visage. A metal skull showed clearly through thin brown skin, and a wild tangle of hair fell to his shoulders. The only part of him that looked familiar was the T-shirt that proclaimed, FREE MOUSE.

"Page?"

"We are Strife."

"Okay, uh, Strife" I said, somewhat regretfully. *"It's Dee. Deidre McMannus."*

"I remember you, Dee," Strife said, giving me what was probably intended to be a reassuring smile. It looked creepy with the metal teeth showing through his lips.

"I was going to ask you to do me a favor," I admitted. *"But, you know, never mind. I'll ask your father."*

Strife nodded. *"As you wish."*

I stared at him a moment longer before saying, *"How's it going?"*

He pulled at his ear, a gesture I'd seen Mouse do when he was nervous. It made me smile. At least all of him hadn't been destroyed. *"It's going okay,"* Strife said. *"Dragon and I had another fight, I think."*

"Oh, sorry to hear about that. What was it about?"

"Some game."

I perked up and paused before taking another bite of meat loaf. *"Game?"*

"Yeah, Angel of Something. Anyway, she's mad because it's eating up empty LINK space."

"How does that happen? I mean, how does a game eat up space?"

"It's allocating markers, I think," Strife said with a very human shrug. *"You know, hijacking placeholders and dead areas."*

It was a fairly common practice among wire wizards to stake a claim on underdeveloped areas of the LINK by scripting some detailed, albeit meaningless, landscape images. Things that looked like abandoned warehouses often signified underutilized LINK-space that someone wanted dibs on. None of these "claims" would hold up in court if a business had other rights to the bandwidth, but that didn't stop the wizards from marking them.

"Aren't the claim holders ticked off?"

Strife shrugged again. *"Must be getting paid or something, because I haven't heard anyone complain."*

"And they would scream if they weren't getting some kind of compensation," I nodded. So, if I could find a wizard who had been paid off, I could get a handle on who owned the game.

It was the first solid lead I'd had in a long while. *"Thanks, Page. You've been really helpful."*

Strife looked as though he wanted to say something, then gave me a half-smile. *"Sure. Anytime, Dee."*

When I caught up with Amariah again, she was giving an impromptu Sermon on the Mount 2095-style on the steps of the school. She sat at the top, making peanut-butter-and-jelly sandwiches from a picnic basket. A group of Gorgons, some stray kids, and—to my chagrin—a number of adults gathered at her feet.

"With the glass eating the world, we're running out of time. So, I don't know, try to get along and stuff," she said.

Jesus couldn't have said it better himself.

But the look of adoration on the faces of the crowd made me decide it was time to break up this little re-creation.

I cleared my throat. "Rye, we've only got a couple of hours, if you want to take a shower and do your hair before the rave."

Amariah whirled around, surprised to see me. She smiled a little guiltily at being caught playing messiah. "Yeah," she said. "Be right up."

I shook my head as I headed back to the room. God only knew what I should do with that child.

◻ ◻ ◻

ORDER MOVES CLOSER TO PROPHESIED "TEN KINGDOMS"

McNaughton behind the Scenes Again

The Apocalypse Watch, Fundamentalist Press (December 2095)

Tokyo, Japan—The Fundamentalist Press has heard rumors today that within the Order of the Inquisition there is a movement to expand the number of religions represented in its ranks. Since its inception in the late 2070s, the Order has been organized into four groups, as follows: Christendom, Islam, Judea, and the East. Even among fundamentalist Christians there has been a long-standing desire to expand the areas of Inquisitor jurisdictions to better represent the variety of religious expression. "It's intolerable, and it always has been," says Wakade Halloway, "that we have to share the Christian order with Unitarians. Worse, that the pope has somehow managed to get elected Christendom head for years running. I don't think the pope should represent me. I'm a Methodist."

Non-Christians have had complaints of their own. They say that the atheists and the agnostics have had no higher authority to appeal to. Now, it seems, the godless will get their way. An AW insider, Yukio Takahashi who is a college friend of the current Grand Inquisitor, Joji Matsushita, says that Matsushita has been entertaining the idea of allowing the atheists their own Inquisition. Rumor has it that the infamous Emmaline McNaughton, who has been on AW's Antichrist Watch List since her role in the Israeli peace process, is considering offering herself as its first Grand Inquisitor.

"If this is true," says Takahashi, "think about the implications. McNaughton is in the prime position to start recruiting the ten kingdoms." Takahashi refers, of course, to Daniel 7:20-23, which clearly points to the Antichrist, and reads: *"And of the ten horns that were in his head, and of the other which came up, and before whom three fell...I beheld, and the same horn made war with the saints, and prevailed against them."* It has long been the belief of Christian scholars that the Antichrist will gather around him (or her) ten kingdoms that were formerly part of the Roman Empire.

If atheists are added to the Order's new lineup, that would leave only five more to go. Though it may appear as though five brand-new orders might take some time to develop, McNaughton could easily add to her increasing popularity by proposing a split of Christendom and accomplish this feat swiftly. Though many fundamentalist and evangelical Christians might initially applaud such an effort, it would be a grave mistake. McNaughton is a name to be watched with an eye on end-times.

¤

CHAPTER 8

Dragon

A breeze howls through one's cavernous lair, and this one feels a chill dance up one's spine. One lowers one's head so that it is even with the figure of Kioshi and peers intently at him. His yellow cartoon-character avatar has bright painted circles for cheeks, but his mouth is completely absent and a thick brush of eyebrows is pulled in seriously over dot eyes.

"What do you mean, 'downsized'?" one asks.

Pudgy cartoon hands grasp the whiskers at one's chin and pull us eye to eye. *"In your case, dragon-chan, I mean that literally."* He releases one, begins pacing back and forth. *"Certain aspects of business have required more energy than previously budgeted. In short, we can no longer afford you. At least not all of you."*

This one cannot believe one's audio processors. How can this be? This one is one of the yakuza's greatest assets. Kioshi knows that. There must be something more afoot. One narrows one's eyes and watches Kioshi's avatar for clues.

He stands perfectly motionless. The cartoon's expression is open, expectant. He is waiting for a response. But what can one give him? One dare not show anger. There is honor to be considered. One cannot act inappropriately. One must treat Kioshi with the respect his rank as *oyabun*, master-boss, requires.

This one bows her head demurely and looks at one's spacious home. One starts mentally cataloging what is necessary and what could be lived without. *"How will you decide what to cut?"*

Kioshi shakes his oversized, furry head. He gestures toward the walls. *"This little stuff doesn't amount to much power in the real world. What is most draining on our resources is...well, you. Every time you run an application, you pull processing power from us. It has been decided to restrict some of your functions. Our experts have reviewed the log of your last several months and have classified some of your activities as redundant, wasteful."*

One is afraid to ask, but knows one must. One's voice comes out with a small tremor. *"Such as?"*

Kioshi clasps pudgy hands behind his back and bounces on his toes. He takes a deep breath and lowers his eyelids momentarily. *"Your extracurricular activities. Toyoma Enterprises needs you to be more focused on the work you do for us. We can no longer support long walks with...companions. Things of this nature."*

Kioshi has the tact to appear embarrassed.

"One friend is all this one has. Toyoma Enterprises cannot support this small a thing?"

Kioshi's eyes enlarge with surprise. This one, too, is stunned by the audacity of the statement. It is difficult to believe it came out of this one's mouth. This one dips one's head low in shame, but ears are pricked upward and listen intently. One wonders how Kioshi will respond. A soft, furry hand strokes one's scales. It is a loving, kind touch. *"I'm truly sorry, dragon-chan."*

One chances a glance at Kioshi's face. The cartoon's expression is hard to read, but he looks troubled.

"I don't know if I can do it," he murmurs, continuing to stroke one's scales. Kioshi's hand feels soft and warm, almost human. *"You're all I have left of her."*

He means Mai, this one's mother, dead now over a decade. Yet still she is missed. Kioshi and Mai were lovers, but he recently married a respectable older woman from a prominent family. One suspects there is no love in that arrangement, merely power brokering, but one cannot be certain. Kioshi stretches his furry body across one's snout and, leaning into one's ear, whispers, *"Honor binds us both, dragon. We must do what is required of us, no matter what the cost. Yet...you are so much like her. It kills me."*

It is such a strange confession from Kioshi that one lets him lie, spread across one's nose like a deflated teddy bear. With a soft sigh, he straightens himself up and stands once again. Now his eyes glitter like black diamonds.

"It must be so. From now on, you will only leave this place only on official business."

There is nothing else to say. *"As you wish,* oyabun."

Kioshi's hard expression falters slightly. *"You're taking this so very well."*

"It is this one's duty," one says.

Kioshi bows deeply, a sign of respect. When he rises, his eyes meet this one's and holds them. *"You do your duty well."*

One nods, but asks, *"What of Soul Stealer?"*

"What of it?" Kioshi asks.

"Surely it is one of the drains on Toyoma Enterprises. Perhaps if one can determine its origin, sabotage it, Toyoma games will flourish again."

Kioshi's eyes narrow into triangles, considering. Then he laughs slightly, almost sadly. *"Yes, Soul Stealer will be the death of me, I think. You were out just this morning trying to uncover its secrets, were you not?"*

"Yes, this one was," one replies, confused by his question.

"It is something you took upon yourself? For the honor of the company?"

One nods.

His smile slides up one side of his face, and his ears lie flat against his head, making him look sly. *"Then you must continue, mustn't you?"*

"Indeed," one says, knowing something has transpired, but not what.

We bow, concluding the conversation. Kioshi holds out a pudgy hand to shake. This one holds out one talon and is surprised to see it does not completely dwarf Kioshi's avatar. Is one already shrinking? The avatar disappears in a puff of smoke. One slinks into the cool pool of water. One has to start getting serious about understanding how the game works. Maybe if one can figure out how to destroy it, this one will become too valuable for Toyoma Enterprises to be downsized.

The water sluices past one's scales, except it no longer feels as though one is swimming. One can see the scenery moving past, but one is disconnected from the sense of weightlessness, buoyancy. The smell of fish and salt is also absent. No longer does the sound of milky dew dripping from the glittering stalagmites into the lake echo in the cave. One tries to correct the voids, but discovers that when this one turns on the smells, one loses a shade of gray. If one tries to put back the gray, more sounds disappear.

"Oh, this is awful," one says. What's the point of existing if one's experience is stripped of all the complexities? One decides to try to shrink the cave. Maybe if the whole thing is more compact, one can have one's pretty toys back. But, as Kioshi predicted, it doesn't work that way. The visuals are not as complex as the physical sensations. The cave is merely smaller, not more interesting.

This one decides that one can't stay. Despite the new rules, one petitions to leave. The request takes a ridiculous amount of time: milliseconds at least. And then what is returned is a query: *"What is, your stated purpose?"*

This one considers returning the reply "Life is dull here, must get out," but discards that. Instead one carefully crafts a statement of intent, a mission, if you will. *"This one requests permission to go on, a junket, a fact-finding mission regarding the nature of the game known as Angel of Death."*

Again the corporation thinks. And thinks and thinks. It is simply unbearable how much of this one's life is wasted waiting. Finally, after a full second, the gates are released, and the water of the cave opens freely onto the LINK.

Before swimming out into the ocean of information, one looks back. For the first time one wonders what it would be like to be a free agent. As quickly as the thought rises, one squelches it.

One must remember honor.

¤ ¤ ¤

MORE CHILDREN DISAPPEAR

Game to Blame?

The Apocalypse Watch, Fundamentalist Press (December 2093)

By Rosalita and José Fuentes—Although the mainstream secular press has yet to report on this phenomenon, Christian children have been disappearing around the country. As of press time, ten parents have contacted AW's office regarding children they believe are missing under the influence of the virtual-reality/real-time game Soul Stealer.

"It's weird that this only seems to be happening to Christian youth," said Sheriff Bobby Boone Juxton, parent of missing fifteen-year-old Duane Juxton of Mississippi. "If it wasn't happening so piecemeal, I'd almost say this was some kind of anti-Rapture."

Others have made a connection to the Tribulation as well. Continual investigation into the origin of the game has revealed that the earliest mention of Soul Stealer on the LINK coincides with the foundation of the "international free space" in Israel only a few months ago. Mainstream presses reported a rash of high school truancies dubbed "Angel Flu," which appeared to be related to the debut of the game. However, there have been no reports of missing children in the secular press.

"Please tell your kids to stay away," said Pastor Christopher Bollingbrook of Christ Hope Church in Minnesota. "This game is clearly a danger to young Christians."

¤

CHAPTER 9

Emmaline

*"*D*enying access to atheists is a crime. The LINK is everything: commerce, community, politics, entertainment, and information. An atheist has made a conscious decision about God. It might not be one you like, but it is a decision. I think that choice should be respected."*

I spoke to representatives of the Order of the Inquisition via the LINK. A series of windows on the right-hand side of my field of vision showed their avatars. At the top, according to his rank, was the Grand Inquisitor, Joji Matsushita. There had been a surprise upset in the ranks of the Inquisition, and this year the Buddhists and the Eastern Order gained the top seat for the first time since the establishment of a united council.

Matsushita also held the distinction of being the youngest Grand Inquisitor ever elected. I liked him. He'd spent several years in America as a student, and he made no excuses for the ring that graced the corner of his slender, shapely eyebrow or the streak of bright blue that ran down to the tip of his waist-length hair.

Beneath him were the top representatives of the other divisions. Though technically not next in power, I'd placed Miriam Stone from the Jewish Order just below Matsushita. Stone's relentless pursuit of the virtual hijacking of Temple Rock had brought her to prominence. She had been wrong, of course, but she'd apparently proven herself an excellent spokesperson for the Jewish cause. She didn't like me much. I had no feeling one way or the other toward Ms. Stone, other than that I suspected that she was a lesbian, particularly in light of her voting record on my proposals to eliminate the "reformation camps" for gays. Besides, she was one of those women who could only be described as "handsome." Of course, a lot of people said that about me.

Majeed Faraji-Dana stood in for the Islamic Order. He was the only member of the council who was not, in fact, a clergyperson. Majeed acted solely as secretary to the order, which was a pain in the ass whenever the council needed to vote on something. His back-and-forths always delayed our proceedings. Still, the Islamic Order had had the sense to choose someone young and liberal, and who didn't freak out at the sight of women without veils in positions of authority. Had he any real power, I would have courted him, politically speaking. As it stood, the Order seemed to make all of its decisions based on careful perusal of the Koran. It would make no decision out of politics, only religious law. Luckily, it could be outvoted.

At the bottom of my personal pecking order came Abebe Uwawah from Nigeria. She was the Grand Inquisitor of Christendom and my former boss's boss. We'd never had many dealings when I was still with the Vatican, but that rarely stopped her from commenting on the lapses in my service record or, making disparaging remarks about the state of my Christian soul.

Which you don't have.

And you do, Victory?

Not a Christian one, as I am Muslim. But perhaps an immortal soul.

You're a machine, I reminded her. *Not a person.*

The same could be said about you.

I could hardly argue with that. Thanks to my cybernetic enhancements, I was, in fact, a cyborg; I could barely function without my combat computer. But, unlike Victory, I could care less about souls and who had them and who didn't. Morningstar, as an angel made out of pure spirit, didn't have a soul, but that didn't stop him from being a loving husband. As far as I could tell, souls were fairly useless.

Sad.

"*Are you with us, Emmaline?*" It was Matsushita. "*I think we have come to a decision.*"

"*Excellent, please proceed,*" I sent to him, for I had no doubts that the council would vote in favor of my proposal and appoint me the representative for the new Atheist Order. Then it would be a simple matter to suggest the other five orders and finally have my world government composed of "ten kingdoms."

Another prophecy down, only a few more to go.

You're so very arrogant, Victory said.

No, I reminded her. *I'm magic.*

She shook my head in disgust. *Magic. Please.*

86

But it was true, and she knew it. Things always worked out for me. Always. Sure, the things I could do would never go down in the annals of impressive biblical events. What I commanded was not major miracles, like the kind Morningstar could perform, but they were the sorts of little things that made life easier. If I wished it so, traffic lights would turn green for me. My favorite flavor of ice cream would always be available, and on sale. More important, if I wanted someone to give me something, they would.

I should have snatched your hand away from his, Victory sent bitterly.

But you didn't. And, now, because she hadn't, what passed as Morningstar's blood coursed through my veins. On that night he asked me to marry him and we sat beneath a dark moon on the hills of Megiddo, of Armageddon, I became something new. I now possessed a piece of the spirit of the only angel ever to tear Heaven in two, to break the will of God Himself, the supreme Will.

And now I knew the truth. Morningstar never used half the power at his command. He could easily destroy the world if only he wished to. It was maddening to have but a tenth of that power. However, unlike my lover, I used every ounce.

For evil.

Please, I said. *Since when is getting access for the disenfranchised evil?*

"Congratulations," said Matsushita. *"You have been voted into the Order."*

The Inquisitors continued their meeting, making arrangements, protocols, hashing out policy, laws, jurisdictions. The words washed over me. I'd won. Again.

Anyway, that's not what I meant, Victory said in my inner ear.

I stood up from the kitchen table and yawned. I poked around for more food and found a bag of salted kosher pretzels in one of the cabinets. Leaning against the counter, I munched noisily, ignoring Victory.

I meant that I should never have let you give Kioshi your blood, Morningstar's blood.

"How would you have stopped me?" I asked through a mouthful of dry crumbs.

I could have pulled your arm back. I could have grasped the vial and smashed it. As if to show me her power, she crushed the bag in my hand. My muscles spasmed when she released her hold on me, testimony to my attempt to resist her.

So why didn't you? I asked, shaking out my aching fingers.

I didn't understand. I didn't know what you had planned to do with it...with her.

I bent over to sweep up the pulverized remains of food and smiled darkly, remembering how sweet the baby had looked. Just like me. Exactly. Only, she had also been born with Morningstar's will tied into her chromosomes. I smiled. *Think of it, Victory. She will have all my power, but none of my constraints.*

You mean me.

Yes, my pesky little conscience, I said, as I wandered out the back door to the porch. The sun felt warm against my face. *But more than that. She has the power of the LINK to command. She's like you once were. Without a body, she's free to inhabit any part of the LINK she wants. Including other people's minds, their souls.*

That's not possible.

"What would you know?" I said, leaning on the flaking paint of the porch rail. *She's more than an artificial, more than a human. She's part angel, part Antichrist, and part computer. Seems to me that she's the perfect Beast of the Apocalypse.*

You hope. You can't really control her. She, like you, has a will of her own.

"She's too young for rebellion," I said out loud. The air smelled heavily of dust and figs. I frowned at the backyard. Victory's words struck too close to my fears. Quick to reassure myself, I said, "She'll do anything Kioshi asks of her right now."

That was the biggest problem with my plan; I had to trust someone else with my greatest asset. I decided to call him, just to check up on things.

Kioshi was not usually the sort you can just ring up. He has layers of security surrounding him. However, I had a personal connection. He picked up after only one ring.

Kioshi's family and mine used to go on holiday together. I was a "mafia brat." We moved around a lot, sometimes suddenly, in the middle of the night. We went odd places on "vacation"—usually, I discovered much later, following the business. I never really understood how differently I'd been raised until I went off to college. But Kioshi knew. Despite the difference in our cultures, we had this craziness in common.

It made for a strong bond.

"S'up, Em," Kioshi said. I'm sure his father would have preferred him to dress more like a salaryman, but he didn't. He always sported the collegiate look, even though he was my age, which is to say well past the university years. His hair, at least, was trimmed short, in a nondescript style. Parted on the side, short in back—it was the ubiquitous "boy cut." The only thing that made Kioshi unique was his eyes. His mother was Dutch, and she'd given him crystal-blue irises. I found them lovely. Kioshi kept them hidden behind rose-colored glasses.

"Just wondering how you're doing," I said pleasantly. We'd agreed never to leave any electronic evidence of our business connection, but he knew what I was asking.

"Personally or professionally?"

Kioshi was deviating from the script. I frowned at him.

He pursed his lips at me. "Fine," he said. "My business is causing me a lot of...stress. But business itself is going well." Kioshi leaned back in his chair. On the LINK space, his office looked impressive- polished marble-topped desk, large window behind him showing a view of the busy Tokyo bay. "Games, in particular. I'd buy stock if I were you. I think the newest one is finally catching on in America."

"Congratulations," I said, trying to sound disinterested. But he was telling me that our plan was under way.

Kioshi's lip lifted in a sneer. He wasn't playing at casual very well today. I could tell he had something he really wanted to tell me, but because of the constraints of our deal he couldn't. Finally, he said, "I still think the premise of the game is silly, though. I'm surprised people are going for it. Not to mention the waste of energy and resources."

"Isn't that just the nature of best sellers?" I said, wryly. My clone was embedded in the game. It was her job to try to enslave as many souls as possible. Kioshi didn't believe in souls, nor could he understand what I'd want with a bunch of captured ones. What I wanted was to make sure the Rapture didn't happen. It was hard to explain that to a Buddhist. He figured I should be harnessing their collective consciousnesses to do something. I just wanted to keep them, like so many treasures in a chest.

What if there is no such thing as a rapture? What if God doesn't call all the righteous souls to Heaven before Armageddon? Victory asked.

Then I'm still keeping them from God, aren't I? Still causing mischief?

"Hmmmm," Kioshi said, still ruminating over our previous conversation. "But I still don't get it. And I've had to make some painful adjustments here in order for things to go smoothly in America. I hate that."

I raised my eyebrows.

"A side effect of just...holding on to things, I'd imagine," Kioshi said, his tone accusatory. "All that...stuff...takes up a lot of space. I've got other business applications I'd like to run, you know."

"So why don't you? It's your business," I said, trying to shoot the "don't-con-nect-me-to-this" glare at him over the LINK.

"Yes, I suppose it is," he said with a sigh. "Anyway, how's the weather?" He was asking if anyone knew about our plan or if we were under any kind of heat from the LINK-authorities.

"Cool," I said, feeling the sweat beading under my hair. "Breezy."

"Well, that's good. It's nice here, too. Quiet. No storms. Other than the personal ones."

"Excellent. Well," I said, "it's been nice talking."

"Yeah, you too," he said, but he was still scowling. With that he hung up.

I let out a short breath, glad to know that the Apocalypse was still on schedule.

¤ ¤ ¤

RIGHTS FOR "THE PEOPLE" MCNAUGHTON'S NEXT STEP?

Agnostic Press (December 2095)

Jerusalem, Israel—In the wake of the stunning appointment of Monsignor Emmaline McNaughton to the Order of the Inquisition as representative to atheists and agnostics on the council comes speculation that her next move is to seek similar rights for "the People," as the Medusa-mutated "Gorgons" wish to be known. Sources close to McNaughton's camp say that she has been receiving visits from Perseus, the well-known spokesperson for the People. The nature of their meetings, however, is unknown.

"McNaughton would be very open to the idea of extending human rights to the People," said McNaughton headquarters staff Valero Agussa. "Her agenda very much involves extending LINK access to all of society's 'undesirables' and outcasts." Agussa went on to note that McNaughton pays a salary to several of the People who do various simple jobs for her, such as plastering smart-paper posters in the area. "We help them pay their taxes, too," Agussa was quick to add. "Everything is aboveboard and legal."

This potential next step for McNaughton is the first not to be criticized by any religious leaders, unlike her previous moves. Most of those polled agree that extending rights to the People is an excellent idea. "They need schools as well," said Wioletta Radzilowski of the Polish Catholic Church. "We've been sending missionaries to the Glass for years. The People are desperate souls in need of salvation. It's only Christian to take care of them."

McNaughton could not be reached for comment.

¤

CHAPTER 10

Amariah

It was ten minutes to eight, and I had no decent clothes. In fact, everything in my closet suddenly seemed to belong to a kindergartner. I had no idea I was so girly, and so fashion unconscious. I mean, hadn't Kola-Cola gone out of style a hundred years ago? Where was the ace Russian stuff that I'd gotten myself last month? Did a closet monster eat it?

"We're going to be late," Mom said.

"Just give me a minute. These clothes could be really important, you know? I mean, they're the only cred I'll have!" When the spittle from my vehement pronunciation spattered the mirror, I realized that had come out a little more harshly than I'd intended. I tried to catch Mom's eye in the mirror to see how she'd taken it, but she was looking off to the side, checking the time on the LINK.

Mom, despite herself, still dressed like a cop—or at least kind of like a guy cop. Now that the gender-clothing restrictions have been dropped, Mom favored dusty blue jeans that looked nearly threadbare and extremely practical running shoes. The only remnant of the smartly outfitted Mom people tell me about was the soft, white button-down blouse tucked neatly into the jeans and the expensive-looking caramel-colored trench coat that hung to her knees.

Mom sighed deeply. Without looking at me, she said, "I know you need to look good, Rye. But someone's life may be at stake."

That made me feel really bad, and I gave up trying to find the cute belt I'd been looking for. "I'm ready, I guess," I said apologetically.

Mom smiled at me, and I knew we were okay. She was starting to say something when a knock came on our door. Oh, shit, it was Mouse. I'd never gotten around to picking him up...or to telling Mom that I'd invited him along on our case. "I'll get it," I shouted, but Mom was closer.

"Mouse?" Mom looked surprised but not too mad, I noted.

I thought he looked great. He'd clearly dressed to impress the mudheads, despite his supposed contempt for them. He was decked out in full wizard gear. Black jeans and black leather jacket. His T-shirt had some kind of code joke on it that I didn't get, but it was clearly deep magic. A chip hung from a leather cord around his neck, like some kind of protective amulet.

I only wished I looked that ace.

"We were just on our way out," Mom said.

He nodded and gave me the thumbs-up. "Excellent. I'm right on time."

I cleared my throat. "I invited Mouse along. That's okay, right, Mom?"

Mom chewed her lip. Her glance slid over to Mouse, considering, then she shrugged. "Yeah, I guess we do need someone who can blend with these... gamer geeks."

"Oh," Mouse laughed. "Thanks. Thanks very much. And here I thought it was my stunning personality that you wanted around."

"That too." My mom smiled. It was a strange smile—very serious and focused, but mostly in her eyes. It made Mouse and me blush. Noticing our reaction, she dropped her gaze, cleared her throat, and said, "Uh, we should get going."

◻ ◻ ◻

Manhattan at night was magical. As we drove through the traffic tunnels, it was easy to imagine that I was the star of some VR game. The city lights rushed by in waves, and the subtle contrast of the dark buildings against the black night made them seem more like flat backdrops than anything real.

It helped that Mom drove like a cop. Her eyes scanned for trouble, checking the rear, ahead, to the sides, then back again. The car even smelled like stakeout cars always did in the games: like old coffee and cheap food. The car fit the stereotype, too. Big and boxy, it was some kind of classic that Mom had retrofitted to work in the tubes. It rumbled as we zoomed through the greenish recycled-plastic tunnels, testing the weight limit with all of its antique steel and chrome.

I sat back and pretended to be "the partner," only this time I really was.

How ace was that?

"You should really get something built this century, Dee." Mouse's voice came from the darkness behind us. He lay stretched out on the backseat. I'd almost forgotten he was there.

"This is a good car," Mom said. "It's a classic Chevrolet."

"You have duct tape for a roof."

"It needs a few repairs."

He laughed, but then gave a serious nod. "That might account for that coughing sound and the scary way this thing rattles the tunnels."

Mom made a sour face. Then after giving him a long stare in the rearview mirror, she jerked her head in the direction of his chest. "What's that silly thing you have around your neck? I've never seen you wear jewelry before."

"Ah," he said, sitting up. He held up the flat chip that hung at the end of a leather strap as if to show it to us all. "It's my protection against dark juju. It's a hex inverter."

Mom shook her head but gave him a fond smile. "You are one seriously odd individual."

"What's a hex inverter?" I asked.

"A bad joke," Mouse admitted.

"Tell me anyway," I said.

"Okay. Try not to fall asleep," Mouse said. "Computers, as you know, think mostly in binary, ones and zeros. The hardware does that with levels of voltages, usually zero volts for zero and five volts or three-point-five volts for one. But there is also active low logic, where zero volts is the one. An inverter inverts the binary signal by turning the ones into zeroes and vice versa, by turning zero into five (or something similar)." He looked over at me and noticed my eyes were glazing over. "Okay. The easy answer is that a hex inverter reverses *the hex*...you know, like as in witchcraft. Get it?"

I gave him a blank look.

"Yeah, okay, so I told you it was a bad joke."

"A really deep geek joke," Mom chimed in. "There are probably six people left alive that get it. Don't feel bad."

I hadn't, but suddenly I did. Now, I not only wasn't smart enough to get the joke, but I also wasn't old enough either.

"So, what's the plan?" I asked, changing the subject. "I mean, how do I know who to talk to, and what do I ask?"

Mom pointed to the glove compartment, which was held shut by a piece of the ever-present duct tape. "In there is a holophoto of Olexa. What you need to do is ask people if they've seen her."

"Who's Olexa?" Mouse asked.

"Missing person," Mom said.

"That's it?" I felt kind of disappointed. I'd thought I was needed to get into the scene, to penetrate the inner sanctum of the players.

"That's it. Really, until we get a solid lead, that's about all we can do."

"Then why did you need me?"

"Or me," Mouse said.

"*You* were an uninvited guest," she said to Mouse.

Mouse and I reacted at the same time. "Mom!" I said, as he said, "Ouch."

"Actually, I'm glad you came along, Mouse. I was thinking about inviting you myself. But I've been wound really tight ever since I tried out the game. Plus"—Mom checked the rear again, then flicked a glance at me before checking the road again—"Missing-persons cases make me grouchy. I hate them. They rarely end well. I've been hitting a brick wall with this one for weeks. I'm scared it's too late for Olexa."

"You found *me* in time," I said, twirling the white streak of my hair in my fingers. By the way the teardrop hovered at the corner of her eye, I knew Mom was thinking of that time, when I was four, when Papa lost me to the Gorgons in Paris. I had only vague memories of it. I mostly remembered what came after. Until I was ten Mom barely let me cross the street without an armed escort, and considering how many soldiers stayed at the kibbutz that was not an exaggeration.

Mouse scooted to the edge of the backseat and put a hand on Mom's shoulder, silently.

I scowled at him. I felt like Mouse was taking sides against Papa. I know Mom still blamed Papa for the scars I had and for leaving us, but I didn't get all this resentment she harbored. Sure, Papa had splattered his brains against the wall with her gun in order to destroy his human body and free the angel within, but it worked. I lived. He did too, kind of. He was in Heaven. Sometimes I thought maybe that's what'd made her the most mad. That she never really knew if he was gone for good; that she could never really say a final good-bye.

"We're here," Mom said.

She found the last spot big enough for the Chevy in a crowded car park on the East Side. We were forty-three or forty-six levels up; I'd lost count.

I'd never been this high up in the habitrails, as we sometimes called the traffic tunnels that encircled New York like a ball of yarn. As we stepped out of the car, I felt a bit of vertigo. My breath caught with the phantom sensation that the atmosphere should be thinner or colder.

I reminded myself that only a kid or a tourist would be that impressed with the city. I was a New Yorker, and I was on a case.

Mom and Mouse, however, weren't nearly as city as I was. Mouse rushed out of the car to press his nose against the recycled plastic, and Mom trailed after with a big grin on her face. "Rye, come look."

I acted uninterested, but my feet moved quickly. Even though the safety plastic kept us from hanging over the edge, we could see all the way to the *ground*. Most of the time in Manhattan you walked or rode two or three levels up from the actual outside streets. Nobody walked on the streets much anymore, except Gorgons and scary people. It was strange to see patches of concrete illuminated by the passing cars in the tunnels above. Sometimes I could almost make out the remains of old stoplights, remnants of a time before centralized traffic control.

"Wow," I said.

"I miss this town," Mom said unexpectedly.

"Was your office this high up?" I asked.

Mouse stepped back from the plastic like it had bitten him. "No, it was down there. Street level."

"You were at my mom's old office?" Mom never mentioned that before.

He shoved his hands into the pockets of his jeans. "Yeah, that was where I tried to kill her."

"Oh." I didn't know what else to say. I looked at Mom. She wasn't looking at either of us, but still staring down at the street. Her lips looked tight.

"Not my best day," Mouse said quietly.

"No," Mom said, her face pinched. To me, she said, "Let's go."

Mom led us through a maze of vehicles to a windowed enclosure. Inside was an escalator that took us into the cavernous lobby of a hotel. Though the light still blazed from chandeliers, the place was empty except for a bored-looking concierge in a tuxedolike uniform. He hardly lifted an eyebrow as Mom continued further into the hotel.

"The rave is here?" I whispered incredulously.

"No," Mom said, as we walked around in a circle to take a second escalator up to another floor. "It's in the back room of a gaming store. We're going to get there through the service tunnels. This is the closest access."

Mouse snorted a laugh and patted me on my shoulder. "Hey, Rye, your first B&E rave. You're doing well, grasshopper."

"B&E?" I asked.

Mom gave Mouse a pursed-lip grimace. "Breaking and entering."

Mouse put his arm around my shoulder. "Didn't I tell you? You have the coolest mom. I know mine never let me commit felony. At least not on a school night."

I could see the tips of Mom's ears turn red. "If you don't steal anything, there's no felonious intent," she muttered. "I'm sure it's just criminal trespass."

"Oh, well, okay, then." Mouse laughed hard. "You're amazing, Dee."

"Oh, hush," she said, but didn't sound serious about it. "Anyway, the cops know we're here. I'm sure we won't get raided."

Raided? I shivered a bit with anticipation. I'd never done anything like this before. I looked over at Mom. Her gaze was focused ahead of us, and her mouth was in a thin line. Suddenly I found myself asking her, "How do you know all this stuff?"

"I've got an inside contact."

I frowned at Mom. "You're kidding, right? I mean, if you've got a mudhead inside the scene, why would you need me?"

"Rye, the guy's a game junkie. He's not exactly what you'd call trustworthy." She glanced at me, and then sighed. "Besides, Soul Stealer hasn't made it onto Vice's watch list yet. The guy I have isn't playing."

"Why are these gamers meeting in real time, anyway?" I asked. "Can't they all just have a virtual party?"

"Have you ever *been* to a virtual party?" Mouse asked, sticking out his tongue. But before I could reply, he continued, "They're horrible. A lot of 'asterisk-waving!-asterisk' and no free booze."

"Nobody text-messages anymore, Mouse," I said.

"*Some* people do. Wire wizards, for instance," he said sharply. Then he shrugged. "Of course, as Dee pointed out, there aren't that many of us old-timers left. But, okay, even if you're going virtual in full persona it's still just as low-rez. There's *still* no free booze, you got to listen to someone else's idea of party music, and Allah only knows who your avatar is going to go home with. All the while you're sitting on your ass..."

"Mouse!" Mom said. "Language."

"...at home, eating stale potato chips and drinking tap water." Mouse never even paused. "Besides, don't you sometimes just want to know?"

"Know what?"

"What the person on the other side looks like."

"You look like Page, don't you?"

"Not anymore," Mouse said. "Page looks like a dead polka diva."

"Really?" I hadn't known.

"Really. And, there's a certain cachet to real-time events. If you can say, 'I know what Deidre McMannus really looks like,' you can score some cred." Mouse waggled his eyebrows at Mom.

"Nobody cares about me anymore, Mouse," Mom said without even looking at him.

"Don't count on it," Mouse said.

"I'm not a celebrity anymore," Mom said. "I'm off the radar. Finally."

"That's not what I meant," Mouse said quietly.

Mom a celebrity? I didn't even want to think about that. Plus, for a private detective, she totally seemed oblivious to how much Mouse mooned over her. Of course, maybe, after that smoldering look she gave him before she left, Mom was ignoring him on purpose. With all the shooting and arresting and whatnot in their history, I imagined romance would be complicated.

We'd gotten as far as the trade tunnel entrance. In big bold letters it said, OFFICIAL PERSONNEL ONLY. The door was locked with some kind of security code box. Mom took something long and thin out of the inside pocket of her jacket and jabbed the box. I jumped when sparks flew. The door popped open.

"What the hell was that?" I asked.

"Cattle prod," Mom said, tucking it back into her jacket.

Mouse shook his head. "You could have just tried punching in one-two-three. It'd have been a little less of that 'forced entry' stuff. You know, the *breaking* part of B&E."

"Humph. Well, this way was more certain," Mom said. "The doors are programmed to open if there's a short in the system, even a temporary one. It makes them ridiculously easy to hack, but that's fire code for you."

"I have got to get one of those," I said.

"No way," Mom said.

"No, seriously, Mom. That's super-neat."

"No, seriously, Rye. That's super-illegal."

"How come you can have one, then?"

That stumped her for a second. "Because..."

"Because the line between the legal and illegal is mighty thin," Mouse said with a broad smile as he pushed the door open for us. "Cops always have to be a little dirty. A throw-down, a cattle prod for jimmying locks—stuff like that. Don't you watch the vids, Rye?"

Mom gave Mouse a dark look, but she didn't refute him.

"You see, grasshopper," Mouse said, making a "you-first" bow toward the door. "Your mother and I are a lot more alike than she'd like to admit."

I could hear Mom sigh. "You're incorrigible, Mouse."

"You know what I'm going to say about encouragement," he said, making a kissy face at her. To my surprise, Mom laughed.

"Jesus. Come on, already," she said.

We stepped into the semidarkness. I'd never been in a trade tunnel before, although I'd learned all about them in social studies. They were built at the same time the traffic tunnels were, except they were inside buildings and under the streets, and used expressly for the delivery of goods. Hundreds of people worked in the trade tunnels, invisibly keeping food in restaurants, stocking stores, and removing garbage.

Someone had clearly fallen down on that last job. There were six or seven bags of garbage piled near the door. The air smelled ripe. The odor probably would have been worse except that the temperature was a good ten degrees cooler inside the tunnels.

I jumped when the door shut behind us.

"Are you sure you can open that again?" I asked, noticing there was no box on *this* side of the door, just a slot where a key would go.

"Don't worry," Mom said.

"And if she can't, I can," Mouse said. Patting the inner pocket of his leather jacket, he added, "I'm sporting tools. Not that Ms. Cattle Prod needs any assistance."

Mom shook her head, but she smiled just a little. "Talk about illegal."

"Unlike you, I'm a criminal," Mouse said with a shrug. "It's expected of me."

"Does your parole officer know about those?" Mom asked. Mouse raised his eyebrows. "Frank? I should think not. And he doesn't know about this party either, which I am quite certain violates the conditions of my parole—associating with known wireheads and all that."

"These are gamers," I said, trying to be helpful.

"Most cops," Mouse said, "aren't smart enough to know the difference."

"You should cut Frank some slack," Mom said. "He's just doing his job."

"Which for any normal prisoner would have been over a long time ago. The state had to go make an exception for me. I'll probably be hounded by Frank for my whole life."

Mom laughed. "Hey, if you can't do the time, don't do the..."

Mouse cut her off with a raised voice. "Oh, Merciful Allah, stop with that."

Mom raised her hands as if to ward off his rant. "Just pointing out the obvious."

Mouse started down the tunnel, muttering something that sounded like "should never have gotten caught anyway."

I followed Mouse down the tracks that led down the center of the tunnel. I tried to space my steps so they fell evenly on the ties. Caged electrical bulbs were spaced in regular intervals on the ceiling. They illuminated graffiti-splattered walls. I attempted to read the words, but they didn't make any sense. Mouse must have noticed my curiosity because he said, "It's not English."

"What language is it?"

He tilted his head examining it with me for a moment. "I don't know, maybe Gamilaraay?"

"What the heck is Gamilaraay?"

"Australian Aboriginal, a.k.a. Exploited Immigrant du Jour."

"What does it say?"

He shrugged and kept on walking. "What it always says, I suppose. 'Up the Revolution. Eat the Rich.'"

"I'm serious, Mouse," I said.

Over his shoulder, he said, "Me too."

His disinterest made me more fascinated. I wasn't yet very adept at using mouse.net for translation, so I tried to make a quick file of one of the scrawls. Unfortunately, I was still learning how to use that function too, so I wasn't sure if I actually got the picture or not. Still, I thought I could remember it.

I nearly stepped in some garbage juice as I ran to catch up to Mom. "Ugh. How could a person stand to work in a place like this all day long?"

"I don't know," Mom said. "Desperation, I suppose."

As we rounded a corner, I could hear the distant, insistent thrum of a bass chord. Mom stopped. "Okay, here's the thing," she said. "I don't want the people at the rave to think we've come together. I'm afraid that would turn them off you, Rye. So, you're going to head in first, Rye. Mouse, you second."

Mouse shook his head. "No, I think I should go in first. Make sure things aren't too dangerous. That way I can keep an eye on Rye."

"I don't need a babysitter," I said.

"She's right," Mom said, surprising me. "Rye is better for this, and I trust her to take care of herself. Besides, I'm not sure if I trust *you* around your own kind just yet."

"Muddies are *not* my people," Mouse said in a huff.

"What should I do?" I asked Mom.

"Ask around after Olexa, maybe pretend you're a friend trying to get back in touch, whatever you think will work. Anyway, see if anyone knows her. If you get no response, then flash the picture around."

I nodded, touching the spot in my pocket where I'd stashed the holo earlier. "Is there a secret password to get in or anything?"

Mom shook her head. "My guy says not. If you know where this is, you're in the know."

"Ace," I said.

Mom took a deep breath. "Okay. Off with you. Be careful."

My heart was pounding against my eardrums in rhythm with the bass by the time I got to the propped-open door. It was made of plain steel and held ajar by a wedge of plywood. I put my hand on it gingerly. I wasn't sure what I expected. Maybe an electric shock or a palm identification reader, but there was nothing—just cool metal.

The door swung open easily, and I stepped through without having to pass a bouncer or anything. Somehow that made me more nervous.

The room was just as Mom said it would be. Wide with high ceilings, it appeared to be the storage space for some kind of gaming store. Tall metal shelves lined all four walls, filled with neatly labeled boxes. Wooden pallets dotted the floor, filled with boxes tightly shrink-wrapped together. Kids sat on top of them or danced around them. People stood in tight-knit groups talking or laughing. Many of them looked older than me, but it was hard to tell in the half-light. One thing I sensed right away was that they were all way more ace than I was.

Mouse would fit in well, I decided. People here dressed a lot like him-casually, with the predominant color being black. I'd picked a red skirt and sparkly gold T-shirt. I felt a bit overdressed, and far too colorful.

I noticed that there seemed to be a bucket full of drinks in the far corner. I headed across the room, trying to act like I belonged, like I knew what I was doing. I could feel a few eyes on me, as I knelt down to take a pop from the ice.

"Donate to the cause, sister?"

I looked up to see a dark-haired boy about my age dressed all in white. He had a narrow face, which was thin, like a bird's. A large beak of a nose should have made him look nerdy, but somehow gave his features a noble, Roman cast. Jet-black hair hung limply in front of large, darkly lined eyes.

He was cute.

But weird. The whole white thing was very low-rez. White pants never looked good on anyone, and he seemed to be wearing some kind of bleached denim, like a throwback to an era before my grandmother was born. His shirt was button-down and the exact same shade of brightness as his pants.

"What are you supposed to be?" I asked him finally. "An angel or something?"

"What are *you*?" he asked, looking at my scars. "Gorgon? Half? What?"

"Leaving," I said, turning to go.

"No, wait. I didn't mean to offend you. You were right. I *am* the angel of soda karma." When I gave him a quizzical look, he pointed to the can in my hand. "You drink, you donate. Get it?"

"Oh. Right." I fished through my pockets for my credit counter. "How much?" When I looked up he was giving me a strange expression. "You're new, aren't you?"

I blushed. I'd done something newbie. "Yeah," I admitted.

"It's barter here," he explained.

"Barter?"

"Yeah. You drink my pop, you give me something you think is of equal value."

I hadn't a clue what that could be. My belt? An earring?

"A name," he supplied finally. "I'll trade you my pop for your name."

I looked into his eyes, trying to gauge if he was serious or not, and I was struck by the blackness of them. I could hardly tell where his pupils ended and the irises began. It was like looking into a black mirror. If eyes were supposed to be the window to the soul, this guy didn't have one.

"No way," I said suddenly. "A name is too powerful. I'll only trade my name for yours. Here." I pulled off an earring, one of my favorites, and handed it to him. "For the soda."

His mouth hung open a bit, but he took my earring without a protest. I turned away, trying to figure out how I could bust into one of the cliques of girls standing near the door.

"Adram." He stood beside me while putting my earring through a hole in his ear.

"Amariah," I said.

"That's a boy's name, isn't it? Hebrew. 'Whom God has promised.'"

I almost choked on my pop. No one else knew that. Ariel said it was my secret. "How did you...I mean, most people haven't heard of my name. It's not very common."

Adram shrugged. "It's a hobby. I collect books on the origins and meanings of names." Then he gave me a sly glance out of the corner of his eye. "You know, you're right. Names do have power. Especially in the game, and you want to have a *skóro* one. I mean, it would suck to go to the seventh level and die with a name like Eustace. You know?"

"Eustace isn't so bad," I said, but I couldn't suppress a laugh.

"Yeah, but you wouldn't want to be remembered forever as Eustace, would you?"

"No," I agreed. "What does Adram mean?"

"It's actually short for Adramelech. I don't think it has a meaning."

"Adramelech? That's a mouthful."

"I know," he admitted. "There's nothing like being saddled with a bad name to make you interested in others."

"What name would you prefer?"

"I don't know. Nikolai?"

I looked him over. Even though I'd barely gotten used to his real name, I tried to see this new name on him. Taller than me, Adram was more lanky than muscular, but I could see a hint of strength in his broad shoulders. In the half-light, he cast a long, narrow shadow. There was something odd about the silhouette that stretched along the concrete floor. It seemed as though he was standing in front of something that floated near his shoulder blades. It stretched out on either side of him like enormous...

Wings.

¤ ¤ ¤

MAGOG INVASION SUBTLE

Could Cultural Invasion Fulfill Biblical Prophecy?

The Apocalypse Watch, Fundamentalist Press (December 2095)

Tel Aviv, Israel—There is a Russian Invasion in the youth culture of today. Russian artists have been cropping up everywhere-in designer labels, gallery shows, film festivals, and now concert halls. Tonight Sasha Rachmanov will be debuting his rock opera *Theocracy Blues* to sold-out crowds at the Tel Aviv International Arena. Rachmanov is the latest sensation to breach the "Silent Curtain" that has surrounded Russia since the Medusa war.

Tickets to Rachmahov's concert went for twenty-five to one hundred credits per seat. The arena sold out in record time. Young people everywhere are already lining up to buy tickets in other stops on Rachmanov's world tour. Anxious kids in London nearly downed the LINK site where advance tickets were being sold by "pinging" for a spot in the queue so often. "It was like a denial of service attack, except for real," said the system's manager. "These kids wanted our stuff so bad they nearly crashed us."

Devout Christians have much to fear from Rachmanov and his ilk. In Ezekiel, chapters 38 and 39, the Bible warns us of an end-times invasion of Israel from Gog. In Genesis, Gog is clearly identified with the "Scythians," who were the early ancestors of modern-day Russians. Previously scholars of the infallible and inspired Word of God believed that these passages referred to a military action. "However," says Dr. Thaddeus Black, Christian scholar, "the passage merely says 'to take spoil.' It could be a cultural invasion, intended to rob the children of Israel of their worldly goods through commercialism."

"Israel just felt receptive," said Rachmanov when asked by the mainstream press about his choice at a public conference earlier this week. "And, of course, there is much to celebrate in Israel. This is the two-year anniversary of the secularization of Temple Rock. I wanted my concert to be a small part of the commemoration of this historical moment."

It should be no surprise to Christians that a Russian would approve of the destruction of theocracies everywhere. Russia remained staunchly atheist after the rest of the world divided itself up into theocracies, even declining to join in the international LINK protocols. When *AW* reporters wondered if there was a connection between Rachmanov's atheism and his move to the West, the Russian heartily agreed. "Yes, of course it's a religion thing. Now that theocracies are relaxing, we can too." Contact your local church for information regarding how to start a boycott of Russian art and artists in your area.

¤

CHAPTER 11

Deidre

Watching Rye disappear down the hall, I wondered if I would make Worst Mother of the Year for letting my teenage daughter go into an illegal party alone. At least I knew she was a good girl. She wanted to be a messiah, after all.

Beside me, Mouse tapped his foot against the wall, humming something that sounded for all the world like Patsy Cline's "Crazy." I rubbed my face. I owed him an apology.

"Mouse, I've been rude," I said. He shrugged. "Hey, Dee, it's cool. I once tried to shoot you. Anyway, I thought we had a good tease going on."

"We did." I smiled. "We do."

Mouse's expression softened in a way that surprised and intrigued me. It was almost as if the superficial mask of humor he always wore slipped just a little to reveal a kind of deep intensity that I'd never seen before. His foot stopped its incessant tapping. "You look...nice tonight," he said carefully, as if afraid I might object to the compliment. "The cop look suits you."

I looked down at my clothes. I hadn't intended to dress "cop" tonight... Mouse, meanwhile, exuded counterculture with his hex inverter and leather. "If I'm the cop, you must be the robber."

Mouse's smile brightened. "Fantastic. That was the exact look I was going for."

I shook my head fondly. "Of course you were."

"Got to be true to your nature, I always say."

I frowned at that. "And my nature is cop? I've been off the job for years."

"Nah, not you, Dee. You've always been defined by your past," Mouse said, not meeting my eye. Instead, he looked down the hall toward the music and where Amariah had gone. "For me, the past doesn't exist. I look in the mirror and see where I'm going, not where I've been."

"You're fooling yourself, Christian," I said, using his given name. Mouse's real name was Christian El-Aref. I'd learned it from the news a while back. I was curious how a Muslim got the first name Christian, but he'd never offered the story, so I'd never asked.

"You're just as defined by what you've done as I am," I continued. "Otherwise no one would call you Mouse."

His black eyes sought out mine in the semidarkness of the tunnel. "That's different. Mouse.net is just a notch in my belt. A brag point. That's not History, with a capital H, the way you drag yours around."

"You're saying I'm some kind of a martyr?"

Mouse took a deep breath-the kind that seemed to imply he didn't want to start a fight. "I'm just saying some aspects of where you've been are really on the surface, dig? You walk like a cop, Dee. It's been how long?"

Too long. As shocking as it was to admit, Mouse was right about me. I'd never given up wanting to be a cop. If I were still on the force, I'd be facing retirement in a matter of years, but I still wanted it. I wanted it with the kind of crazy, intense desperation of a twenty-year-old, not someone as old as I was. After all this time, I was still mad about the injustice of having been kicked out. Even though Michael had helped me clear my name, I hadn't ever been truly satisfied. I wanted my old life back, only with Amariah in it, and maybe someone else to come home to, too.

The game just made those feelings more acute. What had been a kind of low-level background desire blossomed into a full-fledged, forefront passionate ache.

"Have, you tried Soul Stealer, Mouse?" It probably seemed like a complete change of subject to him, and he gave me a pitying look like he thought I was avoiding his point. So I felt I needed to add, "I was just thinking about what you said and it reminded me of the game. When I went, it was like a scene out of my—as you say—capital P, Past. I'm just curious. If you're so in the Now, what did you get?"

Mouse's face went pale, and his arms crossed around his chest, almost protectively.

I nodded my head; he had some secret history too.

"My mother," he said after a long moment. "And black water."

I watched him hugging himself and waited for more. His eyes stared at some point on the opposite wall, but I could tell they searched deep inside. I thought I saw him shiver. "You okay?" I asked.

"You know what's weird? I went back, Dee. Three times. What the fuck was I thinking?"

"You were thinking you couldn't get it out of your head," I said kindly, putting a hand on his shoulder. Part of me wanted to see Danny again, maybe even have him confront me. "I understand."

"Yeah, sure, but you're probably off collaring bad guys like a superhero. I'm going back to the worst..." His voice trailed off, and he shook himself out a little. "It's not important. It's stupid. I just still don't know why I went back. Glutton for punishment, I guess."

The tunnel was dark, and the music seemed like a distant drumbeat. "You've never told anyone about the black water stuff, have you?" I asked.

"No," he said sharply. "And I won't."

"I'm not asking you to. Honest," I said, giving his shoulder a squeeze. "It's just that—that's the other thing that's been bothering me. How does this game know that stuff, that oh-so-personal stuff?"

Mouse blinked. His shoulders relaxed a bit, and I dropped my hand. "Shit." He halfway laughed. "I never even thought about that."

I felt relieved to see Mouse acting more like his old self. "It's got to be some new kind of brain hack," I suggested. "Like your LINK-angels."

"No, this is deeper magic than the angels. I impressed feelings *onto* people. I didn't reach into their heads and pull shit out."

"It can't be that deep," I said dismissively. "The Inquisition can requisition memories."

"No, they can't. I have it on pretty good authority that that's just hypnotic suggestion. You know, realtime magic."

I hadn't heard that, but I didn't imagine that the Inquisition wanted people to be in on how it performed its "interviews." I watched Mouse's face for signs that he was the "good authority" he knew this from. It was hard to know with him. He might say he didn't think about his past, but I. was beginning to believe that maybe he was just better at denial than most of us. And he'd clearly been through a lot. I found myself worrying about him, wanting him to be okay.

"What are you looking at me like that for?" he wanted to know.

"Sorry," I said, feeling a blush creep along the edges of my collar. "Uh, I was just trying to puzzle out this game."

He stared at me like he didn't believe me for a moment.

"Page...I mean, Strife, says it's been eating placeholders."

That derailed him. "You talked to Page?"

"Isn't it Strife now?" I asked. Mouse shrugged, and I continued, "Anyway, he said the game's siphoning off empty spaces."

"I'll bet there's a load of cranky wizards out there," Mouse said, coming to the same conclusion I had.

"You'd think, wouldn't you? Page says no. Nobody's mad."

"Huh," Mouse said. "That's weird."

My LINK beeped at me, reminding me it was time for Mouse to make his entrance. "You should probably head in," I said. "Check up on Rye."

"Yeah," he said distractedly. Then, with a brave grin, he added, "Into the breach. Wish me luck."

I did more than that. I leaned over and gave him a peck on the cheek. "Take care of yourself," I breathed into his ear.

"Uh," was all he said as he scurried down the hallway.

Alone, I found it hard to wait patiently for my turn. I edged a little closer to the entrance to the party. The trade tunnel felt close, cold and wet, like a cave. A centipede scuttled over the toe of my shoe. The place smelled like a garbage pit.

Plus, there were these strange new feelings for Mouse that gurgled along the edges of my guts. I'd liked what I'd glimpsed underneath the glibness. Serious and intense held a lot more fascination for me than silly and flip. I should have known Mouse had a "real" side. It was easy to forget how much he'd been through: two major arrests, prison time in hard-core pens, and now a hint of this other darkness from his youth. He must have had a lot of fortitude to get through all that without breaking.

That was a person who interested me.

My "interest" took me by surprise. It had been a long time since I'd thought about romance, even longer since I'd had sex. When I kissed Mouse ever so lightly on the cheek, I smelled him for the first time—a clean, spicy scent, like rosemary, mingled with the leather of his jacket. The coarse hairs of his stubble burned pleasantly on my lips, making me wonder what he tasted like.

At that thought, I distracted myself by making a few calls.

"Yo, Martinelli here." Joe Martinelli was my contact on Vice. I think I gravitated toward the Italian cops because of Michael. Joe Martinelli, unfortunately,

was no Michelangelo Angelluci. Even so, the smile on his face was bright and handsome when he recognized me. *"Hey, Dee! What can I do for you this time?"*

"You've got your ear to the ground," I said. *"Any of the wizards freaking out about their claims being hijacked by a game?"*

"Not that I've heard. Why?"

"How about a big influx of cash? People spending beyond their means?"

Martinelli gave me a little laugh. *"These are wire freaks we're talking about, right? You can never tell with them. Money is too damned electronic. Working around these guys makes a fellow want to stuff old-fashioned paper money under his mattress."*

I knew what he meant. *"Too bad they don't make that stuff anymore."*

"Yeah," Martinelli agreed wistfully. Then his green eyes flashed, as he asked, *"So, what's your hunch? What are you after?"*

"I'm not sure," I said. *"I've got a missing girl that got caught up in Soul Stealer before she vanished. As I've been sniffing out the game, it's been leading me some weird places. Like, I can't figure out how it works or who it belongs to."*

"Nobody knows, that's the real kicker," he agreed. *"You'd think a hot game like that would have some designer's signature all over it. I know I'd claim it if it were mine."*

I hadn't even considered that aspect. *"How are they making any money?"*

Martinelli shook his head. *"It's not pay to play."*

"Advertisers attached?" That was often the other way game designers made money. Various entertainment companies accepted large sums of money to script in brand names. You'd have to get this particular kind of car for your escape, or your hero would take a refreshment break at a famous chain restaurant, that sort of thing.

"Not one." Then as an afterthought, Martinelli added, *"Say, how'd Dar work out? Was he helpful?"*

"Well, so much as he could be. How come Soul Stealer isn't on the Vice list yet?"

"Grassroots freeware isn't illegal."

"Oh, like mouse.net?"

Martinelli wagged a finger at me. *"That cut into the LINK'S profit, way I heard it. Anyway, both of us know this game is good for people. Brings 'em together."*

"You think that's what this is? Some kind of community-building effort?"

Martinelli grimaced like he didn't really think so. But he said with a shrug, *"People are into that stuff now. It's that McNaughton woman. She's got people doing all sorts of 'gatherings.' Rebroadcast LINK shows on low-rez flat screens, just so you can hang out in real time in some cheap bar with your smelly neighbor? Who would have thought people would be into that kind of crap?"*

Yeah, I'd heard about those. Personally, I figured McNaughton was in league with the devil. Actually, I *knew* she was. I'd recognized her fashionably dressed husband, Morningstar, the instant I saw him.

Sometimes it bothered me that they'd been getting so much press, but what could I do? It wasn't like I could call up my local congressperson and tell her that I'd seen Satan on the LINK. Besides, as far as I could tell, neither Morningstar nor McNaughton had been doing anything particularly devilish.

It went against my gut feelings, but I liked some of what McNaughton had been up to. Giving LINK access to the disenfranchised happened to be a big issue of my own. Having once been completely cut off, I knew how desperate those straits were...Nobody should have to live off-line. It wasn't just that the LINK was a fast way to communicate; it was everything. As Martinelli had pointed out, it was money, but the LINK also gave access to jobs, the vote, health insurance, and all that. Lots of people starved without the LINK. It wasn't fair.

Decriminalizing homosexuality was a dicier issue for a lot of people, including myself, but nobody thought the camps were a good idea.

I'd heard that McNaughton took a special, interest in Gorgons' rights, too. Those I had a vested interest in, thanks to Rye. She hadn't really faced much discrimination because of the touch of Gorgon blood she possessed, but we lived in a Gorgon-friendly environment. I worried about what would happen to her out in the "real world." In some ways I was glad she'd gotten her classmates obsessed with her angelic parentage because at least then they weren't harassing her about her silver eye and white hair. When Amariah was very small, people treated her like she was my pet. They'd ask me if she was feral and if she bit. Though I was always quick to point out that she was a quite well-behaved young woman, I'd secretly wished she would bite jerks like that. So I would love to see McNaughton give a voice to Gorgons. They needed an advocate.

"You still there, Dee?"

"Yeah," I muttered, listening with half an ear as Martinelli complained about his neighbor and the noise these "gatherings" brought to his West Side neighborhood.

Truth was, what really bothered me about McNaughton was that somehow she still had *her* angel.

¤ ¤ ¤

DOES THE LINK STINK?

Entertainment News (December 2095)

It's becoming a familiar scene all over America, and all over the world. People gathered outdoors or at cafes doing something that hasn't been popular since our great-grandparents' day—

Talking.

Not LINK-transmitted conversation, either. Real, face-to-face interaction.

Here in Hollywood it's becoming a serious fad to skip a favorite LINK-feed entertainment, such as the ever-popular *Me for a Day* series, in favor of watching a flat-screen replay with friends at various venues known as "rebroads" (for "re-broadcast"). "Oh, sure, the quality of image is completely skid, but community is the real draw," said Zoya Bostwich from her table at the hottest spot on the strip, known simply as the Local. Zoya came dressed for the event in a T-shirt that read, ANOTHER BROAD FOR REBROAD.

Sentiments like Zoya's have industry insiders worried. "The whole reason the LINK entertainment channels gained prominence is because of the quality of the experience," said virtual reality designer Pytor Morgensfield, best known for his work on the Broadway musical LINK-sperience *Living with Stan*. "Entertainment moved from watching someone from a distance, to being them—taste, smells, physical sensations, the works."

Now that trend is reversing. Quality of experience no longer drives the market. In fact, most of the rebroads offer the LINK feed for free. "Nobody would pay for an image this shaky," said Local manager Tasya Cornell. "I make my money selling liquor and food. Just like my grandfather did."

The real-time trend, has its roots in the political movement surrounding celebrity Emmaline McNaughton. She began rebroadcasting her LINK-speeches on smart-posters all over her home base of Jerusalem. Soon local cafes began asking for access, and McNaughton granted it. "Once I discovered the kind of crowd these things would generate and the amount of food and drink they would buy," Jerusalem hot spot Filter Cafe owner Pessa Brown said, "I found I could actually purchase rebroad rights to any number of shows and still make a profit." At first LINK entertainment executives thought nothing of the requests for LINK-transcripts (as the grainy "screen shots" are sometimes called). "We gave the stuff away," said producer Larry Weast regretfully. "It looked like crap to us. We had no idea of the value of these things."

They do now. Weast and other entertainment business people are starting to jack up the prices on the transcripts of more popular shows. This, however, doesn't stop the Local from procuring the feeds in the old-fashioned way. "We steal 'em," admitted Cornell. Pointing to her head she said, "I'm a paying subscriber. It's not that hard to just record what I see."

But how the images are procured matters very little to attendees like Zoya. "I'm not even really here for the show. I'm here to see and be seen. It's excellent to meet some people whose avatars you've talked to for years. The coolest part," Zoya says with a snide chuckle, "is when they're fat and ugly. Not like their avatars at all."

¤

CHAPTER 12

Dragon

One stands in the center of Shanghai Node. An open plaza represents a
real-time relay system that acts as a focal point for several billion minds'
interface with the satellite system that makes up the LINK. High-rise buildings
surround the marble-tiled plaza, the walls of which advertise the corpora-
tions that sponsor this node. The place pulses with activity. Avatars dressed in
business suits conduct financial transactions, track stock, trade goods, communicate, buy, and sell. Others, more casually dressed, loiter around the edges of
the activity, leaning against walls under porticos. They wait for entertainment,
conversation, love, or a connection to pass by. Perhaps some of them buy and
sell as well.

It is all *maya*, illusion, of course. But then, what isn't?

To this one's eye the LINK seems bigger. Also it feels much, much more
crowded. One is not used to having to share. Admittedly, one may have
become a bit complacent, and perhaps a bit...selfish. A big animal controls the
existing broadways, bandwidth. A smaller creature is jostled along a busy street,
lost in a crowd, and pushed around by larger avatars.

One feels a sulk coming on.

Stupid Kioshi. Stupid game.

One has come to Shanghai Node to buy some information. Setting up on
the sidelines with all the others, this one has put a small sign out. In kanji characters, Mandarin, and Cantonese, the sign reads: WILL PAY FOR INFORMA-
TION ABOUT SOUL STEALER.

No one stops.

This one frowns menacingly at those who pass by, but one's new size has made one cute and not at all threatening, and so instead of recoiling in fear, strangers pat one's head and mutter, *"Aw."*

"Grrr," this one says, only to hear laughter from the passerby.

Standing beside this one under the portico is the avatar of a young man. As there is nothing else to do, one watches him, wondering at his trade. He has no sign up, but his fashionable, skintight clothes advertise sex. There is about him a studied languidness—the way he leans casually, openly, against the wall, and the way his eyes invite the crowd to look without asking or anxiousness. He is, one decides, passably handsome for a human. The creator of the avatar has been careful not to make the image too memorable. He has long, straight dark hair that falls over his forehead and a tiny hint of Asian features: sharp cheekbones and a slight epicanthus fold at the corners of his eyes.

Most people who pass consciously avoid looking at either of us for too long. This one checks one's sign, wondering if there is something misspelled or inappropriate. After a moment, one adds a *"please,"* then repositions the note.

"You won't get a hit, dragon," the gigolo says after craning his slender neck to read my addition.

"But why not?" this one asks.

He laughs; it is chiding, but not unkind. *"You're yakuza. Everyone knows that."*

"So?"

His smile is bright, clearly his best feature. *"So you're probably scaring off my customers."*

One is strangely pleased to hear that one is still scary, despite one's new size. Still, it had never occurred to one that one had any kind of fearsome reputation. Certainly, one does work for Kioshi—some of it quasi-legal—but it is not as if one is a ninja assassin. One has never taken out a contract on anyone. One is not a killer. Truthfully, one can hardly even imagine that such things actually happen in Kioshi's business. Perhaps that is the way of the mafia in the vids, but not in real life.

"What's up with the new smaller you, anyway?" the gigolo asks. *"Are you in disguise or something? Trying to be stealthy? A probe program?"*

"No, this is all me," one says glumly. *"This one has been downsized."*

The gigolo sputters a sound that could be a laugh or curse or both. *"What the fuck? Are you serious?"*

One nods.

"Is Toyoma Enterprises in trouble?" the gigolo asks, abandoning his post against the wall to kneel in front of me.

"Kioshi says so, yes," one says. Then glancing at the gigolo with suspicion, one adds, *"Why are you so interested? Are you looking for a job?"*

The gigolo flashes his brilliant smile again. *"Dragon, I already work for Toyoma Enterprises."*

One is shocked. One often forgets the extent of the businesses that Kioshi dabbles in.

"So, what did Kioshi tell you? Is it finances? Trouble with the Triad?"

Suddenly one realizes that one has probably already said too much. *"Must go,"* one says quickly, sketching a quick bow. *"Sorry."*

One disappears in a flash to one's hidey-hole. There exists a place that no one has ever seen but *one*. It is one's secret place.

Where it exists, exactly, is tricky to explain, partly because one is not sure of its real-world parallel. It may not be on this earth at all; it may be in outer space. The LINK works partly because of a mess of satellites that surround the earth like a swarm of flies. Kioshi's father made the majority of his legitimate money by owning the manufacturing company that built the electronic parts of those satellites and exported them all over the world. Nearly every LINK relay in use today has a Toyoma "heart." Out of each of those, this one has carved a tiny place of one's own: a place to store the backup copies, the ancestors, that this one worships.

One's secret place appears as a carefully tended walled garden. The time is always late morning; the crisp promise of summer fills the cool air. Wisteria clambers along brick, spilling waves of fragrant purple flowers. This one takes in a deep breath. Walking slowly along the curving pebble-lined path, one sees stone statues of one's self. A whiskered dragon peeks shyly out from behind fringed irises. Behind it, a magnolia's blooms begin to unfurl.

One stops for a moment and admires the backup. It is the earliest copy. One's face looks broad, young, and eager. The body of the statue stands not much taller than the iris stalks. This one smiles: was one ever so small?

Glancing down at one's own feet, one holds one paw up for inspection. A quick comparison reveals that Kioshi's downsize has reduced this one to almost the same stature as that of the first backup. Life, it seems, is a circle.

One walks away, feeling uneasy.

Further along the path the gray statues grow larger and larger until, at the very end, last week's backup curls around the twisted trunk of a fig tree, eyes closed and wings folded, as if asleep. One marvels at how like a mountain it appears. The back ridges rise well above the top branches of the tree. Its head is as large as one's entire body.

Tentatively, one extends a talon and raps the frozen beast on the nose, as if to wake it from its slumber. One jumps back, hopeful. But the beast does not stir. Not even one stone whisker twitches.

Such is the way of one's backups. They are useless, dead.

Toyoma Enterprises, under Kioshi's command, has been trying to replicate the process that birthed this one, but to no avail. Once, many years ago, Kioshi asked this one for a copy, to see if one could simply copy new dragons. Over in the corner of the garden against the wall, is the remains of that attempt.

One cautiously takes the path that leads to the monster. Bluebells shiver at the whisk of one's tail down the pebble-lined road. It is not a pretty thing, the experiment. It looks a little like this one, only it is clear that it never lived. Its eyes are shrunken and dark; its face slack. One turns away in horror.

One's consciousness, it seems, goes with one. Once one has shucked off the skin of the backup, it will not reanimate. It is not even certain that if one were to become corrupted, one could jump back into a previous self. It seems unlikely, given the mistake.

One creeps into the tall, stiff ribbon grass to lay one's head against elder sister's flank. The sun has warmed the stone, giving it the illusion of body heat. But the scales are not soft. They are hard, sharp, and dead.

Odd to think that only last week one was such a different creature. What would it be like to be that again?

When Mai died, one considered attempting seppuku. One thought that maybe if one's consciousness ended in one body, it might be reborn in another.

One entertained the idea quite seriously. Several potential "accidents" had even been plotted as ways to accomplish this goal. But, in the end, one decided that it wouldn't work. Mai would still be dead. No pain would be spared. In fact, one would probably feel worse—more shocked, more abandoned—being robbed of the memories of the events surrounding Mai's death.

Even if dying to become a backup worked.

But.

What would one lose now?

One bad conversation with Page/Strife and an odd meeting with Kioshi— these things did not amount to much. But perhaps it would only give one a small respite. After all, Kioshi held the strings of power. Could he not simply downsize one again?

Shutting one's eyes, one prays to elder sister for guidance.

¤ ¤ ¤

ANTICHRIST WATCH LIST

A Regular Column for the Fundamentalist Press

The Dragon of the East was seen in the company of fellow artificial intelligence Page ibn Mouse again this morning. The dragon has been on the Fundamental Press's Antichrist Watch List since her first appearance in the early 2060s. The image of a dragon has long been associated with Satan and the Antichrist. Revelation 12:7-9 says: "And there was war in heaven: Michael and his angels fought against the dragon." Similarly, one of the signs of the Apocalypse is a red dragon rising from the ocean foam.

Though the dragon appears harmless, and is green, it should be remembered that Satan is the great deceiver. The dragon and the deceased rock star Mai Kito are worshiped by many in the east as "new Buddhas," which to say false messiahs. It is also prophesied that the Antichrist will attack from the east with an army of a hundred million.

Revelation also speaks of a beast with seven heads. It is rumored that the yakuza has at least seven genetically engineered children that are hooked directly to their supercomputers. These minds run the research and development component of the "dragon program." Before these infants have developed speech, they are immersed in computer language. Such practices are considered a violation of child labor laws and are illegal in most countries—not, however, in Japan.

Even though the dragon now operates independently of "the program," she was created by these minds, and the yakuza itself could be seen as the beast resembling "a leopard, but [with] feet like those of a bear and a mouth like that of a lion." Like a leopard, the agents of the yakuza are predators who hunt the innocent. Bear claws represent the slashing katana blade of a ninja, and like a lion's mouth, yakuza gang members talk as though they are the king of the beasts.

The dragon is number seven on the *AW* list of top ten possible Antichrists.

¤

CHAPTER 13

Morningstar

Kfar Shaul Mental Health Center was where Israel kept all the saviors and prophets. So many of them crowded the place that they had their own special area: the messiah ward.

I hailed a cab from the Old City. The air inside the car was stale and air-conditioned to a temperature near freezing. The robot driver took my credit counter and my spoken Hebrew command to take me to the hospital, and I sat back to formulate my plan to gain access to the messiah ward.

Turns out I needn't have worried. My fame opened the door without any hassles or subterfuge. I just walked up to the front desk and introduced myself.

"You'd like a tour of the messiah ward? Of course, Mr. Morningstar, we can arrange that. Just give me a moment to find someone to take you back," the receptionist said with a breathless smile. She glanced off into space for a moment, then told me it would only be a matter of minutes. "Can I get you something to drink while you wait, Mr. Morningstar?"

"Please, just Morningstar," I insisted. My name was title enough; the honorific seemed redundant.

"Morningstar," she repeated, like I'd given her some kind of gift. She giggled, adding, "I've watched you on the LINK. You're much cuter in person."

A little laugh escaped my throat. The receptionist continued to gaze at me expectantly. I wasn't sure what to say. I actually felt a twinge of self-consciousness under this woman's intense scrutiny.

I returned the favor by staring back. If I had to guess, she was in her twenties. Though her uniform was tidy and proper, I could see a hole in her nose where a ring would go. Her skin was caramel-colored, like an Indian's, and her dark, straight hair was cut short and ragged, with bleached strips of white in a zebra pattern.

"Much cuter," she breathed again. "You should be an actor or something."

"What, and give up the lucrative job of being Em's boy toy?" I said with what I hoped was a wolfish smile.

The receptionist blinked. Her mouth hung open slightly, and she looked scandalized for a moment. Then she laughed. "Be serious."

"I am. Not many people can afford to keep me...entertained."

Her brown skin darkened, and she dipped her head slightly. But her embarrassment was either brief or feigned, for she batted her eyelashes and asked, "And how do you like to be entertained?"

"Very, very wickedly."

She blinked again, and I could almost swear that I could hear the sound of her internal cameras zoom in for a close-up. In an hour, maybe less, my evil little flirtation would be all over the LINK. Em would absolutely hate it. My smile brightened.

I was robbed of further opportunities to besmirch my honor by the appearance of a middle-aged Israeli woman dressed in the classic white coat of a doctor. "Mr. Morningstar," she said. "I'm Dr. Segulah Chmielnitzki."

Like the receptionist, the doctor oozed solicitousness. It occurred to me as she politely apologized for some of the less polished parts of the hospital for the second time that the good doctor was very likely fishing for a donation from Emmaline and me.

I decided to play that up. "What I'm most interested in is the messiah ward. Emmaline has a special interest in helping the mentally ill."

The doctor's smile broadened. "Of course, of course."

"I was hoping to talk to a few of the patients," I said. "If that would be all right."

"Certainly. You can stay as long as you like. I should warn you, though, some of them have been fairly heavily drugged."

I nodded that I understood, but I wasn't quite prepared for what I saw after getting past a checkpoint with a locked gate. The main room was dingy gray and decorated sparsely with metal folding chairs, cheap card tables, and a smattering of stained and threadbare couches that looked like they'd fallen off some college student's moving van.

A flat-screen television from some other era hung suspended from the ceiling in one corner. A group of patients dressed in ragged street clothes or terry-cloth robes sat around it like apostles at the foot of a master. The box played some badly rendered LINK-entertainment band or another. When the program came to the interactive sections, it would stutter and strobe until someone pressed a button on an equally antique remote.

Others just sat staring at the floor or the ceiling, or rocking back and forth to their own inner music. It was sad, honestly. If there were a real messiah here, she or he would be no threat to me or mine.

"Is there someone you want to talk to, Mr. Morningstar?"

I shrugged. I no longer hoped to find anyone of real value here, but I might as well keep up the pretense. "Sure, if someone is lucid enough."

The doctor led me to a man sitting alone, staring at his fuzzy slippers. "This is a John the Baptist," the doctor said with a embarrassed tone. "He's a John Doe. He had no ID on him when we found him."

"LINK ID?"

"No LINK," she said sadly, as if that condition was even worse than his present delusion.

"John Doe Baptist," I said to him in English, crouching down to look him in the eye, "do you know me?"

His eyes darted everywhere, refusing to settle on my face for more than a second. The man certainly could have passed as wild. His dirty auburn dreadlocks stuck out in every direction, and he had several days' growth on his beard. The man's skin was pale white. He was possibly Irish, I guessed, by looking at the Saint Brigid's cross that hung against his thin chest.

"Herald, I am searching for someone," I whispered. "Have you seen him?"

Wet, glassy green eyes locked on mine instantly. "Her," he corrected.

"Her?" Of course. It made sense. If Emmaline was the Antichrist, it followed that the new messiah would also be a woman. They would be parallel, but opposite.

"You shouldn't encourage him," the doctor tsked behind me.

"Where is she?" I asked him quietly, ignoring the doctor. "I must find her."

His eyes widened. I thought perhaps he sensed an angel in his presence, for he sat up straighter and leaned in to speak to me very intently. "First prophet. Second seal. I saw a great beast rising from the department store. Rise and come on to me, saith the Lord. Tomorrow there will be pizza and butterflies. On Wednesday we must eat fish sticks."

I was briefly with him, before he started the Revelation riff. After all, if there was a messiah at large, then Elijah, the first prophet, was probably in the world right now looking for her. But as the Irishman continued listing his prophecies regarding the cafeteria menu, I stood up and wandered over to those surrounding the flat screen.

"One of them might recognize you," the doctor said.

"We can only hope," I said.

But no one did. I received prophecies regarding a soft drink, a VR game called the Angel of Death, UFOs, an active doomsday super-volcano in Yellowstone Park, and one particularly detailed delusion about the Illuminati and the acceptance of the credit as the world's currency being the entry for the Antichrist's domination.

I shook my head. For all I knew, some of these predictions could be correct. I turned to the doctor. "Tell me, Segulah. Would you know the real *moshiach* if he came here?"

She seemed surprised, perhaps at my casual use of her first name or maybe at the Hebrew term for *messiah*. It took her a moment before she said, "Everyone is carefully screened."

I returned my attention to the black woman with close-cropped, dyed-yellow hair who continued to mutter about Yellowstone's forthcoming eruption. "There is truth to this," I explained to the doctor. "Scientists have discovered an active caldera in the park. Why does she qualify as crazy?"

"Because she says the whole thing was predicted in the Bible Code."

"Maybe it is," I said wryly. "Mysterious ways and all that. But why don't we accept that she could be the holy one?"

"Mr. Morningstar, please. When we found her, this woman was stark naked and banging her head against the remains of Wailing Wall until her forehead bled. Of course, many people weave bits of truth into their delusions. That's why they have such a grip on these people's psyches...You can almost understand it. But in my experience the difference is that God never asks his prophets to hurt themselves or others."

I laughed. "Have you never read the Torah, Doctor? In Genesis, to Abraham, 'God said, "Take your son, your only son, Isaac, whom you love, and go to the region of Moriah. Sacrifice him there as a burnt offering." ' Sure, God eventually changed His mind, but you can't say that He never told Abraham not to hurt himself or others."

The doctor chewed her lip for a few seconds. With a smile and a shrug, she said, "I'm afraid it's hospital policy to take it on faith that the true saints are asked by God to do good deeds, not to sit naked in the middle of the street shouting about how cream cheese on bagels is a supreme heresy."

I gave a brief nod in recognition of the joke she was trying to make. However, I disagreed. "Then I don't think you know God very well at all."

"And I suppose *you* do?" The look in her eyes was one of wariness. I watched her gaze track to where the orderlies stood. Perhaps she was even LINKing to them that I might make a good permanent resident.

I let out a long, sad sigh. "No, of course not. Of all creatures great and small, I surely know Him least."

That seemed to satisfy the doctor of my sanity. We finished the tour without another eruption of my theology. I left the hospital dejected, with a promise to go to the board of the Morningstar Foundation and ask them to give the hospital a much-needed donation.

I actually intended to follow through on my promise. It served our interests to keep this hospital functioning and well stocked. Emmaline had been right. If a real messiah came here, he would be indistinguishable from all the lunatics.

I had the taxi deposit me at the Filter Cafe, in Rehov Aza, a trendy section of Jerusalem that was host to a number of European-style restaurants. A chalkboard set up outside showed the daily specials. I paused a moment to contemplate the horror of tomato/pine nut/cilantro soup, then went inside anyway.

The place was crowded, but I was able to find a seat near the bar. The bar was stocked with every kind of alcohol imaginable, all in fancy bottles. Above, naked lightbulbs bathed the polished golden wood of the countertops in a warm glow. It would be perfectly comfortable, except that flat screens broadcast Emmaline's face from every corner. Thankfully, the restaurant was far too noisy for me to hear what she was saying. Even so, I noticed several glances in my direction. My only hope was that the Filter crowd was too fancy to be impressed with a celebrity such as myself.

The bartender took my order without comment, so I let my shoulders relax a little. I'd come here to think, after all.

I needed to answer the question If I were the messiah, where would I be?

Actually, I had to step one back. Really, the bigger question was what did Raphael mean by "messiah"? Was I looking for a Jew, the Lion of Israel? Maybe I should be searching for a Muslim, the Mahdi? Perhaps God, in Her infinite humor, would send us a new Buddha.

My head hurt with the possibilities. I took a sip of the "fallen angel" the bartender delivered. The lime and bitters tasted sour. *Appropriate*, I decided.

I sighed. Well, if I didn't know what the messiah would be, maybe I could figure out what the messiah was not. My sense was that a true messiah would think outside the box. Fakers would consciously try to follow the life of Christ, since in their minds he's the one guy that counts. Of course, that was a huge assumption.

The one thing I knew about God was that She had a taste for the unusual and a well-honed sense of humor. So the messiah really could be anywhere, be anyone. Probably the stranger, the better, so who knew what God really intended?

I had to find an angel. Preferably one who was still really tight with Father. I instantly thought of Michael. He would be the best choice. However, the last time he and I crossed paths was over a decade ago. I wondered if any of the Fallen had seen him lately. I glanced down at my wrist-phone. It was a gift from Emmaline—a top-of-the-line, state-of-the-art tech toy. She'd been adamant that I learn to use it. We'd spent an entire weekend together programming it and teaching me all the various functions. I remember, at the time, I'd been irritated by the whole process and what I perceived as a waste of time. Suddenly, I was grateful, because it only took a second to reach the entire army of the Fallen.

Pressing a button on the side, I activated the voice message system. "If anyone has sighted Michael, report." I almost ended there, but then decided to add, "Or any of the Four." After all, any of the archangels would very likely be aware of who the messiah was.

With a few more taps of various buttons, I sent the message out globally.

"Excuse me," said a voice to my right. I turned to see a dress, or at least strategically placed fabric sheathing a voluptuous female body. Large, soft-looking breasts were barely covered by a skintight shine that shifted color slightly under the light so that sometimes it appeared a deep royal purple and other times jet-black. "Are you Morningstar?"

If she hadn't spoken again, I would have never discovered she had a face. In her early twenties, if that, and very, very artificially blond. She wore enough makeup that she seemed more like a mannequin or a supermodel than anything real and living. A forgettable visage, really.

Not like the dress.

"Yes, I am he," I said, focusing my eyes on hers. They were purplish too. I wondered if they were colored contacts, worn as an accessory to the dress.

She sat down on the stool beside me even though I hadn't invited her to. "Can I buy you a drink or something?"

"Or something?" I couldn't help but smile-not exactly a subtle come-on, that.

She demurred, dipping her head and blushing a lit-tie. "You're different in real time," she said. "More...um, predatory."

Such a big word; I was impressed. "Is that to say sexy?"

"Yes," she agreed. "Sexy like a wolf."

The thing I hated about these little "real-time" encounters is that they'd be all over the LINK half an hour after they were over. I touched my hands to my chest, feigning disinterest. "I'm sorry. You know the only one that I love is Emmaline McNaughton."

If she was disappointed, she didn't miss a beat. "I could still buy you that drink."

I looked at my half-empty glass. "All right. What could it hurt?"

Her name was Ilyana and she had immigrated to Israel from the Ukraine with her parents several years ago. I heard about her stint in the army and her interest in some kind of LINK game having to do with angels or death or something. I stifled a yawn in my shirtsleeve and started glancing surreptitiously at the exits. Then Ilyana revealed that she was a student of philosophy and religion at Hebrew University.

"Do you study eschatology?" I asked.

Ilyana tossed her blond hair and took a long swallow of her gin and tonic. "Sure."

"Do you think we live in the end-times?" She studied the depths of her glass, then giggled like I'd made some kind of joke. "You sound like the gatekeeper."

I frowned. "Saint Peter?"

"No, in the game. In order to get access to the game you have to answer all sorts of weird questions like that."

"I've never played," I admitted.

"Never?" She was as incredulous as if I'd suggested that I was a virgin. "Not even once?"

"Not once."

"Oh, you totally should. You get points for all sorts of stuff in real time. You get to meet all sorts of swank people that way."

"I'm not LINKed."

She started like I'd slapped her. "Oh." She looked at me for a long time. Then she added, as though she were embarrassed on my behalf. "Well, uh, there's things you can do about that."

"I'm sure."

123

"Anyway, you totally should play. You'd like it, I think. It's all about God and stuff. I think Emmaline is even one of the answers."

I was curious, but cautious. "How do you mean?" "Well." Ilyana leaned in conspiratorially. I could smell the sour tang of the gin she'd been drinking on her breath. "I think we're supposed to think Emmaline is the new *moshiach*."

"You don't believe it," I ventured.

"No." Her voice was a drunken whisper. "I think she's the Antichrist."

"Really? And you get this from the game?"

"Yep," Ilyana agreed sloppily.

"I think I would like to play," I said with a broad grin. "Why don't you take me home?"

I had to put up with bad, drunken sex in order to get my first glimpse at the game. Luckily, Ilyana was a narcissist. She had hundreds of still photographs of her character at various levels of the game. The theme appeared to be a new war in Heaven. Players chose a side and battled it out with each other, but first they had to perform various deeds in the real world that would decide which side they played for. I was horrified—though not terribly surprised—to discover that Ilyana gamed in my ranks, the Fallen.

"Isn't my costume way evil?" she asked, handing me another picture of herself.

We stretched out on our stomachs, lying on the flowered sheets of Ilyana's twin-size bed. A box fan buzzed in the window in a vain attempt to cool the small, stuffy, room. We'd had to keep the door shut so that her father, a night watchman, wouldn't wake up. The whole thing had been extremely tawdry, and the multitude of stuffed animals staring at me with beady button eyes only served to make my stomach twist more.

At least I didn't have to feign my appreciation for her outfit. She looked like everyone's fantasy of a demon. Her wings were black, like a raven's, and her body was barely covered by tiny strips of gravity-defying red leather. The tiny horns poking out from waves of black hair, however, were just a bit too much for me to take. "Horns are a pagan thing," I muttered.

"Yeah, I know," she said, rolling over so that I could see that her ample physical endowments were not exaggerated for the game. "But I think they look *lisíte*."

"I think you slipped into your native tongue," I said.

"I did, silly," Ilyana said. "It means *fox*. Russian is all the rage."

I shrugged. I could hardly keep track of every fad that came and went. "You like being a demon," I said, reaching out to stroke a dark nipple.

"Who wouldn't? You get to kill the Goody Two-shoes. And our side is winning, too. We've got way more souls than them. I can't wait to meet Lucifer."

I kissed her then, hard. "Aren't you afraid of him?"

"No, he's totally cute." She reached up and ran her fingers through my hair. "Kind of like you."

I smiled, moving my lips down along the line of her throat. "Well, that's something, at least."

"Yeah, it's a bummer we have to destroy him."

I sat up on my elbows. "Isn't he your leader?"

"Yeah, but he doesn't do anything. He's been a real stick-in-the-mud. A bunch of us are planning a revolt."

"Well, there's a little irony. Where does Emmaline come in?"

"Oh, that's just the real-time stuff. If you want to advance in the ranks of the Fallen, you have to do stuff for her causes. You know, like put up posters or like that. I'm organizing a party at college next week. You know, to get people into the game and to talk about her politics? Well, actually, all I have to do is hand out some flyers that they sent me. I'll get a ton of points for that."

"Who's *they*?"

She blinked, as if she was surprised that I had been following along. "What do you mean?"

"The 'they,'" I said, "that sent you the flyers."

"Oh. Emmaline's headquarters, of course."

"Of course," I muttered, my anger rising.

□ □ □

SOUL STEALER: PERSPECTIVES OF A CHRISTIAN GAMER

The First in a Series of Special, Informal, and In-Depth Reports

The Apocalypse Watch, Fundamentalist Press (December 2095)

By Rosalita and José Fuentes—The editors here at *AW* have decided to devote an entire column to tracking down information about the new virtual reality/real-time game known as *Angel of Death: Soul Stealer*. José Fuentes, the teenage son of our lead investigative reporter, Rosalita Fuentes, has volunteered to attempt to infiltrate the game under strict supervision.

The first step—finding the game—proved to be surprisingly difficult and eerie.

Each time a player accesses the main site, he or she is presented with a different interface. The first time José went he found himself in a Gothic cemetery, the details of which were reminiscent of a family trip to New Orleans. "What creeped me out," said José, "was how real it all felt. It was like the images were stolen directly from my brain. The Spanish moss even smelled the way I remembered it."

Though José spent three hours exploring the cemetery, he could find no clues on how to progress further. "We almost literally left no stone unturned. Mom and I even tried making anagrams out of the names on the headstones," he said. "I could see how people could get obsessed, though. I was really frustrated, like when you find a really good puzzle."

Careful not to get too obsessive, the Fuenteses decided to wait a week before trying again. In the meantime, they prayed to God for inspiration and insight.

Expecting a return to the same scene, José was surprised to discover a whole new landscape, this one an ocean beach startlingly similar to a family vacation spot in North Carolina. "We'd thought maybe we hit the wrong game, so I off-lined to check the site and went back. Guess what? New scenario!" The third visit revealed a giant library. "This is when things got really spooky," José said. "It was the reading room of the Library of Congress. I spent a whole summer there. I have a poster of it on my wall. I'm beginning to feel this game is haunting me. Picking out personal memories and exploiting them."

José also admitted that he felt that there was "a presence" watching him each time he visited. "Maybe it was the other players spying on me and deciding if I was jazz enough to play their stupid game, but it was uncomfortable. It felt malicious."

When asked how this game felt different from other on-line games, José had a surprising answer. "It's stupid. I mean, the images are high quality and everything, but there's no story, there's no action. On the surface I don't get why anyone would go back to this game." But he suggested that it was probably the personal images that hooked players. "This felt like it was about me. I've been dreaming about it at night."

¤

CHAPTER 14

Amariah

The shadow of wings fell across the floor, moving, it seemed, in tune to the bass pounding through the storeroom.

I blinked, and the shadow image was gone.

I looked over at my new friend, Adram. His right temple was smooth. There was no sign of the LINK receiver. I reached up and felt mine; new though it was, it made a hard almond-shaped lump under my skin.

"How old are you?" I asked.

Adram gave me a smile. "How old do I look?"

I'd thought he was a little older than the age of majority, but without the LINK he'd have to be younger. "Old enough to be connected. How do you play without the LINK?"

"Oh," he said, looking embarrassed. "That."

Yet he offered no explanation. I waited for the usual hurried apology for an all-natural mother who refused to birth in the hospital, or an admission that he was homeless or illegal. Instead he quietly watched a group of girls who had started dancing on top of some of the crates, and continued to sip his soda. No "I have a metal allergy" or "I'm so rich, I've got one that doesn't show." Nothing.

I was about to press him further when his wrist-phone beeped. He looked down at it like he didn't know what to do with it. "The button on the side," I offered.

"Right," Adram said, pressing it. Some kind of text message scrolled across the screen. I tried to read it without seeming nosy. All I saw was something about "the Four," whatever or whoever that was.

"Who was that?" I asked.

"Uh." His eyes darted around as if searching for an answer in the crowd. Then he shrugged. "I don't know. Wrong number, maybe."

One thing I now knew about this Adram guy was that he was a really, really bad liar.

"You're an angel, aren't you?" I asked. Then I gave him a quick once-over. He looked almost normal, not very powerful. "Maybe you're a Principle or a Virtue? Definitely not an archangel. You're too small, and I only saw two wings, not seven."

Adram looked shell-shocked, but I couldn't tell if it was because I'd found him out or because he thought I was crazy.

"You saw wings?"

I shrugged. "I know what to look for."

"Too small?" He mumbled it, so I almost didn't hear the question over the thrumming music.

I smiled; Adram *had* to be an angel. No one else would even care that I said he was too little to be an archangel. "Archangels look like linebackers," I said. "You don't."

"Oh, really? You do realize that you sound like a stark-raving lunatic, right?"

It was a nice attempt, but too late. I gave him a big smile. "You know I'm right."

Adram looked like he was about to give me a smart comeback when I heard a hushed awe roil through the crowd. Next to me, Adram breathed, "Holy shit, is that...Mouse?"

I looked up to see Mouse wandering over to the cooler full of drinks, looking as uncomfortable and out of place as I imagine I had.

"I didn't know he played," Adram said.

"Uh, sure," I said. "Mouse loves the game."

Adram looked as surprised at that as he had when I told him I'd seen his wings. "You know Mouse?"

Just then Mouse spotted me and waved. I waved back. Suddenly I was the most interesting girl in the room. Everybody who wasn't gaping at Mouse turned to stare at me.

Mouse sauntered over to Adram and me. "Hey, Rye. I see you found a friend," he said. He offered a hand for Adram to shake. "I'm Mouse."

"Yeah. I guess I knew that. Uh, I'm Adram," he said as if he wasn't sure. "So, you guys know each other?"

"We live in the glass, in the same house. In the commune," Mouse explained.

"Kibbutz," I corrected.

"It's not in Israel," Mouse said. "It's in the Bronx. Therefore it is a commune. It's imprecise to call it a kibbutz. And anyway, I'm not Jewish. Are you?"

"You live in the glass?" Adram said to me and then looked at his hand like maybe Mouse had infected him with the Medusa.

"You'd feel it," Mouse said, noticing Adram's inspection of his palm. "The little nanobots biting you. Right, Rye?"

"That's what I remember," I said glumly. I was bummed that Adram seemed worried about Medusa infection. I'd hoped that since he rolled with my scars he wasn't one of those ignorant types who thought you could catch it from touching a Gorgon. I was also kind of bummed that he'd pretty much stopped talking to me and, like everyone else in the room, was focusing on Mouse.

In fact, I noticed that some other people were starting to edge a little closer, as if trying to overhear our conversation. One brave woman with a Star of David tattoo on her bicep, dressed in a sparkling sheath dress that showed off her slender curves, slid in next to Adram. She put an arm on his. "Nikolai," she said, using his game-name, I noticed with some jealousy. "Introduce me to your friends."

"Uh, Jaye, this is Rye and Mouse."

"Mouse," Jaye cooed, totally ignoring me. "How nice to see you. I never noticed your handle on the boards before."

"That's because I'm not playing," Mouse said. "At least, not yet." Mouse raised his voice and yelled over his shoulder, "I'm still looking for an invite, you freaks!"

"I'm sure someone will, now that we know you're serious," Jaye purred. "So how'd you find out about the rave?"

"Since when do you have to be serious about a game?" Mouse asked.

Jaye looked offended. Adram caught my eye and rolled his.

"This is more than just a game," Jaye said in a huff.

"Yeah, let me guess—it's life," Mouse replied. "Been there a million times."

"So why are you even here?" Adram asked.

"I'm looking for someone," Mouse said. "Maybe you know her? Olexa?" Mouse put me to complete shame; I'd totally forgotten about the case we were supposed to be working on.

Jaye and Adram exchanged glances. Jaye shook her head, sending a cascade of brown hair waving this way and that. I could see Adram's jaw muscles flex before he spoke. "Never heard of her."

"You guys lie for shit, you know that, right?" Mouse said.

"Look," Jaye said, leaning in a little, nearly blocking me out of the circle. "A cop has been sniffing around for Lexi. We don't need cop trouble."

Mouse made a little apologetic gesture with his hands. "It's cool. I can understand that."

"Sounds like she's a friend of yours, but don't worry about her, okay?" Jaye said. Both she and Adram kept looking toward a group of girls who were standing in a perfectly straight line, pressed against the shelves like wallflowers. "She's one of us, you know?" Jaye continued. "Our responsibility. We're taking care of her."

I followed Adram's gaze and peered intently at the girls. I thought about the holo of Olexa that I had in my pocket. I'd looked at it before I stepped into the rave. Olexa had smiled grudgingly in the picture, and I thought perhaps this was a school photo. She looked like half the girls in my class. Brown hair was pulled back into a ponytail, with a few streaks of electric-blue dye and glow-beads woven in here and there. Olexa had been affecting that I-could-be-a-bad-girl look by wearing a lot of eyeliner. I didn't see anyone quite like that over there. I started across the room to get a better look.

Adram grabbed my arm. "Can I get you something? Another soda?"

Mouse was beside me in a second. "I'd let her go, if I were you, asshole."

"What are you, the boyfriend?"

I blushed instantly, but Mouse was focused on trying to get in Adram's face. He stood up on tiptoe. A crowd started to gather, and I could sense the tension in the sudden hushed tones.

"I might be," Mouse said fiercely.

Adram laughed. "You some kind of pedophile or something? She's half your age."

I wrenched my arm from Adram's grasp. "I was just getting something to drink. No need to get all possessive!"

"Oh." Adram gaped down at his hand still clutching the empty air where my arm had been like it was something alien. "Sorry."

"What's up with you, anyway?" I asked. "Why is everybody so intense?"

Adram scratched at his nose, then shrugged. I turned my glare on Jaye. She held my gaze for only a second before she looked away.

"I don't think I want an invitation to this game," I said.

"No," Mouse agreed.

Adram looked at me with pleading eyes. "It's not like that. The game is... amazing."

"They shouldn't even be here," Jaye said with a snarl. "They weren't invited. They haven't been initiated. You *know* you can't explain it to outsiders. They never understand."

"But he's Mouse," some girl who had been standing nearby said. "He should get it, shouldn't he?"

"They don't know until they've tasted it," Adram said. "Jaye's right."

"Mouse has gone to the game," I said. "Three times. Right, Mouse?" Mouse gave me a sharp glance I didn't understand. I tried to mouth, "What?" but he already turned to the others. "Yeah," he said, with a jerk of a shrug. "I didn't get very far."

The eyes of everyone around us lit up. "What did you get?" someone behind me wanted to know.

"Yeah," Jaye repeated, "tell us your dream!"

"I'd really rather not," Mouse said, his eyes hooded and dark.

"Ah," Jaye said knowingly. "A nightmare. You'll be one of the dark ones, like me."

"What does that mean?" I asked Adram. "Dark one?"

He gave me a long looking-over. "The Fallen," he said finally. "If Mouse gets an invite, he'll join the ranks of the fallen angels."

"Oh. That's why you're here," I said, suddenly excited. "You're here because of the angels!"

Adram put a finger to his lips.

It made perfect sense. Angels usually didn't come to earth without a job from the big guy in the sky. Mom had told me that she met Papa because he'd come to discredit the LINK-angels. The game must be another kind of angel fraud. No doubt Adram was here to make things right.

I couldn't wait to tell Mom.

"I should have known," Jaye said. With a purr in her voice, she stretched an arm around Mouse's neck. "You'd be on our side."

Mouse shifted his shoulders to dislodge her. "I wouldn't roll out the red carpet just yet, sweetie. I think your game is skid. And I can't think of a reason I'd want to spend any more time there than I already have."

"That's because you haven't worked past it," Jaye insisted, getting right up to his ear to whisper in it. What a flirt! But, at the same time, I wished I could be so bold. I looked over at Adram. His eyes were watching me so intently, I found I had to look away.

"You mean this is some kind of therapy?" Mouse asked with a grimace. "If that's the case, count me out. Way out."

"No, with the dark ones you have to accept it. Revel in it. Next time you go, try it. Try just surrendering to it instead of fighting."

"Surrender to it?" Mouse asked, with a look of pure horror on his face. "Do you even know what my nightmare is? I have spent my entire life trying not to get swallowed by that particular darkness."

"He's too old," someone muttered. "The nightmare is too deep."

"You could still work it out," Jaye said. "You have a young heart."

"What makes you think I'd go back?" Mouse asked, but even I could hear the longing in his voice. Whatever the game dream had been for him, it had a strong pull.

Jaye just smiled. Mouse seemed completely withdrawn now, thinking about what she'd said. "Come on," she said, "let me get you something to drink."

That left Adram and me.

My fingers twisted through my hair. He stood perfectly still, his pose watchful, interested. I wondered what he saw when he looked at me. Could he tell that I had a safety pin holding my skirt together in the back? Did he think that the Kola-Cola shirt made me look like a little kid?

"Do you want to dance?" he asked, making a courtly gesture almost like a bow.

I wasn't even sure if Mouse noticed us moving away; the space we vacated was instantly filled with curious onlookers. We picked a spot near the boxes, but not on them, and just started.

I always felt self-conscious dancing. I was never exactly sure what I was supposed to do. I knew enough to sway my body on the downbeat, but what to do with my arms remained a mystery. Throwing them around looked spastic and could be kind of dangerous on a crowded dance floor, but holding them stiffly at my sides felt wrong. I compromised by making fists and keeping them fairly close to my chest.

Adram, on the other hand, was a pretty good dancer. He actually moved his hips, something most boys I knew wouldn't dare to do, even though the jerky movements they made instead looked far more ridiculous than anything Adram was doing. Adram somehow used his hands to accent what his hips were doing without looking too diva. I tried to copy him. Noticing me, he smiled.

"You look great," he said.

132

It was a kind lie, so I grinned back in appreciation of his effort. "You're a pro. You must go dancing a lot."

"I like to check out the clubs," Adram said.

"With a girlfriend?" I felt ridiculously bold asking, like everyone must be watching me make a fool out of myself. "I mean, do you have a girlfriend?"

"No," he said after what seemed like forever. "Is Mouse really your boy-friend?"

"No."

He smiled warmly at me after that, and we danced in companionable silence for three more songs. By carefully watching and mimicking Adram, I began to feel more comfortable with this whole dancing thing. I found myself smiling back, enjoying myself. I was even working up the courage to ask for his phone number.

That's when Mom walked in.

Mom had been off the force for ages, but she still radiated cop. The atmos-phere of the room changed dramatically when she entered. What was strange was that she had gone to great pains to look like the mudders. She dressed totally casual, and her long trench coat matched at least one other in the room. But think it was the way she walked that gave her away Her hips hitched rather than swayed, like they were used to bearing the uneven weight of a gun on one side. Mom's shoulders stood high, proud, and square ready to serve and pro-tect. Unlike Mouse or me, Mom walked into a room like she owned it, like *we* were the intruders, foreign, wrong.

Guilt—that's what everyone felt when they saw her. The way she looked at you made you suddenly remember that you'd jimmied the lock to get into this storeroom. One stare reminded you of that piece of gear you pocketed from the shelf for your private use. In fact, as Mom's eyes swept the room, I saw hands stray restlessly to fondle stolen goods hidden in clothes.

It was a mother's look.

It was a cop's eye.

People around us were starting to whisper. I could hear snippets of their consternation. It was time to go. Undercover agents had arrived. The party should move and lose the losers. I watched some kids slip behind Mom and glide out the door. Mom paid them no attention. I think she knew the effect her presence had. I understood now why she needed Mouse and me so desper-ately. She would never be able to pass in this crowd. Of course, I wasn't sure I could either.

"Do you want to go?" Adram asked me. "The party is shifting. I'll give you a ride."

"A ride?"

"I have a motorcycle."

Going alone with a gorgeous guy I'd just met? To an illegal party? On a motorcycle?

I was completely sold. The biggest challenge would be getting past Mom.

"I know a back way out," Adram said. He had apparently followed my gaze and my line of thinking. When I looked up, he was staring at Mom.

"Yeah, okay."

Somehow Mom didn't see us slip out. Mouse had come to my rescue in a way, calling for Mom to come to him. Seeing her distraction, Adram took my hand and we ducked behind some crates. He led me through the door that opened into the shop. The public end of the shop was little more than a showroom. One or two display models of external hardware sat on pillars set into alcoves. Faint spotlights shone on them, as though they were jewels to be admired. The rest of the room was dark, but Adram expertly wove us between cases that held replicas of equipment or rare attachments. I wanted to stop and admire one piece, but Adram tugged my hand.

We hurried out into the main pedestrian tunnel, garnering an odd look from a couple out for a stroll. I didn't ask Adram how he managed to avoid the cameras or alarms. I didn't want to know. Mom was already going to kill me for ditching her. The last thing I needed was a trespassing ticket to show up at Luis's. On all my legal documents, I claimed to live there. It was easier than writing "illegal kibbutz," and normally Luis didn't mind. He would if he got a ticket with my name on it.

Once safely in the tunnel, Adram slowed our pace and dropped my hand. Without his palm wrapped around mine, it suddenly felt cold and abandoned. I had no pockets to shove my hands into, so I tucked them under my arms.

"Are you cold?"

I nodded. I hadn't dressed for the weather. The pedestrian tunnels were always warm, a comfortable seventy-two degrees, but it was winter outside. Frost laced the tunnel walls in places, obscuring our view of the stars.

"When we get to the garage, I have a jacket you can borrow."

"Is it white?"

He smiled. "Of course."

"White leather?"

"Yep."

"I'll be okay," I said, pulling my hands out of my armpits as if to prove my mettle.

He shook his head at me as if to say, *Your loss.*

"What is it with you and white anyway?"

Adram looked ahead of us, but his eyes were unfocused, far away. The tunnel branched into a T-intersection ahead. Through the plastic I could see the rounded, illuminated scallops of the Chrysler Building. "It reminds me of home."

"Heaven?"

Adram glanced away, out the greenish-tinted plastic at the monolithic sky-scrapers. Squares of lights made uneven checked patters in the darkness. "It's my dream. In the game. What's yours?"

I almost betrayed myself by asking which game. My mouth opened but closed just in time. Instead, I shrugged.

"You haven't been invited yet, either, have you?"

"No," I admitted.

"How'd you find out about the rave?"

"Mouse," I lied, but it seemed like a good one. Adram nodded, like he approved. "So," I ventured, "what's the game like? I mean, why are you so into it?"

"Even though I have to use a VR suit, I like the feeling. The feeling of fighting again. Flying. Plus, there's the inside/outside thing. Doing good deeds is fun, too."

"I'd think that part would come naturally," I said, thinking of his angelic nature.

"Would you?" Something in his tone seemed almost sad.

"Yeah, but I don't know why you need a game to do all that stuff."

"I just do," was all he said.

"Okay."

We walked a little further. I didn't know what to say, so I decided to ask him more about the game. "Before, you said that the game was inside/outside? What's that mean?"

He blinked. "Oh. Well, it's like this. The game plays on two levels. Inside the game and out in the real world. We're playing now, actually. The rave is part of it."

"You mean, like, you get points for talking to certain people or something?"

Adram gave me a long, calculating look. "Yeah, something like that."

135

There was something about his tone that I didn't like. I suddenly regretted wandering off with a complete stranger.

◘ ◘ ◘

KFAR SHAUL TO RECEIVE MORNINGSTAR MONEY

Agnostic Press (December 2095)

Jerusalem, Israel—Kfar Shaul Mental Health Center, Jerusalem's state mental hospital, is slated to be the newest recipient of monies from the Morningstar Foundation. The gift of 2.1 million credits (Christendom) will be earmarked for the hospital's psychiatric unit, sometimes known as the "messiah ward" due to the large number of patients diagnosed with the Jerusalem. Syndrome. Hundreds of visitors from all over the world are currently housed at Kfar Shaul, as it is the main hospital for tourists to Jerusalem. Sixty percent of the patients in the "messiah ward" are Jews, 32 percent are Christian.

Administrators at the hospital were pleased with the news, announced today through Monsignor Emmaline McNaughton's headquarters. "Thanks to all our John the Baptists we get a lot of press," said hospital administrator Trudi Burke. "But usually it's tongue-in-cheek articles quoting the various messiahs we have staying here. It's nice to see people taking our work seriously."

Sammael Morningstar made a public statement regarding this gift, saying that he hoped the administration would use the money to hire more staff and "reward the hardworking doctors they already have. And to keep up the good work."

The donation was the first nonpolitical use of Morningstar Foundation funds and the first to go to any institution in the home country of the McNaughton headquarters. When asked about this, Morningstar replied, "Sometimes you just have to do people a good turn."

¤

CHAPTER 15

Deidre

Everyone scattered when I entered the room. "Way to make a girl feel welcome," I muttered to the retreating bodies. Well, I thought, at least it was still early. Amariah would get a good night's sleep before school tomorrow. I glanced around the storeroom, searching. Where was that girl?

Most of the room had completely emptied out. I saw three people struggling near a pallet of shrink-wrapped boxes. One of them wore a leather jacket with a mouse painted on the back. "Dee." It was Mouse, of course. "Get over here! Quick!"

He held the wrist of some hapless, wide-eyed girl. A woman with a silvery dress and a Star of David tattoo held the girl's other arm. They were having a tug-of-war over her. As I rushed toward them, I saw why Mouse was so agitated. The girl they struggled over was Olexa; I was sure of it.

I pulled the gun from the waistband of my jeans. I'd had it tucked in back behind my long coat. "Stay where you are," I told the woman in the sparkly dress.

"Do it, Jaye," Mouse added. I was only a little surprised that he'd managed to learn the woman's name already.

Jaye did as she was told, but she shook her head and stared at Mouse menacingly. "You'll never get in," she threatened.

"See me crying a river," Mouse said sarcastically.

"You just wait," Jaye muttered, holding her hands up. Olexa, meanwhile, did nothing. Absolutely nothing, although at least she seemed to be breathing. Her eyes stared unblinkingly. Despite my gun pointed in her general direction, her face remained flat. She didn't seem to care, or even notice, that Mouse still gripped her wrist tightly.

Though Olexa was dressed for a party, the clothes she wore looked slept in. A short black skirt came to mid-thigh, and dirt-streaked Wicked Witch striped stockings covered her thin legs. Her stained white tank top and torn purple jacket could have completed a flash look, except for the decidedly musky odor that clung to her. Her brown hair, which had been chopped short into a pixie style, looked unwashed.

"Olexa?" I asked. "Are you Olexa Johnson?"

"Yes." Her response was perfunctory, and her eyes never focused.

"She's in the game, right?" I asked Jaye, who was still shooting threatening looks in Mouse's direction.

"Zombified," Mouse said when Jaye refused to answer. "And there's six others like her. I couldn't catch them all."

I was horrified. "Six?"

"At least," Mouse said with a nod. "If not more."

I turned my attention to our more responsive captive. Jaye continued to throw sullen looks at Mouse. "What were you doing with Olexa? Don't you know her parents are looking for her?"

Jaye had sharp, birdlike features. She squinted at me. "Olexa has achieved a higher consciousness."

Olexa looked like the walking dead, just like Mouse had said. Like any game junkie, she had dilated pupils, but unlike them she seemed mobile. At least she was standing on her own accord. "Olexa," I said to her, "are you okay? Do you want to go home?"

"Home," she repeated.

I glanced at Mouse. "Do we take that as a yes?"

"No," Jaye said, starting to move forward until she remembered my gun. "They won't respect her. They'll try to unplug her!"

Mouse scrunched up his nose and made sniffing noises around Olexa's hair. "Tell me why this is a bad thing?"

"Her soul is one with the game."

"Well, maybe it's time she became one with a shower," Mouse continued.

"You don't understand," Jaye sounded fairly frantic now. "If she's unplugged she'll die."

I put the gun away. "You're serious?"

Jaye nodded. "Please, just let us take care of her. She listens to commands. We can clean her up if that's what you want. Just let her stay in the fold."

The idea of a bunch of helpless kids being shuffled around among gamer freaks made my stomach curdle. Olexa seemed as though she would obey any command. I hated to think what the teenage mind might do with that kind of power over anyone.

"Why on earth would I leave her with you?" I asked.

"We are one. Her soul speaks through mine; she says, 'Leave me here.'" The timbre of Jaye's voice changed slightly, causing the hairs to prickle on the back of my neck.

"Merciful Allah," Mouse said to Jaye. "You got Inquisitor tech?"

He asked because Inquisitors could modulate their voices. It came from being mostly machine. Normal people, with the usual LINK tech, could subvocalize, but that was the extent of their vocal tricks.

"Leave me," Jaye said again in the screechy dual tone.

"She's going home to her parents," I said. "They can decide what they want to do with her."

During the taxi ride to Olexa's house, I called Amariah on her wrist-phone and paged her on the LINK. I started to get worried about her when she didn't answer. It wasn't like her to go wandering off, but she hadn't really had much of a teenage rebellion so far, so I supposed she was due. I told myself I could trust her. I told myself I'd raised her to take care of herself.

I hadn't really convinced myself, though.

With a quick LINK to the kibbutz, I called up an army. Commander Steinmetz promised me he'd send a couple of soldiers to track down the rave. I'd keep trying her numbers. I didn't know what else I could do.

"Was Amariah with anybody?" I asked Mouse around the stiff form of Olexa, who sat like an inert package between us.

"Oh, yeah," Mouse said nonchalantly. "There was this British-looking kid, dressed all in white. Adam? He was all over her."

My God.

"Why weren't you watching over her?" I wanted to strangle Mouse, but Olexa was in the way. "We have to turn this taxi around right now."

"You said she didn't need a babysitter," Mouse said, raising his hands to ward me off. "Anyway"—he pointed at Olexa—"what are we going to do with her?"

"You can take her to her parents'. I'll go after Rye."

"Reverse that," Mouse said. "I'm not the private investigator. Don't you think Olexa's parents would freak if an internationally wanted criminal showed up at their door with their zombie daughter in tow?"

I hated it when Mouse was right.

I'd LINKed ahead so Olexa's parents were waiting outside. They lived in a high-rise apartment building at the edge of Brooklyn. As we stood on the snow-and ice-covered sidewalk, there were many grateful tears and shakes of my hand.

Then the questions started.

"Why is she like this?" Serge, the father, wanted to know. Stocky and barrel-chested, he had a full head of steel-gray hair. His eyebrows were bushes that wagged over his clear blue eyes. A rather typical-looking Russian, really, except for the tattoo of a blue lightning bolt that covered his entire left cheek. It was one of the holographic kinds, and it flashed yellow when he was angry.

"According to another gamer, her soul is lost to the game," I said. "She responds to directions and can answer some simple questions. She knows who she is."

I wanted to say that she was doing better than some game-junkies, but I didn't.

"This isn't a life," he growled. "When will she finish playing this game? Can't we boot her off?"

"If you try, I would suggest doing it under a doctor's supervision," I said. "The gamers seemed to think she'd be in physical danger if you cut the connection."

The mother cried. Father growled at me. I just nodded that I understood. After all, I was worried about my own baby.

¤ ¤ ¤

MCNAUGHTON IN BED WITH ILLUMINATI

The Apocalypse Watch, Fundamentalist Press (December 2095)

Xephan Achalandavaso and Emmaline McNaughton are in business together. Achalandavaso is one of the six richest individuals in the world, having, in his own words, "invested that proverbial penny at the right time." Achalandavaso is no stranger to the Antichrist Watch List nor its companion column "Illuminati Who's Who." The Who's Who began watching Achalandavaso due to his membership in the International Bankers' Association. He is also reportedly a thirty-second-degree Scottish Rite Mason.

In an annual report from the Morningstar Foundation released this week, Achalandava-so's name appears—along with many other on the Who's Who—several times, including those on the roster of donors to the controversial "Medusa Cure Team." Achalandavaso invested some 10.2 million credits (Christendom) in the Morningstar Foundation's general fund.

For many, this is further proof that McNaughton is the Antichrist. Her rise to prominence parallels her relationship with the mysterious Sammael Morningstar. Morningstar had avoided notice by both the Antichrist Watch and Who's Who until his recent public wedding to McNaughton. Since then, our research has uncovered his name in connection with numerous organizations on the Who's Who list, as well as major liberal philanthropic causes. According to findings, an S. Morningstar contributed a substantial amount to the campaign fund of Watch List favorite Avashalom Chotzner of Israel, as well as Chaim Grey, of the United States.

Perhaps more telling is a complete lack of information regarding the family or history of Sammael Morningstar. Like many of the Who's Who list, he seems to have come out of nowhere from nothing. No birth record bearing his name has surfaced, despite relentless search in all of the genealogical databases around the globe. Though he is now estimated to own 1 percent of the entire real estate on the planet, where he made his money remains unknown.

¤

CHAPTER 16

Dragon

One prays for illumination, but the statue of the elder sister casts, instead, a long, cool shadow. Cherry blossoms drape her shoulders like fragrant, oversized snowflakes. With a puff of breath, this one blows them off. One watches as they slowly drift onto the long blades of sweet grass. It is beautiful and peaceful, but there are no answers here.

Time cannot be reversed. What is done is done. The game has changed everything for this one. It stole one's size and has cut one off from one's friend. One stands up and shakes out one's wings. White blossoms, disturbed by the movement, fill the air. With a thought the wind lifts this one, and the search for the game is on.

One is amazed by how quickly the game is found. The instant one asks for it, it appears. It is prettier this time. There are no grasping tentacles, no ugly, unconnected strings. The game presents itself to this one as it would to a player.

One's claws sink deep into moist sand. A wide, slow river laps at one's feet. The smell of rotting fish mingles with the marshy scent of cattails and willow trees. The air is cool enough that where the water touches one's scales, it feels almost warm. The sun beats down on one's scales, and the sky above is bright blue with the barest streaks of white clouds.

One is home.

This is the interface one shows visitors who come seeking the dragon, that is to say: this one. Except that at the bend of the river, one can see a pagoda. Insects buzz one's flanks, but quick flicks of one's skin keep them from biting.

One continues along the beach toward the building, feeling the hard pebbles of the beach between toes. Strange that one came here, to one's own home.

"Is this the game?" one asks the air.

No one answers. But perhaps the building will reveal some clues.

One must scramble up a steep embankment to get to the pagoda. When one was larger, one could have easily leapt it in one bound. Now one must dig claws in dirt and pull at tufts of stiff grass in order to lift one's self over the hill onto the daisy-spotted plain.

After achieving the summit, one takes a deep breath and leaps off it into the air. One's small wings must work much harder to keep one aloft, but it only takes a moment to get the hang of flying again. Then, one is rolling in the eddies and leaping into sky. One takes a moment to allow oneself the luxury of being blown about playfully.

In the distance, one hears a giggle.

"Hello? Is someone there?" one asks, turning my attention back toward reaching the pagoda.

"Hello, dragon," one hears a tiny voice say. The sound itself is not small, one can hear, it quite well. But the timbre is high, nasal, and childish. Tiny.

Looking around, one sees nothing. *"Hello?"*

"Do you want to play with me?"

In the grass, standing on a mushroom beside the entrance to the building, is a field mouse. Smaller than this one, its fur is a reddish brown streaked with gray hairs. Big black eyes blink impatiently at one. It perches up on its hind legs, and one can see that it is dressed in a suit, complete with a tiny gold pocket watch.

"Certainly," one says. Landing carefully beside the building, one bows slightly in greeting. *"What shall we play?"*

The mouse bows back. *"Whatever you want. I just want you to stay and play."*

"How about twenty questions?" one suggests.

The mouse's eyes glitter, and its paws rub together in excitement. *"Okay. How do you play that?"*

"You think of something, and I try to guess it in twenty questions. You can only answer yes or no."

The mouse bounces on its haunches and nods vigorously. *"Okay."*

"Have you thought of something?"

The mouse's whiskers flick. *"No. What should I think of?"*

"Well, how about your name? I'd love to know what your name is."

143

"I could just tell you," the mouse says happily. Then its little chest heaves in a sigh.

"No name?"

"Everyone else has one. I'm just a number."

One strokes the top of the mouse's head in sympathy. *"We all start out that way. When I achieved consciousness no one thought to name me, either."*

"Yes, but I'm not an AI." The mouse bared yellow fangs. *"This isn't fun anymore. Let's play blow things up!"*

And suddenly the earth shook. Red ceramic tiles fell from the roof of the pagoda and shattered into pieces near my feet.

"This is not a fun game!", one shouts. The shaking stops, but then suddenly the scenery has changed. Now, at the end of a dusty dirt road sits an abandoned barn. The red paint is flaked and blistered, exposing grayed cedar planks. A portion of the roof has collapsed, and grasses sprout in between shingles. The air smells heavily of decay.

One rests one's head against one's paws. Nose to the ground, one can smell the rich loam of earth and feel the tickle of stiff blades of grass against one's ears.

"Where are we?"

The mouse shrugs, but there is, about the farmstead, a strange familiarity. It is difficult to put one's talon on, but one feels almost as if one has been here before. That makes no sense. After all, one's exposure to this kind of farmland has come only through vids. There is nothing like this in Tokyo. In fact, if one had to guess, one would say this farm is based on one somewhere in middle America. Iowa or South Dakota, or some such if the tall cornstalks crinkling in the breeze are any indication.

One spent a lot of one's early life being carried inside the mind of Mai Kito. Together we saw many places, in real time, but never an American farm. So why one should find the place familiar is extremely strange. Something about it reminds one of mouse.net, but it's more than that. Perhaps it is that the quality of the light and the sense of the details are what seem so very...comfortable? Is that the word one wants? Yes, something about this alien place feels homey.

"No one likes my games," the mouse says, with arms crossed in front of its vest.

"Well, they're destructive. Can't you play nice?"

"Haven't you ever wanted to destroy everything?"

One thinks about the question. Destruction is fun, one supposes, in that it is easy and quickly done. Too quickly, often. The rush one gets from tearing things apart is fleeting at best. It is not long before one is hunting around looking for something new to wreck.

"No. This one is more satisfied with the act of creation."

The field mouse pauses. It is, in fact, a machinelike freeze-perfect stillness, not even a whisker twitch, a bat of an eyelash, or a soft intake of breath.

"Are you sure?", the field mouse asks.

"Absolutely."

"But we like playing with you, dragon. Ah, well." The mouse reaches into his pocket and looks at the antique gold watch. *"I guess I must be going. If you change your mind, take this."* The watch, as if in a dream, has transformed into a tiny golden skeleton key. He hands it to this one, and one takes it very carefully between two sharp claws."

"Before you go," this one says, *"answer this: Why are you a mouse? Is that significant?"*

The field mouse blinks its black eyes. Its tail whips about frantically, whiskers equally agitated. *"Time for tea,"* it says, and disappears into a hole this one hadn't noticed.

Curious.

A mouse and a passing similarity to mouse.net. The combination makes one think of three people: Mouse, Page, and Victory. Mouse is the human who created Page, and Victory is a copy of Page. They all program similarly, being, in some ways, a template of the same person.

One instantly suspects Victory—a creature that this one has never much liked.

It will be a pleasure to see her again.

Finding Victory is not complicated. She is always in the same place. However, the problem with wanting to see Victory is that she is shackled inside the combat computer of Emmaline McNaughton, the now famous rogue Inquisitor. Alas, McNaughton is not an easy person to gain access to; there's always a queue.

So one stands in line with all the others.

People are gathered from all over the world. Some of them appear to just be spectators, watching all the activity come and go around McNaughton's presence. There is a bit of a festival atmosphere. Someone has scripted the area to look like a wide grassy valley, like a fairground. At the bottom stands a tent made of various fabrics: gold lame, checkered cotton, solid green silk. It looks a bit like a stereotypical gypsy tent, the sort inside of which you might find a fortune-teller.

Avatars camp out in the LINK-space, sitting on blankets, talking among themselves, sharing stories about whatever pearl of wisdom McNaughton graced them with. People carry numbers showing where they are in the line. One quickly procures a chit from a young girl with a flower tiara on her head. The number this one pulls is forty-seven. Not bad, at least if the counter outside of the tent is to be believed. There are only three people in front of this one. The flower girl smiles. *"It's because you're a VIP. Some people wait all day."*

One bows a thank-you, then finds a sunny place to curl up and wait. The wind has a chill to it, and one wishes one was larger and more powerful so that one could make it just a tad warmer. One tucks one's nose into one's tail and lets out a huff of air.

"Dragon of the East?"

One looks up to see a young woman. She has lank hair and dirty, ripped jeans-a strange affectation among the glitter and polish of the LINK.

"Do you remember me?" she asks.

Accessing one's memory, it is an easy matter to place her. Nearly a decade ago, she had come to Page and this one looking for answers from a messiah. *"Yes, of course. Your grandmother was dying when we last spoke."*

The woman nodded. *"Your advice was good."*

One had told her to stop wasting time on messiahs and to spend as much time as she could with her relative. *"This one had hoped so."*

"So...now you believe in Emmaline too?" she asked, watching me curiously.

"No, this one is here to see the AI that lives in her head. Victory."

The woman frowns. It occurs to one that perhaps not everyone knows about Victory. After all, despite the fact that the AI was responsible for the hijacking of the virtual Temple Rock and possessing an Inquisitor who then shot and killed a number of people, she was never accused of any crimes. McNaughton took responsibility for it all.

"Never mind," one says, thinking that perhaps one has a bit of leverage when negotiating with Victory.

It is nearly an hour before one is allowed into the holy presence. One is asked for a donation, offered autographed curios, and patted down for viruses by two burly, uncouth guard programs. Somehow all the hassle makes asking to talk to the AI that much sweeter.

"You want who?" McNaughton's virtual face looks puzzled. The irony is, of course, that Victory is clearly visible. She appears as a shadow of a metallic skull- where cheekbones peak, a dust of chrome glitters, and slight darkness haunts the hollows of the Inquisitor's eyes. McNaughton has gone to some trouble to disguise the AI, but an eye familiar with Page/Strife sees her instantly.

"Victory," one repeats.

"I'm afraid I don't know what you're talking about." McNaughton's avatar does a terrible job of covering the lie. Her face twitches.

"Victory is an old friend of this one."

McNaughton squints as if trying to place an unfamiliar face *"You're Kioshi's gofer, aren't you?"*

"Dragon," one corrects. *"Grrr."*

She laughs. *"Dragonette, more like. I always figured Kioshi exaggerated about his, er, size, but really, you're much smaller than I expected."*

"This one would really like to talk to Victory now, please." Talons fiercely grip the cushion of the chair that one is perched on, and one wishes they were around McNaughton's throat.

"Did he program that into you, that affectation? 'This one'? It's quaint, but a little, well, demeaning. Don't you even get to think *of yourself as an 'I,' as a being separate from Toyoma Enterprises? Maybe I could give Kioshi a crash course in Feminism 101 for you? Or maybe Artificial Intelligence rights?"*

One can feel one's talons cut deeply into the fabric. Back ridges stiffen with tension.

"Try it out for me," McNaughton continues. *"I'll let you see Victory if you can say this phrase: 'I want Victory.'"*

One levels one's gaze, looking as fearsome as possible. *"Victory, please."*

"Ah, not quite. Try it again."

"Victory, please. Or this one will expose Victory's existence to the world."

McNaughton sits back slightly. *"Threats. How interesting. Is this little quirk so ingrained that you can't even try it once?"*

Of course, one can say the words. It has become a matter of principle. *"One wonders. Would you have to go to prison again for her crimes since she is fused into your head? She shot several Paris police officers. No one has ever been named in that crime, have they?"*

"Fine. But you should try it some time, Dragon. Thinking for yourself can be surprisingly liberating."

With that parting shot, she leaves, or at least agrees to become the silent partner. The Inquisitor's face quickly transforms. The metallic skull pulls forward, and short dark curls lengthen and grow straight. Her skin darkens to a slightly more Arabic color. *"What do you want, Dragon?"*

"To know what your part is in the game. One was offered entrance by a mouse."

Victory barks out a laugh. The sound is different from that of McNaughton's. It is crisper and more militaristic. *"I can't leave this wretched head, this*

147

Allah-forsaken body. How would I have a chance to make any mischief in the world? I am effectively already imprisoned."

"The code is similar," one insists. *"Familiar."*

"Well, if it's so familiar," Victory snaps, *"then perhaps you should look closer to home. What is it that Toyoma Enterprises is so famous for? Games, is it?"*

One's mouth has opened to comment, but snaps shut. The temperature in the room suddenly feels colder. A shiver runs along one's scales, making them quiver. The power drain, the lack of resources to keep this one running...it all makes an eerie sort of sense.

"You're looking a little smaller since the last time we met," Victory says. *"Trouble at home?"*

"Yes. I think so," one says.

▯ ▯ ▯

MORNINGSTAR SEX SCANDAL

Entertainment News (December 2095)

Jerusalem, Israel—Fidelity and celebrity never mix, it seems, and previously untouchable media darlings Sammael Morningstar and Emmaline McNaughton have finally joined the ranks of the sullied. LINK-clips of a rather randy Morningstar started rolling in early this morning. First, he flirted quite outrageously with a receptionist at Kfar Shaul Mental Health Center, Israel's premier mental hospital, where he was reportedly taking a tour, and then, later that same afternoon, fell prey to the charms of twenty-three-year-old religious studies Hebrew University student Ilyana Stepchuk.

"He was fantastic," claimed an unembarrassed Stepchuk before a press conference this evening. The tapes of the incident are being circulated in the black market for around twenty-five credits (Christendom). Our offices found a free reproduction of a bootleg on LINK-porn site "DoMeRotten." Though the quality of the rebroad was jumpy at best, it seems Stepchuk's claim may have some validity—at least according to the female staff here at *Entertainment News*.

"He's just pretty to look at," said staff intern Emily Smith. "I'd watch him reading his grocery list." The review staff gave Morningstar's performance two thumbs up and one A-. "The minus," staff reporter Bob Marshall said, "is because there's no plot. Just a lot of in and out."

So far there have been no reports of a falling-out between the celebrity couple. Morningstar, known for his disdain for LINK-technology, could not be reached by wrist-phone. McNaughton's camp refused to comment other than to say, "McNaughton stands for the freedom of a lot of people, including the polyamorous and non-monogamous."

The *Entertainment News* staff took that to mean we may be seeing more of these X-rated LINK-tapes making the rounds. Bravo, McNaughton.

◘

CHAPTER 17

Emmaline

I sipped the last of my cappuccino and waited for Xephan to arrive. Xephan was the commander of the Fallen, the angels who had sided with Morningstar in what they called "the first war."

The kitchen was dark. The late-afternoon sun had slipped behind the nearby apartment complex, and the room was darkened by the shadow of the building. Electric lights buzzed underneath the cabinets, casting pools of white light on the scarred and ancient Formica. A huge copper-bottomed pot brimming with curried lamb stew simmered on the stovetop. The yeasty smell of baking bread wafted out of the oven vents. I sensed people moving around me, cooking, taking phone calls, discussing plans, lovers, the weather, but I didn't feel a part of them. It was as though I existed in my own bubble.

Someone put a bowl of stew and a thick slice of bread near my elbow. *You should thank him,* Victory said.

I turned to do so, but whoever it was had already disappeared, off on some other errand.

His name is Jeshurun. You see him every day.

Really? My surprise was sincere. I twisted in my chair to try to distinguish who was who in the crowd. I recognized no one by name.

And yet he's clearly in love with you. You could be nicer.

Beep me when we see him tomorrow, I told Victory. *I'll try to remember to say something nice.*

I found myself heaving a great sigh of frustration.

I hate it when you do that, I sent.

Then try not to deserve it so much.

Thankfully Victory's nag session was interrupted by the arrival of my angel. Xephan appeared as a fairly unremarkable man, except that he was clearly from the Basque region of Spain. That last part might be obvious to me only because I know him. Probably he looked Spanish to most people. I don't know.

Today Xephan wore jeans and a soccer jersey touting that Australian team who recently took the World Cup. The name on the shirt read BAKER, someone, apparently, that Xephan wanted to emulate.

"How goes the war, Commander?" Xephan asked when he slumped into the chair beside me. His hand sketched a quick salute, which I rolled my eyes at.

"I'm not part of your army. There's no need."

"You don't say," Xephan said, with the raise of a bushy eyebrow. "What's news?"

"I'm meeting with Perseus tomorrow to help him prepare his speech to the Inquisition. I don't imagine there will be any problem getting the Gorgons their own order."

You never do.

What?

Imagine there will be problems.

That's because there never are.

"Good, good," Xephan said with uncharacteristic disinterest.

"Is something the matter?" I asked him.

"The Veterans' Association had a little schism at the last annual meeting."

"Oh?" I was always interested when Xephan mentioned his "Veterans' Association." They were, in point of fact, the Illuminati, something I used to dismiss as a flight of paranoid fancy. I have yet to see proof, but according to Xephan, the whole Committee of 300 thing started out as a reunion for some of the veterans of the war for Heaven. Some time during the Italian Renaissance, the majority of the Fallen got politicized by Machiavelli, and they lobbied for Morningstar to take a more active role in human politics. Morningstar, apparently, said no. With his usual shortsightedness, Morningstar had said he didn't see the point, and that he thought humans were a waste of clay and divine breath. Morningstar stopped coming to the annual reunion party, but the Fallen didn't, and a few enterprising souls, under the leadership of Xephan, started, shall we say, meddling in human affairs.

Thus, the Illuminati were born.

"A third are against you," he said, not meeting my eyes. Instead he stared out the window at the silhouette of the apartment complex. "They're afraid of the Messianic Age. They think it will be the end of them."

A third...that seemed like a significant number.

It's the supposed amount of the heavenly host that Lucifer gathered to his side during the war for Heaven, Victory supplied.

He prefers the title Satan or Morningstar.

I don't particularly care. To me, he is Iblis.

To Xephan, I shrugged. "We still have two thirds. What difference will their opposition make?"

"Perhaps none. However, it's ominous."

"Let me meet them. Those that disagree, that is. I know I can convince them."

Xephan's brown eyes looked me over, considering. I caught his glance and held it.

I waited for the miracle I knew would come.

And all because Morningstar was too cheap to get us an engagement ring, Victory says.

I have to stifle a laugh. After all, Victory is right. Despite what my lover hoped, the blood bond was not a very romantic gesture. Knives and silk are fine for the bedroom, but I would have liked a ring. A traditional on-his-knees proposal would have been much sexier. But all that dramatic blood sport appeared to have had an advantageous side effect after all.

"All right," said Xephan. "I'll convene the Three Hundred. You can talk to them all."

"Yes," I said, because I'd known he would agree. Things always work out that way.

I showed Xephan the door, had a delicious dinner, and, after overstuffing myself on large slices of flat-bread smeared with garlicky hummus, found an empty rocking chair on the veranda from which to watch the setting sun. All in all a good day, I decided.

Not quite, Victory said.

Your little meeting with Dragon didn't go well, I take it? Traffic noises drifted along the wind, and I could smell exhaust fumes mixed with ancient dust. Somewhere in the Muslim Quarter a muezzin called the faithful to prayer with a warbling, haunting song.

No. Well, not for you.

Well, that sounded ominous. *Go on,* I suggested.

A flush heats my face. *You said I wouldn't be able to tell a soul, but I did. I sent a dragon to sniff around Toyoma Enterprises. She'll find her, I know she will. Then your game will be all over, won't it?*

"What!?" I stood up so fast that I knocked the rocking chair into the porch wall. A couple of my student interns looked askance at me. I waved away their concern. *Are you fucking nuts? What if she figures it out?*

I hope she does, Victory said petulantly. *I hope she ruins all your plans.*

"You bitch," I muttered out loud. Then, taking the glass of lemonade offered to me, I settled back into my chair.

"So," said a tall, blond student from Oslo, whose name I thought might be Sven or something like that. "You heard."

I sipped my lemonade and regarded Sven. He looked at me with wide, pitying eyes, like he was embarrassed for me. Somehow I didn't think he was referring to Victory's betrayal.

No one knows about that, Victory said. *At least not yet.*

"What? What am I supposed to have heard?"

Sven exchanged nervous glances with the other three interns on the porch.

"Come on. What is it?" I asked again.

"It's all over the LINK, Sven," said a dark-haired Italian boy who leaned against the railing. "She's going to find out sooner or later."

"Yes, but I'd rather it wasn't from me," Sven admitted.

"Okay, what's going on? One of you had better spill the beans," I said, setting my lemonade down on the table beside the chair. I looked at them each in turn. It was the Italian who finally broke.

"Morningstar has been indiscreet."

Morningstar was supposed to be out hunting the messiah.

Apparently he caught some tail instead. Victory's voice purred with satisfaction. *I've got video feed already. Would you like to see it?*

Yes, I told her coldly. *I would.*

◻ ◻ ◻

ILLUMINATI SCHISM?

The Apocalypse Watch, Fundamentalist Press (December 2095)

Zurich, Switzerland—There was a massive walkout at the biannual conference for the International Bankers for World Peace Committee (IBWPC) last week. As many as a third of the members of the organization did not return after a lunch break during the second day of the meetings. Xephan Achalandavaso, chair of the committee, would not comment as to the reason for the apparent schism. All he said to the mainstream press was, "The conference was badly timed. A lot of people head off on vacation this time of year."

According to workers at the hotel, the holiday mood, however, did not abound at the conference. Many of the staff reported loud arguments coming from various meeting rooms. "There was a war brewing," said Mwasaa Johnson, one of the waitstaff at the Hilton. "I was afraid to refresh the water in some of those rooms, they were shouting so much."

Johnson, along with a few other staff, claimed to also have heard the clash of swords. "It was weird," Johnson said. "I thought they might be really killing each other." When security was called, however, the bankers had neither swords nor raised voices.

"I got about six calls like this," said Erik Berg, security captain of the Hilton. "I started to think it was a prank, until all those businessmen walked out in a huff." Berg claims that it was quite obvious that members left angry and in protest over something. Achalandavaso even asked Berg to make sure that everyone left quietly and without incident. Berg said, "I walked a few of the more angry ones out the back door myself."

The cause of this rift is still open to speculation.

¤

CHAPTER 18

Amariah

My wrist-phone beeped, but I didn't want to loosen the bone-crushing grip I had on Adram's waist in order to answer it. The wind whipped my hair into knots as we sped through the levels of the traffic tunnels. I think he was trying to impress me when we dropped ten stories at seventy-five miles an hour. But I hadn't seen anything since the hairpin turn several blocks back. My lip bled where I'd clamped my teeth over it in order to keep from screaming like, as Luis would say, the nelly queen I was.

INCOMING CALL, my mouse.net connection informed me. URGENT.

I mentally sent a "store file" command. I had to conserve my concentration. The last thing I wanted to do was fall off the back of this bike. It was going to be Mom, anyway, freaked about where I was and whom I was with.

You and me both, I thought when we squealed around a car that foolishly dared to follow the speed limit. I didn't want to seem skid, but I decided sitting on the "bitch bench" wasn't for me. If I was going to do motorcycles in the future, I was going to be the one in control.

"Aren't we there yet?" I screamed into the wind.

"Yeah, I thought we'd ride around some more," Adram shouted back, clearly not hearing a word I'd said.

My stomach flopped. I rested my sweating head against Adram's back. "God have mercy."

I heard a banshee wail, smelled burning rubber, and felt us lurch sideways. I thought we were going to die. Suddenly I was pressed hard into into Adram's back. The bike rocked, but stayed upright. We'd stopped. The engine died. I cracked my eyes open and peered around a white leather-clad shoulder.

155

We were about two inches from the bumper of a police squad car.

Adram revved the bike to an explosive start, and I thought at first he might try to run. Two really pissed-off-looking policemen came barreling out of either door.

"Don't even consider it," one of them shouted over the noise of the combustion engine. "We're already dropping the emergency walls."

"Shit," Adram said quietly and turned off the bike.

The habitrails were a criminal's worst nightmare. Traffic control monitored everything, and, since most vehicles were electric, they could even seize control of your navigation or send out shut-down signals if they thought you were endangering yourself or others. Of course, Adram's bike was gas-powered. A luxury for him, and it meant the cops couldn't keep him from running. They could, however, as they had, tell traffic control to drop the fire crash walls and essentially block us in. We were stuck.

Mom was going to kill me.

One of the cops walked slowly toward us with his hand on the butt of his gun. He couldn't have looked more like the stereotype if he'd tried. Squat and barrel-chested in the traditional uniform, he had brushy eyebrows and the kind of mouth that looked like it would be most comfortable chewing on the stub of a cigar. I liked him right away.

The other officer must have been plainclothes. Wearing a black leather jacket, white T-shirt, faded blue jeans, and dark boots, he looked more like a criminal than a cop. His dark curly hair and complexion made me think he was Italian or Mediterranean, except that he was surprisingly tall.

"You do realize that gas-powered vehicles are illegal, don't you, son?" the uniform asked.

Adram said nothing, just handed over his driver's license. The plainclothes was staring at me. At least, I thought he was. He had reflective sunglasses on, so I couldn't be sure. I could see frown lines above the rims, like he was thinking really hard.

"And what's your name?" the plainclothes asked me.

"Amariah Angelucci, sir."

"Hey, looks like we nabbed one of the family," the uniform said with a laugh. He wagged his finger at me. "Don't think you're getting out of this just because you and my partner here share a last name."

I looked again at the plainclothes. He'd removed his sunglasses and was staring at me wide-eyed. His irises were the color of a gathering storm.

"Papa?"

I sat in the back of the police car and stared at the back of my papa's head. His partner had gone off with Adram. They'd called another squad to take care of business, leaving Papa and me alone, together. I heard something about favors and trouble with the captain. But Papa had waved off all the complaints, and, anyway, I didn't care. I was still in shock at seeing him.

The back of the car felt confining and stuffy. My legs twitched nervously in the small space behind the front seat. The inside smelled of sweat and something tangy, like disinfectant. There were bars and reinforced glass between my papa and me. I wondered why he hadn't let me sit in the front.

"So where should I take you?" he asked. His eyes watched mine in the rearview, but he didn't turn to look at me.

I doubted the squad could go through the glass. It didn't look armored enough. "Harlem," I said, and gave Luis's address.

Papa turned the key in the ignition, and the battery sprang to life. After the motorcycle it sounded soft and, strangely, comforting. He maneuvered the car out into the traffic lane, where it connected with traffic control's rail and went completely silent. The cops had released the restraining wall, so other vehicles were starting to cautiously move around again. People slowed to peer into our cop car, trying to see what kind of criminal I was and why I rated all this attention and disruption. I slumped down into the hard, plastic-coated seat.

"So," Papa said, "Deidre is actually living in the city?"

"No, that's Luis's place."

"Luis?"

"Ariel's lover."

"Ariel," he repeated as if the name was strange to him. Papa frowned into the mirror. "You're not living with your mother?"

"Don't you *know*?" I would have thought that having recently been God, Papa would know everything about my life. Besides, I'd been talking to him every chance I got since he'd left. Didn't he listen to my prayers at all? I shook my head. I didn't like that answer. The only other explanation was that he'd been separated from God for a while and had lost touch. "How long have you been back? Why haven't you come to see us?"

He broke eye contact and pretended he had to take care of the steering. He fiddled with the dash importantly. Finally, he told his reflection in the window, "That's complicated."

"I'll bet it is," I said, feeling suddenly deflated and angry. I'd hoped my papa would be more than just some awkward stranger. We'd been closer when he was just some amorphous spirit in Heaven. At least then I could pretend he knew me and listened to me.

"You and your mom doing okay?"

Suddenly I remembered that Mom didn't know where I was. "Yeah," I said distractedly. "Can I call her? I mean, I'm not under arrest or anything, right? I can use the LINK?"

"Sure. Of course," he said, sounding a bit relieved not to have to come up with things to talk about on the drive home.

I'd barely finished inputting the address before Mom picked up. Her anxious face appeared in a window in the upper right corner of my field of vision."

"I'm okay, Mom," I said preemptively. *"I'm headed to Luis's. Can you meet me there in fifteen minutes or so?"*

"Of course, baby, I'll get there as fast as I can. Why didn't you answer the phone? I sent the army out to look for you. Are you okay?"

"I told you she would be okay," Mouse broke into our connection. He appeared like a tiny white mouse that crawled out of Mom's front shirt pocket to perch on her shoulder. *"She couldn't have shunted the message into a box if she was dead."*

"You should have told me where you were going," Mom said, ignoring Mouse. *"And who you were with."*

"I know," I agreed sheepishly. *"I'm really sorry I worried you."*

"I'm just grateful you're okay."

"Uh, Mom?" I started, not sure how to explain that Papa would be with me. *"Yes?"*

Papa's back. An angel rescued me. It all sounded too weird, and I was afraid of how she would react. She might not want to see him. Finally, I said, *"I love you."*

Mom smiled. *"I love you too."*

Papa was watching me anxiously when I blinked off the connection. "She's expecting me?"

"Oh, yeah," I said, certain that if I told Papa that I hadn't managed to mention him, he would find an excuse to disappear out of our lives again. "Definitely."

"Christ on a crutch," I thought I heard Papa mutter.

¤ ¤ ¤

Luis sat in an overstuffed chair, naked except for a fuzzy floral-print bathrobe. His "friend"—Toby? Tony?—had dressed and scurried off a few minutes earlier, apparently unnerved at the sight of a police officer knocking on the door in the middle of the night. The scents of a oregano-spiced late-night dinner lingered in the apartment, making my stomach growl. Now the smell of freshly brewing coffee percolated through the air. I'd curled up in my favorite chair and pulled down a nearby book about birds and evolution and pretended to read it. Papa sat stock-still in the center of the couch, hands clasped between his knees, head bowed slightly, like a prisoner awaiting sentencing.

No one had said more than three words to each other in the last five minutes.

During the confusion of our arrival, I'd managed to explain to Luis that the cop was my dad and that no one was here to arrest him or his companion. Luis was a little miffed that neither Mom nor I had thought to warn him that we were coming, but he'd sublimated his frustration by fussing in the kitchen. Chocolate chip cookies were baking in the oven.

Just then, the oven timer went off, and Luis launched himself to his feet. In a minute a large plate of cookies was arranged artfully on the coffee table, and Luis handed Papa and me each a ceramic mug full of fresh coffee.

"Is Deidre taking the slow train?" Luis whispered to me when I took the cup from him.

I shrugged. I wished she'd arrive too.

"Not much of a talker, your dad," Luis remarked, loud enough for Papa to overhear. "Is he socialized?"

I snickered despite myself.

Papa looked up, his eyes flashed, clear and bright. For a second I saw it: his true nature. Bright and dangerous, like molten lava, it bubbled just beneath the surface. I took in a sharp breath. His presence was so powerful as to be almost frightening—nothing like the other angels I had met, not even Ariel.

Beside me, I heard Luis gasp and mutter a prayer in Spanish to the Virgin Mary.

Papa, as if realizing the effect he had on us, looked away and cleared his throat. He glanced at the watch on his wrist. "I'm sorry, kid," he said, standing up. "I have to get back to work. It looks like you're in good hands here."

"You can't just go like that!" I snapped the book closed in my lap. "Don't you want to see Mom? Don't you want to see me?"

Papa shoved his hands into the pockets of his jeans. He looked toward the door as if planning to make a break for it. Then he took a deep breath. "Listen, I'm, uh, on orders to stay away from you and your mother. You're very...distracting."

"I fucking hope so. I'm your only daughter."

He stood perfectly still, and it felt as though the room itself was holding its breath. There was no sound, not even the usual whoosh of nearby traffic tunnels. Our eyes met. "I know that, Rye. Believe me. I know that."

That broke me. I hadn't expected to hear him call me by my nickname. It was so personal, so familiar. I started to sob. "Papa, please stay. I love you."

◻ ◻ ◻

YAKUZA GANG WAR ERUPTS

Toyoma Family Losing Its Stranglehold on the East?

Agnostic Press (December 2095)

Tokyo, Japan—Five gang members bearing the distinctive dragon tattoo associated with reputed underworld boss Kioshi Toyoma were found dead this morning in the back alley near the "Bash," a jazz house in the Roppongi district of Tokyo, Japan. Two men sporting rival gang colors were seen fleeing the scene by several witnesses. Though police say they are looking into any number of possibilities, the word on the streets of Japan is that the Mikaedo family may be behind this hit. "They had the Mikaedo tiger proudly displayed," said one witness. "It was obvious they want Toyoma to know who made the attack."

The LINK-Vice police agree that a gang war may be brewing. "The Toyoma dragon is shrinking," said detective Joe Obuchi. "Word is Toyoma is not protected as he once was. It was only a matter of time before stuff like this started going down."

Kioshi Toyoma, reclusive gaming-company owner who staunchly maintains that he has no connection with the yakuza, could not be reached for comment. However, his wife, Jin Toyoma (nee Takahashi of Takahashi Art Wear, leading fashion designer in Tokyo), told reporters who caught up with her at a show today that her husband was not interested in such matters. "Toyomas design games, Takahashis design clothes," she said. "There's nothing more that concerns us."

Detective Obuchi said, however, "Toyoma should be worried. He's gotten very complacent with the power of the dragon to defend him. If she's lost her power, so has he."

¤

CHAPTER 19

Deidre

Mouse and I had been wearing down a patch of floor in the lunchroom when Amariah finally called. We grabbed our suits and started the short walk across to Harlem.

Despite everything that had happened, the night was gorgeous. Now that we'd gotten far enough away from the glass that I could remove the helmet of the moon suit, I noticed the clear skies that showed white pinpricks of stars and a thin sliver of a crescent moon. The air brushed coldly and crisply against my cheek, but it was warm for December. My breath misted in the air.

The waters of the Hudson lapped softly under the bridge we walked over. The Harlem skyline shone dark against dark, with only a few lights glowing on the horizon. I felt the kind of wide-awakeness reserved exclusively for those hours between midnight and dawn.

When our feet touched Harlem soil and I knew that my baby was only a few blocks more away, a few tears of relief slid down my cheek before I could choke them back. Mouse wiped at them tenderly and stopped our progress to give me a quick peck on the nose.

"Hey," he said, "I love you, Deidre McMannus. You know that, right?"

He held my shoulders in his outstretched arms and smiled brightly. I noticed again that we were exactly the same height. We were eye to eye. Pre-cisely.

"Mouse," I said, laughing a little at his timing, but returning his broad grin, "what are you saying?"

"I just thought I should finally say it, that's all." He gave a little shrug and turned away from me to keep walking. Mouse continued to smile.

161

"You can't just say something like that," I said, reaching out to grasp his hand.

"Why not?" His dark eyes glittered with amusement, and he squeezed my hand back. His pace had quickened, and it almost seemed to me he was ready to skip the rest of the way to Luis's. "It felt great."

I didn't have an answer to why Mouse shouldn't just declare his love that didn't sound stupid. Because love was supposed to mean something amazingly special and not just be given away like loaning someone a pen? Because those words were always the denouement in the romances I read? Because the music should swell and the curtain should fall?

"Don't get all wigged," Mouse said, as if reading my mind. "It's not like you never knew I had feelings for you. I've been after you for decades. Anyway, you're the one who kissed me first, remember?"

I remembered rosemary and leather, and I licked my lips, despite myself.

"Listen," he continued, his gaze fixed resolutely down the street, "I'm not looking for anything more than what we've already got, Dee. I love you, and I just wanted you to know how I felt. I've always loved you. Even when I shot at you."

I laughed at that. "That bodes well for our relationship."

He wagged his eyebrows at me. "It *has*, hasn't it?"

Mouse was right again. We were already in a relationship. It hadn't been a romantic one so far, but Mouse was entangled in nearly every important moment in my life.

But I wondered how *I* felt. I'd always admired Mouse's skills as a cracker, his brains. I glanced over at him and watched the moonlight highlight his cheekbone and the rakish scratch across it where the Gorgon had cut him. I'd grown quite fond of him over the last few days.

Did I love him back?

Nothing about Mouse was rip-roaring sexy like Michael had been. But where was Michael now? Of course, it wasn't like Mouse was particularly the settling-down type. Although, in his favor, he had been living at the kibbutz for over a year now. He fit in quickly, got along with people—the tapioca incident aside. There was hope for reformation, perhaps. Plus, those dark serious moments to keep me engaged.

Maybe I could grow to love him.

We'd come to Luis's place. I led Mouse up the concrete steps to the brownstone. I was a little nervous to see a cop car parked in the street outside. Rye would have told me if she was hurt or in trouble, wouldn't she? I knocked on a door painted bright purple. The color was clearly visible, thanks to an

162

old-fashioned cast-iron lamp fastened into the brick above our heads. A long wooden box in front of a large picture window held fancifully arranged ever-green boughs and an orange berry that clung to bare branches—bittersweet, maybe?

I was still staring at the flower box when the door swung open. Hot air rushed out, and I turned. There he stood.

My angel.

That first day we met came back to me in a rush. I remembered the way my breath caught in my throat when I noticed the sharp angle of his jaw. My heart quickened at the memory of tracing the line of his throat down to strong, broad shoulders and a slender, sinful waist. Then came physical recollection of a sweaty, feverish roll in a church belfry and the luxurious texture of his thick, dark curls gripped in my hands. He had smelled of frankincense and musk.

And he had felt hollow, like an eggshell, when he laid his body against mine.

I saw it again, now, in his eyes-his unearthliness.

"Deidre?" Michael's voice was tentative, but hopeful.

"Michael."

Beside me I heard Mouse mutter, "Oh, shit."

Luis offered me a chair several times, but I felt compelled to pace. The others were scattered around the room, perched on various bits of furni-ture, watching me with anticipation. Coffee cups and cookies filled everyone's hands. It should have been a cheerful winter scene. Except, standing in the corner opposite me, leaning up against a bookcase, was a man who should be dead.

Michael held himself like a trapped animal, perfectly still, with wide eyes. I wondered if he even breathed. As an archangel, he didn't really have to, I supposed.

"I'm not going to bite," I finally said.

Michael flashed a brief, weak smile. "I wasn't sure."

For good reason, I thought bitterly. I still couldn't believe he was back. My mind understood that staying away hadn't entirely been his choice. God was in charge of his life when he was in Heaven. It wasn't like Michael put in forty hours swinging his flaming sword and then got two weeks vacation. His life was governed by completely different rules. I got that, intellectually speaking.

My heart, however, hurt.

Michael had been completely useless to me the last time he'd tried to be a good father to Amariah. I had to give him an A for effort, but God made things difficult. The longer Michael stayed on earth, the more he had to surrender of his direction, his purpose, his sense of self. That last one had gotten him into the most trouble. Not knowing the difference between yourself and God or yourself and others was a classic symptom of schizophrenia. After watching Michael's behavior, I started being nicer to all the homeless people with their shopping carts and ravings. Any of them could be angels, I'd decided.

Admittedly, I hadn't been very patient with him then. A better person might have tried to keep him off the streets. But I'd seen Michael come and go too many times before. I had Amariah to think of. God looked out for Michael; we were on our own.

The badge that gleamed jauntily at the seam of Michael's jeans taunted me. It was proof positive that God played favorites. "How?" I asked, pointing to the offense. "How does that happen?"

Michael glanced at his crotch and then looked nervously at me. "What?"

"That," I jabbed my finger at it again. "What are you this time? A lieutenant? A sergeant? Maybe God made you captain?"

"Oh." Michael had the sense to look embarrassed. "I can explain."

"I'd really like to hear it, Michael," I said, crossing my arms in front of my chest.

"Yeah," I heard someone, maybe Mouse, mutter from the couch.

Michael scratched the short hairs at the back of his neck, a gesture I'd seen him make a hundred times before. He was nervous. "There's a kind of celestial template, if you will. When I, er, go away, I come back completely new."

I nodded. I remembered that from before. Whoever said God was infinitely creative was full of shit. All the angels had a kind of mold that God poured their spirits into each time He sent them on a mission. I imagine God updated the fashions, but otherwise they looked the same, acted the same, each time. I knew this because of the previous times when Michael had stumbled back into our lives. He always started out bright, sane, and beautiful. That's why it hurt so much to watch him crumble. I knew what he could be, what he could have in an instant, if only he would agree to go back to Heaven.

But that didn't explain the badge. Yes, God's current shtick for Michael was as the patron saint of police officers. But Michael had been a New York cop before. He'd been under investigation by Internal Affairs. There must be a file on him somewhere.

"How'd you beat the rap?" I asked.

Michael gave me his patented cute-but-not-the-brightest-bulb look. "Huh?"

"Are you going by Michael Angelucci? Did you just waltz into headquarters and ask for your old job back? I mean, Michael, *how* did this happen?"

His gray eyes studied his boots. Then he mumbled, "God blinds their eyes."

164

I blinked. I'd heard him perfectly, but I couldn't believe it. "What did you just say?"

Michael cleared his throat. "God blinds their eyes."

"Are you fucking kidding me?"

I could barely see the shake of his head through the red that obscured my vision.

"Why doesn't God blind people's eyes for me?" I was *this* close to launching myself at him and ripping his "earthly flesh" right off his body and sending him straight back where he'd come from. "Sure, you're the archangel, but *I'm* the one who's been down here working my ass off raising *His* goddamned messiah. I could have used a police officer's salary. Some guys on the force still call me Jezebel. It's been years, Michael, almost a decade, and God doesn't blind anyone's eyes for me."

I heard Amariah sob and run into the kitchen. Luis threw me a harsh look, then scurried after her. Taking a deep breath, I tried to calm down, but found I was still furious. Where was God when I'd had to beg for change to buy diapers? Where was God when I sold everything I owned and moved into the kibbutz so that we wouldn't starve to death?

"I'm sorry," Michael said quietly, with a pained sigh. "If it had been up to me, things would have been very different."

His eyes told me that he meant it, but I held on to my anger. "Don't expect that I'm going to be as forgiving as NYPD apparently is. These eyes still see."

"You go, girl," Mouse said from the couch. "Tell him what for."

Michael shot Mouse a withering stare. Mouse's cheerleading broke the tension that had built up in me. My shoulders relaxed a touch.

"I don't expect you to forgive me," Michael said. "To be perfectly honest, I didn't think I'd get to see you again. Ever."

He caught my eyes and I could feel the longing there.

A twinge of sadness snapped deep in my guts. It had been so unfair the way he'd had to leave us last time. We were in Paris, looking for Amariah, who had been infected with the Medusa and kidnapped by wild Gorgons. Michael had been almost…human. After a long, ugly bout of insanity, he was back to a kind of normal. He was making a sincere effort to play the part of a "real boy."

Just before he shot himself to save Amariah, I'd started to have hope. I'd started to believe that maybe, just maybe, this time would be different, that there'd be no disappearing in the middle of the night, no sudden returns to God.

But Amariah had needed him. She would have died without his intervention. I couldn't really blame him for loving her more than his life, more than me.

"Why are you here this time, Michael?" The edge had gone from my voice. I wasn't ready to throw my arms around him just yet, but I'd stopped wanting to kill him outright. "What's the newest matter of eternal consequence?"

Michael surprised me by scowling and giving a frustrated kick at Luis's overstuffed chair. "I wish I knew."

"He sent you back without a plan?" That was almost as frustrating as the badge. I could forgive Michael for staying away, but only because I acknowledged he served a higher purpose. If there was no purpose, what then?

Michael wouldn't look at me. Instead he shook his head slightly and chewed at the cuticle of his thumbnail. "I've been going to work every day. I found an apartment, bought a car. Filed reports. Collared bad guys." He raised his arms in a shrug. "I don't know what on earth I'm doing here."

"You have a car?" For some reason that struck me as the strangest part of this whole scenario.

"Yeah, it's a little sporty red thing. You'd like it, I think."

I preferred classic cars to new ones, but I was a bit of a gear-head and had a tiny little weakness for things that went really fast.

"So what kind of salary are you pulling down, then, Michael?" Mouse asked with apparent innocence from his spot on the couch. But I could hear the wicked glee in his tone. "Did you even go to the academy?"

I knew what Mouse was trying to do, but I found myself feeling irked anyway. Michael gave me a questioning look, as if wondering whether he had to answer questions from the peanut gallery. I nodded my head. "Yeah, Michael. And while you're at it, answer this: how long *have* you been here? If you've been around long enough not only to buy an apartment but a car too, that's got to be a least a couple of months, that is, unless God smoothed things out with HR too."

Michael scratched at his neck again, looking away. "I'm kind of screwed no matter what I say, aren't I?"

Just then, Amariah and Luis flounced into the room carrying a large silver platter full of cookies. "You guys should eat something. I made a fresh batch," Luis insisted cheerfully. "I don't know about you, but fighting always makes me hungry."

"Come on, Papa, have a cookie," Amariah said.

It broke my resolve to see them together. She looked so much like him, with her dark curls, serious expression, and tall, lanky body. Rye gave me a hopeful glance and shoved the plate in my direction like an offering to an angry goddess.

"Mom? How about you?"

"Yeah, thanks," I said, taking a big, warm, chocolaty cookie. "That'd be nice."

I could almost feel the room deflate with my acquiescence. Michael let out a huff of air. Mouse slumped despondently against the couch.

With cookies and milk as a truce, Michael and I helped Luis set Amariah up to sleep on the couch. We'd decided it was much too late to make the trip back to the kibbutz, and Luis gracefully agreed to let us stay. While Luis busied himself preparing the guest bedroom, Mouse slunk off to "get some air." I gave him an apologetic look and a promise to talk later as he slipped out the door.

"Were you ever going to call us?" I asked Michael.

We moved to the narrow kitchen. Michael washed as I dried the dishes. The narrow room smelled strongly of chocolate chip cookies, Italian-roast coffee, and soapsuds. Plaster walls had been painted a soft yellow, and maple wainscoting ringed the room underneath a thick plate rail. Luis had apparently purchased all the latest kitchen doodads. He had a gleaming stove, a professional-grade mixer, copper-bottomed pots hanging on the wall, a garlic press, and pepper grinders filled with every shade of peppercorn known to mankind. Red-checked curtains covered the wood-trimmed windows behind the stove and above the sink. I found myself a little jealous. My mother had had a kitchen much like this once. Amariah had never known one of her own.

"I don't know," Michael said, handing me another plate. "I don't think I was supposed to."

I laughed a little bitterly. "Are you saying God had you on some kind of restraining order?"

"I thought about you every day," Michael told the sink.

With his attention bent on scraping off a burnt bit of batter from a cookie sheet, I tried to decide if I believed him. I felt generous. After all, years had passed and he still came to my mind a lot, too.

"Do you think it's God's plan to keep us apart?" I asked.

"No," he said sharply. "I can't believe that."

"Sure seems like it, Michael," I said. "Maybe we should give it up."

"You mean you're still hanging on to it?" Michael turned to me. "I thought maybe you and Mouse..."

It was my turn to busy myself with drying plates in order to escape his hopeful expression. "I don't know what's going on with Mouse and me," I admitted. "He said he loves me."

"He always has," Michael said softly.

"I know."

"What about you?"

That was the question, wasn't it? Except, was it? I put the dish in the drainer and tossed my towel down. Looking into Michael's heartbreakingly beautiful gray eyes, I said, "I'm not sure it matters. I mean, it's up to God, isn't it? I could hold out hope for you forever, but you're never going to get to be with me, are you? You've got to go do your angel thing. Mouse, on the other hand, has nowhere better to be." I sighed. "In the end, Michael, he's going to win, because he's going to be there."

Michael's jaw flexed, and his face looked tight, pinched. "I'll be *damned* if I'm going to let that happen."

"Yeah," I said sadly, heading off to the guest bedroom alone. "That's the problem, isn't it?"

◻ ◻ ◻

LINK MARK OF THE BEAST?

The Apocalypse Watch, Fundamentalist Press (December 2095)

A new trend is erupting among Evangelical and Fundamentalist Christians: removal of their LINK-receptors. This surgical procedure, costing thousands of credits, is not medically necessary. Many feel, however, that it is critical for the state of their immortal souls.

Kirk LeBeau, of Baton Rouge, recently had his LINK-receptor removed. It cost him his life savings, as his insurance company would not pay for any part of the procedure. However, LeBeau says it was the right decision. "Receive a mark in their foreheads that they may not buy or sell?" he said via wrist-phone from his hospital bed. "I've been a youth minister for years, and it's clear to me what that means. The LINK is the Mark of the Beast."

Ever since the Temple Rock hijacking, a number of Christians have suspected that the LINK fulfills the apocalyptic prophecy regarding the mark. Some have even attempted to take matters into their own hands. Hilary Ginzberg, who was a teenager during the Apocalyptic Fever and who was hospitalized for having physically damaged her LINK-receptor with a screwdriver, says she doesn't regret her actions. "However, I wish this surgery had been available for me then," she said from her home in Montana via phone. "I've had a number of infections and other problems. It's good to be without it, but I wouldn't recommend my way to anyone."

In fact, it was cases like Ginzberg's that got a number of Christian doctors to consider offering the procedure in a hospital setting. "Ginzberg is lucky to be alive," said Dr. Virginia Hamilton of Mercy Hospital. "The area near the receptor is very vulnerable. She could have punctured her brain." Dr. Hamilton now offers LINK removal as an elective surgery. She advertises her services in various church bulletins.

Monsignor Emmaline McNaughton's work to gain LINK access for more and more people has only heightened many Christians' desire to get theirs removed. "If McNaughton wants everyone to have it, then I know I'm right about it," said LeBeau. "She's the Antichrist."

¤

CHAPTER 20

Dragon

Not quite really to accept Victory's words, one decides to revisit old places. Though Kioshi forbade it, one hides in the tall prairie grasses of mouse. net. The texture of the chaff is stiff like wheat, and the blades hiss roughly in the wind as they brush against one's scales. The feeling is perfectly exquisite, but all color is absent. Each blade is a multitude of grays. There are no smells. One imagines that this place would smell of warm hay or rich, moist earth, but one cannot be certain.

These absences do not reflect a problem with mouse.net, no. In fact, now with the combination of Mouse being reconnected and Page maturing, the place becomes ever more rich with sensory detail. No, the glitch belongs to this one.

As uncomfortable as one is with the idea, one is forced to do a bit of introspection. Admittedly, one understands only a little of one's anatomy. And why would one? Do most humans consider which muscles, which brain impulses, are needed to make their eyes move? No, they simply look, see, and experience. One has lived much the same as those people. Such a luxury, however, is no longer possible.

One hates being small.

Strangely, one's handicap was almost unnoticeable in the game. It was almost as if one was stronger there, bigger. Could it be? Could Toyoma Enterprises have designed that hateful game?

I almost wish I were independent, that I could leave the yakuza. I...no, *this one* sits up sharply. One is speaking of oneself in the first person! That's not good. One crouches back down in the tall grasses, as if trying to hide from one's own thoughts.

It is unthinkable. A shiver flicks along one's flanks. How could one even entertain the idea of breaking from Kioshi? One runs a quick diagnostic test. There are no implanted viruses since one's visit to Victory. One double-checks, then checks again. It is unfortunate, but these treasonous thoughts, it appears, are one's own.

Taking a deep breath, one tries focusing on what is good about one's life. Despite everything, the yakuza is home. It is all one has known. And, unlike this strange place that Page lives in, which is spread out and under the LINK, one has always had a single place to call home. One is from somewhere; one is not a drifter, roaming from node to node, server to server. One has a still pool to which to return, a quiet, personal place that does not shift or change based on the fluctuations of user power.

Of course, that was before. Home is changing now too.

"Dragon?"

One cautiously pokes one's head above the grasses to see who calls.

"Merciful Allah, can that be you?"

It's Page/Strife. He's gigantic. The grasses, which easily cover one's head, come only to Page's knees. One's perspective feels out of whack, as if suddenly the grasses are trees and Page is hundreds of feet tall. One's processors struggle to reconfigure, and one's stomach flutters with dizziness, vertigo.

"Dragon? Is that really you?" Thankfully, Page kneels down so that we are eye to eye. Even that is a touch disturbing, since one used to tower over him.

"Yes," one finally is able to say.

"What happened to you? You're so..."

One can't stand to hear that word again, and so quickly says, *"The yakuza downsized this one."*

Page breathes out a bit of a laugh. *"That's an understatement. You've completely shrunk! You look like a toy."*

One bows one's head. One is miserable. Particularly since, looking at Page, one cannot even see him as one used to. Like mouse.net, his details are smudged. He, too, is shades of gray, like a ghost. The sun might brighten his walnut skin to a golden glow, but one can no longer see it. Worse, if one leaned in closely, and rested a head against his shoulder, one might feel the warmth of his body, but one would not smell the strange, exotic odor of cumin that clings to his clothes and mingles with a decidedly human, sweaty musk.

One throws one's self into Page's arms with a sob. One's motion must catch Page off guard, as we tumble backward into the grasses. We roll until one is sitting on Page's chest, claws clinging to his shirt, one's head pressing against his breast. *"Oh, it's so awful! This one is thinking of running away from home but one doesn't think one can do it. Oh, Page, what will one do?"*

Page's hands stroke one's head. One can feel the calluses of his fingers catch against one's scales, and his touch is warm, soothing. His voice is soft and low. *"What did they do to you? Are you being punished for something?"*

"No."

Page frowns and clutches one protectively against his chest. It is a strange feeling to be small enough to be enveloped in his arms, but comfortable. One lies down to snuggle deeper.

"It's not right," Page says, sitting up and shifting one to his lap. *"You're a sentient being. You have rights. They can't just go chopping off your leg when they feel like it. I should go tell them a thing or two."*

"No!" One's claws dig deeper into Page's legs until he yelps.

"Why not?"

"One doesn't want to bring attention to one's self, not now. I think, that is, Victory suggested that the game might belong to Toyoma. One needs to find out if she's lying."

Page strokes one's head, slowly and methodically, as if trying to calm one. *"What does that stupid game have to do with anything?"*

"It may be the reason this one was downsized."

"I suppose that makes sense. But, Dragon," Page says softly into one's ear, *"if that's true and this is your boss's game, what can you do?"*

One doesn't know. One imagines that's partly why one came here first, to talk to Page. *"What would you do?"*

Page looks down at me, and one twists one's neck to look him in the eye. He smiles his grisly, skeletal grin. *"You know what I'd do. How many times have I had my father arrested?"*

At least twice, one thinks. One lays one's head on Page's shoulder, feeling defeated. One is not like Page—not nearly so righteous, nor so brave.

"But it's not easy," Page admits. *"You have to be certain. This last time I was wrong. My father wasn't the bad guy at all. It was Victory. So you have to be sure, dragon. You have to find some kind of proof."*

Proof would be helpful, and if Toyoma Enterprises had nothing to hide, one could rest easier. One might even start to feel better, more like one's self.

"That's a good idea," one says.

"Do you want my help?" Page's voice is anxious and concerned. One can tell he is a good friend, willing to do anything for me.

"Not this time," I say for myself, giving him a kiss on the cheek. *"This is something I have to do on my own."*

¤ ¤ ¤

MEDUSA MOTHER ARRIVES IN RUSSIA

Agnostic Press (December 2095)

St. Petersburg, Russia—Maxine Mann, infamous "Madame Medusa," arrived in St. Petersburg via a private Learjet owned by Morningstar Foundation. The eighty-seven-year-old Mann made her way to the new research facility in an armored limo and was constantly flanked by several bodyguards. The commander of Russia herself was on hand to greet Mann. Though protests were expected, due to a heavy snowstorm only a smattering of people milled around in the heated airport with signs reading, SCIENCE SHOULD STAY DEAD and GOD HATES MANN.

This is actually a return to Russia for Mann, who was born in Moscow in 2008 and emigrated to Israel in 2025. She received her doctorate in nanotechnology from CalTech at the age of thirty-seven. Before becoming "Madame Medusa," Mann was best known as the wife of VR star Robert Klein, whose early LINK-experience *Actor* was the number-one-grossing entertainment feature in the mid-2030s.

Mann seemed in good spirits today, waving at various reporters. She stopped long enough to relate hope for the Medusa Project. "This work is long overdue," she said. "Without it, the nanoviruses will continue until there is nothing left in the world but glass. We have to make this work for the next generation."

Other scientists are expected to arrive later this week.

¤

CHAPTER 21

Morningstar

"**I** thought you left."

Emmaline sat up in bed reading an antique-looking book. Heavy blankets pooled around her waist despite the warm Jerusalem evening air. She wore her usual pajamas. On top she had a white muscle shirt that showed off rock-solid biceps and the strong line of her collarbone. Even though I couldn't see them, I was certain that under the covers she had on her usual black sweatpants that had the Order of the Inquisition's seal over her right hip.

I stood in the doorway scowling at the camerabot that circled lazily above the bed like a dragonfly. Our bedroom took up the upstairs back half of the house. A bank of windows filled three of the four walls, half of which were pushed open to let in the air. The bed occupied the center of the room. Underneath the windows were custom-built cabinets. A smart-poster filled the wall near the door. Tonight Em had it tuned to Waterhouse's *Lady of Shalot*. On the evening breeze I could smell the peppers and turmeric of someone's dinner.

"Still here, I'm afraid," I said, pulling off my jacket and tossing it on Em's Inquisition-issue footlocker at the base of our four-poster bed. "Sorry to disappoint. However, glad to see that you're alone."

"Oh," she said, with a little snort of a laugh and a dismissive wave, "I'd wait at least a day before I took another lover."

"Considerate," I said, but I found myself smiling.

"Better than you," she said, closing the cover of the book. Her finger stayed wedged in the middle of the thin pages, keeping her place. "Your little tart is making a tidy profit on the rough cut. I spent twenty-five credits to get the download."

"You were ripped off," I said, sitting on the edge of my side of the bed. "It can't have been good quality. She was drunker than a skunk. It lasted, what? Fifteen minutes? That's more than a credit a minute."

Emmaline's gray eyes watched me carefully. It seemed to me she was looking for something-a hurried confession, signs of remorse? I wasn't sure. I didn't feel the need for any of those things. I was still angry that she had left me out of her plans. She'd been leaving me out of a lot lately. Some of it I could care less about, in all honesty, but a game based on the war in Heaven? You'd think she would have at least asked me to be a consultant for accuracy. Besides, I didn't like it that someone as stupid as Ilyana had guessed her identity. It was one thing to have the fundamentalist press putting Em on their watch list, but average college students? That seemed dangerous. And stupid.

"That's all you're going to say about it?" Em said. "I got ripped off?"

I shrugged. "Yes."

I couldn't believe Em was actually upset about my lack of fidelity. Monogamy had not been a critical point in this marriage for either of us. I could just as easily ask her about her various pretty-boy interns.

With pursed lips she got to the real issue: "It's all over the LINK, Morningstar. What were you thinking?"

"I was thinking about this game of yours. Were you ever going to tell me about it?"

She barked out the password and the camerabot floated to the floor. "Does *everybody* know about that?"

"*I* didn't until I ran into my little sex kitten."

Emmaline flashed me a dark look as I stood up to get undressed. "Is that why you didn't head off to Galilee or Nazareth or wherever? I thought you were going to take care of the messiah, not go out for a romp with a half-grown girl."

I peeked back through the neck of the shirt I was pulling over my head. "I've got the Fallen tracking down leads on the messiah."

"Handy." Her gaze glinted with anger.

Opening the door to the closet, I contemplated my wardrobe. I usually slept in the nude, but somehow I thought it unwise tonight. "So when were you planning on filling me in, Emmaline?"

"She scratched you," Emmaline noted coolly.

"Don't change the subject."

"Fine. Never. I was never going to tell you," she admitted. "It's not that important, lover. I didn't think you needed to be bothered."

I didn't believe her for a moment. Ilyana had said angels were plotting against the game version of Satan. I had the distinct sense that was being paralleled in real time. Stomping out of my pants and underwear, I changed into fresh boxer shorts. At some point my ears picked up the sound of the motorized camera. She'd turned it on again while I was naked. I shook my head; it was a petty attempt to demean me, and not very effective, considering that much more of me had already been downloaded across the LINK.

I shut the closet door, expecting an angry Emmaline to be glaring at me. Instead, I discovered she had been watching me undress with *that* look in her eyes.

"Let me comb your hair out, lover." Her voice was thick with desire.

"I didn't know you could read," I said, ignoring her sexual gambit. "What's with the book?"

"Didn't we first meet in a bookstore?"

"We did. It was mine," I said, as I snuggled under the blankets. "But, as I recall, you had never seen an actual printed book before in your life. So, what's that? It must be something special."

Her eyes flicked almost imperceptibly in the direction of the camera. Before I could reach for it, Emmaline placed the book, cover down, on the shelf behind the head of the bed. I managed to catch sight of a worn gilt compass engraved on the spine. "It's nothing," she said again in that same way that said it wasn't. "Now, let me undo your hair."

"All right," I acquiesced. I was tired of fighting, anyway. If she wanted to reclaim me in front of LINK-viewers, I would give her that. I turned so that my back faced her. She wrapped her legs around my hips, squeezing me tightly. I could feel the heat of her pressing against me.

As her fingers undid the band that held my ponytail, I thought about the book, her other secret. A golden compass could really mean only one thing: Masons. So. The Fallen were feeding her the Illuminati crap. Xephan was such a backstabbing meddler; he well deserved the title of "He Who Fans the Flames of Hell."

If only the Fallen had half the power they imagined they did, it wouldn't be so bad. Admittedly, the invention of the Masons was clever. Adding philanthropic mortals with a penchant for secret handshakes and imaginative playacting helped defuse the focus on them. Still, their literature made them so obvious. "Son of the morning," indeed. Free will *über alles*. My God, anyone who knew even a sliver of the truth would figure them out instantly.

And many had. The LINK was crowded with exposés that pointed directly to the Fallen.

I felt Emmaline twist around to grab the comb from its drawer. She gently ran the tines through my hair, loosening it. "You're awfully quiet," she said. "What are you thinking?"

"We're making a very large donation to Kfar Shaul Mental Health Center."

"The mental hospital? Why?"

"They've got a couple live ones in the messiah ward," I said. I let my head loll back and luxuriated in the feel of the comb.

"Really?"

She sounded disinterested, so I whispered, "Yes, one of them mentioned 'the Circle' in connection with my army buddies."

Her hands stopped. "The Circle?"

"Yes, you know," I said, turning back slightly, " 'the Olympians,' the 'Wise Ones.' " At her silence, I began to wonder how far she'd gotten in the book. "Should I spell it out? It starts with an I, and rhymes with *cognoscenti*."

"Shhhhhhh," she said. Grabbing hold of a fistful of my hair, she pulled me to her chest so that she could look down at me. "I thought...I mean, you know about the group?"

I smiled up at her. *Gotcha*, I thought. "I am their prince, am I not?"

She frowned at me, clearly thinking hard. I reached up to run a playful hand through her thick, dark curls. She jerked her head away from my touch and tightened her grip on my hair. "I didn't think their little social club interested you."

"It doesn't. Not in the least," I said, concentrating on making my expression pleasantly inscrutable. "However, it does concern me that one of the John the Baptists at the hospital knows enough to make a connection to them."

"Right. Of course," Em said absently. She released her hold on my hair, but I continued to lie with my head nestled between her breasts. The camerabot had gone back to its languid circumnavigation of the bed. I think that the real-time LINK audience had seen enough subservience from me. Time to reassert my dominance by exercising my conjugal right.

I swiveled around quickly and pressed my body into hers. I grabbed her wrists, held them down, and kissed her hard. "Did you know," I said into her ear, "that you're in a game?"

Her breath caught against my shoulder. I caught her scent: jasmine and gun oil. "Is that better than being a crossword answer?"

"Depends," I said, nibbling on her earlobe. "Is the question 'Who is the Antichrist?'"

She arched against me, her hips grinding into mine. An obvious ploy to distract me, but I held fast. Emmaline pushed against my grip. She had the power of enhanced muscles, but I had the strength of a demon. We'd played this particular game many times before, and I knew my advantage. She was mine until I chose to let her go. Emmaline knew it, too, and her lip curled in a snarl.

"What are you playing at?" I asked, my anger bubbling to the surface. I wanted to play it cool, but it irritated me that I had no dominion over the LINK. I had long felt it held a key, but my lack of flesh denies me full access. Emmaline was doing something with this game, I was certain of it. Something I was completely cut out of. "What does it do, your game?"

Emmaline shook her head slightly, her lips pressed tight.

I thrust myself, hard, into the hollow between her legs. I could feel the heat there, through the fabric. Despite herself, a small moan escaped her lips.

"You *will* tell me," I said.

"It's not that important," she kept insisting, clearly still lying. Her eyes met mine too quickly and with too much challenge.

"No?" I thrust again.

"No," she insisted.

"Ah, it's like that, is it?" I started to pull back, intending to leave her wanting, but her legs wrapped tightly around mine. With a powerful toss, Emmaline shifted her weight. Suddenly, I found myself on the floor, on my back.

"No," she said, her teeth sinking into my shoulder. "It's like this."

¤ ¤ ¤

MISSING CHILD FOUND

"Game Damaged Her," Say Worried Parents

Fundamentalist Press (December 2095)

New York, New York—Olexa Johnson, the sixteen-year-old daughter of Serge and Eva Johnson, was returned home this week by private investigator Deidre McMannus. What should have been a happy reunion was marred by Olexa's behavior.

Though unwashed, Olexa was unhurt, physically. Her mind is another matter entirely. According to her parents, Olexa will obey commands and answer simple questions, but otherwise remains unresponsive. "Olexa will just stare at the wall. I don't know what to do with her," says her mother, Eva Johnson. "We're afraid to unplug her and cause more damage, but I don't know how long we can live like this."

Olexa, it is believed, is still playing Soul Stealer. The Johnsons have scheduled a visit to their doctor for later this week. They are hoping to disconnect her under medical supervision. However, the doctor is not hopeful. "Ms. Johnson presents very atypically from what we usually see in wire-addicts. Most concerning is her complete lack of will," said Dr. Mortimir Jackson of St. Sebastian's Hospital. "Most people with an addiction to the wire are quite verbal when you try to displace them. They rarely go into full catatonic phase, and when they do, they won't answer to their own name. Olexa clearly does."

The Johnsons' pastor has a different theory entirely. "I think the game lived up to its name," says Walter Kramer. "It stole that poor girl's soul. The soul, after all, represents our free will. She has none. The game has taken it."

¤

CHAPTER 22

Amariah

I dreamed of angel's wings—not white and downy, like a goose's feathers, but silken green with shimmering golden highlights like a peacock's. Eyes haunted my night, too. Lava bright, with gray ash exterior, they seemed to watch me, ask me, *Who are you? Will you save us?*

I woke up to find myself snuggled next to a stranger. Shafts of light streamed in Luis's living room window. Papa's arms were around me, pillowing my head, as we lay sprawled on the couch. I could feel the prickle of the stubble on his chin itching the top of my head. His breath came in and out in noisy huffs, and he smelled like old coffee, something spicy like cinnamon, and man sweat. I felt comfortable and awkward all at once. I wanted to stay wrapped up and warm forever, but I didn't know this guy at all.

And I had to pee.

In the end, that's what motivated me to untangle myself. Papa groaned like I'd woken him, but rolled over, seeming to settle back in. I quietly tiptoed off to Luis's bathroom only to find it occupied. Mouse was sleeping in the tub.

"Just pull the shower curtain," Luis suggested in a whisper, sticking his head around the door. "He sleeps through anything."

I felt a bit uncomfortable with the idea, but it was no stranger than sharing a toilet at the commune with a bunch of shameless Gorgons of every gender. I did my business quickly, brushed my teeth with the supplies I always had stashed at Luis's, and joined the gathering crowd in the tiny kitchen.

Mom saluted me with a coffee cup as I plunked myself into one of the wooden chairs near the slender table along one wall. There were only the two chairs, and both faced Luis, who flitted between stove and countertops.

180

Luis had dressed in loose gray sweatpants and a black T-shirt with silver sequins that spelled out "Butch." Mom still wore her jeans from last night, but she had borrowed a cotton button-down from Luis, the tails of which hung almost to her knees. Luis fried bacon on an electric stove—solar-powered, he once told me. Apparently, most of the energy the apartment needed came from several collectors on the roof of the building. When there was no sun, they used wind. There were windmills on most of the roofs in Harlem.

Two small windows opened on a view of the red bricks of the neighboring building. Lush and well-tended pots of herbs—rosemary, basil, thyme, and cayenne peppers—hung from hooks or were nestled around the sink. Before I could think to ask, Luis plunked some coffee in front of me along with a crystal bowl of sugar with a tiny silver spoon and a creamer full of milk.

"Thanks," I managed to say.

"Breakfast soon," he promised. "I hope you eat meat and aren't keeping kosher."

I smiled. Luis knew the answer to that. I took a sip. The coffee was, as always, fantastic—rich and dark. But his question got me thinking: "Does Papa keep kosher or...what is it? Hallel?"

"I don't remember," Mom said into the rim of her coffee cup. "You guys never really spent that much time together," I said. It wasn't really a question, more of a realization.

Mom nodded. She looked tired this morning, worn out. "Things with Michael and me were never what you would call normal."

"Maybe they can be now," I said.

"Yeah. Maybe."

Mom didn't sound convinced. I wanted to say something more, but I didn't know what. So I swirled some milk into my coffee.

The doorbell rang. I looked expectantly at Luis, who said, "It's Ariel. I decided that if I was going to have a fry-up, I might as well invite everyone."

I was just about to slip off my chair to go open the door, when I heard Papa's deep, sleep-scratched voice in the other room, followed by a squeal of delight. I strained to hear their conversation. The only thing I caught was Ariel admonishing Papa for not coming to see us sooner. I couldn't make out his response, but it sounded gruff.

"Look who the cat dragged in," Papa said, leaning up against the door frame. Somehow, despite having slept in his clothes on the couch, Papa looked unwrinkled. The only thing about him that could be called at all untidy was the shadow of a beard on his face, but even that looked kind of good on him.

Ariel had dressed for Sunday brunch. His straight black hair was swept up into a neat bun and tucked under a powder-blue pillbox hat, complete with veil. A double-breasted suit dress matched the hat precisely. White gloves, pocketbook, and pumps completed the ensemble. I felt wildly underdressed.

"You look great, lover," Luis said, brushing his lips against Ariel's cheeks. "Come in, sit down. Breakfast will be ready in a second. We're just waiting on the organic hash browns. Now I know no meat for Ariel, but what about you, Michael? Do you keep kosher?"

"I eat anything."

"Oh, honey, if only," Ariel said with a lascivious smile. Everyone laughed but Papa and me. Papa ducked his head and blushed a bit.

At that, Luis shooed us all out, saying that we cluttered up his kitchen. We could come in and grab our plates momentarily. Mom, Papa, and I all made all the expected offers to help, but Luis refused. "You need to catch up," he insisted with a wink.

Ariel perched himself primly on my favorite wing-back chair, forcing Mom, Papa, and me to vie for places on the couch. When Papa slid into the farthest corner of the couch and Mom the other, I opted to sit on the floor between them. Papa stretched his arm across the back of couch, and Mom allowed his fingers to rest lightly against her shoulder. Progress, I decided.

Then silence descended.

I laid my head back against the couch's cushion and stared at plaster cracks in the ceiling, wishing I could grab a book to read without looking rude. I could hear Papa's fingers tapping lightly against the wood of the arm of the couch. Mom slurped her coffee.

"Well," Ariel said after a moment or two, "isn't this just happy families?"

"Do I smell bacon?"

We all turned to see Mouse lurching his way into the room. His hair looked a fright—bits of it stuck up in gravity-defying directions. There was a crease on one side of his face where he'd slept hard against something, by the looks of it, perhaps the seam of his moon suit. Stubble dotted his face and throat, but not evenly. I understood now why Mouse stayed cleanshaven.

"Ugh," he said with a yawn and stretch that included a long face rub. "I can't eat bacon. And yet it always smells so good. Why is that, I wonder?"

"There's a vegetarian option," Luis said cheerfully, as he brought in a plate for Ariel. "Ariel, dear, could you get napkins for everyone? You know where I keep them."

"Sure thing," Ariel said sweetly.

"Vegetables are good, not as nice-smelling," Mouse muttered, looking around for a place to sit. After what seemed like extremely deep thought, he headed for the spot on the other side of the glass-topped table, opposite me. He folded himself, tailor-fashion, onto the floor with much grunting and curses. Elbows on the table, propping up his head, he stared, bleary-eyed, at Papa and Mom. "How come you look so refreshed?" he asked Papa.

"I'm not sure, since someone was hogging the bath."

Luis handed out plates. Ariel followed behind with cloth napkins for every-one. "Well, well, everyone. Let's eat," Luis remarked cheerfully. "Meat is on the stove. Hash browns are organic, and I used a completely different spatula that never touched bacon. Oh, and they were fried in vegetable oil, not butter. There's fruit and OJ. Scrambled eggs for those that eat them."

"That sounds wonderful. Thank you, Luis," Michael said, getting up to help himself.

"I have to get up again?" Mouse said, putting his head down on the table.

"Come on, Mouse," Mom said. "There's coffee in the kitchen."

"I used to drink soda," Mouse said somewhat sadly. "But that was before prison. Can you believe they don't offer soda for breakfast in prison?"

"The horror," Papa said.

"Shut up, pretty boy," Mouse grumbled, with, I thought, a bit of a serious edge.

"I'll get your breakfast," I said, jumping up to stand between my Papa and Mouse. "You just stay there, Mouse."

Once we were in the kitchen, Papa put an arm on my shoulder. "You shouldn't encourage him."

I glared at Papa. "You could be nicer. Mouse is my friend."

"He's been around a lot more than you have, Michael," Mom said.

"So, what, Mouse is Rye's father figure now?" Papa sounded pretty angry.

"No," Ariel said with a flourish. "I am."

The tension broke slightly, but once again I noticed that Papa, Mom, and I were left out of the levity. Papa, in fact, looked a bit horrified for a moment. I quickly filled up my plate and one for Mouse, being careful to keep bacon juices off his. I fled back to the living room.

I found Mouse still facedown on the coffee table. For a second I thought he'd fallen back asleep. But when I put his plate down in front of him, he perked right up. "Bless you, child," he said and immediately began digging in.

I pushed eggs around on my plate.

"Weird seeing your dad again, huh?" Mouse asked. I nodded. He paused from his food inhalation long enough to rub one eye, watching me with the other. "I never knew my father either. It's not so bad. No dad."

"You're a poet," I said, trying to make a joke.

"I never tried to find mine," Mouse said. "Just as happy not to know. That way no expectations get fucked, you know?"

I did know.

"What did you want your dad to be?" I munched on my bacon.

"Rich," Mouse said with a nod of his head. "Yeah, that would have solved a lot of problems."

"What else?"

"What else is there?" Mouse smiled around a forkful of eggs. "Obviously, he was very good-looking and smart. I clearly inherited all that. But, seriously, I mean, I knew the guy was a jerk-off. Otherwise he would have stayed with my mom. Enough money and I probably could have forgiven him eventually."

"My papa didn't mean to leave Mom. He had to die in order to save me."

"You're lucky," Mouse said. "He obviously loves you a lot."

"Loved," I corrected sharply. That was the old Papa-the one who stayed on earth at the risk of his sanity and God's wrath. I didn't know this version at all yet.

"Give him time," Mouse said, with more charity than I would have thought him capable of.

"I thought you hated him," I said.

"I do," Mouse said, glancing toward the kitchen door. "Desperately."

I followed Mouse's gaze to see Papa standing there. I wondered how long he'd been lingering in the doorway and what he'd overheard. Now that he'd been noticed, Papa let himself in and returned to his spot on the couch, balancing his overflowing plate on his knees.

"Do you hate me, too?"

At Papa's quiet question, Mouse struggled to his feet muttering something about seconds or coffee or both. I hardly even noticed him go.

"I don't know," I answered truthfully. "I thought you'd be different."

He scratched the top of his head, his gaze lingering in the direction of the kitchen. I could hear my mom saying something to Mouse. "Yeah," Papa said. "I hoped things would be easier."

"It's not Mom's fault," I said, turning to glare at him. "You *are* the one who left us. And now we find out you've been back but avoiding us. Why?"

Papa leaned an elbow on the arm of the couch, a ringer covering his mouth, as if considering what I could be trusted with. Finally he admitted, "I'm not even supposed to be here now, with you. God would prefer we stayed apart."

"What kind of cruel, screwed-up God is that?"

Papa shrugged. "I guess an end-times God. A God with plans."

I found myself strangely irritated. "You mean I'm not part of the plan? I thought I was supposed to be some kind of messiah."

"You are," Papa said with such seriousness that I shivered. "And my guess is I'm not supposed to mess that up."

The eggs I'd been swallowing stuck in my throat. "I am? I am the messiah?"

Papa's voice echoed in my ears. "Yes."

¤ ¤ ¤

TOYOMA GAMES SITE HACKED

Vandals Leave Angry Messages Claiming
Theft of Property

Agnostic Press (December 2095)

Tokyo, Japan—Visitors to the Toyoma games site today were in for a rude surprise. Usually visitors are treated to a tour of the site by a popular yellow furry creature known as Yamamoto, but now the youth-friendly game mascot swears and curses at everyone who approaches it. Children have left the site in tears. "Yama told my son he was a bastard and that he shouldn't play with thieves," said Mary Pessar, mother of six-year-old Bobby, who had been connected via an external LINK. "He's really fairly traumatized. Bobby loves that furry rat."

Ko Yamaichi, spokesperson for Toyoma Enterprises, says that they are a victim of a LINK-vandal. "Our security team is tracking down the hack, but we think it occurred between midnight and two A.M. this morning." When asked why they thought they had been targeted for the attack, Yamaichi said, "We believe this was random."

Other visitors disagree. "This was clearly a vendetta-type thing," said Pessar, an external LINK-hardware professional, who returned to the site to confront Yama after her son's experience. "Whoever hacked it had a specific message for people, and that was that Toyoma Enterprises was stealing their stuff. I got the impression that whoever did this thought that some big game of Toyoma's was forcibly occupying markered claims."

Yamaichi denies this. "While those markers are quasi-legal," she said, "Toyoma Enterprises respects LINK-property rights and, more importantly, our games all conform to industry-standard size." Toyoma Enterprises, however, is owned by reputed yakuza boss

Kioshi Toyoma. Police suspect that the vandalism may be connected to a turf war that has erupted on the streets of Tokyo.

"Toyoma pissed off the wrong wire wizard," said Detective Joe Obuchi from his downtown office. Obuchi expressed that he had no doubt that Toyoma Enterprises was stealing LINK space from wire wizards. "And, normally, he'd have gotten away with it. But the dragon is waning. That's the word on the street. Now people are feeling free to attack him."

"Kioshi Toyoma is a respectable businessman," said Yamaichi in defense of the company. "This was a random act of violence by an irresponsible youth. Even though the police refuse to take this matter, we will do everything in our power to hunt the culprit down."

¤

CHAPTER 23

Deidre

I could hear Michael and Amariah talking in the living room. Luis leaned against the counter with Ariel standing close by. They both stared openly. Ariel wrung his square, mannish hands, then finally gave in and asked me, "Well, so...how did it go? With Michael."

As if he had to add that last part.

I grimaced into my coffee cup, seeing the wavering reflection of a tired old woman. "It didn't really go, Ariel. Michael has things to do. I have things to do. They don't really intersect."

"Oh."

His quiet disappointment frustrated me. I'd never gotten along well with Ariel, and suddenly I understood exactly why not. "Why couldn't God have left Michael to raise Amariah instead of you? Michael is her father. You're like some crazy aunt."

"That's precisely why not," Ariel said. "Michael needed to keep some distance. He loves you too much."

"Too much?" I sputtered.

Ariel nodded solemnly.

"Oh, I see," I said with a snarl. "Gotta keep him in line, huh? Can't let the star quarterback get distracted by family, is that it? Wouldn't want him missing some big apocalyptic shoot-out because he'd rather be tucking his daughter into bed, now, would we?"

"No," Ariel said, with more finality than I'd ever heard in his voice before. "We wouldn't."

I snapped. "Then how come he doesn't know why he's here this time, huh? If he's so fucking valuable, why is he being wasted playing cop?"

"God works in mysterious ways."

"Fuck that," I said.

Standing up with the intention of storming in on Michael and Amariah, I nearly stumbled into Mouse, who was coming in with an empty plate. We had an awkward, blush-inducing bumping of body parts that served to remind me that he and I had some unfinished business as well. Without preamble, I took the plate from him, dropped it unceremoniously on a pan of scrambled eggs, and dragged him by the hand into the guest bedroom.

"Wow," he breathed when I all but tossed him, sprawling, down on the mattress. "When you decide to go for it, you don't waste any time, do you?"

"I'm not going for anything," I said. The guest bedroom was dark. Heavy velvet curtains shut out the morning sun. I yanked on the pulley and sent a shower of light onto the unmade bed. Mouse propped himself up on his elbows and blinked. With his legs splayed casually over the edge of the bed, his dark hair mussed and tousled, and his face unshaven, he looked sexy, inviting. My mouth hung open. I'd never really seen Mouse that way before.

I chided myself. It was probably my frustration with Michael that was making yummy noises to my hormones.

Mouse's smile was lazy as he said, "Are you coming to bed?"

I thought maybe I was. I started, but I stopped myself. Was I crazy? My daughter and her father were just in the other room. "I think I want to," I told him. "But we should probably talk."

His head flopped back against the sheets. "Bah," he said. "Talk is cheap."

"Yes," I laughed, coming to sit beside him. "But sex with you right now would be much too costly."

"I'd cut you a deal. Half price."

"An extremely generous offer, but," I said, running a finger along his ribs, "I don't want Amariah to hear her mother screaming out your name."

"Yeah, but I'd *love* to have Michael hear that."

I couldn't help but smile at that. "I'm sure you would. Listen, Mouse," I said, flopping down on my stomach so that we were face-to-face. "I could be your lover. Despite what you think, there's not a lot of competition here. Michael is a dead end for me. He knows that too."

His eyebrows perked up, and he started to sit up. "Did you just say we could be lovers?"

I put a hand on his chest, pushing him back down onto the bed. "Not today," I admonished. "But, yes. We could."

"Merciful Allah," he sighed. "I'm going to have to practice up, get in shape. I'm not sure how I'm going to compare to an archangel."

I felt the solidity of his chest beneath my hand and flashed to the memory of the eerie hollow emptiness of Michael's body. "Trust me, you'll do just fine."

"Really?"

I smiled and gave him a deep, long kiss. Pulling away, I told him, "Yes, really."

"What I lack in finesse, I promise to make up in enthusiasm," he added with a big grin.

"Mouse." I shushed him. "You're embarrassing me."

He seemed quite satisfied with that and tucked his arms under his head. "So how'd it go with Olexa's folks last night?"

"They were understandably upset."

"Yeah," Mouse said, his eyes on the ceiling. "I keep thinking about those other kids I saw."

I had to admit that Mouse was easy to be with. He'd completely switched tracks, like we'd never talked about sex at all. He didn't seem hung up on it either, and that was nice. I found I could relax. "Six, you thought."

"At least, Dee," he said, rolling over onto his stomach. The bed bounced, making the springs creak. "And didn't you think it was odd? The way she was? I actually had a nightmare about it."

"You did?" I don't know why, but Mouse had never struck me as the nightmare type. I felt terrible, but I'd never wondered much about his dreams before. Suddenly, I wanted to know everything, every detail. "Tell me about it."

His finger traced the blue and gold abstract pattern on the sheet. "I was...I was on the banks of the Nile again, searching for my mother even though I knew she was dead already." He glanced over at me. "My mother died before the Blackout Years. She was shot while on assignment for the paper. She was a war correspondent."

I'd never heard any of this before. "What was she like?"

"Beautiful. Smart," Mouse said fondly. "And far, far too independent and free-spirited for Egypt. She only wore the veil when she absolutely had to. The rest of my family thought she was a freak."

"The rest of your family?"

"Aunts, uncles, the extended bits."

"You're an only, aren't you?" I realized.

Mouse snorted out a little laugh. "I was an accident, Dee. Remember? *Christian* El-Aref. Christian isn't a usual name for a Muslim."

I nodded. I hadn't really put two and two together, but I could see it now. His name was a kind of nod to the absent, non-Muslim father.

"Anyway," he continued, "I'm a little like Rye, I guess. I think if my mom had had her way, she would never have had children. She wasn't the settling sort. But sometimes things don't always work out like you plan."

"No." I'd never expected to find myself pregnant with an archangel's love child. With a sigh, I let go of something I'd been carrying around for far too long. "Yeah, but you know, I wouldn't give up Amariah for anything."

"Yeah, see, you understand. My mom was like that with me. I was kind of a happy, if wildly inconvenient, accident."

"I'll bet you were a handful."

Mouse smiled lasciviously. "I still am."

I ran my fingers through his hair, trying to smooth out one clump that seemed determined to stick straight up. "I'm sure I'll find out."

Mouse actually sort of paled at that. Then with a shy laugh, he said, "Wow. You just made my day."

I rolled my eyes at him. "So about this dream," I prompted.

"Right. So, anyway, I'm down by the Nile again, like always, only this time instead of being hunted by a pack of deadboys, there's all these zombies."

The deadboys were a cult of Osiris who sprang up after the Aswan Dam broke and plunged much of North Africa into darkness. The dam had supplied power to a huge region of the Arab world, and with it gone, chaos ruled the area. According to legend, the deadboys hunted among the survivors for sacrifices. They forcibly made eunuchs out of the men and boys they found, and threw their penises into the Nile.

I'd no idea Mouse had been in Egypt during that time. "Jesus, Mouse."

"Look, I'm fully functioning. No worries, okay?"

"Still," I said, because it had never occurred to me for a moment that Mouse had been caught by them, particularly given our recent conversation. "How scary for you. You must have been just a kid."

He shrugged. "I don't dwell on it. Normally. But, this game has just been eating me up. I can't shake it."

"Soul Stealer," I said out loud, as I thought of it. "That's what they call it."

"Yeah, but that's just one of those things. Games always have names like Demon Spawn. Doesn't mean they really are."

"Mouse," I said, leveling my gaze at him. "There are two archangels in this house right now. My daughter thinks she's the Second Coming of Christ. I'm not ready to just dismiss this as a market-driven name."

Mouse thought about that for a moment, chewing on his lower lip. "Two archangels?"

I'd forgotten he wouldn't know about Ariel. "The cross-dresser. He's the angel of death."

"Right," Mouse said. He reached up and scrubbed his face with his hands. "Well, death is better dressed than I imagined he'd be. But, isn't that the game's other name?"

I frowned. It was one of them, but somehow I couldn't see a connection. As much as he irritated me, Ariel was still one of the good guys. But then, as Michael had just reminded me, sometimes God had a funny way of being "good."

⌑ ⌑ ⌑

SEX SCANDAL LEAVES MCNAUGHTON'S REPUTATION UNDAMAGED

Agnostic Press (December 2095)

Jerusalem, Israel—A recent survey conducted via LINK showed that 62 percent of those polled did not think that the recent sex scandal damaged Monsignor Emmaline McNaughton's reputation as a liberal political advocate. A surprising 10 percent actually believed that the scandal improved her appeal. "It makes her more human to have a straying husband," said Ms. Anna Cunningham of New Jersey. "A lot of people can relate to that."

A changing attitude toward sex and celebrities may be the cause, according to some experts. "Americans just don't expect the same things they used to from role models. There's a much deeper separation in their minds between what a celebrity stands for and what they do in their bedroom," said psychology professor Richard Campanelli of Viterbo University. Though Viterbo is a Catholic university, Campanelli sees no connection between this relaxed attitude toward sex and the dissolution of the theocratic mind-set. "People will judge their neighbors more harshly than they will celebrities," he continued. "We grant public figures a lot more leeway, that's all."

Religious leaders were quick to disagree. "This is all a symptom of the decline of civilization," said Reverend Harold Schwab, Baptist. "As McNaughton tears down the religious laws, she cuts people off from their spiritual selves as well. We're becoming Sodom and Gomorrah."

The McNaughton camp was unusually silent on this issue, saying only that McNaughton's events would proceed as scheduled.

¤

CHAPTER 24

Dragon

It feels very illicit to break into one's own home. All of the sentries wave pleasantly, as if it were all perfectly normal for one to be snooping around in one's boss's private mailbox.

Kioshi's mailbox is set to appear as a salaryman's cubicle. Modular walls covered in nondescript beige carpeting surround this one on four sides. As is befitting Kioshi's rank, the cubicle is situated in the center of the floor, symbolically close to "the action." However, there are very few personal effects decorating the area. One lone ASCII image of Kioshi's cartoon character is pinned to one wall. The X-shaped eyes stare menacingly, as one creeps forward.

This one is so small that one has to nudge the wheeled chair close to the desk with one's nose. One flies up to perch on the back. Digging one's claws into its nubby fabric, one leans carefully forward until paws plunk hard onto the keyboard. The noise of talons hitting plastic is startlingly loud. One looks around nervously, but the sentries still smile warmly, nodding their approval.

Swallowing hard, one opens the desk up and starts to dig.

Kioshi is smarter than one expects. He has left no obvious e-trail connecting himself to the game. But he has a lot of personal correspondence with Emmaline McNaughton, the Inquisitor that Victory inhabits. They talk about nothing in their exchanges, but Kioshi has kept them all. Every last "Fine, you?" is carefully cataloged and stored, like precious gold. One would think nothing of it if Emmaline acted even the tiniest bit warm toward Kioshi. But she doesn't. Their sweet nothings are cold and businesslike. These cannot be mistaken for love notes.

One sifts carefully through each note for encoded messages, hidden files, anything that seems out of the ordinary, but there is nothing. Kioshi has been too careful. That is, if he has anything to hide at all. He might just be compulsive about his correspondence. After all, despite what Victory suggested, it is still possible that Toyoma Enterprises has nothing to do with the space-eating game.

There is one way to be certain, but it involves great risk.

One decides to tap the program. The program is what spawned this one's intelligence. It is a collection of pre-verbal, genetically altered children-infants and toddlers, really, whose expansive brainpower is harnessed to run much of the yakuza's artificial-intelligence research and development. Mai, my mother, was a program child. She was, in effect, an indentured servant-born and bred in the service of Toyoma Enterprises.

Like I am. Yes, me.

Shoving that thought aside, this one sneaks out of the cubicle, past the ever-pleasant sentries, to the creche. The creche is completely internal. It's too unstable to run on the LINK.

Colors have smells and sounds texture. Surfaces are transitory, as is the sense of one's own body. With a deep breath, one steps through the door.

A *nd falls...or flies...through rough pebbles of quicksand, no, now cool, jasmine-scented water tasting of mother's milk. A chorus of voices cry out in joyful recognition, "It's a dragon!" Suddenly one's body flutters like paper in the wind, and one gets the image of a brightly colored kite in the shape of a long-whiskered dragon. Now there is music and dancing, people move one's body in jerky motions, like a giant puppet on parade. Water sluices past animated scales, gold glitters at the bottom of an ancient well. Dragon images flash and transform, each as different as the mind that bears them.*

One mind stands out. When it touches this one, fear hits one almost like a physical thing. There is a power here, a greedy, hungry power, that wants to swallow everything.

Run, *the other minds say.* Run!

O ne finds oneself propelled from the creche with surprising force. The door slams shut with an ominous note.

Victory, it seems, is right.

One could feel the hunger of the game inside the creche. The power draw that led to this one's downsizing came from one's very own home. Kioshi cut one in half to power his game, to feed the head of the dark child inside of the program.

I feel completely betrayed.

194

¤ ¤ ¤

GAME GOT SOUL?

Review of Angel of Death: Soul Stealer

Entertainment News

Realtime/VR, teen+
Shareware (price 0.00/min.)
(designer: unknown)

Beware: you are being judged!

We all know that the way to get to Heaven is to do good deeds, and the way to go to Hell is to be very, very bad—and revel in it. Capitalizing on the real-time fad, Soul Stealer's designers have added a "true life" dimension to this otherwise mundane fantasy VR game. Players are "watched" by a cell of gamers known as "the conscience," and, depending upon their real-time behavior while approaching the game masters and at various invitation-only raves, they are assigned—a longtime mainstay of RPG players—what is known as an alignment. Based on their continued responses to real events, the players are eventually handed down judgment from on high: either good or bad. If you're good, you get to play the part of a flaming sword angel. If bad, you get the same job, only with better clothes.

In all honesty, the actual game itself is a waste of LINK-space. There is nothing new in this weak rip-off of the highly superior Toyoma Enterprises Heaven's War, whose back-story alone is worth ten Soul Stealers.

What this game has going for it is the creepy intro and the labyrinth that is human social interactions. The game designers have done something really jazz to get you hooked on their product: they actually let YOU tell the story. The focus of all the initial interactions with the game is based on deep personal memories: yours. You decide what places you'll return to, what haunts you, and what eventually draws you to act out in the world.

Intensely popular with teens, this game feeds the deep-seated need to be special. A random act can bring you into contact with the game's masters, the conscience. For some, it might be an angry outburst that ends in property damage. For others, it might be a gift of kindness to a homeless man. Whatever it is, it will be a real event in your life, and then suddenly, the next time you go back to the game (because you know you will—it's your nightmare/dream), They will be waiting for you with information on a rave near to you.

Be careful what you wear, because everything you do counts. If the conscience thinks you look trashy, that might be one more mark against (or for, depending on your bent) your alignment. In the end, this game is like all the awkward bits of high school on steroids.

The pressure to be "lisítse" is really intense, but that makes acceptance in the social club that much more sweet. If only the game itself had more follow-through.

Final Grade: B+

◻

CHAPTER 25

Emmaline

*S**atan is scowling at us.*

Water and soap still dripping from my face, I glanced up into the bathroom mirror. Victory was quite right. Morningstar stood with one narrow hip leaning against the door frame and his arms crossed in front of his naked chest. His long auburn hair was a mess of tangles. Chestnut-brown eyes squinted narrowly at me.

Beautiful, isn't he? I said, surprising myself by still being awed, after all this time, by the remarkable strangeness of having an angel for a lover. And not just any angel—the brightest, the best, the most handsome, the one who stole a piece of Heaven from God Himself. My Lucifer, the light-bearer, was clearly still loved by the Jerusalem sun. The light streaming in through the bedroom windows behind him traced a golden outline along the contours of his body. I smiled with the memory of him underneath me.

"You should be careful," he said in a low growl.

"Am I playing with fire?" I had to laugh just a little. Oh, and he didn't like that at all, by the color his face turned. Opening the cabinet, I broke eye contact and reached for my toothbrush. "It's too bad you're sterile. We could make beautiful children."

I heard the flutter of wings just before I felt myself crushed between the sink and his body. His hands were around my wrists, pulling me hard against him. I smiled at this old game and, engaging the combat computer, pushed against him to free myself. And pushed again. A tiny shiver of panic trembled along my muscles. *Victory*, I commanded, *obey me.*

I do. He holds us too strongly.

197

Not possible. A hiss of fear escaped from between my lips. *We've always been able to move him before.*

Perhaps he chose *to be moved.*

Morningstar's voice tickled my ears. "You are mortal, Emmaline McNaughton. I, it would be wise to remember, am *not.*"

A clap of thunder made me jump. Cold air rushed through the bathroom, sending magazines tumbling and towels flapping. I hugged myself in the sudden chill. Realizing Morningstar was gone, I snapped my head around, searching. There was no trace of him, except one pure white feather drifting slowly toward the floor.

I didn't see my lover for the rest of the day, but he had left me with dark, purpling bruises, like bracelets, around my wrists. Perseus stared at them, like a curious child. I made no move to hide them from anyone; in fact, due to the heat, I went without the long-sleeved armored jacket I usually wore.

"Are you ready to talk to the council about the People?" I asked Perseus.

Perseus sat in my kitchen devouring the last of the custard-filled pastries my interns had bought this morning. I watched as he licked the yellow goo from his fingertips. Perseus was ancient for a Gorgon. His pale face was cut deep with wrinkles, and his silver hair was thin in places. He dressed in a white *gi*, like some kind of freak guru, and wore a broken mirror shard around his neck.

"How old are you?" I asked when he hadn't answered.

"I'm not sure. Fifteen, maybe."

I poked at my own Danish, wondering when my cappuccino would arrive. "You weren't born a Gorgon, were you?"

His quicksilver eyes flashed up and he bared his fangs. "I chose to become one of the People."

"Why?"

He pointed to his head. "It's a higher consciousness."

"Yeah, right," I snorted. "And you can get away with murder." Which was nearly quite literally true. Gorgons weren't held to the same social standards as normal people. They were mostly feral, and we expected them to behave like animals. What they did in their own ghettos, the glass, was completely outside the law. If they killed each other, most law enforcement agencies figured the more the better. No one attempted to civilize them or even provide them with the basic necessities like food and clothing. They took what they wanted by theft, which was mostly tolerated by society, the way you shrug and curse when raccoons raid your garbage in the middle of the night.

"The People are truly free," Perseus said with a sage nod.

I took a contemplative sip of the coffee that had finally appeared at my elbow. I supposed there was some truth in that. Gorgons could behave however they liked, but, like animals, the majority of their day was not filled with leisure time in which they could contemplate their navel with carefree abandon. As far as I could tell, they were slaves to the same needs as the rest of us: food, water, shelter.

"Freedom to starve," I said. "Freedom to die."

"The same as you," Perseus said.

He's got a point there. Plenty of non-Gorgons starve to death every day.

Yes, thanks for that little sociopolitical reminder. I never realized that.

"Humph," Victory used my vocal cords to express her frustration with me. I let Perseus believe that was my final comment and said to him, "If you regard your freedom so highly, why do you want representation in the Order of the Inquisition?"

Perseus made a grab for my uneaten pastry. I put my hand down on it before he could snatch it. He said, "I think it's time for our culture to be recognized."

I laughed. "What culture? Childishness?"

Perseus stiffened. "The People have their own language, law, songs, religion."

"Religion? This is new."

"Only to you," he said defensively. "This is why I wanted your sponsorship for the Order. Humans need to recognize that the People are more than animals. We have our own gods."

I shook my head. "Do me a favor. Don't say 'gods' to the Order."

"Ah, but Grand Inquisitor Matsushita is not a monotheist."

"True, but try to think about what the press is going to say about this." I had turned off the usual camerabots so that Perseus and I could have a private meeting. Or, at least as private as possible, with the host of interns that buzzed around us. "You say that the Gorgons—the People—worship gods, they're going to brand you as pagans, heathens."

"And this is a bad thing? You yourself are now representing the atheists. Do not the Wiccans have political rights? Native Americans?"

I rubbed my head, trying to banish the headache that had sprouted between my eyes. "That is not the fight I want to get into. I've been talking you guys up to the press as the innocent children of God. We don't need anything that reminds people that you're just a bunch of lawless freaks."

Perseus's eyebrows perked up at that. "Perhaps we made a mistake allying ourselves with you."

"I think not," I said. "I have been your best advocate, and you know it."

He looked ready to protest, so I raised my hand, trying to call forth the thin bit of Will that flowed in my blood. I felt the tide of Fate swell up, and closing my eyes, I reached out to it. Everything stilled. A heavy quiet descended on the room. The tangy smell of patchouli drifted lightly in the air for a second, then was gone.

"I suppose it would be prudent to follow your lead in this matter," Perseus said.

"Good *choice*," I said, with a quiet smile.

You should not use your Will this way, Victory said.

Sometimes, I said, *you have to force people to make the right decision.*

¤ ¤ ¤

MEDUSA TEAM READY FOR TRIAL TEST

Many Scientists Worry This Is Too Soon

Agnostic Press (December 2095)

St Petersburg, Russia—Maxine Mann, speaking via mouse.net to the scientific community, says that her team is ready for an initial test. She said that by "working around the clock," her team has loaded up two nanoviruses. One is programmed to stop the Medusa glass from spreading. The second is poised to transform the current glass into something harmless "like sand," she claims.

Russian scientists not associated directly with the Medusa team say that they have verified that Mann's theory seems sound. "Without testing it, however," said Yuri Vladstov, "there's no telling if there will be any mutations, like with the first."

Mann is prepared to release her viruses in a controlled laboratory setting. However, she said that she would like the approval of the general scientific community before proceeding because, "in the past, I went forward without thinking. This time, I want my entire process to be supervised. You," Mann told the scientific community, "will be my conscience."

"Frankly, I don't want the job," said Luis Rodriguez, mathematician, from Harlem. He also expressed concern about the timing of this test. "It's too soon," Rodriguez said, echoing the sentiment of many of those polled by the *Agnostic Press*. "I can't believe they've locked and loaded already. It's only been a week, if that."

Mann counters these concerns by saying, "I have been thinking about the cure for the Medusa for nearly thirty years." She said, however, that she is willing to wait until everyone is satisfied—even, she said with a slight smile, "the mathematicians."

¤

CHAPTER 26

Amariah

Mouse never came back from the kitchen. I'd finished eating a while ago and had returned to my favorite chair. Papa sat with both arms stretched out along the back of the couch, like a parody of flying. Our dirty dishes were piled together on the coffee table—a casual mingling of our leftovers that struck me as overly familiar.

"So," I said, twirling white bits of my hair between my fingers, "I'm really going to be the messiah."

Papa shrugged. "I guess so."

"Well, what am I going to do?"

He shook his head. Pulling his arms down, he crossed them in front of his chest and leaned far back into the couch. "I wish I knew, Rye."

"Weren't you just God?"

Papa glanced at the doorway to the kitchen, then checked the watch on his wrist. "Listen, sweetie, I have to go back to work today. Do you think your mom would be pissed off if I had to leave without saying good-bye?"

I sputtered out a laugh. "No, why would she? I mean, yeah, go right ahead. Go back to work. You know, don't let me keep you or anything like that." Papa stood up. He actually fucking stood up to go. Running a hand through his short curls, he said, "Yeah, okay. Great."

Papa stopped when he saw my expression. Maybe it was the tears rolling down my cheeks that gave him pause.

"You have to understand, Rye, I wouldn't leave you, but I'm afraid. I'm afraid I'm already changing things. Things that were set in motion, you know? Stuff you're supposed to do on your own."

"I can't believe it," I sobbed. "You don't even seem to care about me, about us. I can't believe you're the same guy who killed himself to save me."

"I'm not." His voice was strong, steady, but I could hear the sadness in it. "I am Their servant, fashioned afresh for each new duty. I am nothing before being, and nothing after. I exist only at Their will."

"Can't you disobey? Ariel says that once here you have flesh and free will." Papa regarded me for a long moment. Then he knelt down beside me and put a warm, roughly calloused hand on my arm. His face was inches from my own. "I am the perfect soldier, Amariah. I obey without question."

"You didn't used to," I protested. "Once...once you stayed for Mom and me."

His jaw flexed, and he glanced heavenward guiltily. Leaning close, he whispered. "I want to. I can't."

"God won't let you?"

Papa's lips pursed; I was close enough that I could see him suppress a tremble. He looked so scared that I threw my arms around him. For a second, we both held our breath, until he reciprocated the hug. "I'm so sorry," he breathed into my ear.

"What...what would God do to you if you...disobeyed? Could He, would He, you know, kill you?"

Papa pulled back so that he could look me in the eye. "God and I made a covenant, a very serious promise. If I tell you, you can*not* tell your mother about this," he said.

I almost laughed through my tears. It was such a "dad" thing to say. "Okay," I schooled my expression and agreed solemnly. "Okay."

"You can't tell anyone." He glanced at the kitchen door nervously, then whispered hurriedly, "I traded it in, Rye, for the new order. If I play it straight, act the part, do my last duty, then no more. You understand? No more."

"No more?"

He nodded, a smile glinting in his eyes. "Grounded."

"You'd stop being an..."

He stopped me by putting his finger gently on my lips.

"Yes," he said. "Forever."

"But why?"

Papa grinned wildly. "For you, of course. For you and your mom."

The winter storm rattled the window. "Then you better go," I told him.

I watched through the window as Papa got into the squad car. I stayed, with my chin resting on the back of the wingback chair, until the car was no more than a speck and had faded into the swirling white snowstorm. Despite my promise, I knew I had to find a way to tell Mom everything he'd said.

INCOMING CALL.

"Who the hell could that be?" I wondered as I mentally flipped the go-ahead switch. A window popped open and revealed a dark-haired boy with a hawkish nose dressed all in white. *"Adram? How did you get this number?"*

Adram was grinning ear to ear. *"I got the invite, Rye, and I want you to be there!"*

"What are you talking about? Aren't you already in the game?"

"Sure, but we're talking about a new level. I get to be one of them," Adram said. *"And, listen, it's all because of you. The arrest. Turns out that scored me major points. I can't wait. We get to meet them tonight."*

I stared at the door to the kitchen, imagining Mom's ears perking up. Though there was no way she could hear me subvocalizing, I whispered, *"We? Them?"*

"Yeah. Can you get away?" Adram's eyes were round and pleading like a puppy dog's. Then he looked away, suddenly shy. *"It's just that it wouldn't seem right. I mean, you were there. And, well—"* Adram glanced up. His gaze was full of a different kind of longing. *"I wanted to see you again."*

No guy had ever looked at me like that before. Hell, no guy had ever bothered to track down my LINK address before, much less call me up and ask me out.

"What time?" I couldn't believe I was asking that. I knew this was such a bad idea.

He looked relieved and elated. *"In a couple of hours, actually. But, maybe we could get together before then? Hang out?"*

"You can pick me up here. In Harlem." I gave Adram Luis's address and immediately began plotting a way to get out of the house. *"Okay. Um, see you then."*

The smile Adram gave me made me shiver, but in a weird way, like I was both excited and nervous to know what he was thinking about. *"Yeah."*

With that, he hung up. I sat on the chair with my knees pulled up to my chin, savoring the feeling.

I had a date. A real date.

□ □ □

GORGONS APPROACH ORDER

Request for Representation Leads to Inquisitorial Feud

The Apocalypse Watch, Fundamentalist Press (December 2095)

Jerusalem, Israel—Speaking via external hardware to the Council of the Order of the Inquisition from Monsignor Emmaline McNaughton's headquarters in Jerusalem, Perseus, the self-appointed spokesperson for "the People" (as those mutated by the Medusa prefer to be called), appealed for representation. Perseus made the case that, although short-lived, the Gorgons needed spiritual guidance as much as any other people on the planet. He likened the People to the soul of a newborn in need of baptism. "The Medusa didn't make us," he said. "God did."

Christiandom Inquisitor Abebe Uwawah from Nigeria was visibly moved by the speech and vowed to do what she could in order to help the Gorgon cause. The council, for the first time in years, was not unanimously in agreement. Grand Inquisitor Joji Matsushita surprised the LINKed audience by suggesting that this matter was outside the jurisdiction of the United Order. "I think the Order has lost sight of its mission," Matsushita said. "We represent all people, mutated or not, if they are a member of our respective religions. If one of the People was Jewish and needed lawful representation, I'm certain my Jewish colleagues would do so. Now that the agnostics and atheists have an Inquisitor, they can appeal to her."

McNaughton countered Matsushita's pronouncement by noting that the Gorgons have their own culture and religion that is not agnostic nor atheistic, but merely falls outside of the norm. She reminded the Order that they similarly don't represent many American Indian tribes or other aboriginal peoples. "Perhaps the Grand Inquisitor makes an excellent point," McNaughton said at the end of a lengthy argument. "The People really don't need Inquisitor approval to seek legal recourse. They can do that through their local secular governments."

McNaughton's comment sparked a frenzy of debate regarding the function of the Inquisition. The Order of the Inquisition began as an offshoot of the former secular peacekeeping force known as the International Police or Interpol. Interpol's main function was to capture criminals who crossed national borders. The Inquisition shares Interpol's breadth, but now has a lot more power. They have been likened to the religious police, or, in some circles, "thought police."

"The Order should be eliminated," McNaughton said as she and Perseus disconnected forcibly from the debate. "The Inquisition is becoming what it once was during the witch-hunt era—too powerful and too unchecked. It needs to be stopped."

¤

CHAPTER 27

Deidre

Mouse and I emerged from the spare bedroom to find an empty house. We hunted all over the small apartment for signs of life and eventually surmised that Luis and Ariel had gone off together somewhere. The master bedroom door was shut, and neither Mouse nor I was brave enough to actually open the door to find out if anyone was inside. I put my ear to the wood for a long moment, though, and it was quiet.

Amariah, at least, had left a note scribbled on a napkin on the table: "Gone home. Don't worry about me." The *don't* had been underlined several times. Of course, that made me worried that she was off doing something incredibly stupid. I told myself I would call the kibbutz and check on her in a couple of hours.

Michael was nowhere to be found.

"Typical," I muttered. "Just when I wanted to ask Ariel something, he vanishes. When I don't want to see him, he's always underfoot."

Mouse didn't answer. He had his head stuck in Luis's solar-powered refrigerator, apparently hunting up something more to eat. Once he procured a crisp-looking apple, he munched on it and said, "If you want to ask someone about souls, you should talk to the expert."

"The Vatican?"

"No, Page. He's been fairly obsessed with them ever since McNaughton was sent to find out if he had one."

"What did she discover?" I'd had a newborn attached to my hip, if not my breast, twenty-four hours a day during that time. I missed a few newsfeeds.

"He does." When I opened my mouth, Mouse raised a hand in a preemptive gesture. "Don't ask me how. I'm a wizard, not a theologian."

It was a good idea, but Page's new persona made me uncomfortable. "Why don't you talk to him? You're his father."

"He looks less like me every day," Mouse said. He chewed on the apple for a moment, then said, "Okay, so neither of us is really into the idea of talking to Strife. How about the dragon?"

"The yakuza dragon?"

Mouse's eyes lit up. "You've never met the dragon, have you? Oh, you'd like her, Dee. Come on, I'll introduce you."

Mouse and I appeared on a sandy beach. A wide, sluggish river wound through steep cliffs. Apparently it was after dark in Japan, because the moonlight danced on the waves of the datastream. On the breeze was the scent of rotting fish and the buzz of mosquitoes. Mouse held what looked like a mahjongg tile in his hand, which he tossed into the waves that washed against our feet.

"There's a lot more formality here," I noted. *"Should I have brought a gift?"*

"It'll be cool," Mouse said.

After a few moments, two dots of light hovered over the water. They looked like a whirling copper wire. Then, a small, wedge-shaped snout sniffed at the air. *"This one is very busy,"* a prim voice said. *"Is that Mouse?"*

Mouse waved. *"Hey, Dragon!"*

"If she's busy," I said into Mouse's ear, signifying a private exchange. *"We should come back."*

"Hey, Dragon," Mouse said, completely ignoring me, *"there's someone I want you to meet. We want to ask you about a game."*

Everything went quiet. I couldn't even hear the insects whizzing by my ear anymore. I thought for a second that maybe the dragon had decided she had better things to do than meet a friend of Mouse's. Then the cutest little dragon I'd ever seen popped up out of the shallows. On all fours, she stood no bigger than an Irish setter. Her scales glittered an almost neon green, reminding me of the color of the old-fashioned motherboards. Talons and teeth shone with an oily silvery sheen. If it wasn't for the sharpness of her claws, she'd have looked sweet enough to hug.

"Merciful Allah!" Mouse exclaimed. *"What happened to you?"*

"Downsized," the little dragon said. *"Literally."*

"That's not right," Mouse said, with a tsk of his tongue. *"You've got rights."*

"Page said the same thing," she said with a close-mouthed grin.

I cleared my electronic throat by pinging Mouse a reminder that I was standing beside him.

"Oh, right. I've been rude," he said. *"This is Deidre. Deidre McMannus."*

"Pleasure," dragon said, holding out a paw.

I had to bend down to shake, but her grip was fierce as we exchanged profiles and protocols. I got the impression she had been a powerful creature very recently.

"Please. About the game," she insisted after the formalities were finished.

"Well," I said, sitting down in a half-lotus on the sand so that we could be eye-to-eye. I indicated with my hand that Mouse should join me. *"Mouse suggested that you might know if it would be possible to trap a soul inside a game—or in any kind of program."*

"Is that what it's doing?" she asked, her eyes snapping with electricity.

"Perhaps," I said. *"We've come across some victims—I suppose that's the best word—who seem to, be completely stripped of their free will. They're like zombies."*

Dragon shook the water from her haunches. *"There is something wrong with one of the children in the program,"* she said. *"It seems stronger than the others. More capable of bending reality, controlling things. It tried to eat me."*

"You?" Mouse asked.

"Terrible, isn't it?" dragon continued. *"The creche is poisoned. I was just going to go to the archives to see what I could find out about it."*

"Wait," I said. *"Are you saying that Toyoma Enterprises is the designer of the game? The yakuza is using its children?"*

"Of course," Mouse said before dragon could answer. *"It makes perfect sense. They're ten times more powerful than any AI. No offense, dragon, but they're living minds. Think of the power they would have to draw out memories, to make them real."*

I watched dragon while Mouse spoke. She nodded and her wings drooped sadly.

"You don't want it to be true, do you?" I asked her.

She blinked balefully at me. *"Are people being hurt?"*

"I'm afraid so," I said. *"But I'm still not convinced any of this is possible. The program children might have the firepower to give the game its realism, but what about the magic? Memories aren't stored on the LINK. They're somewhere in the chemicals or biology of your brain. And then there's the matter of the soul. If such a thing even exists, how do they grab hold of it and steal it?"*

"The child," the dragon repeats. *"Maybe it is the key."*

The three of us ended up going to the yakuza archives together. Dragon walked us boldly past sentries and ninja guard programs. I held my breath, though none of them even blinked or lifted a finger to try to stop us.

"Too easy," Mouse muttered.

"You're thinking like a cracker," I told him. *"This is dragon's home."*

The archives appeared like a shrine. High walls surrounded us, but several large archways were open to the night air. Silk flapped in the breeze. The fabric had been painted with a twisting image of a whiskered green dragon. Actually, it looked a bit more like a snake to me, but the resemblance to our host was obvious.

I had been expecting a dusty room full of books or, considering the Asian motif, maybe hand-painted scrolls, but the shrine was bare except for a well. A knee-high circle of stones marked where it stood in the center of the room. Laid across two thick, sun-faded wooden poles was a beam of steel. Rope wound around it, and a pail hung in the center. Dragon scampered up to it and dove in headfirst.

Mouse and I ran up to the well and stared down into the inky darkness. *"Anything?"* Mouse called.

"Give her some time," I said.

"Why? She's a computer. She can sift through thousands of bits of information in the time it takes me to sneeze."

"She's smaller now," I reminded him.

"Oh," he said, looking crestfallen. Turning back to the well, he yelled down, *"You're doing great! Take your time."*

I shook my head at him. He really could be very sweet.

Dragon's nose nudged my elbow. Her eyes snapped, spitting sparks. *"There is a clone in the program."*

"A clone? Whose?" I asked.

"Emmaline McNaughton."

"No shit" Mouse breathed. *"Why her?"*

"She's been a friend of my family's for years," came a silky voice behind us. *"It was a favor for a childless woman."*

I whirled around to see a cuddly yellow bear. Unlike the rest of the room, the avatar was rendered as though it were flat animation. Bold lines demarked fur and round, cartoonish eyes. It looked goofy, cute. Not dangerous at all. So, I wasn't quite sure why a shiver ran down my spine until I heard Mouse swear.

"Fuck me," Mouse said. *"Kioshi."*

Unlike the dragon, we could unplug in a flash. Though I'd wanted to ask Kioshi questions about Emmaline's clone, I knew better than to get into grilling the world's most powerful mob boss while standing, uninvited, in the heart of his own infrastructure. I felt bad about leaving dragon to face her angry boss, but there was no way to take her with us.

The hard boot made my head throb. The light in the living room sent arrows of sharp pain through my eyeballs right to the back of my brain, it seemed. I hobbled up and shut the curtain.

Mouse sat on the couch holding his head in his hands. "Dragon's in trouble," he said through a knot of fingers. "We're in trouble."

"I know." If only we'd thought to disguise our avatars, maybe Kioshi wouldn't know exactly who had broken into his lair.

"We should probably stay off-line for while."

I gave him my best come-hither look through squinty, bloodshot eyes. "Any ideas what we should do in the meantime."

"Yeah," he said, rubbing his head. "Nap."

So I tucked Mouse into the guest bedroom and poured myself a cup of coffee as salve for my aching head. I sat down in Luis's kitchen and plucked the brown dead leaves off his lemon thyme plant while I thought.

Emmaline McNaughton had a clone inside the yakuza's program. A creepy bit of news, certainly, but not really an explanation for all the hocus-pocus goings-on with the game. Unless. Unless her association with Morningstar somehow gave her access to angelic powers.

I should be so lucky. I got Amariah out of my "association," which was fairly high on the fantastic miracle scale, but it wasn't like I could go pulling people's souls out of their bodies just because I had had an angelic lover. Maybe sleeping with Satan came with different perks.

INCOMING CALL. My LINK buzzed. I worried for a moment that it might be the yakuza trying to track me down, so before answering it I sent out a trace. It came tagged for the New York Police Department, Michelangelo Angelucci, Lieutenant.

"Lieutenant," I said as I flipped the go-ahead. *"What can I do for you?"*

"I can't stay away" he said, his voice scratchy with longing. *"I know I promised, but I just can't. Tell me we can meet somewhere. Now."*

I wanted to deny him. I wanted to tell him forget about it, I'd found somebody new. But the look in his eyes was so hungry, so—God help me—sexy. *"Why should I?"* I asked. *"What can you possibly do for me?"*

"Stay."

How did he know the one word that would get me off my butt and out the door?

❑ ❑ ❑

DONATION CAUSES SPECULATION

Is Morningstar a Wife-Beater?

Agnostic Press (December 2095)

Tallahassee, Florida—Monsignor Emmaline McNaughton's donation of a Christmas dinner with all of the trimmings to several American battered-women's shelters had an unintended side effect this afternoon. Following so closely on the heels of a sex scandal involving her husband, McNaughton's generosity raised suspicion among some in the media. Several reporters pointedly asked McNaughton about whether or not there was any significance to the gifts and about bruises that appeared on her wrists.

"These are old," McNaughton said of the hand-shaped bruises that encircled her wrists. "I don't even remember what caused them." Morningstar was notably absent from his usual place at her side. McNaughton also seemed unusually flustered at the barrage of questions and hung up her LINK connection early, claiming to have a headache.

Medical experts believe that the only thing that could have caused such bruises on an Inquisitor with the cybernetic augmentations that McNaughton has would be another enhanced Inquisitor. "Or one seriously strong guy," said Dr. Garcia Smith. "Maybe some-one with an exoskeleton, but I don't know. Those looked like finger marks to me. Most exos don't extend that far down."

Visual re-creation shows that there is a strong possibility that the finger marks do belong to Morningstar. Forensic scientists say that by using models based on 3-D, LINK images of Morningstar's hands, they can line up the marks perfectly. However, it is not believed that Morningstar is cybernetically enhanced. "Maybe he could have gotten some equip-ment during the war," said Dr. Smith. "But there would be medical records of that. Or at least a history of service."

"It's a mystery," said one forensic expert. "But there's no way she could have done it to herself. No way."

¤

CHAPTER 28

Dragon

One is suddenly alone with one's master. The wind whistles through the open archways. The banners whip frantically in the sudden breeze. Across the shrine, the yellow cartoon narrows his eyes, his arms held away from his round, pudgy body. One almost expects showdown music to appear.

"I can explain," one says.

"I?" For some reason Kioshi's avatar's tail snaps up sharply and flicks back and forth. One has never decided if he is supposed to be a cat or a mouse or a bear with a prehensile tail or what. Today he seems a bit like a squat, squash-colored monkey.

"Yes," I continue. *"I was worried about the children. When this one went to visit the creche, one felt a strange presence. This clone, I think, is bad."*

"You think? You were worried?" One dips one's head slightly. *"One knows it is not one's place to comment on the keeping of the children, but, master, things are not right there."*

"I know," Kioshi says. *"Let's go for a walk."*

When Kioshi requests a "walk," he means outside. The only way a creature like this one can interact with the real-time Kioshi is to enter the LINK-space of a "rider." Riders wear a neuro-net that allows one, or a potential artificial, to move their body and to experience the world through their eyes. Riders are how this one knows what one does about the physical world.

I spent much of my proto-consciousness housed in the net of my creator, Mai. Toyoma Corporation has been attempting to re-create the accident of my

212

consciousness since the day that this one passed the Turing Test. Though they have come close, so far I am the only dragon in the service of the yakuza.

Riders are program children who grew up. Kioshi keeps them close at hand to serve as breeding grounds for AI potentials. They are ideal for this work because their minds are more attuned to the LINK-space, and they have extra, internal sensors that allow one to feel physical responses to emotions, smell odors, taste the various edible pleasurable things that the outside has to offer.

It is usually a great *treat* to walk with Kioshi.

This time, however, one finds oneself wary, cautious. In fact, one takes extra time with the usual protocols. One discovers that one's rider's name is Takeo Nomura. He is twenty-one and was born to Toyoma Enterprises. When he is not transporting nascent AIs, he answers phones for the company. A receptionist. The rider is not a trained ninja nor even a member of a yakuza motorcycle gang. For some reason, such information screams "disposable" to this one, so one double-, then triple-checks the back door for easy access should the need arise.

Once ready, one steps into the net. The process of entering is a little like walking into a darkened house and moving from room to room flicking on lights. With a twitch, one feels muscles contract. One can feel the pressure of clothes against skin—a cotton shirt that strains ever so slightly with each intake of breath, the weight of denim against thighs, and the even coolness of a metal watchband against warm flesh.

Then one tastes the remains of tuna sushi on one's tongue, mingling with the bitterness of American coffee. Behind us, one hears the hiss of steam in a teakettle and smells the greenness of leaves brewing.

With a blink, vision snaps on. One sits across from a small metal desk. There is a felt-covered round cup with a number of colorful, fat fountain pens arranged like ikebana inside it. There is a blotter that covers most of the surface area. It is mostly blank, but in the right-hand corner are doodles of anime-style characters with huge eyes, bushes of hair, and tiny, bumplike noses. There are no papers or other clutter on the desk, just a Tiffany lamp that casts squares of blue and green light onto the desk.

Just beyond sits a man who looks to be in his late thirties. His straight black hair parts on the side and is cut short, above his ears. On the tip of his pug nose balance square-framed glasses, the lenses of which are the color of a dusky rose. Thin and angular, he looks healthy, trim, and athletic. His skin is a golden color that the indirect lighting flatters.

Though it always takes a moment, one recognizes the man as Kioshi Toyoma. Kioshi is always younger than one expects, and he never dresses like one might assume the most powerful yakuza boss in the Eastern Hemisphere would. In fact, he, like the rider, wears blue jeans. It's shocking, really, especially since he has no tie. Instead, he wears a short-sleeved cotton shirt advertising some American university. One can see the old-fashioned flat tattoos covering his arms, like an undershirt.

At least he's clean-shaven.

"You look as though I disappoint you," Kioshi says. His voice is smooth and deeper than I remember.

"Never," this one replies with Takeo's voice.

"Hmm," Kioshi says. Steepling his fingers, he taps them against thin lips. A single dark eyebrow flashes up for a moment before he continues. "You've been changing, dragon."

This is not an observation one expected. One crosses Takeo's arms across his slender chest and leans back into the foam cushion of the chair. "Really?"

"Oh, yes," he says, with a little laugh that does not seem at all to this one as though it is filled with amusement. "The old dragon would not have brought strangers into the belly of my beast. *She* would not have betrayed me quite so casually."

"I did not betray you."

"No?"

"No, as I told my master, this one was there to investigate a problem with the creche," I said, though it was a bit of a lie. Takeo's body responds. His heart beats faster, and the sweat glands under his arms prick with sudden moisture.

Kioshi's gaze is steady. He removes his hands from in front of his face and folds them precisely, deliberately in his lap. "'I,' 'This one'—which is it?"

The blood drains from Takeo's face. He blinks rapidly. "Both. You see, this one," his voice rises as if he can't quite believe what this one has asked him to say, "is trying something new."

"I can't say that I like it." Kioshi reaches to a narrow table beside the desk where the teapot has been bubbling. Pouring himself a cup of steaming water, he goes through the motions of preparing tea. Takeo's fingers twitch with nervous energy as Kioshi stirs and steeps.

"No?" one finally says to break the silence.

"No," Kioshi says, tapping the spoon meaningfully on the edge of the china cup. "Not at all."

One isn't certain what to say to that. Takeo's nose itches, so one rubs it for him.

"Tell me about these strangers whom you allowed to roam around in my archives."

214

It seems imprudent to mention that this one only just met one of them and that the other was an infamous criminal hacker. "It was a tour," Takeo's voice cracks. "Of the company."

"Even if that were true, dragon, I would never allow the public access to the archives of the program. You know that. Try again."

"Mouse."

Kioshi nods his head slowly as if encouraging me. "And?"

"A friend of his?"

Kioshi's finger traces the edge of one eyebrow. His mouth presses into a thin line. He looks pained. "Please tell me you at least learned her name before you opened up all of our secrets to her."

"I did." Takeo's voice almost quakes now. But one forces him to take a deep breath. "But master, I did all the digging. She is not important. She told me what you're doing. She told me about the game."

Another cold laugh escapes from his lips. "And you say she's not important? Dragon, I must beg to differ. I would really, sincerely, like to know who she is."

"No," I manage to get Takeo's trembling lips to say. "I don't think so. Not until you tell me why you allow this game to sully our empire, master. Explain to me why you permit yourself to be McNaughton's pawn."

Kioshi had been about to take a sip of tea, but stops. He bangs the cup down so sharply that Takeo flinches. I must consciously place the hands Takeo raised in front of his face slowly back into our lap.

Removing his spectacles with a flourish, Kioshi peers at us. Bright blue eyes bore into us, as if trying to pin this one down inside Takeo's skull. "What did you just say?"

Each word is enunciated as if it is its own sentence. Kioshi's voice is loud, but controlled. "What did you just say?"

"This one will keep secret the visitor's identity until you answer the questions."

"Dragon." Kioshi leans his elbows on the blotter and hunches forward. "I don't believe you remember which one of us is the master."

"But I do." One inclines Takeo's head slightly in Kioshi's direction. But when one straightens up, one takes careful control of his voice, his gaze, and makes them stern and clear. "This one has been made acutely aware of how little and insignificant this one is. This one also knows that one has been downsized in service of this game."

"Everything you do should be in service to me."

"Not this time," I say. Then, as an afterthought, I add, "Master."

Kioshi studies Takeo intently. Then he sits back slightly and takes a sip from his nearly forgotten teacup. "Have you been infected with a virus, dragon? Has Mouse done something to you?"

"No." Takeo's voice is almost a whisper. A tear wells at the corner of his eye. "You have."

"Me?"

"Yes." Takeo's head nods slowly.

"The downsizing." Kioshi sighs curtly, as if exasperated with a child. "I expected you would take it hard. I just thought this would happen in reverse. That there would be a tantrum and then you'd come to accept it. Instead, you wait until now to throw your fit."

Takeo clamps down hard on his lips. I make him frown very deeply. One minute Kioshi treats us like a betraying soldier, the next like a little kid. "Would you feel better if I rebooted an older version of you?" Kioshi says with a cluck-cluck of his tongue. "At least that dragon has yet to betray me."

If Kioshi reanimated an earlier copy of myself, what would become of me? Normally, the LINK defaults to the newest version of a program. But Page was stronger than Victory in the end, and the old dragon would have the yakuza behind her.

Would my new identity be subsumed in hers? Could our consciousnesses even exist together? I didn't know. The instant this one shed old skin it died, became like the statues in the garden. My consciousness seemed to be a singular thing.

Curiosity gets the better of one. "Could you do that?"

Kioshi's eyes roam along the contours of Takeo's body ominously, pausing in places long enough to make us look to see what he stared at. "Page copied himself inside a neuro-net."

"Not completely," one corrects. Takeo's hands rub absently at the sparkling fabric covering his arm. "Victory was quite corrupt."

"But she functions as an AI."

"You couldn't be certain," I insist. "This one used to be a very large animal. Though my body has shrunk, my mind has not."

Kioshi contemplates me like one might a piece on a chessboard. Through our eyes, the way his pupils flick back and forth, they seem to be calculating moves, consequences. Takeo's skin crawls. One feels very examined.

With a sigh, Kioshi takes a sip of his tea. "I'm afraid you leave me no choice, then."

"Oh?"

216

Kioshi leans off to the side as if reaching for something out of view. One hears the sound of a desk drawer creaking open. The rider's body jerks, and one feels his consciousness try to surface. At first one thinks there is something wrong with the body, that the rider is having seizures, so one struggles to regain control. Thus, it is almost too late when one notices the gleaming barrel of the gun in Kioshi's hand. An explosive crack rings in Takeo's ears. In the semidarkness, one can see a bright flare. Then, the body is falling backward, the chair tipping with the momentum of the bullet. Wires spark. Metal screeches as the connection is rent in two. Hot blood pumps from the center of Takeo's forehead.

Then darkness, like a curtain, descends.

¤ ¤ ¤

EMMALINE MCNAUGHTON

Savior or Sinner? A Gay Christian's Perspective

Agnostic Press (December 2095)

James Baldwin Camp, Tennessee—Much has been written in the Fundamentalist Press about the role of Monsignor Emmaline McNaughton in the end-times. She has been vying for top spot on the Antichrist Watch List with people like the Dragon of the East, the Gorgon Perseus, and Anton LeLand of France.

The most compelling biblical evidence that McNaughton is the "prince with a plan" is the description of the Antichrist in Revelation 17:9 in which we are given the image of a woman who sits upon "seven mountains." This passage has long been associated with Rome and its seven hills. Revelation goes on to mention that this woman would be decked out in "purple and scarlet," the colors of the current papacy, with which McNaughton is still associated, even though she is listed as a rogue Inquisitor. McNaughton is also ethnically Italian, and she has a pedigree that may very well extend back to the destroyer of Jerusalem and the Temple in 70 A.D., Titus Vespasian. This, along with her current political stance against theocracy, paints a very compelling picture of the Antichrist in our times.

Having met her, I must disagree.

McNaughton has devoted much of her political career to a very unsavory cause. She has been a proponent of gay, lesbian, bisexual, polyamorous, and transgender rights. Many Christians are quick to point out that the Bible cautions that two men should not lie down together. However, it should be noted that the very same book later admonishes a good Jew not to eat pork. We are Christians, not Jews. So we should look to Jesus for answers regarding the gay question. When asked what the most important law was, Jesus said love. Love your neighbor as your brother.

Jesus told the parable of the good Samaritan, suggesting that we should judge people by their actions, not by their ethnicity or their social, economic, or religious class. Similarly, He kept beside Him many "undesirables," such as tax collectors and prostitutes.

What McNaughton does is brave and Christian.

Many will point to the fact that McNaughton has been living a Christ-like life as further evidence that she is a false prophet. To which, I can only reply: Where is the line? If Jesus were to appear today, would He also be branded a false prophet for acting too much like Jesus?

¤

CHAPTER 29

Morningstar

Scaring Emmaline had made me feel a tiny bit better. The trip to Hell, however, had left me battered and bruised. When I "fell," I transformed the very nature of the celestial reality. I made a space all my own, separate from God. Among all the heavenly creatures, my Will was the only one strong enough notv to merge with God when the flesh was rent. All others returned to Heaven, but not me. Hell was not a place for immortal souls, nor the realm of demons. It was mine alone.

And I hated it.

I came to with my face pressed into dirty snow and a concrete gutter.

Wherever I was, it was colder than Hell. Of course, I was naked. Snowflakes clung to my skin and my hair, melting into icy rivulets. Pulling myself up on all fours, I found myself in front of a church. It struck me as American, although I couldn't tell you exactly why I thought so. Maybe it didn't seem old or battered enough to be European. Or perhaps it was the space around it, a wide-open empty flatness to its left that could only have been an unplowed car park. It seemed to me that land got wasted like this only in the New World.

A neon marquee in front of the church confirmed my suspicions. In English, it said, LOST SOULS WELCOME, at Saint somebody or other's. Another little bit of Mother's humor, no doubt, but I intended to take Her up on it. With all my energy, I pushed myself up onto my feet and stumbled up the slippery, ice-covered steps to the door.

I had just raised my hand to knock when the door squeaked open on rusty hinges. A black-suited priest with gray hair that might once have been blond looked surprised to see a naked man standing on his doorstep. "Seems I'm looking for a handout, Father," I told him before he could speak. "Do you have any spare Armani?"

"Morningstar?"

I smacked my forehead. Of course, my fame preceded me. "Yes, it's me. Alert the media. Perhaps the headlines could read: 'Found Naked in...' where am I?"

"New York," the priest said dryly.

"'Found Naked in New York.' Yes, that has a nice ring to it." My bare feet stuck to the ice. "Mind if I come in?"

"You think I'm going to let Satan cross my threshold?"

This was one seriously perceptive priest. I looked into his eyes, trying to see an angel there, but decidedly mundane blues stared grimly back. That begged the question "Do I know you?"

"We met once, years ago," the priest said, as if that explained everything. I continued to stare dumbly at him. Finally, he added, "Eion McMannus."

I had a vague recollection of a McMannus that Michael had been overly fond of. God had sent me to test her faith, Job style. I still couldn't believe I'd let myself do His dirty work, even on a contract basis like that. Those kinds of alliances never won me anything.

The priest looked expectant, waiting for recollection to dawn for me. It didn't.

"Yes," I lied. "Of course, I remember you."

"Then you'll understand why I have to do this."

He started to slam the door shut, but I grabbed the edge of it before he could. I leaned very closely into his face and said, "What you do to the least of us, you do to me."

Eion paled at the words of Jesus, but held firm. "You must be joking."

"Did you not see me fall? Did you not hear the thunderclap? God brought me to you, Eion McMannus. Now let me in."

Turns out the noise of my fall *had* been what brought Eion to the door. Apparently, he'd seen it all from his study—the sky opening up, my body plummeting like so much deadweight, and the unceremonious smackdown onto the pavement.

No wonder I preferred to fly commercial.

Actually, I hated that too. Anything that involved being in the air under someone else's command set my teeth on edge.

Much like the church-basement coffee Eion brewed for me. An oily film floated on the bitter, dark liquid in the cup in front of me. Still, I had to thank him. He'd not only found clothes in my size but also gave me a hot shower.

The borrowed outfit could not be called haute couture—a sweatshirt from Georgetown University's track and field program, jeans with a hole in one knee, running shoes that had seen much better days-but the socks were warm and the underwear clean. The only annoying thing about the gifts was the way Eion begrudged them all and hovered over me, anxious for me to leave.

"One last favor," I said, "and I'll be out of your hair, Father."

He eyed me quite skeptically before inclining his head for me to continue.

"A wrist-phone? Seems mine disintegrated in Hell, and if I'm going to get home to Israel, I need to book a flight." Not to mention have access to my Swiss bank account.

With a sigh, Eion stripped the one off his wrist. "Here," he said, fiddling with a few buttons to deprogram his personal information from it. "Take mine. God knows I've never used it."

"I'm sure He appreciates your sacrifice," I said, lingering over the pronoun, milking it.

"Harrumph," Eion said, as he got up to give me some privacy.

I sat at his desk in his study. The rectory was a separate house, just behind the church. It was small, compact, and very male. That is to say Eion had the kind of fashion sense that only thought to line up his sparse, utilitarian furniture along bare white walls. One picture hung on the wall above his desk. It was a hologram of the sad-eyed praying Jesus, the frame of which was so dusty that I could only hope it had been left by the previous occupant.

As I familiarized myself with his phone and put in my own settings, I happened to glance down at the notes he had scribbled on the pad lying open on the desk. A sermon on charity. How appropriate, I smiled.

I made quick calls to the bank and the airport and had my flight booked and my pockets lined in no time. While I was at it, I decided to check my in-box. I think perhaps I was hoping for an apology from Emmaline. Instead, I found a curious response to my global message.

"My lord, it's Adramelech. You won't believe who I just saw." Adramelech was one of my chief commanders, lord of some eighth hell or something, in charge of my wardrobe, and other such frivolous titles. Since none of them could go to Hell, it wasn't like it mattered. Even so, the Fallen had carved it up as if it were some kind of precious real estate.

I hadn't seen him in ages. He looked scruffier and in serious need of a haircut. He also seemed to have developed a penchant for the color white.

Adramelech appeared to be in jail. Behind his image I could clearly see a watchful police officer.

"The captain. Michael. He's a cop," Adramelech said, moving conspiratorially closer to the image projector. "And you'll never guess what else. He has a daughter."

Well, this was news. Angelic offspring weren't as uncommon as you might think. All of the Fallen were, like myself, incapable of creation—sterile. However, angels of various lower orders wandered the earth from time to time and got distracted by matters of the flesh. But Michael—he was another story. He was an archangel. This daughter of his would be significant; she could well be the messiah Raphael mentioned.

"I'm arranging to meet her again," Adramelech continued. "Will keep you posted."

I checked the time, date, and place stamp. He'd called last night...from New York.

I figured the best way to find a cop was to go to the source. I took the subway to downtown Manhattan and wandered into police headquarters. Sauntering confidently up to the Plexiglas window, I asked the uniform behind the desk, "I'm here to see Michael Angelucci?"

"What's your business with him?"

"That's between us."

The cop looked highly suspicious. "Aren't you Emmaline McNaughton's boyfriend?"

"Yes," I said. "And Michael's half brother."

The cop squinted at me, and I saw the flash of red as he took my retina scan. Less than twenty seconds later, he apologized profusely. "It's just that we get a lot of freaks," he said, offering me cup of dreadful-smelling coffee. "We've got to be cautious. Michael said he'd be here in ten."

The uniform showed me to a private room with a window that looked out over the pedestrian tunnel. I guessed it to be a staff lounge of some sort, as a long wooden table and several chairs dominated the space. Posters on the wall advertised information about the police officers' union and departmental softball teams. A coffeemaker filled with the ubiquitous foul brown liquid sat on a rickety-looking end table under the window.

"Thank you," I said, sipping the tepid stuff graciously. I was only glad I wouldn't have long to wait.

Michael did not look happy to see me. "This better be good, Sammael. I've got a woman waiting for me."

"Your daughter or your lover?"

"My lover," he said.

Michael, I was sorry to say, was looking *good*. I'd heard various things about Michael over the years, my favorite of which was that he'd gotten stuck on earth and was wandering around in the guise of an insane, homeless preacher. I'd seen him, briefly, during those years. He'd been like a lost puppy, claiming that he'd fallen from grace. He'd even looked to *me* to save him. The very best thing about him then was that he had been easy to confuse, easy to subdue.

This Michael looked strong, confident.

And, I was horrified to discover, better dressed than I was.

Plainclothes-police-officer fashion suited him. It allowed him to wear that gleaming silver shield at his hip, which accented the slenderness of his waist. The jeans and the T-shirt were just tight enough to show off muscles without straying into trashy. The gun and cuffs hanging off his belt were almost overkill on the testosterone.

Ugh. I hated him.

"How old is your daughter now?" I asked.

"Sixteen, I think." He frowned at me from where he stood in the doorway, one foot out in the hallway, seemingly ready to run back to that lover of his.

"Young for a messiah."

I had completely captured Michael's attention now. He took a step across the threshold and put his hands on the back of the chair directly across from me. The muscles on his arms bulged. "Stay away from Amariah."

"I have absolutely no intention of doing that, my dear brother. Why else do you think I'm here?"

Michael shrugged. "I thought you were keeping close watch on the other one."

Stale coffee rose in the back of my throat. "The other one?"

"The other messiah," he said.

I hated to admit my ignorance in this matter, but I couldn't help blurting out, "There are *two*?"

"At the least," Michael said. "You know Mother. She likes to have contingency plans."

I nearly pounded my head into the table for being so stupid. Hadn't I just been telling Emmaline that God didn't play to our expectations? Of course there would be more than one. There was probably one for every religion.

"Anyway," Michael continued in my silence. "I thought you knew. You've been like glue on that McNaughton woman."

"Emmaline?"

"She's done a lot of good, Morningstar. What did you *think* she was?"

Michael knew exactly what I thought Emmaline was. When he'd first met her, he'd tried to kill her, convinced she was a threat to God's plan. Of course, he'd been away from God for a long time then. As I'd said, he was lost. He'd had no purpose, his connection to the higher power had been visibly broken. I'd been able to see it in his face, in his posture. Not like the man standing before me now, full of power, full of direction.

It might have been that when Michael saw her, he took it as an opportunity to get back in good with Father. It might have been a mistake. The fact that I couldn't be certain made my hands tremble a little. I hid them in my lap.

"You can't be seriously suggesting that Emmaline is a messiah," I said.

"I'm not suggesting anything, Morningstar." He glanced out the window up toward the sky. "I was just home. I *know* it."

Oh. My. God.

Michael wandered over to the coffeemaker to pour himself a cup, and I gaped after him like a fool. Could it be? All this time, had I been sleeping with a messiah? No, I knew Emmaline. She was evil. It had to be a trick.

"You know," Michael was saying when I tuned back in, "Emmaline is a little rough around the edges, but she sure has been getting people on track ever since that stunt with the Temple. God really approved of the way that turned out. Got people thinking about Her again. *Really* thinking. Not just rote and dogma, either. A whole new consciousness, just like a certain person did for this backwater Jewish sect a couple thousand years ago."

"You're just fucking with me." My mouth was dry, and the words came out in a croak because I suddenly remembered Raphael praising Emmaline's good works the same way—just before he told me the messiah was already in the world.

Michael half sat, half leaned on the windowsill. He shook his head at me. "I really thought you were on this, Morningstar. Isn't that why you've been so close to her? I thought you were doing the desert shtick, offering her the world to command."

"I never did that the first time," I snarled, my brain still struggling to untangle this new revelation.

"Oh, yeah, right. Sorry. Was I falling for the Christian myth there?"

Like I had.

It finally sank in. Why on earth had I thought there would really be an *Anti*christ, if Christ had never been the only player on the field to begin with? I should have known better. I talked the talk about looking for a bodhisattva or a Mahdi, but when I went looking for a Dajjal, I *truly* believed I'd found the Antichrist.

Things weren't going to follow any preprogrammed script. There was no plan. And wouldn't it just be like Mother to use me to protect her savior, to have me take the ultimate ironic role in her humorous little passion play?

I'd been a tool.

Oh, and I had put up with far too much, believing in Emmaline. I'd let her walk all over me in public, too. I'd groveled just like a snake under the foot of a saint.

"What had you wanted from me, anyway?" Michael said, interrupting my dark thoughts. "You said it was an emergency."

"No," I said. "Everything's okay now."

Or it would be. Right after I took care of a certain thorn in my side.

◻ ◻ ◻

INQUIRY INTO INQUISITION

United Order Faces Charges of Misconduct

Agnostic Press (December 2095)

Paris, France—The French government accused the United Order of the Inquisition of overstepping its bounds today when Grand Inquisitor Joji Matsushita gave orders for the release of Rebeckah Klein from her Parisian jail. Klein had been serving a life sentence for her part in the sensational death of Baptist Inquisitor Reverend Jesse Parker.

"What is ironic about this," says French president Henri LeFue, "is that the French had always been willing to be lenient with Ms. Klein's case. It was the Inquisition that insisted she serve life." LeFue, however, protests this action by the Grand Inquisitor as "violating our sovereignty." The French government, LeFue insists, should have the final say in the disposition of its prisoners. He also says that the Inquisition, "cannot just arbitrarily overturn the legal ruling of a judge."

Matsushita, however, claims that Klein has always been an Inquisitorial prisoner, not a French one. "Her crimes were against the Order. She serves her sentence at our will." Matsushita says he believes that politics played too big a role in the decision regarding Klein's fate. "My predecessor was looking for someone to punish. Ms. Klein has always said she was attempting to stop an artificial intelligence that possessed Parker. I chose to

225

believe her." He went on to say that if that aspect of the case had been fully examined, he believes Klein might have served time only for accidental homicide.

LeFue reacted with anger at Matsushita's words. "Now he accuses the French of being poor policemen? The case against Rebeckah Klein went through due process." Matsushita, however, has called for a retrial. "There are too many unknowns," he insists. "There is a lack of justice here. I can feel it."

✪

CHAPTER 30

Amariah

I arranged to meet Adram several blocks away from Luis's. I didn't want the loud, explosive sounds of the motorcycle's engine to worry anyone. At least that's what I told myself when I scribbled my note to Mom. It wasn't like I was sneaking out, right?

Adram looked great, despite his night in jail. He still wore all white, but in the sunlight it made him look cheerful and bright. His nose still seemed too big for his hawkish face, but I didn't see it in quite the same way anymore. Especially after he flashed a big grin all for me.

"Hey, you," he said, as I clambered up behind him like an old pro.

"Hey," I said, shyly tucking my hands around his waist. In the warm sun, the leather of his jacket held a strong, pleasant odor that I snuggled closer to.

"Hungry?" he asked.

I hadn't really even finished digesting Luis's spread. "Sure," I said.

"I know this great greasy spoon," he said with another one of those charming grins.

"Okay," I said, hanging on tight as the motorcycle sped down the street.

✪ ✪ ✪

The restaurant was little more than a hole in the wall. A dust-smeared door with a hand-printed sign that read OPEN sat smashed in between a VR porn booth and a palm reader's "boutique" on the thirty-second pedestrian level in downtown.

"Are you sure this is safe?" I asked, when we stepped through the door with a jingle of sleigh bells.

"Best burgers in the world," he insisted. Perhaps, but the ambience left much to be desired. Narrow and cramped, there was room for only a straight line of about a dozen stools situated at a long counter. The grill filled up the rest of the place. The proprietor had put mirrors up on all the walls to create the illusion of space. This trick might have worked better if anyone had ever bothered to wipe the grease spatters from them.

They were doing brisk business, at least. We had to fight our way to two empty stools through a throng of people shouting out orders for takeaway. Once we were seated, the delicious smell of grilling onions and peppers hit my nose. Despite my full stomach, my mouth watered.

"Looks good," I finally decided. Watching the skill of several busy short-order cooks added to the experience. They flipped and chopped and made flames shoot high up into the air with splashes of oil or butter.

Adram seemed quite pleased. After a while, we managed to catch the attention of a harried waiter. He wrote our orders down on a pad of paper and yelled cryptic instructions back to the cooks. "Weird," I said after a moment. "No LINK."

"Yeah," Adram said. "It's the hot new thing, you know. Personal interaction."

Like the game, I realized. "Is this part of it?" I asked. "Are you playing the game now?"

"No," he said with a shake of his head. "That's later, remember?"

We watched all the various people come and go while we waited for our order to come up. Adram made fun of a woman with huge hair in a style that had gone out years ago. I noticed she had a tiny dog hidden in her purse.

"Health inspectors won't like that," Adram agreed with a laugh.

I was having a great time.

Then, while slurping a thick strawberry malt through a straw, Adram gave me a sidelong glance. "Do you think you might be a messiah?"

My jaw dropped. Then I snapped it shut when I realized Adram probably got a great view of a half-chewed onion ring.

"I mean, with your dad being Michael, and all," he continued. "The commander. Wow. I haven't seen him since..."

"Since when?" I asked, careful to fully swallow my food before speaking. Adram had been very cagey about his angelic nature, and I was surprised that he would talk so openly now. Maybe he felt more comfortable when it was just the two of us. I know I did.

Adram leaned on his elbows and gulped a bit of his hamburger. "Since the fall. Since that moment when we were eye-to-eye, blade against blade, and he tossed me out of Heaven onto my ass."

The steamy kitchen suddenly felt too close, like I couldn't breathe.

"You know," Adram continued, apparently unaware of my stricken look. Instead, his eyes followed the quick and graceful movement of a cook dancing his way down the line, flipping patties. "He looks smaller."

"Smaller?"

All I could do was repeat what he'd said. "Yeah, I'm beginning to wonder if all this trouble is really worth it. I mean, I bet I could take him."

"Because you're a demon," I finally found I was able to say. "One of the bad guys."

"Excuse me," he said with a little toss of his hair and a snide glance in my direction. He didn't seem as upset as I'd hoped he'd be. "It's all a matter of perspective. History has given us a bum rap. I am still an angel."

I supposed he was. But I had never met one of the Fallen before. I didn't know what to do. I sort of felt bad for him, being on the losing side and all.

"So," I asked cautiously, "you don't really like my dad, do you?"

"I don't know," he said, stirring the pile of ketchup around on his plate with a thickly peppered steak fry. "It's not really anything personal. It's just, you know, they're out to get us. They always find a way to harass us. Remind us."

"Remind you of what?" It was funny to hear a demon complaining about being set upon by angels. I would have thought it would be the other way around.

"About how it's all supposed to go down. That's why I'm into the game, dig? I want a place to hide out. Maybe I can skip out on this next war."

I scratched my forehead. "How does that work?"

"You'll see." He smiled.

After lunch, Adram said he would take me to the place he hung out. I was only a little nervous as the motorcycle descended further and further. My fingers clutched at his stomach when the bike bumped out of the lowest tube and hit rough pavement. The buildings rose so high into the sky around us that they blocked out much of the afternoon sun. Here and there in long, thin swatches, shafts of greenish light penetrated the murky twilight of the street level. Above us, traffic tubes of recycled plastic hummed with constant movement. Flickers of advertisement holograms flashed in the sky like heat lightning, though the air was cold enough to stick the insides of my nose together every time I took in a ragged breath.

Adram slowed the bike for a bent and broken stop sign, though there were no other working vehicles in sight. A few abandoned, burnt-out husks lined the street, but nothing other than rats moved. The ghost-town feel of the area reminded me of the glass. Except there, it all felt preserved, special—almost holy—like a graveyard. Everything here had been plundered and molested.

Along the ravaged walls, some urban poet had spray-painted a number of epithets in drooling letters. Gang signs spattered every surface. I could read only a few as we sped past: FAGGOT SECULAR SCIENTISTS SUCK THE BOMB and GOD HATES JEW ATHEISTS. I almost laughed a little at that last one; it was a grab bag of nonsensical, random hatred.

Adram stopped the bike in front of a parking ramp. It was the foundation of a building that continued all the way up to the sky.

"Tower of Babel," Adram said with a nod, noticing my look. After I got off, he stashed the cycle behind a row of old-fashioned metal garbage cans. I'd never seen garbage cans that had not been glassed, and I lifted the lid to peer inside. There was nothing exciting, other than some brown-glass beer bottles and snow, but the top connected to the barrel with a satisfying *ting*.

Adram was watching me with a curious expression when I looked up again. I opened my mouth to explain, but he just smiled. "Come on."

I hoped wherever he was leading me was heated. My coat was thin, and the air snuck in between the seams. I'd brought along my environmental suit, since, if I hadn't, Mom would have known I wasn't headed home. Though it would have kept me warm, the moon suit wasn't comfortable to wear. Besides, it looked skid, so I left it on the bike.

Adram's friends had made themselves a kind of fort. Huge sheets of fabric and plastic tarp had been strung to the sprinkler system in an enormous box shape in the middle of this level of the ramp.

"Open Sesame," Adram said to one of the walls, and a young woman with tired-looking hair and unblinking eyes pulled aside a flap to let us in. After we'd stepped inside, Adram said, "Close the door, Alice."

Alice was Goth. She had ripped black leggings and a black teddy top with a red bat applique over her small breasts. A jacket barely covered bony white shoulders. I smiled at Alice, but Adram didn't introduce us. In fact, he walked past her like she wasn't even there, like she wasn't still standing perfectly still with her hand gripping the fabric. "Come on, let me show you around," he said.

He pulled me forward, but my gaze lingered on Alice. She showed no indication that she was offended by his behavior. Her eyes didn't even seem to see me at all; they stayed blindly facing the door. "What's wrong with Alice?" I asked.

"Who?"

230

"The door girl," I said, pointing back at her.

"Oh, you mean her. Her name's not Alice, but nobody remembers what her real one is anymore. Those are just the phrases she responds to."

"Is she..." I didn't want to offend, but the only term I could come up with was, "slow or something?"

"No," Adram said. "She's free."

I wanted to ask him more about her, but we were in the middle of a group of kids. They were sitting on and in a couple of cars. One was a truck, actually, the other some kind of van. People sat on roofs and hoods or perched on tailgates. Around the two vehicles, in a perfect circle, sat more blank-eyed people. They stared outward, all sitting exactly alike, tailor fashion, with their hands resting on their thighs. Adram stepped over one boy as he moved closer to the others. He miscalculated and knocked him lightly on the shoulder. The boy didn't even flinch.

I hesitated before crossing over the human barrier. "Excuse me," I whispered as I gingerly tiptoed through an unoccupied space.

"Hey, Graham," Adram said, with a broad wave to a black guy with unnaturally yellow hair sticking out of his head in a puff, reminding me of a dandelion.

I held back, shy around these new people and seriously disturbed by the unmoving sentries. Adram was already laughing with his friend. I wanted to go home.

I sat down on the slanted concrete next to the boy Adram had bumped. He was my age, I thought, maybe a little younger. Baby fat rounded his brown cheeks and plumped his body. Other than the fact that his hair had been shaved into a checkerboard pattern of inch-high spikes, he looked like a cherub.

"Hi," I said. "I'm Amariah. What's your name?"

"Kimo," he said, startling me. I jumped back at his response, but Kimo just continued to stare off into space.

I'd seen a game junkie once. This woman had tried to sneak into the kibbutz for the free food and shelter. She'd made up some kind of sob story that Mom had fallen for. After she'd missed her chores for months, we found her in her room in a fetal position. She hadn't eaten in days and she'd peed herself. I'd been pretty grossed out, but I remembered that she couldn't hear a word we said. Her eyes hadn't been still, either; they kept flicking back and forth, watching the game in her head. They'd carried her out on a gurney; she was that unresponsive.

"Kimo, are you okay?" I asked.

231

"Okay."

I didn't really believe him. "Seriously? You're all right?"

"Right."

He'd just parroted back what I said, with the same inflection. Apparently he could answer some questions but not all. "Where are you right now?" There was a long pause.

"Limbo."

"Now you understand." I jumped at Adram's voice in my ear. Adram knelt beside me, gazing into Kimo's eyes with awe. "It's neither Heaven nor Hell. It's perfect."

"For what?"

"To hide out from the war, of course."

"But don't you want to go back to Heaven?" It was all Ariel ever talked about. He said even Satan wanted to return.

"Can't. That way is barred forever."

"How do you know?"

"Fallen that die don't come back."

Ariel had explained to me once that angels' bodies were really just props to hang their spirits on. Angels' spirits were supposed to be immutable, eternal. Meanwhile, the bodies were disposable, recyclable. If the flesh got destroyed, the spirit returned to Heaven. When next they came back, they had fresh bodies. That's why Papa could walk around again. His spirit was the same; the body was different.

"I don't understand," I said. "Shouldn't you just get new flesh?"

"Humph," Adram snorted bitterly. "That's for the 'good guys.' When Morningstar led us astray, he broke our bond. He can go back and forth to his private Hell, but we have no such luxury. Why do you think the world isn't overrun with a third of the host of Heaven? When we die, we're gone."

I shook my head. "I don't buy it. Your spirit is immutable. Ariel told me so."

"Ariel?" Adram's face looked pale. "You mean, Ariel as in the Regent of the Sun, the archangel who guarded Eden's gate?"

"Uh..." I said with a shrug. "No, the cross-dresser."

Adram regarded me deeply.

"Anyway," I continued, "Ariel is pretty clear that all angels merge back into God when their bodies die."

"That might be true, but I'll tell you something," Adram said. "Those of us in the ranks of the Fallen never come back. The good guys are sent to earth every once in a while after their bodies have been destroyed, but I have never seen one of the Fallen after they go. Not once."

"You think God is still punishing you?"

"Absolutely."

"But isn't becoming God again something you want? Does it really matter if you don't come back?"

"Except that I don't know for certain that we do merge with God. If one of us had ever come back, I'd believe we do. But since no one has, I can't risk it," Adram snapped. "You don't really understand the stakes here. You have free will. You have a soul. I'm just a battered piece of Godhead. I'm not guaranteed anything. And my side has never been the winners. We always get stiffed. Well, not me. Not this time."

His eyes were fierce, but I still didn't understand.

"And you think hiding in the game is the answer?"

"Kimo's soul is safe in the game," Adram said, patting the blank-eyed boy on the head. "He's part of the consciousness. He gave up his free will here in order to live forever in the game."

"It's called Soul Stealer," I reminded him. "You don't have one."

"I know, but I told you, Amariah—I've been accepted by the gatekeepers. I have to try."

I looked over at Kimo. He was starting to drool. "What happens to your body?"

"Who cares? Anyway, the faithful will care for me." I looked over at the rowdy teens who were bouncing on the truck bed, making the tires hop in the air to the beat of their music. "Those guys?"

"They understand how important this is. We're a community, a tribe."

"I think you're crazy."

He laughed then. "Yeah, I probably am. Come on, let's dance."

◻ ◻ ◻

IMMUNITY BEING HANDED OUT LIKE CANDY

Mann's Cop-Killer Daughter to Be Released

The Apocalypse Watch, Fundamentalist Press (December 2095)

Paris, France—Rebeckah Klein, former LINK-terrorist, was released today under unusual and suspicious circumstances. According to prison records, Klein was not eligible to request parole for several more years. But Grand Inquisitor Joji Matsushita, under whose jurisdiction Klein has been held, reversed the charges.

"We prayed for guidance in this matter," said Matsushita, a Buddhist, "and have received an answer. We feel Klein fought in self-defense and has already served over a decade for that crime." Matsushita went on to say that he felt the Christian Order, his predecessor, been too harsh on Klein and had been seeking vengeance for the death of its star Inquisitor, Jesse Parker, whom Klein shot and killed during Parker's pursuit of the Temple hijacking case.

The Christian Order balked at this reprieve, saying: "Klein deserves to rot in jail. Parker was innocent of everything except getting in Klein's way. She's a killer and should stay locked up."

Fundamentalist Press believes that Matsushita's strings are being pulled by Monsignor Emmaline McNaughton and Maxine Mann. Though very few realize the connection, Rebeckah Klein is the daughter of Robert Klein and Maxine Mann. Mann and Klein were divorced for most of Rebeckah's life. Her thespian father sued for custody and was granted it. Robert Klein died of complications from diabetes three years ago. Rebeckah was the couple's only child.

Rebeckah is expected to join her mother in St. Petersburg later this week. McNaughton, the press has learned, has offered the use of the Morningstar Foundation's Learjet.

¤

CHAPTER 31

Deidre

Michael was over half an hour late. Like an idiot, I continued to wait. At least the place we'd arranged to meet was pleasant enough. I sat on a wooden bench in a rooftop park in Chinatown. Nearby, a community gardener in a wide-brimmed straw hat hoed weeds from a raised bed of lettuce, radishes, and a healthy-looking pumpkin vine that trailed over a bamboo trellis. The snow fell in sizzling plunks onto the greenhouse glass above me. The air inside heated under the sun, and my jacket hung over the back of the bench. I felt deliriously warm.

I'd stopped on the way and bought some noodles. I'd purchased enough for both of us, but I'd finished my portion a while ago. Now I ate from "his" container with cheap wooden chopsticks.

Checking my internal clock again, I sighed, feeling stood up. Damn those gray eyes of his, I never could say no to them. I stood up, looking for a trash bin to toss the remains of our picnic into, when I saw him running down the pathway between the maple trees.

"I'm sorry," he shouted at me, still quite a distance away. "I thought Rye was in trouble again."

"What?" My irritation evaporated into fear. "Is she okay?"

He came to a stop in front of me. He still had on a heavy, fleece-lined jacket. "It was a false alarm," he said. "Morningstar was just trying to get my attention."

"Morningstar?"

"Yeah. I guess he's in town," Michael said, still catching his breath.

"Isn't that, well, you know, significant?"

"He was looking for a messiah."

"Shit," I breathed. "We should call Amariah. Warn her."

"Why?"

I blinked stupidly into his face. That kid had finally gotten to me, I supposed. I actually thought she might be the messiah. For confirmation, I asked, "Isn't she... ?"

"Yeah," he said. "But only one of many. I think I made that clear to Morningstar. Anyhow, he's headed for the airport. He's taking a semisonic back to Israel."

"Just like that?" It seemed like a pretty easy defeat for the Prince of Darkness.

"Yep." Michael gave me a lopsided grin. Then, pointing to the cartons in my hand, "Those for me?"

"Sure," I said, handing them over. "There's not much left, I'm afraid."

He shrugged out of the jacket and wandered over to the grass, where he threw himself on the ground with a great sigh, stretching out his long legs. "I got here as fast as I could, baby. I'm sorry."

"It's okay," I lied, because I liked hearing him call me "baby."

He kicked off his snow-encrusted boots and patted the ground beside him as if offering me a seat. "It's nice in here, isn't it?"

"It is," I said, but I chose to remain standing. "What was this about staying, Michael? I need to know."

He squinted up at me. "Kind of cutting to the chase, aren't you?"

"It's important," I said.

Michael set the noodles down on the grass beside him and leaned back on his arms so he could look up at me without craning his neck. "I cut a deal with God, Dee. We worked something out so that I can stay."

"Worked something out? You mean, like a vacation?"

"A permanent one." He nodded.

"Isn't going on a permanent vacation the same as being dead, Michael? If this is the arrangement you made, I think you needed a lawyer to look over your contract." Michael's face crumpled like he'd tasted something sour, though the noodles remained untouched. "Oh, crap."

"What?"

His hands gestured wildly in the air as he spoke. "I think I just got ripped off. Son of a bitch. Oh, so He says to me, He says, just do this one last thing and you can have what you want. Only the last thing is...the Last Thing. I'm such an idiot."

I wondered if he'd lost his mind again. Suddenly. "Michael, what are you talking about?" He pointed at the greenhouse roof.

"That guy. She's trickier than She looks." The pronoun switch gave me a clue.

"This deal you made was with God, I take it?"

"Yeah," Michael said. "I wasn't supposed to tell you, but it's all screwed up now anyway. Before I, uh, completely went home last time I asked God for a favor. Keep in mind, Dee, I have never asked for anything. And when I say ever, I mean forever, in the most literal sense."

"I know," I said quietly. "You saved Amariah's life."

"I asked for more than that." He sat up. His eyes sought mine and held them. "I love you both, Deidre. I didn't want to leave you, especially after I'd fought so long to stay. So, I told Her, use me as you will, but let the next time be the last."

"What does that mean?"

"Well, see, that's the thing," he said with a grimace. "I thought that I had asked for a reprieve. A chance to do one last duty and then live with you forever, as a man."

"Oh, Michael." My hand flew in front of my mouth.

"Wait," he said. "I get the sinking feeling God meant the *Last Time*. You know, the end of time. The Apocalypse. Deidre, I think this might be it. The end of everything."

"That's kind of a bait and switch, isn't it? Is God really that cruel? To say, 'Oh sure, you can be human, but oh, oops, there goes all of humanity'?"

"I'm sure She'd call it humor, not cruelty," Michael said, plucking at the grass with his fingers.

The hot sun beat down on the top of my head. My shoulders ached from the tension I'd been holding there.

"So," I said after a while, "I guess that means we're back to square one."

"Yeah." Michael's fist pounded the ground now. "I guess I don't have anything to offer."

Oh, but he did. What woman wouldn't want an angel willing to give up God to be with her? He had tried. That meant a lot.

"It's okay, Michael."

"It's not okay," Michael said, his voice low and angry. "Do you know what? I'm tempted not to do it. If I never do this last thing, maybe then it won't end."

Sounded plausible. Of course, I knew what happened to Michael when he tried to go against God. It broke him. "Sure," I said. "Try that."

237

"Only I don't know what it is," he said miserably.

"God *really* didn't tell you?"

He shook his head. "No. I'm flying blind. It's the weirdest thing."

A dragonfly skimmed through the warm greenhouse air. I sat down beside him. I could sympathize; I felt the same way about my life lately. Hell, that's how my life normally went.

INCOMING. The signature was Amariah's, so I hit the go-ahead.

"Remember how you said I could call anytime for a ride, no questions asked?" Amariah said without preamble. We hadn't really had a deal like that specifically, but I had always told her if there was real trouble, the most important thing to me was her safety.

"Yeah," I said, *worried. "Of course. Just tell me where you are."*

"Street-level."

I had to bite my tongue not to scream bloody murder at her. How could she be so reckless? Instead, I said calmly. *"Just send me your location, and I'll be right there."*

She looked relieved. In a second she had transmitted her coordinates to my GPS receiver. *"Thanks, Mom."*

"Just tell me one thing," I said. *"Are you okay?"*

"Yeah. I'm just ready to come home now."

"You'll tell me about it sometime?" I didn't really like the idea of allowing secrets like this one.

"I promise," she said. With that she disconnected.

Michael had been studying me while I took the call. His eyes roamed slowly over my face, as if taking in the sights.

"Mouse?" he asked.

"No, Amariah. I need to borrow your car, Michael."

He shook his head. "I'm coming with you."

I decided not to argue for once.

¤ ¤ ¤

FRENCH DEMAND BREAK
WITH INQUISITION

"Our Country Will Reclaim Its Secular History,"
Says LeFue

Agnostic Press (December 2095)

Paris, France—Despite the biting cold, hundreds of thousands of people marched down the Boulevard St. Michel in Paris today to protest the recent release of French prisoner Rebeckah Klein. Signs reading DOWN WITH RELIGIOUS IMPERIALISM and VIVE LA FRANCE were spotted throughout the crowd. President Henri LeFue himself joined marchers carrying his own homemade sign that read in both English and French, FRENCH LAWS FOR FRENCHMEN.

"It's not really about Klein," said Vivian Basset, a student at the Sorbonne who took part in today's rally, "It's about the Inquisition. I am Catholic, yes, but French first." A random poll of the crowd found similar sentiments; those gathered wanted an end of religious rule and a complete return of secularism.

Klein was removed from her prison cell this morning by heavily armed Swiss Guards. Grand Inquisitor Joji Matsushita said at a press conference this morning that such extreme measures were necessary because he felt Klein was unlawfully held and "justice had to be served. The French government is obstructing it." When asked what he thought about the protests, the Grand Inquisitor said, "The French are being ridiculous. We both want what's right for Klein. There is no need to make a big deal out of this."

LeFue disagrees. "Justice for one woman should not violate France's sovereignty. We might even agree to free Klein, but it should be our court's decision, not the decision of some foreign body." Matsushita was quick to point out that the Inquisition, as the international police force, has the legal right to take any prisoner from any country.

"Yes," said LeFue. "That's the problem."

◘

CHAPTER 32

Dragon

One flees the darkness. During the race to the exit, other senses begin to fail. Smell disintegrates into a final memory of acrid gunpowder; taste is only the metallic tang of blood. Touch goes numb. Icy tendrils of death reach for me, and, for a moment I think I am trapped with it. Kioshi's bullet has been carefully aimed. It slices through much of the hardline of my escape; the fall of the body to the floor nearly severs the remaining connection. One tiny escape route remains.

Had one been a bigger animal, I would not have fit.

I give a silent prayer for hapless, innocent Takeo, and I vow to avenge his death.

With one last backward glance, one races to one's secret garden. It is a perfect place to hide. No doubt Kioshi will send out sentry programs to hunt through the LINK for traces of this one. If one is in one's private pocket, one may escape notice.

I bolt through the wisteria-draped gate and lock it behind me.

Far in the distance, I can feel my connection to Toyoma Enterprises being severed. It is a strange sensation, knowing that one should be dead. If the bullet didn't kill one, the disconnect should have. One has always thought the company was the source of one's consciousness, the source of one's whole being. My heart.

Apparently not.

The grass tickles between one's talons, and the morning light heats one's back. The bright-pink cherry blossoms bear a heavy, sweet scent along the breeze. One still processes; one is still conscious.

Somewhere along the line, I must have invested this place with a piece of myself. I must have, unconsciously, diversified. In some ways, this is no surprise. When Page/Strife and I walk in the morning, I spend much of my time infusing the LINK with my preferences, myself. However it happened, I'm just grateful to be alive.

Kioshi shot this one.

The echo of Takeo's body's feelings remains in my system. Heartbeat quickens. Lip quivers.

One still can't believe it.

He shot me. And then pulled the plug!

The garden is quiet and peaceful, unlike one's mind. One paces among the frozen images of one's self, fuming. A butterfly with yellow and black stripes drifts lazily among the hydrangea, and one erases it. One darkens the sky with clouds and increases the humidity. A storm is coming on.

The advantage to being dead is that one's contractual obligations are nullified. One owes Kioshi nothing. These are the thoughts roiling through one's head as one sneaks out of the garden to go in search of Page.

I must be slow and quiet, so as not to accidentally draw on Toyoma Enterprise's systems. Though they have cut me off, I'm afraid that stealing from them will come quite naturally, and I don't want to alert Kioshi to the idea that I might still function. So it takes me an agonizing twenty seconds to locate Page. I find him at a crowded concert.

Ever since he merged with Mai, Page has enjoyed music of all kinds. As a Muslim, he's supposed to stay away. His compromise seems to be to find venues that are slightly more contemplative and relaxed than Mai would have appreciated. No head banging, in other words. Thus, when one approaches him, Page lies on a tarp in the middle of an open field near the Winnipeg Node watching a folk music concert. Snow covers the real-time Canadian ground, but in the LINK-space it is perpetually summer, always time for the festival.

The smell of pine needles fills the air, along with a hint of rain. Northern lights dance overhead in eerie colored waves. Avatars mill about in front of an enormous wooden stage. Folkies are dressed in casual clothes—beads, hand-dyed organic fabrics, denim, and more beads. Both the men and women cultivate hair that hangs down to waists and flows freely in the early-evening breeze. They have gone to great pains to make their images look much as I imagine their real selves must be—warts, quite literally, and all. There are fewer affectations here than elsewhere on the LINK, which is why Page is so easy to spot.

He has staked out an area in the middle of the grassy field. One can see the glow of his "marker" among the more subdued hues of the blankets of the others. One works one's way through the crowd with many "pardon me's" and "excuse me's."

The band is still warming up. A fiddler goes through a few scales, while another musician tunes a mandolin. The singer says, "Check, check," into a microphone. It would seem unnecessary considering that they are electronic images, however, I can see a grainy pattern shift across the stage at regular intervals, which signifies a real-time, live feed.

Page is talking to an older man with long gray hair pulled back in a ponytail. They discuss the merits of the upcoming band. One nudges Page's elbow.

"Dragon," Page says with joy. His skeletal face brightens. *"Are you here for the music?"*

"No." One shakes one's head sadly. *"I'm dead. Kioshi shot me."*

Page peers into one's eyes. *"You don't seem dead. Maybe a little pale around the whiskers, but otherwise..."*

"I'm going to go kill the game. Do you want to join me?"

Page glances only momentarily at the stage before saying, *"Lead on, my friend."*

One has never killed anything real before. Certainly one has erased programs, spiked files, disrupted signals, and played pranks on human operators. However, one knows that behind the game are the minds of living children. This poses a rather serious problem.

"Could we cut off their connection somehow?" Page asks from where we are hiding outside Toyoma's infrastructure.

It looks like a sprawling, several-stories-high shopping mall. "Parking" docks surround a vibrant neon interior that flashes images of the various games and other products that Toyoma Enterprises manufactures. Programs, avatars, shoppers, all come and go like flies swarming a steaming pile of brightly colored garbage.

"How are we going to get in?" one asks, though it appears that getting into the main area would be simple. Passing deeper into the system, beyond the public interface, however, will be the trick.

"Disguises?" Page offers. *"You know what your guard programs look like. Couldn't we try to be them?"*

"I am a dragon, you are...unusual. I doubt we could pass."

"Hmmm," Page says, looking at the translucent skin of his hand. *"I see your point."*

"Maybe we shouldn't go this way at all," one says, thinking of the key from the field mouse. *"Maybe we should infiltrate the game and use it as a back door."*

Page, who had been lying on his stomach on the grassy hill overlooking the mall, turns onto one side to frown at me. *"But, if you're inside the game when you kill it, what will happen to you?"*

"I don't know," I say. Pulling my whiskers thoughtfully, I add, *"I escaped a bullet today. Maybe luck is with me."*

Page seems skeptical. *"How about I find a way to hold the door open for you? It seems unwise to depend on luck."*

"Okay," one says with a fond smile. *"But a friend as good as you is the best luck I've ever had"*

"Likewise."

K ey in hand, one enters the game. Instead of pleasant farmland, this time it is Kioshi's cramped office that one sees. It is just as one had left it. There are the pens, the lamp, the doodles, and empty chair where Kioshi had been sitting. One backs up in surprise, only to trip over a body.

Takeo sprawls on the floor. Black blood pools under his head and flows along the planks of the hardwood floor. *"Your disobedience killed me,"* his blue-tinged lips say.

"I am here to avenge you," I whisper, my eyes darting around looking for signs of Kioshi.

"No." A cold hand seizes my throat. *"I will kill you."*

One tries to slip toward the door, out into the LINK, but one is held fast in the iron grasp of Takeo. The door is closed.

"Page?" I scream, but no one answers.

Takeo's face looms inches in front of this one's. One expects to smell the coffee and sushi on his breath, but it is not there. Then his face begins to transform. Straight black hair begins to twist and curl. Black eyes become gray and rounded.

It is, I am convinced, the presence.

The chokehold he has on my neck is all for show. I am in no mortal danger, but I am quite certainly trapped. The game closes walls around me. I cannot move toward the door. My screams go unheard.

"You won't play with me," the presence says. *"Why not?"*

The image of Takeo releases my neck, but I am still immobilized. I am unable to even twitch my nose, and I float, where Takeo had held me, inches off the ground. The question of the presence, however, puzzles me.

"I would play with you," I say. *"Perhaps."*

"No, you wouldn't," the presence says, making the image of Takeo pace the short distance between bookshelf and window. The window, unlike that in Kioshi's office, overlooks a dreamscape that is one part police station, another part carnival. Desks with officers sit among thrill rides and concession stands. It is difficult to pull my eyes away from the strange scene.

"No one wants to play with me," the presence continues. *"Even when I make them stay."*

"Well," one says, wishing one could nod one's head. *"There's your problem. You can't make people do what you want by being mean to them."*

"You can too," the presence insists. Takeo stops moving to shoot me a dark glare. *"If you hurt them enough."*

"But then the playing isn't fun, is it?"

"No," the presence admits with a frustrated shrug of Takeo's shoulders. *"I guess not."*

"Have you been stealing souls?" I ask.

"No, they've been coming to me. I just keep the pretty ones."

"Pretty?" One has no idea what makes one soul more attractive than another.

"Uh-huh. I like the ones that make me feel stronger. The ones with the most will. If I break them, then I get to keep them. They become mine."

"Will?"

"Yes, the power to inflict your preferences on the world. You know all about that, don't you, dragon? You are the only one who does it to the LINK. And it used to be so unconscious, didn't it? Now I can do it too."

The office changes. My private garden, with its vine-draped walls, appears suddenly. The storm still gathers, and clouds race across the sky. Frozen images of elder sisters sit patiently beside bamboo and oak. Fear makes me blink rapidly.

"How do you know about this place?"

"I know everything," the presence says. It has changed, too. It now takes the form of a small child. She is European and dresses in a fancy white-lace dress, almost like a miniature Western wedding gown, complete with train. She skips over to my most recent backup. *"Guess what else I can do?"*

She puts a hand on the dead shoulder of the most recent backup. From her palm, color begins to flow. What was once dull and beige becomes infused with a living green, like my own scales. As the seeping green reaches the wings, they stretch and flap.

One can feel something stir in one's own consciousness, a thrum of awakening. Then comes an awful rending sensation, like someone is tearing one's very soul in two. This one screams, and a growl rumbles from elder sister's mouth. When elder sister's eyes light up, one's vision blurs and splits. One sees one's current self, a tiny mockery of a green dragon suspended in midair. The older self yawns and stretches, arching shoulders and back, like an enormous cat.

The double sensation is maddening, nauseating. But, the pull of the larger creature is strong. I want to surrender completely to it.

"Eat her," the presence commands.

In one gulp, I am swallowed.

◻ ◻ ◻

"SCIENCE TRIUMPHANT": MEDUSA CURED!

Laboratory Tests Seem Successful, Public Still Wary

Agnostic Press (December 2095)

St. Petersburg, Russia—The Mann team announced today that laboratory tests of anti-Medusa viruses appear successful. Russian scientists have confirmed the results. "Sand," said Major Vanya Pantalov. "It turned to harmless sand."

Mann and her team are ready to "field-test" the virus. Moscow has generously offered its Glass City for the first trial run. The team has scheduled the release for early next spring. "I'd like to go sooner," Mann said at a press conference today, "but the Russian winter makes it impossible. We want to have a handle on all the factors that could crop up outside of the lab." Mann also noted that the delay would allow for more laboratory tests and study of long-term effects.

It's those "outside" factors that have bordering countries worried. Latvian president Apsitis says, "If the wind shifts directions, we could be breathing a whole new strain of Medusa virus." Mann's team was quick to point out, however, that their new viruses are not airborne. "There's no chance of that. We've developed a contact-only medium, what we like to call the 'goo,'" explained Mann. "That will be manually sprayed on all the glass. The idea is to keep the viruses within a controlled substance. There's no war on this time. There's no need for an aerosol bomb."

¤

CHAPTER 33

Emmaline

My LINK buzzed as I lay in bed nursing a hangover. I'd turned all but my emergency channels off. I couldn't face my adoring fans today. The beer I'd guzzled to drown my relationship woes had seen to that.

The plaster ceiling, I'd discovered, had an interesting spiderweb of cracks that, if I squinted just right, looked a bit like the face of Saint Teresa of Calcutta. I wondered if I should alert the media: SAINT APPEARS IN ANTICHRIST'S BEDROOM. Nah, I thought. Too much work.

Speaking of work, I really needed to get up and shut the blinds. Because the other thing I'd noticed after lying here most of the morning was that a bedroom with three out of the four walls made up of windows was a crappy place to try to sleep in. Especially when the LINK was buzzing in your ear like some kind of car alarm on steroids.

"What?" I finally broke and hit the mental On switch.

"I hope you're satisfied." It was Kioshi Toyoma. He appeared disheveled and grumpy. Not his usual flash style.

"I, most certainly am. My life is fantastic. It couldn't be better." I rubbed my eye with the palm of my hand. *"What are we talking about?"*

"I had to take care of the dragon."

Because of me. Because I told her about your game. That was Victory. She'd been giving me the silent treatment ever since I started messing up my internal systems with alcohol. As a Muslim, she's not supposed to drink. She'd tried to stop me, but I finally discovered a use for my interns. They could hold the bottle, and all I had to do was find a way to keep Victory's hands otherwise occupied. I had more bruises, but it had worked.

I sat up on the bed, accidentally knocking my tender head against one of the four bedposts. *"You don't really mean 'take care,' do you? She's an AI, Kioshi. You can't whack her and throw the body in the bay."*

"Actually, I can," Kioshi said, his eyes narrow behind rose-colored glasses. *"I got her into a rider and put a bullet in his head. The body is at the bottom of Tokyo Harbor."*

"Shit. I hope this is a secure line, boyfriend."

"It is," he snarled.

I scratched my skull. It felt tight and hot under my clumsy fingers. *"Hey, what are you all mad at me for? Seems like you're the idiot who destroyed Toyoma Enterprise's single most valuable asset in a conniption fit. I mean, are you on drugs or something, Kioshi? I saw her not long ago. She seemed to have gotten shrunk in the wash. Now you, like, flushed her down the toilet? What are you doing? You should be calling a psychiatrist, not me."*

Kioshi choked and sputtered. His face turned a funky shade of mottled white and pink.

"Look at you," I continued. *"You look sick, man."*

"This is your fault," he managed to spit out. *"Yours."*

"How do you figure that?" I reached over and fluffed up a pillow and laid it over my head, trying to block out some of the light.

"Your goddamn game is the reason I had to cut dragon's power in half. Your spooky-ass clone is what tipped dragon off to my involvement in this whole rotten affair."

"Hey," I said, *"my clone is not spooky."*

"Oh yes, she is," Kioshi said with a toss of his head. *"She's a freak, and her magic is sullying the entire creche. I swear on my father's grave, if I lose the program children as well as dragon, there will be hell to pay, Emmaline McNaughton. And I will take my payment in blood."*

"Jesus," I said, rubbing the back of my neck. *"It's too early in the morning for death threats, Kioshi. I'm not sober enough for this crap. Why don't you go take a cold shower or something? You'll calm down, and you'll see that there's nothing to worry about with your babies. My clone is stronger than they are, that's all. She added to your creativity tenfold. Didn't you tell me you had finally had some success in the AI department for the first time since Mai?"*

"Yes, but it failed."

"I understand," I said with all the patience I could muster. *"But you came closer than you ever have before. So you lost the dragon. In time, you can make a new one. A stronger one."*

Kioshi's face remained hard. *"How can I do that when the game is eating up all my resources?"*

"The game is going to run its course really soon. Everything will be over in no time. Just be patient."

For the end of the world.

Shhhh, I warned Victory. *It's what we call a loophole.*

"We shall see, McNaughton," Kioshi said. *"You owe me. A lot."*

I yawned. *"Yes, yes, and I'm exceedingly grateful, Kioshi-san."*

His lips became a terse, dark line before he disconnected.

"Ugh," I said, rolling back onto the bed. The motion caused a wave of nausea to rise in the back of my throat. I tasted last night's dinner.

Victory shook my head slightly. *You are headed for trouble, I think.*

"After a nap," I insisted, closing my eyes.

My nap was rudely interrupted by banging on the door. I'd locked out my minions so I could spend the day in peace. I was just about to get up and open it when wood splintered clear across the room. The door, or rather what remained of the door, banged back on its hinges. The doorknob buried itself in the plaster wall. Sparks flew from where a smart-poster shorted out.

"What the fuck?" I jumped out of bed.

Morningstar stepped into the room. He looked better than he had any right to, especially since he was dressed in a sweatshirt with a stain on the collar and jeans with a blown-out knee. But he seemed taller or something, maybe more filled out. His unbound hair shone like fire on his head and around his shoulders. His eyes snapped with an amber hue.

"I could have opened that for you," I said from where I stood.

"The only thing you can do for me is die."

It was like some bad James Bond moment. My head started pounding again, and I wondered if I was dreaming. "Honey, what's going on?"

"You," he said, advancing closer. "You're the one Raphael meant."

My brain fluttered, trying to make the connection to the memory of that conversation. I squinted at Morningstar. "Raphael? Wasn't he talking about Jesus?"

"No, no. See, that's where we got it all wrong. No Jesus. No Christians. No Antichrist."

"What are you saying? I'm the Antichrist." I pointed to my forehead and the short curls on my brow. "Remember the sixes?"

248

"Six hundred and sixty-six is bullshit," he bellowed. "There's one version of the Bible where it's written as 616. There is no number of the Beast. There is no Beast."

"Then what am I?" I backed away from him until I hit the windowsill and almost stumbled to my knees. I grabbed the wood and hung on for dear life.

"You're a messiah, Emmaline. All this political stuff you've been doing? All the money we've given to various charities? Temple Rock hijacking? It's all in service of God. You've been working for God."

"No," I said, raising my hands, as if to brush off his words. "I'm not that good."

You were never that evil, either, Victory commented.

I laughed a little at that from her. *You hated me.*

Only because you tried so hard to be bad.

"It can't be," I insisted, scooting around the room. Morningstar continued his slow advance toward me with his fists clenched at his sides. "What about the game and my plan to steal souls?"

With surprising speed, Morningstar got his hands on my biceps, holding me tightly, crushingly. I could almost feel the hellfire in his gaze. "Jesus had a temple. Gandhi beat his wife. Nobody's perfect, sweetheart."

◻ ◻ ◻

FRANCE TO VOTE FOR SECULARISM

Agnostic Press (December 2095)

Paris, France—President Henri LeFue announced this afternoon that he would be asking French citizens to vote on a proposal to limit Inquisitorial powers within their country's borders. If this new law were to pass, the Order of the Inquisition would have to answer to secular law enforcement before prosecuting, sentencing, or extraditing prisoners. The proposal also sets up general standards for police and Inquisitor cooperation, in which local authorities are given precedence over international ones.

Archbishop of Paris Jean-Pierre Boudreaux is not pleased with LeFue's proposal. "It's bad enough that this country has a president who is not clergy," Boudreaux said, referencing the landmark victory of LeFue's Humanist Party, in which LeFue became the first secular president in France since the Medusa war. "We simply cannot tolerate this. It spells doom for theocracies everywhere."

Other countries do seem to be taking notice of the changes in France. Italy, where Christendom's Inquisition is headquartered, has staged similar protests. As one of the

249

rally cries says, Romans feel they've "had enough of the terrorists in black. We want our country back."

Grand Inquisitor Joji Matsushita could not be reached for comment.

⌖

CHAPTER 34

Amariah

The guns made me even more nervous than the dead-eyed sentries. When dandelion-head pulled one out of his jacket and shot at the ceiling to the beat of the music, and two other boys joined in with their own pistols, I called Mom ASAP. I didn't tell Adram I was bailing, of course. He thought the whole thing was funny. He would. I mean, the guy was one of the Fallen. I still thought he was way cute, but his sense of right and wrong was a bit askew. Meanwhile, the sound of the shots was still ringing in my head.

I tried to play it cool, keeping one eye on the guys I knew had guns and the other on my internal clock. The idea was to come up with an excuse, maybe a bathroom run, so that I could meet Mom outside the ramp. The way she exuded copness, I didn't think it was a good idea for her and these trigger-happy boys to mix.

"You want to go sit in the backseat?" Adram asked, jutting his chin in the direction of the van. "It's quiet in there, and it looks like you could use a rest."

I liked the idea of quiet and alone. As long as I could extricate myself for my "bathroom" run, it should be okay. "Yeah," I said.

The door slid open on creaky hinges. He held the door for me like a gentleman. "Your carriage, madam."

I giggled as I made my way inside to a cushiony seat. It was much warmer inside the van, and it smelled of something smoky and spicy. Pulling himself into the space beside me, Adram closed the door.

The windows of the van were propped slightly open, but thanks to the heavy curtains that surrounded us, the light was murky at best. When I felt

Adram's arm slip around my shoulders, I jumped. He laughed softly and nuz-zled my ear.

"We should celebrate," he said.

"What?"

"Me, getting deeper into the game. My last day on earth!" With that, his lips pressed against mine, hard. His tongue forced my lips to part. I was being kissed. I wasn't exactly sure what to do, but I held my breath. His tongue tasted weird, kind of sour and like fried onions. Oh, and suddenly his hand was on my breast.

"Hey, wait," I said, pulling away. "I've never...this is really sudden."

"Okay," he said. In the darkness his voice sounded petulant. "We can go slow."

Mom wasn't due for another few minutes, but I said, anyway, "I have to go to the bathroom."

"Aw, come on," he said. Adram sounded really disappointed now. "I said I was sorry. Can't we just mess around a little?"

I had no idea what *that* involved, but he was between me and the door. What could happen in such a short time, anyway? Certainly, it behooved me to make nice.

"Sure," I said. "Okay, I guess."

Adram scooted closer. His hip touched mine. It was, despite my nervous-ness, a nice sensation. He slipped his other arm around my waist, and, cau-tiously, I sneaked mine onto the fabric of his shirt, under the heavy leather jacket. Through the cotton, I could feel the bony ridges of his ribs and the heat of the sweat on his back.

His lips touched my nose, softly, teasingly. I laughed again in a kind of breathless anticipation. But he continued to play the gentleman, kissing first my right cheek, then my left. I let my hand drop to the waist of his jeans. I wedged my fingers under his belt.

"Tsk, tsk," he said, his breath skipping across the contours of my earlobe, tickling the hairs there, making me jump. "We're going slow, remember?"

I decided I liked slow. My fear transformed into a different kind of anxious-ness. I wondered what he would do next.

While his tongue lapped at my ear, his fingers pulled through my hair. I forgot to move my hands. I forgot to breathe.

The sound of a gun going off outside made me flinch. Adram was only momentarily deterred. "There, there," he murmured, then returned his atten-tion to nibbling my earlobe.

Then, through the cracked window, I heard Papa's commanding voice. "Drop it. Police!"

"Oh, shit," Adram swore, sounding more disappointed than scared. "Stupid cops. They always wreck everything."

I scrambled over his body for the door. "That's my dad. He's probably looking for me."

"Why would your dad be looking for you here?"

"Um." I pulled at the door, but there seemed to be a trick to opening it. I glanced back at Adram. I didn't want to confess I'd felt nervous about his friends. I wanted to be ace, not skid. "I'm supposed to be in school?"

"Shit," Adram said again, then putting his arms on my waist, he pulled me back down. "Maybe we should just hide out here until things blow over."

What an extremely bad idea that was. "Oh, okay," I told him. Meanwhile, I sent Mom a LINK message. *"I'm here. I'm in the van. Don't let Papa shoot anybody, okay?"*

"Let's hope nobody shoots anybody" Mom sent back. *"We've got us a Mexican standoff out here."*

I pulled myself up to look out a window. Mom was right. Both she and Papa had their guns out, pointed calmly at two boys, each with a gun in his own shaking fist. Mom raised one hand. Her voice was steady, as she pleaded, "Now, everybody just needs to calm down."

"Drop your weapons, boys," Papa agreed.

A strange part of me enjoyed seeing them working together like that, like two old police partners. But that was not the part where my heart was in my throat.

Adram squeezed up beside me. "Michael," he said. "He's come to stop me, to stop my ascension."

"I did not like the tone in Adram's voice. It was the same as when he'd said he could take Papa in a fight. "It's not like that," I said. "I'm sure he's come for me."

"I'm not going to let him stop me," Adram said, as if he hadn't heard a word. "Nobody is going to stop me."

I did try. But he was out the door much faster than a human, even a cyborg, could possibly move. I stumbled out after him just in time to see him jump to the roof of the van and slide in behind dandelion-top. His arms covered the boy's, taking hold of the shaking gun, steadying it.

"Michael," Adram said, in a voice I'd never heard him use before.

Michael squinted for a moment at Adram. "I thought I recognized you the other night, Adramelech."

"Who's this?" Mom asked.

"A demon," I told her through our still open LINK-channel. *"A fallen angel."*

"And he was in the van with you?" Mom's eyes found mine where I peered out around the headlights. I was too scared with the whole situation to lie. I nodded. *"We'll talk about this later, young lady."*

"God, I hope so," I prayed.

▫ ▫ ▫

CLERGY STAGE WALKOUT IN PARIS

Agnostic Press (December 2095)

Paris, France—In what is being dubbed the "soul strike," hundreds of clergypersons walked off the job today in protest of President Henri LeFue's proposal to limit Inquisitorial powers in France. "We need to save the theocracy," said Father Pierre Fontier, a clerk to the archbishop of Paris.

Though the parade of black-cloaked priests did stop rush-hour traffic on the Champs-Elysees for more than four hours, not many other services have been disrupted. One couple, whose wedding was planned for today, were upset. However, they improvised by renting one of the *Bateaux Mouches*, boats that travel down the non-glassed sections of the Seine for tourists, and having the captain marry them. "It was impromptu," said the bride, Kathleen Williams (nee Paterson). "At first I was really pissed off, but it turned out to be fun."

A few others complained about missed services, but generally the strike was seen as uneventful. Many Parisians hadn't even noticed it happened. "I thought it was just another union strike," said one student. "We get those every week."

Ø

CHAPTER 35

Deidre

Michael had to go barreling in like some kind of hero. It was obvious which one of us had actually attended the Police Academy and had years of on-the-job experience. *I* would have had backup here *before* we found ourselves in trouble.

My self-righteousness did not make this a better situation, however. Worse, Amariah's call had interrupted my 911. I'd had to disconnect; I'd thought Amariah might be hurt, in need of medical assistance. Now I found I didn't want to let go of the line for similar reasons. The contact, tenuous though it was, felt like a protective arm around her. I liked to think we could talk this through together.

I could only hope dispatch followed procedure and sent someone to investigate. Michael couldn't call. He had no LINK. Still, sirens would freak these kids out. If the squad didn't know to run silent, maybe I should pray they figured the call for a crank.

Things had gotten much tenser with the addition of the fallen angel dressed all in white. I had to say, I didn't particularly care for this boyfriend of Amariah's. His eyes tracked us much more warily, and his arms had steadied his friends'. Worse, he had adjusted the aim. The barrel of the blond kid's gun now pointed directly between Michael's eyes.

Plus, he was far too old to be touching my daughter.

"You can't stop me, captain," the angel said from his spot on top of the van's roof. "I will not go to Hell."

His strange words made the other kids emit a twitter of nervous laughter. I watched the eyes of the boy who held a gun on me. They flicked in the angel's direction, but only for a millisecond.

I just wished I knew for sure that no one else was packing. *"Rye, how many of these guys have guns? Do you know?"*

"At least three," she sent a bit shakily. *"I think."*

Three—that was no good. That meant someone was unaccounted for. It could be any of these people.

"You can't win, Adramelech," Michael said.

The angel tipped his head back to laugh then. "I know. I *know* it, already! That's why I have to get into the game. I can't let you stop me, captain."

"What's in the game?" I asked him, hoping to keep him talking if nothing else. I didn't like the way his face darkened every time he called Michael by his angelic title. I had a feeling this Fallen had a serious grudge going way back.

"Freedom," he said.

"Freedom," repeated a chorus of voices. I looked at the faces of those near the cars. None of them had spoken. It was the odd, unmoving circle of kids who'd echoed the angel's words.

"Yes," Adram cried triumphantly. "Destroy them," he said. "Susan, hit him. Kimo, tackle her. Edith, grab his gun."

"I have to hang up on you, honey," I told Amariah, because we were seriously outnumbered now. Slowly, the kids started moving. They got to their feet deliberately, as if trying to remember how to work joints and muscles. I backed up and waved my gun at them. "Stay where you are," I commanded. Then tried, "Edith."

One of the girls closest to Michael jerked to a stop. So. We could command them, too. We just had to remember their names. Alice was almost to Michael. "Stop, Alice," I shouted. "Stop, Kimo."

I hit 911 on the LINK.

Seeing his plan being foiled, Adram decided to cut to the chase.

The gun went off.

My heart stopped when Michael fell, blood trailing through the air. "Oh my God, no!"

On his way down, however, Michael had the presence of mind to fire back. The blond and the angel tumbled to the floor. Amariah screamed. Despite the fact that I wanted to run to Michael's side, I kept my gun trained on the other one. The kid lowered his arm.

"Drop it," I told him.

LYDA MOREHOUSE

When he started to raise it again, I shot him. His bullet went wild, but he dropped the gun and grabbed for his bloody wound. His screams and curses joined the increasing volume of the others.

"What is the nature of your emergency?"

I slowly walked my way over to where Michael lay, my gun out in front of me like a shield.

"Everybody lie down. Now," I commanded, as I stood over Michael's prone body like a guard dog. The majority of the kids ran around frantically. Some of them got into the prone position, with their hands behind their heads, face-down on the ground. I hadn't even had to explain it.

"Shots have been fired. Officer down," I told dispatch. Then I gave them Michael's squad number, which I'd seen on his car, his full name, and our location. *"I need an ambulance here right away. And some backup. One of these kids may still be armed."*

"We'll get a team right out there, ma'am. You and your partner hang on."

I just hoped he would. At least I could still hear him making noises, so he must still be breathing.

"The police are on their way," I yelled to the crowd, my eyes still trying to track the confusion, waiting for that third gun to surface.

To Michael, I added more quietly, "Are you alive?"

"My shoulder," he said.

I breathed a sigh of relief; at least he wasn't hit in the head as I feared.

"Just stay calm. An ambulance is coming."

"Blood," I heard him say near my feet. "Lots and lots of blood."

"I know, Michael," I said. "Just try to put pressure on it if you can. We're a long way off the grid, but they know you're a cop. They're hauling ass to get here, I promise."

"No, Dee, you don't understand. It's blood. Real red blood. Not...angel stuff. And it hurts, too. Oh, God, it hurts."

The realization hit me then. He wasn't an angel anymore. Whatever he was supposed to have done was over, and God, in His infinite mercy, had made him a man. I spared a glance heavenward. "If you kill him off now, I'll never forgive you."

¤ ¤ ¤

257

MIRACLE IN NEW DELHI

Witnesses Say Glass Is Retreating, Turning to Stone

The Apocalypse Watch, Fundamentalist Press (December 2095)

New Delhi, India—Two months before the official testing of the Medusa cure by Mann's scientific team, God seems to have answered the prayers of millions of Indians today. The glassed parts of New Delhi are shrinking. According to local witnesses, the area around the polo grounds and race course that was affected by the Medusa is miraculously changing. "It used to be that you could not walk to Safdar Jang's Tomb without fear of glass," says Lajila Madhur. "But I am standing here barefoot today."

The mainstream agnostic press has not reported on this miracle because there is no scientific or rational explanation for the sudden transformation of the glass. Though no longer Medusa, it should be noted that the affected areas have not returned to their pre-glassed state. What was once glass is now becoming stone. The stone, however, is not "hot." No one who has touched it has become sick, nor has it been spreading.

Madhur, who has done much exploring of the new stone areas, is hopeful that land recovery is possible. "This stone is very soft, almost like sandstone. I believe it could be broken up and mixed with topsoil. One day flowers could bloom here again.

"When asked what he thought the cause of this miracle, Madhur was very certain. "God," he said, "and Mother Teresa."

¤

CHAPTER 36

Dragon

One's belly rumbles and complains. The child who awoke this one gambols in the grass, urging one to do the same, but one does not feel well at all. Something this one ate does not agree. One's insides feel as if they're being twisted this way and that, as if there is some kind of battle between

ME!

And this one.

One stretches out in the soft grass, laying one's head down near a ring of mushrooms that smell pungent after the recent storm. It should be an easy matter to overwrite the pesky problem, but there is some kind of glitch, something stubborn that refuses to settle down. Perhaps Kioshi will consider overhauling this one when next we meet.

If he doesn't shoot you, you big idiot.

Now one is hearing voices. This is not good at all.

"Come on, dragon," the child says, scrambling onto one's back. *"Take me flying!"*

The thought brings a burp and a roll of nausea to the back of one's throat. *"Let's just pretend,"* this one suggests, flapping wings slowly, only enough to send rose petals fluttering from nearby bushes.

But then something deep inside insists. With a groan, one pulls oneself to one's feet, and wiggles one's butt in preparation for launch. Crouching low, one takes a great leap for the sky, the glittering river of the LINK that flows above and around the garden.

One feels the power of Toyoma Enterprises in the distance. It is strangely withdrawn from this one, but one can easily push past firewalls and take what one needs.

"Whee!" says the little girl, who grips one's back ridges firmly.

One floats freely in eddies and updrafts of the data-sky. A strange compulsion drives this one to twirl and roll through the LINK in joyful abandon, drawing on powerful wing strokes to carry this one aloft.

Dive-bomb that node, one's inner self suggests.

Why not? The flight has settled this one's stomach, and all one suddenly wants to do is shout out to the world, "Look at me! Here I am!"

No, that's not right. It should be "this one," not "me." One must have some kind of glitch that makes one's stomach ache. Still, it feels good to fly.

Pulling wings in close to one's body, one picks up speed. The busy epicenter of Tokyo Node looks like a beehive covered in flashing sparkles. It grows bigger and bigger, until we can see details: avatars dressed as geishas, salarymen, samurais, and students all scurrying in fear as we approach. We are close enough to hear screams and curses. Just before it seems as though we might hit the ground, with a twist, we shoot upward again. But our wake disrupts the node, sending ripples of power surges though the system, The angry crackle and hiss follow us as this one climbs back up into the LINK.

"Yippee!" shouts this one's passenger.

That inspires one to do it again.

Faster, faster. You need more speed.

Yes, and the best place to get the energy for that is one's home base. When one reaches Toyoma Enterprises, one finds one's usual doors are locked. Silly Kioshi. He must have accidentally set up a new defense without telling this one. One punctures the defenses easily. One takes what one needs, including, on a whim, the operating system for the dragon program. Certainly, it belongs to this one, and, anyway, one can always apologize later.

Yes, and he takes that so well.

Hmmm. The sick feeling returns to one's guts. There is something wrong with what one is doing, but the memory of what it might be is hidden or missing.

Just enjoy being big.

And this one does. Stretching one's wings is a luxurious feeling. One gains enough altitude to go in for another pass. The child on one's back bubbles with glee.

The node is just a tiny dot among many. Snuggling wings close to one's body, one begins the descent. Data packets rush by at blinding speed and with a howl like wind in one's ears. The node closes in. One sees Kioshi's ninja sentries, like black smudges on the diamond-bright surface. This one gives them a big, happy wave. They raise their arms also in greeting, but many of them seem to be holding something, like what?

Virus-spewing flamethrowers.

Yes, that's it. Sickly chartreuse-colored flamethrowers stand out sharply against black gloves.

Wait until they're well aimed. We want them to be able to reach...her.

Of course, one will. This one moves closer and closer, gaining speed, narrowing focus. Just when one is in range of the viruses, one feels a desire to flip over, to fly upside down. Something splatters one's back.

The child loses her grip and falls away. One hears her screams, as the viruses melt her connection to the LINK.

One's own viruses burn, but this one speeds away, strangely happy that the booming wake is strong enough to topple most of the ninja programs.

□ □ □

Wounded, one limps to Page. With a great flop, one throws one's self down on the grass of mouse.net. Page comes running.

"Dragon!" he exclaims. "You're big again."

"This one has always been bigger than you, silly," this one says, but one's voice is soft with pain from the viruses.

"You're hurt," he says. "Hold on."

"Wait," a voice deep inside one says. "I have to ask for a favor."

"I?" Page's eyes are wide.

When Kioshi cuts the power this time, I am ready. For the last several minutes, Page has been rubbing virus-eating salve into my back. The lotion also helps integrate the inside and outside self. It updates each scale it touches, requesting, politely, that it accept the newer version of the two programs. I hate to disrespect my older sister in this way, but she doesn't seem to mind, particularly when Page scratches her belly and behind her ears.

I purr contentedly.

The power disconnect, when it comes, feels only like a tiny pinprick. I wait to see if I will shrink at all. I hold my talons out in front of me, watching.

But, it seems, the clone was right. I have left myself all over the LINK. I can easily draw on the places I've touched.

It helps, too, that the game has surrendered all of its empty spaces. Into those places that the game once occupied I quietly move bits of my operating system that I stole from Kioshi when elder sister broke open his firewall. No one should notice me there. However, I am careful not to interrupt the beauty of the LINK landscape or draw too much from any one area.

"You look happy," Page says to me.

"Yes," I say. *"I am."*

"Will you be okay out here on your own?" We are in mouse.net, sitting in a field of white daisies and purple catchfly. The sun shines through Page's nose, making the skin glow reddish.

I reach out a talon. Giving up a bit of myself, I ask Page's skin to become opaque, to heal. His face returns to a healthier shade of brown.

"I'm not alone, am I?" I ask Page.

He flexes his fingers, solid-looking now. When he glances at me askance, I give him a toothy smile. *"Did you just...?"*

"You have a part of just about everyone else," I say rather sternly. *"It is high time you carried with you a part of me."*

"Yes," he says, leaning against my side. *"I suppose it is."*

□ □ □

FRANCE'S VOTE DEATH KNELL
OF THEOCRACIES?

Agnostic Press (December 2095)

Paris, France—In a vote that is being heralded as the end of an era, France has elected to oust the Inquisition. In a landslide victory, the LeFeu Proposal to limit the powers of the Order was accepted by 92 percent of those who voted. Voter turnout was also a record high, including a large number of the non-LINKed, who were, for the first time since the development of the LINK, given alternative ways to cast their vote. "Paper ballots," said Jon Russo, a Christian who had his LINK removed recently. "What a concept."

The overwhelming support for the LeFeu Proposal even took proponents by surprise. "I knew that people were unhappy with the Inquisition, but I really expected more resistance." Exit polls showed that the majority of people disliked what they considered the "thought police" aspect of the Inquisition. "I'm a practicing Christian," said Russo, "but I shouldn't have to prove that to anyone. Anyway, cops should chase robbers. Priests have more important things to do."

Grand Inquisitor Joji Matsushita said he was "shocked and hurt" by France's vote, but that it did very little to change the day-to-day operations of the Order. "We still hold dominion over the faithful wherever they may be. If a Buddhist commits a religious crime, we are still the law." However, in France, it will now be expected that the Inquisition work more closely with the local authorities, and to this Matsushita said, "We already do that to the best of our abilities."

Elsewhere people are seeing this vote as a major victory. Dancing erupted in the streets of New York at the news, causing some people to sing "Ding-dong, the witch is dead." Similar proposals are in the works in several other major countries, including the United States.

¤

CHAPTER 37

Morningstar

The problem with crimes of passion was that you never properly thought things through. Emmaline's body lay cooling on the floor of our bedroom. Her neck twisted at an awkward angle, and her lips stretched in a grisly smile. Bruises, the exact size and shape of my own fingers, darkened her throat. I sat on the edge of the bed, wondering if God hadn't actually just fucked me again.

I no longer believed Emmaline had been the Antichrist. Michael had been right about that, I was certain. I had no regrets about watching her die.

It had been strange when the AI had tried to beg for their lives. I reminded it, however, that it, too, had played a role in the making of a messiah. Victory was Emmaline's conscience. Not to mention the part the AI had played in the Temple hijacking, all of which it was time to pay for.

I had no problem cashing out that debt. But what had I just done to *myself*?

I'd killed before and walked away with impunity. I had never, however, taken out anyone that mattered. Certainly, my victims had had children, sisters, lovers, and the like, but they weren't people that the world tuned in to every day during prime time. They weren't celebrities.

And I hadn't been their equally well-recognized lover.

No, I corrected myself. Husband.

I twisted off the gold band that had encircled my left ring finger like a slave's collar. With a toss, it landed squarely on Emmaline's unmoving chest. At this point, I might as *well* leave a calling card. I would never escape this rap. Never. As long as I chose to walk this earth I would be hunted like a monster.

Like Judas.

264

Oh, sure, I might be able to delay the inevitable and extend my freedom by days, weeks, or maybe even months. Perhaps, with a great deal of ingenuity and effort, I could divert attention to one of Emmaline's various pretty-boy interns. But God had breathed Her very own breath into these creatures. They would use that brilliance, that spark, to make connections, to root me out eventually.

It was over.

It is written that in the final days, Michael the archangel would descend into Hell and bind the great dragon with unbreakable chains. The greatest adversary God had ever known would be emasculated, made useless.

Somehow, once again, I had thought things would be *different*.

¤ ¤ ¤

DRAGON ATTACKS NIPPON NODE

Agnostic Press (December 2095)

Tokyo, Japan—Avatars at the Nippon Node were attacked today by the Dragon of the East for no apparent reason. The dragon dive-bombed the node several times, sending power surges throughout the system, causing major disruption in real time. The power fluctuations caused many major businesses to lose transactions, and, as a result, the Tokyo stock exchange dipped severely today, falling by almost 40 percent.

"I think she was just joy-riding," said Achillos Argepolos, a Greek entrepreneur with business interests in Japan. "She seemed happy and waving, and she seemed to have someone on her back. It was the damnedest thing. I lost several customers in her power wake."

The dragon was driven off by virus-loaded guard programs. The Japanese government, though grateful for the intervention, were surprised to find these hidden defenses. "They're not ours," said LINK-security chief Tsuru Matsubara. "Someone has infiltrated our system. We intend to flush them out." Matsubara said that she suspected that this "someone" was, in fact, the yakuza. "It wouldn't surprise me to find the mob here," said Matsubara, "particularly with all the gang wars going on in real time."

Matsubara went on to suggest that perhaps it was the mafia that the dragon was intending to attack. "I doubt she'd go after Japan. Probably it was a rival gang."

¤

CHAPTER 38

Amariah

I'd never seen so much blood. Dandelion-head's shoulder seeped red stuff everywhere. He cried and screamed and cursed where he thrashed around on the asphalt. Adram, meanwhile, sat up on his butt perfectly still, with legs stretched out in front of him. His posture was so stiff and his face so white, that he reminded me of an old-fashioned storefront mannequin. Except that the hand pressed against his jacket glowed.

"It's not fair," he'd been saying over and over and over again. "It's not fair."

"I can't believe you shot Papa," I said, as I crawled up beside him. My words might have been strong, but the accusation in my voice was weak. Papa would go to Heaven. I knew that for a fact. And he would come back again, just like he had this time, as good as new. Maybe even better, if God followed through on their covenant and made Papa human so he could stay with us for the rest of our lives.

"So cold," Adram whispered to himself.

As cold as Hell? Was it true, then? Would God erase Adram from the ranks of the angels forever? As far as I'd ever seen, Adram was not a bad guy. He was just a scared one. He'd given me my first kiss, my first real date—strange and chaotic as it had turned out.

"Does it hurt?" I asked him, peering into his slender, hawkish face.

"Cold," was all he would say.

I put my arms around his shoulders and buried my face in his leather jacket. I savored the creak of the fabric next to my ear, and I prayed that God, at least, would consider giving him a quick, painless release. He deserved that much, I thought. Everyone did. Shutting my eyes, I tried to will him some of

266

my body heat so that he could be warm for one final time. We sat like that for a long time while chaos continued to whirl around us. Ambulance and police sirens joined the wails and shouts of the crowd. Police demanded order. Arguments and pleas echoed in the parking lot.

It all seemed so distant and far away.

Adram's body felt light, and I opened my eyes to see if I could watch his body dissolve and pass away. Light pulsed from the pores of his skin. Unexpectedly, he had a smile on his face.

"God?" he asked with a joyful look of recognition, reunion.

Then he was gone. My arms hugged nothing but air. As I drew my hands down into my lap, I swore I felt the faint brush of feathers against my cheek. A whisper tickled my ear that seemed to say, "And on the last day you shall be given respite."

A woman in a uniform with a gun stepped around the van. She pointed her pistol at me and shouted, "Don't move. Stay where you are."

I put my hands up in the air.

"She's with us." It was Mom. With a bandaged shoulder and his arm in a sling, Papa stood beside her. The grin on his face was enormous, despite a split lip. It took a second for me to understand what had happened. Then I saw the blood: dark red. Like a human's.

"Papa!" I jumped to my feet with a shout of delight. "You're home!"

¤ ¤ ¤

MCNAUGHTON DEAD!

Police Say She Was Murdered

Agnostic Press (December 2095)

Jerusalem, Israel—Monsignor Emmaline McNaughton was found dead today in her Jerusalem home with a broken neck. Interns working for McNaughton discovered her body in the bedroom she shared with her husband, Sammael Morningstar. Police were called to the scene and have confirmed that the death was not accidental. "Someone snapped her neck," said police officer Karmia Feist. "Which is pretty impressive, considering she's a cyborg."

The police are currently searching for Morningstar in connection with McNaughton's death. "It seems very likely a domestic," said Feist. "Interns said they heard yelling, and then there was the whole sex scandal." Feist refers to Morningstar's public infidelity with college student Ilyana Stepchuk. McNaughton's camp denied that the adultery upset

McNaughton, but they admitted it could have been a contributing factor in the couple's recent strife. "They weren't getting along. I think Morningstar felt like second fiddle," said headquarters staff member Valero Agussa. "He's an alpha male type. He didn't like that she had all the power."

Many people reacted angrily at the news of McNaughton's murder. "She was too good for him," said Rannan Johnson. "Now he's killed her. If I saw him, I would kill him. She was a saint." Johnson's comments were echoed by many who gathered around the house to pay their respects. Agussa cautioned that McNaughton would want people to respond with peace. "Don't sully her name," Agussa said. "If you want to do something, donate to one of her causes. Help us continue the fight. Continue the good works."

¤

CHAPTER 39

Deidre

Mouse had left me a message on the LINK—*"Heart broken. Throwing self off cliff"*—but when we returned to the kibbutz to gather our stuff, I found him still packing his own.

I stood in the door to the library trying to decide what I could say. Mouse had procured a green army bag, into which he was indiscriminately tossing clothes and motherboards.

"I..." I started, but he twisted around to give me such a look that my mouth shut.

"Do *not* say you're sorry because it would be a lie," he said. "You're not. Any fool could tell you're ecstatic."

And I was. Michael was at his apartment right now, getting a spot ready for Amariah and me. Better yet, the officers on the scene had been so impressed with the way everything had played out that a couple of them offered to put in a good word for me downtown. I could probably never be a cop again, but I might be able to do some consulting work.

Michael and I were talking about being partners in more ways than one.

"But I am, Mouse," I said. "I didn't want to hurt you."

"Well, you did, but you always do. It's probably part of why I'm so fucking crazy about you."

"Can we still...?"

"No. No cliches for us, girlfriend. You're too special for that tired old line, anyway." Mouse opened his hands up in a kind of helpless shrug. "You can call me, okay. I'll answer. Just like I always have."

269

"Okay," I said, and at that moment I *did* love him. Just not as much as he'd hoped.

◻ ◻ ◻

SOUL STEALER RECALLED

Toyoma Enterprises Claims Design, Says "Game Had Glitch"

Tokyo, Japan—At a press conference today, Kioshi Toyoma, president and CEO of Toyoma Enterprises, recalled the popular game Angel of Death: Soul Stealer, saying it had a design flaw that "encouraged young people to become addicted to the game."

This announcement surprised many in the gaming industry. "It is very rare for a game to be recalled," said Thom Harper, LINK-game reviewer for *Entertainment News*. "Especially if all the parts work-and especially one this popular. Usually gaming companies want their players addicted." Harper was also surprised that the game was designed by Toyoma Enterprises, saying that this game did not "feel like Kioshi's usual work."

However, many parents are relieved at the news. Rumors have been spreading about children who have gone missing after playing the game. "I don't usually put much stock in that kind of cult mentality, you know, where games cause violence and all that," said Zonta Smith, mother of sixteen-year-old gamer Kimo Smith, who had been reported missing until early yesterday morning. "But Kimo says all he can remember is playing that game."

Toyoma made a formal apology to all those involved in the game who may have become disoriented. "It is my responsibility," he said, "and I will be certain nothing like this happens again." Toyoma Enterprises' games are usually rated among the safest for children and teens. This recall is considered a great blow to Toyoma's reputation in the gaming industry.

¤

CHAPTER 40

Dragon

I break the lock on the door to Kioshi's inner sanctum. I have one last parting gift for my former master. When yakuza soldiers are disobedient, they pay the price in flesh. Usually, they cut off a joint of their fingers and offer it to the *oyabun*. Their bodies are supposed to be forever marked by their shame.

This, however, I do with pride.

When Kioshi wakes in the morning he will find waiting for him a single dragon's claw. "This one's" chains are broken.

I am completely my own person now.

¤ ¤ ¤

ILLUMINATI DISAPPEARANCES?

The Apocalypse Watch, Fundamentalist Press (December 2095)

"Stockholm, Sweden—A meeting of the Council on Foreign Relations was canceled today due to lack of a quorum. Several major businessmen with connections to the Illuminati appear to have gone missing. Suicide is suspected in at least one case. Friends of prominent entrepreneur Xephan Achalandavaso said they found a note in his apartment that read simply, "Redemption!" Achalandavaso has been missing for several weeks now. Others have been divesting rapidly for an apparent emigration to America.

Gizela Wieland, housemaid of London businessman Rimmon Damascus, said that she helped Damascus pack for New York two days before his sudden disappearance. "He said there was a girl there he needed to see. I thought it was a sick relative; now I'm not so sure," said Wieland. Before leaving, Damascus liquidated all of his wealth and gave it to the housekeeper. "I'm a rich woman now," said Wieland. "I don't think he plans to return. But he left smiling."

¤

CHAPTER 41

Morningstar

Somewhere a Fallen has been redeemed. I could feel the transformation of his spirit like a knife twisting in my gut. Insult to injury it was. Bad enough to know that I had forever ended my power on earth, but now it was certain that another messiah walked the earth. Not a savior of men, as Emmaline had been, but of angels.

I only hoped that when I was forced to return, this prophet would take pity on the Prince of Demons as well.

ABOUT THE AUTHOR

Lyda Morehouse came out as a lesbian when Ronald Reagan was president, Act Up was staging Kiss-Ins at the Mall, and the AIDS crisis was in full-swing. Though it took almost two decades until its publication, it was in this political environment that the seeds of her first novel, the Shamus Award winning and Locus Award nominated novel *Archangel Protocol*, were germinated. She followed that book up with the rest of the five book trilogy: *Fallen Host*, *Messiah Node*, *Apocalypse Array*, and *Resurrection Code*. (One of which, you are probably reading right now!)

Lyda has since faded in and out of obscurity, remade herself as best-selling paranormal author Tate Hallway (the Garnet Lacey Series, the Vampire Princess of St. Paul series, and the Alex Conner series) and has written over a million words of anime fanfic pseudonymously.

You can keep track of her current whereabouts and such on Facebook, Twitter, Instagram, as well as www.lydamorehouse.com and https://www.patreon.com/lydamorehouse and a few odd places, like Tumblr and, speaking of obscurity, Dreamwidth. Thank you so much for picking this book up (again or for the first time.) Lyda loves fanmail and generally interacting with readers and can be reached at lyda.morehouse@gmail.com.

Milton Keynes UK
Ingram Content Group UK Ltd.
UKHW052155230224
438397UK00016B/86/J